Ephialtes

Paperback edition
by
Reflex Books 2022

ISBN 978-1-9161433-7-1

Version 1.2.0

First published 2015 by parcom entertainment

Copyright © 2015 by Gavin E Parker

This book is copyright under the Berne convention.
No reproduction without permission.
All rights reserved.

The right of Gavin E Parker to be identified as the author of this work has been asserted by him in accordance with sections 77 and 78 of the Copyright, Designs and Patents Act, 1988.

Excerpt from *The Iliad* taken from A T Murray's translation,
public domain

Cover image *blue sunrise, view of earth from space*
© Romolo Tavani / stock.adobe.com
Used under license from stock.adobe.com

Printed and bound in Great Britain by Clays Ltd, Elcograf S.p.A.

www.reflexbooks.co.uk

www.gavineparker.com

EPHIALTES

GAVIN E PARKER

So suffered Ares, when Otus and mighty Ephialtes,
the sons of Aloeus, bound him in cruel bonds, and
in a brazen jar he lay bound for thirteen months;
and then would Ares, insatiate of war, have perished,
had not the stepmother of the sons of Aloeus, the
beauteous Eëriboea, brought tidings unto Hermes;
and he stole forth Ares, that was now sore distressed,
for his grievous bonds were overpowering him.

> Homer, *The Iliad* Book V

CHAPTER 01

The War is Over

He smacked the oak surface twice with an open palm, the *slap-slap* cutting through the burbling speech around the table, reducing it to one or two voices which quickly trailed off to silence. "The president has been delayed for a second time, so I'm just going to kick things off here and get some of this out of the way so we can get right to it when he arrives in," he half turned in his chair and a Secret Service man stepped forward, cupping his hand to his mouth as he leant in and whispered into the senator's ear. The senator nodded 'thank you' and the Secret Service man stood back, scanning the perimeters of the room. The senator continued ". . . the latest we have on that is about three minutes."

The secretary of defence was seated a few places down the large cabinet table. She glanced up from her notes. "What is it this time?"

The senator looked over. "They've had another teleconference on the apron at Love Field. Just straightening out some kinks. Don't worry, this is happening." The senator drew a line through something on the papers in front of him. He looked up over the glasses perched on the end of his nose and, glancing around the table, he cleared his throat. "The time is 15:04 on this January 22, 2241. I've been instructed by President Cortes to open this meeting and brief you all on the historic announcement the president will be making at five o'clock this evening." A brief sound of whispered chatter skittered around the table. "Progress at Jakarta and Mumbai has been good, and what you've been hearing in the news reports is largely accurate. The president wants to make the formal announcement to you himself, but I can tell you the news is good." There was another wave of chatter. For the first time the senator allowed himself a smile. "You can appreciate that this is privileged information and that," he grinned, "for the rest of the afternoon, at least, we remain at war. So if any of you sons of bitches let this out we'll have you for treason." There was good natured laughter, the chatter now louder still and more excited.

The senator spoke again. "One more thing." He glanced down at the sheaf of papers before him on the desk. There was nothing for him to read there but he knew it would add some solemnity to what he was about to say. "It's been a long and difficult road to get to this point. Some of our young men and women have made the ultimate sacrifice for their country, for our safety, and for the protection of all we hold dear. I think it would be appropriate for us to spend a few moments in silent reflection on the great sacrifice that has been made, and on those who made it. Would you please all stand."

Around the table cabinet members began to rise. The last sounds of shuffling feet faded and they stood in silence, heads bowed.

Gerard White slipped into the room as the rest of the cabinet retook their seats. As he strode to his place near the head of the table he caught the senator's eye. "One minute," he mouthed, also making a 'one' hand gesture. As he slipped into his seat an aide quickly placed some documents in front of him, but he paid no attention. He was looking at the senator. "Well, Peter, it's a great day, and a great achievement for the administration, especially your guys up on the hill."

After a pause the senator replied. "A great day indeed. We couldn't have done it without you, Gerard. We're all grateful."

White waved a hand. "Oh, come on now. Team effort. We're all in this thing together, you know that."

The senator gave a stilted nod. "I guess so."

There was a sudden scrape of chairs and, instinctively following the others about them, White and the senator rose to their feet.

President Cortes strode quickly to the head of the cabinet table flanked by two Secret Service agents, his assistant trailing a little behind. "Please, sit," he gestured, grabbing the back of his chair and throwing a commanding glance about the room. "I want to thank you all for coming. I'm sorry I'm a little late, but I guess these things never run smoothly. Anyway, we're all here now, so let's get on with it." As he stepped around the chair one of the Secret Service women pulled it out for him and he sat down. The assistant placed some papers in front of him and moved the pre-poured glass of water two centimetres closer, like she knew that was just where he needed it. He half-turned and nodded 'thank you', picking up the top sheet and quickly skimming down it before he started to speak.

"I have come here this afternoon directly from Jakarta where, as you know, I have been personally overseeing the final stages of the USAN delegation's negotiations with President Tsou, Prime Minister Takisawa and General Nkemjika. This third and last series of mediations has been the most difficult and delicate of all attempts at negotiation so far, particularly in light of the recent incidents in Reykjavik and Boston. There were many moments when hope faded, and it seemed we would walk away with nothing. But, through the great and tireless work of our negotiators, we did not walk away with nothing."

There was a murmur around the table, which the president rose his hand to quell.

"Ladies, gentlemen, it is my proud duty to inform you that at 12:00pm today, 22 January 2241, I put my signature to the accords, along with President Tsou, Prime Minister Takisawa and General Nkemjika, ending current hostilities as of 17:00hrs, Eastern Standard Time, this afternoon."

A cheer rolled around the table and the president allowed himself a smile. "At that time I will make a," he paused to allow the noise to subside, ". . . at that time I will make a public address to the nation and the world, and the fourth world wide war will be at an end." There was a second wave of cheering, stronger this time as at first a few then the entire cabinet rose to their feet, clapping and whooping. The president soaked it in, taking the hands offered to him and shaking them firmly, an automatic politician's response.

"Let's hear it for the president!" The call came from halfway down the table and was met with a huge cheer. The president stood and raised two hands above his head, outstretched, a familiar gesture to anyone who had followed his campaigns. He angled his head down in faux humility and thrust his hands slightly forwards and upwards, the gesture answered by a surge of cheers. He held the pose for a few seconds, then dropped one arm to his side while the other waved to the far end of the table. He looked about the room, making individual eye contact with nods here and small gestures there, working the place like the true professional he was.

The senator held out his hand. "Congratulations, Mr President."

"Thank you, Peter," the president said, quickly shaking then moving on to the next proffered hand.

Presently, Cortes gestured for the cabinet to be seated, and the hubbub died down. "The past few years have not been easy. On this day we can celebrate and, Lord knows, no one should deny us that. But there is still a great deal to do. We have lost so much; men and women, materiel and yes, a little bit of faith, too. We have now to regain our strength, rebuild our countries and redouble our efforts to make these United States and Nations once again into the great paragon of virtue and freedom that we know them to be.

"I have to go now to prepare my address, thank you and God bless you all." He walked down the room to the exit, pausing only once to shake an offered hand and laugh politely at the quip offered with it, then he was gone.

White spoke. "*Once again into the great paragon of freedom.*' So does that mean elections?"

The senator shuffled in his seat and coughed. "This is rhetoric at this time but with the war over there can be no reason to continue with the suspension of elections. I think that's clear."

"And that's going to be in the address, tonight?"

The senator frowned. "Gerard, today is a celebration. The war's over, we won."

"What did we win? Last time I looked at a map, or at a balance sheet, we've won diddly-squat. The latest reports from the treasury show that -"

The senator was holding up his hand. "Gerard, Gerard, what we've won, today, is peace with honour and that's what's going in the address tonight, Peace with Honour. We've had seven very difficult years of fighting, and six difficult months of negotiations, and now here we are, where we want to be, with the fighting over and a new dawn of rebuilding and prosperity around the corner. The suspension of elections is just one of many sacrifices we've had to make in order to achieve this goal. But the war's over now," he could barely believe he was saying the words, "and the suspension of elections is one of many issues we will come to address in the very near future."

White stared across the table at him, trying to read his face, which remained inscrutable. "But for now, elections remain suspended?"

"For now. We'll get to it. I happen to know that the president sees it as a level one priority. He hated to do it, you know. We had to persuade him."

White snorted. "Hated to do it? I hate it too. And I'm going to keep on at this until he makes it right."

"Gerard, you worry too much. This isn't some tin-pot republic. This is the United States and Nations."

White backed down, thumbing through his papers. The senator spoke now to the room, louder. "That's it folks! War's over, you can all go back to bed!" White stood up, gathered his papers and left, mixing in with the assorted cabinet members, aides and Secret Service personnel filing towards the door.

The senator was deep in conversation with one of his advisers, who had slipped into a vacated seat to his right. The adviser was holding a paper on the table in front of the senator, moving his finger across some lines about a third of the way down the page. The senator was shaking his head. "No, no, they have to wait. And it can't go out like that, have Spector re-draught it."

Farrell stood behind the senator and waited for an opening. The senator had seen him approach and was well aware of his presence but made him wait all the same, stretching out the conversation with the aide far longer than was strictly necessary. Eventually he turned and, as though taken by surprise said, "Farrell! You need a minute?" Farrell remained standing.

"I do, actually, Senator."

The senator gestured. "Take a seat, I'll be right with you." Farrell and two assistants took up seats opposite the senator. The room had emptied now. Farrell waited while the senator scribbled notes on the papers in front of him, then handed them off to his aide. "See that he gets this right away," he said, then turned to Farrell. "What can I do for you?"

"It's Mars, Senator."

"Mars?"

"Yes, sir. We've been monitoring communications and modelling population growth and industrial production, and we think there is reasonable cause for concern."

"You do. Why?"

"You're aware of the Kasugai study, published last year?"

"Should I be?"

"Well, the study showed that, theoretically at least, Mars has been capable of total independence from Earth for the last eight years. That is to say, the population is now large enough, and production is big enough and varied enough, for Mars to maintain its current status, in terms of economy, population and production, without any," he repeated for effect, "*without any* input from, or indeed trade with, Earth."

The senator eyed him quizzically. "That's great, isn't it? We've conquered another world, a historic feat."

"Well, Senator, it is a great achievement, I'll grant you that much. But what if the Martians decide *they've* conquered another world?"

"Decide . . ."

"It's like this, Senator. They don't need us. Some of the younger Martians now are fourth, even fifth generation. Most of them have never been here, heck, most of them couldn't afford to come here if they wanted to.

EPHIALTES

They don't feel any allegiance to us. Remember, the most vocal anti-war movement was based on Mars."

The senator brought his hand up to his chin and rubbed it thoughtfully. "And they're talking about this, are they, the Martians?"

"Well yes, sir, it seems they are. We've been monitoring coms across the planet and between planets and it does seem that this idea is out there. The war has alienated lots of people and the idea of Martian independence or a so-called Free Mars -"

"Sheez!" the senator said, unable to help himself.

". . . the idea of a Free Mars has been gaining lots of ground."

The senator took his glasses off and began cleaning them, rubbing the glass with a carefully folded cloth. "So what do we need to do?" Farrell looked at him, momentarily lost for words.

"Well, at the moment nothing. But we do need to be aware of it. I mean, that's what we're here for, to flag up these potential hot-spots before they become actual hot-spots. I don't know what we could do now, practically. Resuming elections would help politically, but with the celebrations coming up -"

"What celebrations?"

"Sometime in the next few months the one hundred thousandth Martian will be born. It's going to be a big whoop on Mars. It may serve to focus minds on just these issues we're talking about. So with that in mind, maybe some counterprogramming might be of use? We could give it prominent recognition here. Have a big parade with an address by the president, or something like that. Maybe we should have sent someone senior over there to lead the celebrations."

"Believe me, Farrell, if I could send the vice president to Mars I would."

"Well, I just think we should be thinking along those lines. Hearts and minds, you know. It's probably nothing, but we should be keeping an eye on it."

The senator stood up and offered his hand. "Thanks for that, Farrell. Thanks for bringing that to our attention." His face cracked into a smirk. "We've just got out of one war, we don't want to be getting into another. Particularly one that's a hundred and forty million miles away - we'd lose home advantage." He winked.

Farrell smiled. "I'm sure it won't come to that, sir. Not if we keep on top of it."

The senator turned and left.

Farrell and his two senior aides got back to his office at the Department of Foreign Affairs around 16:30. Farrell sat at his desk, quickly checking for any notifications on his secure terminal before kicking his chair back and swinging his feet up onto the desk. His silver hair made him look older than his forty-eight years, and his matinee-idol good looks, which he'd managed to kid himself had somehow been a detriment to his political career, were fading. "What time's the address?" he asked the aides.

"Five o'clock".

"Can we get it up on there?" He indicated the blank wall opposite his desk.

"Sure."

"Okay, we'll do that. And do we have champagne, anything like that?" The second aide was looking down at her mobile communication device. "I'm getting on to that now. You want the good stuff?"

"Aw . . . middling? I do *want* the good stuff, but I'll stick to what I can afford."

"Okay. Four magnums of the not-quite-best champagne, on their way."

"Great. Can you get everyone up here for the address? Say, five minutes before?"

"We'll do that. Should be great. You know Shirley?"

Farrell thought, blankly.

"She's assistant to the junior secretaries. Anyway, she has a son in Mombasa. She's going to be in bits. It might make for a great photo, you hugging her and looking understanding?"

Farrell baulked. "Oh come on, you hard hearted-bitch!" he said, but smiled too.

EPHIALTES

"That's the kind of thinking I'm paid for," the aide chirpily replied.

Farrell sunk into thought for a little bit, then wondered aloud, "Are we right to worry about Mars? Is that even our department?"

The woman aide looked up, startled. "Well, it is foreign, isn't it? I mean, how much more foreign can you get?"

Farrell thought. "It just seems, I don't know, different, somehow. So far away that it's not even foreign. And surely it's just part of the USAN, isn't it? I mean, it's not a country or even a state. Marineris is about the size of a small town."

The aide cut in, "No, it comes under us alright. And we're right to be monitoring."

"But there's nothing to it, is there, really? This chatter about breaking away, independence and all that? Armchair warriors and know-nothing kids. They'd shit the bed if we just left them to it, wouldn't they?"

"Maybe. But we're paid to be paranoid, so we are."

"And anyways, they're halfway across the solar system."

"Some of the time they are. Every couple of years they swing by real close - fifty million miles or so. And apparently Helios are this close," she gestured with thumb and forefinger, "to developing usable sized fusion engines which will turn interplanetary travel upside down. You could hop across in your lunch break, almost."

Farrell frowned. "Helios have been about to reveal their fusion engine tech ever since I was a kid. There's no quick or easy way to or from Mars. It's a six month trip, minimum, and even then you have to wait up to two years for a launch window. They need our tech, we need their deuterium, free trade, honour, loyalty, yada, yada, the end. I just wanted the senator to know that, even without a war on, we have stuff to be doing over here. We're on the lookout for any problems, we've got our ears to the floor and our eyes on the horizon and our fingers on the pulse. Forever vigilant." He flashed a big phony smile at the assistant.

"Sheesh," she said, "and you haven't even had any champagne yet."

CHAPTER 02

Kostovich

Dr Daniel Kostovich eyed the barren landscape ahead. Dried brown dirt and the straggliest of sun-beaten foliage stretched before him to a distant and just discernible clump of buildings. It was hot in the suit, and the restricted movement made him feel trapped. He needed to get out of the sun, but he needed to know he was safe. Continuing to scan the horizon for movement he lifted one huge metal leg, then the other, and moved forward. He spoke into the mic. "Stocksy, Bacon. I'm comin' to getcha."

A voice crackled back over the headset. "What about me?"

Kostovich grinned. "Dennis? Time I get over there, Stocksy and Bacon will have taken you out already. If you haven't just fallen over."

"You're a funny guy, Dan. That's why I'm going to kill you last."

Kostovich laughed. "It's great that you still believe you have some worthwhile abilities, Dennis. Despite the overwhelming evidence to the contrary."

Dennis's voice came back over the com. "I'm going radio silent now. Gotta concentrate. Have asses to kick. Out."

Kostovich noted a small outcrop of rocks about two hundred metres from his position. He headed toward them. He brought up a terminal in his HUD, set his mech on an automated course for the outcrop, then brought up a new screen to which he half-whispered a command, "AI

328, scan all channels. Flag and list possibles, report on completion. Confirm estimated time of completion."

A crystal clear and honey-drenched female voice replied immediately. "Scan completion estimated at less than two minutes."

Inside the mech Kostovich stood a little over four metres high. Stood on the ground next to it he would be less than half that size. At twenty-nine years of age he was the youngest department head at Venkdt Mars Corporation. His department was Research and Development. He had been a prodigy at school and often had to deny that his parents, in particular his father, the renowned physicist Craig Kostovich, had modified him in utero to be a brainiac. He'd considered the possibility himself. His dad was crazy, but not that crazy. Dan had just been lucky with his genes, lucky with his nurturing family, who had indulged his 'experiments' and 'research', and lucky to have been around when the settlement at Marineris was still just about a frontier town with people happy to let a little kid ask questions about the place, the landscape and the fancy kit that enabled them to survive there.

He won a prize for his advanced AIs when he was thirteen. That was even reported back on the old home planet, though somewhere near the end of the bulletins.

Kostovich had breezed through school, embarrassing his teachers and alienating his peers. He started on his first PhD (artificial intelligence) when he was just turned seventeen and completed his second (astrophysics) at twenty-two, though that one was just for fun.

He'd raced up the ranks at Venkdt by identifying flaws in their processes and suggesting solutions. Within a couple of years of starting there he had saved them hundreds of thousands and made them millions. In R&D he oversaw all development projects, but his special baby, the thing he got hands-on with (hands-on a keyboard, at least) was AI. Kostovich didn't need to be a great designer of products or processes, though he had the skills to do that, because what he really excelled at was designing AIs that designed great products and processes. With his knowledge of computing networks, cyphers, telegraphy and encryption he could protect that intellectual property from others and rent its power to them.

He'd been head of R&D at Venkdt for two years. The initial thrill had worn off, somewhat. He now found himself correcting tedious and obvious errors in the work of others, and endlessly tinkering with his AIs and monitoring systems. He had risen rapidly, but now there was nowhere left for him to rise to. It wasn't like he could be headhunted by Hjälp Teknik - they had less than a tenth of the resources of Venkdt - and he had no desire whatsoever to go to the home planet, a place he had never been and never wished to. He was fourth-gen Martian, and to him Earth was a foreign and backward looking place, millions of miles away and of only academic interest. He was top of his particular tree at Venkdt, with only the board and Charles Venkdt above him (and they weren't going anywhere soon) and, all things considered, that wasn't a bad place to be. It maybe lacked excitement, but that could be had outside work in things like competitive IVR games.

The honey-voice spoke, "Scan complete. Two anomalies detected."

"Okay. Run AI 14S and AI 14V on the anomalies. Multi-decrypt and report, please give me the estimated time of completion."

"Completion in five to six minutes," came the reply.

Kostovich manoeuvred the mech from behind the outcrop and spied the cluster of buildings. "Thermal," he said, and the vista in front of him changed to a blue, yellow and red child's painting, which he quickly scanned. Nothing. "How long to completion now?"

"Five minutes."

He made his move, breaking from his hiding place and striding toward the hamlet. At pace the mech could travel at around 15km/h. Right now he was vulnerable, but he couldn't stay hidden behind a rock forever. Crossing the open ground he scanned back and forth across the buildings, looking for any sign of movement, his finger held lightly over the trigger in his right hand. At thirty metres out he heard a 'ratatatatata' and a percussive 'ka-boom!' It was difficult to locate, but seemed to be from the opposite end of the hamlet.

Dennis's voice spluttered over the com. "Son of a bitch. Son of a bitch!"

"Morning, Den," said Stocksy. "Thanks for the missiles." Stocksy was now one up on them, and had access to missiles in addition to the machine guns they had each started with.

Kostovich hove closely to the perimeter wall and inched around, trying to get a look down the main street. The buildings were Earth style, above ground and battered. The place looked like some of the news reports from the war on Earth.

"Stocksy?" Kostovich asked into the com.

"Hey, Dan. Don't worry, I've got plenty for you too."

"See you in a bit. Looking forward to it. You seen Bacon?"

"Nope. But when I see him, I'm gonna fry his ass!"

Bacon crackled over com for the first time, "Never gets old, Stocksy, never gets old."

"Probably camped out somewhere," said Kostovich. "Do you want him or shall I do it?"

"Well," Stocksy replied, "if I get him I'll be on guided missiles, Dan. If you get him, it's honours even for the final showdown on Main Street."

"I don't need superior hardware, Stocksy. I already have superior tactics. Take him if you want."

Kostovich spoke to his AI, "How long to completion?"

"Two minutes."

Kostovich knew Bacon liked to camp in buildings. A building with a mech shaped hole in it very likely had a Bacon camping inside it. Bacon's tactics were as obvious as Dennis's, so he'd be facing out into the main street waiting for someone to wander down it. Kostovich continued circling the perimeter, carefully watching all potential danger points as he went. He was just crossing a side road out of the ville when the corner of the building above him exploded into shower of dust and fragments, which rained down about him. Bacon was still on the machine gun; it had to be Stocksy. Kostovich ducked and continued, working over in his mind where Stocksy was. It was a narrow road, so to have hit the back of it he could only be in one specific area midway down Main Street on the opposing side. Glancing to his left as he continued his anti-clockwise orbit of the town he saw some rubble. Bacon.

"How long to completion?"

"Forty-five seconds."

Kostovich pulled back from the perimeter and ran around it in the direction he had been going. As he passed the building Bacon was hid out in he fired a burst of machine gun fire into it, but was gone before Bacon could make the full turn necessary to return fire. Bacon was turning back when Stocksy's missile hit him, and he was out of the game.

"Head shot!" Stocksy declared.

Kostovich made for the top of Main Street. "Completion?"

"Completing in ten, nine . . ."

As the countdown finished Kostovich peered gingerly around the corner and up Main Street, where he could just see Stocksy's missile arm pulling back behind the corner of a building.

"Decryption complete. Competing systems owned. Total time five minutes and forty-three seconds."

"Please run AI M22 on competing system Stocksy."

Kostovich now stepped boldly out onto Main Street and walked up it at a casual pace.

With a flick of the eye he switched the com to Stocksy. "Stocksy? Comin' to get ya, fella!"

"M22 is now complete on competing system Stocksy," said the AI.

"Dan?" said Stocksy, "I hate to do this, but . . ." Stocksy ran across the street, all the while locked onto Kostovich, who implacably strode toward him. Just before the midway point Stocksy's mech juddered as two missiles launched from the forearms, leaving a cloud behind them as they streaked down Main Street. Stocksy had planned to run back into cover on the other side of the street, but on seeing his missiles get away, locked-on and with no reply, he decided to stop and savour his moment of victory. The huge mech skidded very slightly as it came to a stop on the far side of the street.

The missiles streaked passed Kostovich and out of the end of the ville. At first Stocksy couldn't figure out why there had been no satisfying double boom, and the smoky missile trail blocked his view. For a split second he knew something was not right. In the time it took him to figure out what was wrong the missiles had already turned about and had rushed back to the place from whence they came.

Ba-Boom!

The top of Stocksy's mech was totally destroyed. The lower half fell to its knees like it was bowing before its superior.

"Good game," said Kostovich.

"Goddamn, Dan, that's cheating!" said Stocksy.

"It technically isn't," said Kostovich. "If you don't like it we can turn off cyberwarfare next time."

"We should, too," Bacon chimed in. "It gives you an unfair advantage."

"It's advantageous to me, but it's perfectly fair. Only a fool wouldn't play to their advantages."

"I'm done here," said Dennis.

"Me too," said Kostovich. "Laters.

"Laters."

"Laters."

"See you later, guys."

Kostovich pulled off his headset and slumped back into the sofa. He blinked twice and shook his head, quickly looking about the room to re-orient himself.

He glanced over at his terminal screen and could see something blinking red in the notification area. "Put that up on the wall," he said. The terminal appeared on the wall in front of him and he began to read. "Show me that report, bottom right," he said.

"USAN Monitoring?" the AI asked.

"Yes." The report enlarged to fill the wall and Kostovich began to read it, glancing through the lines with a slight frown. He had sent one of his AIs to covertly worm its way into the USAN's secure information systems months earlier. The operation was so delicate that, initially at least, it was not to report back. Its preliminary task was to remain undetected while it monitored the system. Kostovich had programmed it to monitor as long as it felt necessary. Any sort of premature call home risked exposure. The AI was absolutely not to do that until it was convinced it could do so safely.

Like a forlorn lover Kostovich had waited for his AI to return. He had assumed it would take a few days before he heard anything, but very quickly the days had developed into months. He didn't know what might have happened.

There were three options. The first was that the AI had been intercepted. Kostovich found that difficult to accept. From various reconnaissance attacks he had mounted previously he understood the landscape he was going into. He knew there were certain vulnerabilities in the system, and he had programmed his AI to exploit them. He felt sure it had not been compromised.

The second option was that the AI had failed. He could not countenance this possibility. He was a maestro at programming AIs and this piece had been one of his finest works.

Option three was the only one which seemed viable; that his AI was still burrowing around the system undetected. This meant that the crack was much more complex than he had expected. He was willing to concede that much. If the problem was harder than had been anticipated, so be it. He had unwavering faith that his creation was equal to the task. All it needed was time.

The report had been tasked with monitoring all output from the USAN government and military. The AI had the ability to encode messages into standard communications if necessary. If it felt unable to communicate directly it could attempt to do so covertly, via an overlay on some mundane communication.

Kostovich scanned the report.

Nothing.

In the last twenty-four hours the government and military had publicly released over thirty-two thousand communications, ranging from county administration notices to full governmental reports. They were all clean; no coded communications.

Kostovich was tired. He had had a long day and the game, despite being fun, had been somewhat draining. He usually checked for a call from his AI at least twice a day. Every time it failed to call home was a disappointment. This time was no exception. He decided to call it a night.

"Continue scanning," said Kostovich. "Make a report every eight hours. And, of course, ears remain open for a standard call."

"Yes, Dr Kostovich," the terminal replied. "Will there be anything else?"

"Can you order some more Pop-Tarts?"

"Of course, next delivery will be tomorrow at 08:30."

"That's great."

Kostovich awoke at 08:20 next morning. He swung his feet out of bed and sat there for a moment, not quite awake, before rising and shuffling into his living room, slumping onto the sofa. "Anything overnight?" he said through a yawn.

"Yes," the AI said. "AI 2257 reports: '*Success*'"

Kostovich jumped up. "What? Success? Gimme the details. I want them on the wall."

Kostovich's living room wall came alive with the display from his terminal. He could see it right there, in letters twenty centimetres high: '*04.39 Level 6 security owned.*' Kostovich silently punched the air. "Pull me some Level 6 data," he said. "Anything regarding . . ." He thought. "Anything regarding domestic disturbances on USAN military bases in the last two weeks."

"Yes, Dr Kostovich."

Kostovich had to wait only a few seconds before text began scrolling up his screen. Emails, court documents and all kinds of communications were there for him to see. Level 6 was the lowest level on the USAN's security scale. Nothing here would be of the slightest importance or interest. But he was in. The AI was alive and was chewing its way through the security levels. All he needed to do now was wait, and a treasure trove of information would open up to him.

He wanted to tell someone about the staggering achievement he had just made, but what he had done was illegal and, as it currently stood, rather pointless. All the good stuff was still to come. He thought about what he should do. "Get me an appointment with Venkdt," he said.

"Christina Venkdt?" the AI replied.

"I wish. No, fix me up a meeting with Charles Venkdt."

"Mr Venkdt doesn't have any openings until next week. Would you like to proceed with booking the appointment?"

"Sure. It's not important."

Kostovich once again scanned through the lists of uninteresting low-level government communications.

"Your Pop-Tarts have arrived," said his terminal.

"*Oh, yes they have*," said Kostovich, grinning broadly. "Pop some in, would you?"

CHAPTER 03

Welcome Home

Sliding his hand down the rail as he went, he moved in descending circles down the helical staircase. He reached the bottom and strode across to the bar. It was nearly empty now, as he liked it. By Artificial Earth Time it was past 2:00am. He pulled a seat up at the bar and punched a command into his coms device. A robot arm mounted on rails in the ceiling behind the bar glided smoothly past him, its speaker emitting, "Coming right up, sir," as it went. The arm quickly and without error grabbed a shot glass and placed it on the bar, then turned to grab a bottle. It whisked the bottle to the glass at great speed then instantly slowed for the pour. As soon as the drink was poured the speed increased dramatically as the bottle was placed back on the shelf. The arm returned. "This first drink today is complementary as part of your trip. Subsequent drinks will be charged to your account. A maximum of five drinks is allowed in any twenty-four hour period. Enjoy yourself, and drink responsibly."

"Screw you, pal."

"Have a nice day."

He took a sip of the drink and winced a little. At the other end of the bar a solitary older guy was lost in his comdev, prodding the screen and issuing the occasional whispered voice command. He looked up and, after a pause, put the comdev in his pocket. Grabbing the beer in front of him he stood up, half falling from his chair. He sauntered up the bar. "Hey, friend," he said.

Bobby Karjalainen half-turned to him and offered a forced, thin smile. "Hey," he said. The man sat himself down next to Karjalainen and stuck out his hand expectantly.

"Name's Mike, how're you doin'?"

Karjalainen took the hand and shook it. "I'm doin' good," he said.

"Ain't seen you down here before. Thought I knew just about everybody on board."

Bobby shrugged. "Been in my room mostly, or the gym."

"That would explain it!" Mike said, too loudly. "You won't be catchin' me in no gym!" He grinned at his remark and, from politeness, Bobby smiled back. "So you've been holed up in your room, eh? That'd drive me crazy. I have to get out and talk to people. I'm just about stir crazy already. I'm lookin' forward to pullin' in tomorrow. I hate these trips, I really do." Bobby took a sip of his drink. Mike continued. "What can you get up to in your room all day? Beats me how you could do that."

Bobby placed his glass on the bar. "Well, you know. You've got the VR, music, enhanced sleep. Kills the time," said Bobby.

Mike gave him a sidelong look. "Beats me. I have to get out and talk to people. Can't stay cooped up. I hate these trips."

"You travel a lot?"

"Yes, sir, business. This is the third time I've made this trip in twenty-five years. Imagine that! I've pissed three years of my life away, floating through space." For a second he looked genuinely saddened by the thought, but soon picked up. "At least they pay me well for it! I guess it put the kids through school, anyhow."

"That's a way to look at it."

"How about you? First time out?"

Bobby drew a breath. "I've been out once before, going the other way. But I'm on my way home now."

"Way home? You're a Martian?"

"I'd have to say I am. And I'm going home, if you want to drink to that."

"To home," said Mike, raising his glass.

"To home," Bobby echoed.

Mike took a deep gulp of his beer. "So what you been up to on the old home planet?"

Bobby looked Mike in the eye. "I've been serving my country."

Mike took a second to process the information. "The Army? Let me tell you right off, I got nothing but respect for you guys. Nothing but respect. Some of these protesters, well, it makes me sick. The only reason they can parade around with their fancy-dan nonsense is because of guys like you. Where'd you serve? London? LA? I did a year myself, as a reservist. Mainly from home, you understand, but I get it. The discipline, service, honour."

"Lahore."

Mike fell silent for the first time and glanced around the bar as if a script boy would be there to whisper his next line to him. "Lahore?" he said, cautiously. "That had to be pretty rough, right?"

Bobby frowned. "Yeah, it was rough alright. But we'd trained for it. We knew the risks going in."

"Well, I take my hat off to you, sir. I do really." Mike searched for something else to say. "Can I get you another drink?"

Bobby looked at Mike. "Sure."

Mike called out to the robot arm, "Bar keep! I'd like another beer over here and . . ."

"Whisky."

"And a whisky for my friend."

The robot arm zoomed up the bar. "I'm sorry, sir, but we are not allowed to serve you any more alcoholic drinks; today's limit has been reached."

Mike leaned toward the arm. "Now you look here, this is a war hero and we want our drinks, okay?"

"I'm sorry sir. Would you like to file a customer services incident report?"

Bobby cut in. "Could I have a beer and a whisky?" he asked.

"Of course, sir, coming up." The arm whirred off to prepare the drinks.

"See that!" Mike cried. "Even the machines have respect for a war hero!"

Bobby smiled and shook his head. The arm placed the beer and whisky on the bar in front of them. "Your account has been debited. You have two drinks remaining for the current period. Enjoy yourself, and drink responsibly."

Mike grabbed his beer, thrusting it toward Bobby. "To drinking responsibly," he said, with a slight slur in his voice.

"To drinking responsibly," Bobby answered.

After taking swigs they sat in silence for the next few seconds, Mike toying with the edge of a bar mat. He glanced up at Bobby. "What was it like?"

"Lahore?"

Mike seemed ashamed now at having asked the question. "Yeah, Lahore."

Bobby pulled himself back in his seat, tilting his head to one side as he searched for an answer. "It was rough. Like they said. But we held on to it. And some of us got medals, too."

There was a pause, then Mike said, "We're all very proud of what you guys did. I mean," he struggled for words, ". . . thank you. Thank you for your service."

Bobby nodded. "It shouldn't have happened that way, but," he paused, ". . . but we did all we could and we made it in the end."

"People actually died, didn't they?"

"They did. We lost thirteen squads, thirteen commanders. Worst losses of the entire war."

Mike's mouth fell open.

"Thirteen?" he repeated, dumbfounded. "My God . . ."

"Twelve mechs to a squad, with the command drone. You don't want to be losing a hundred and fifty tactical fighting units in the biggest battle of the Fourth World War, but what can you do? War sucks, huh?"

Mike was still staring. "But the people. *Thirteen*. They said it was four in the bulletins."

Bobby smirked. "Well, you know. The first casualty of war and all that. Anyway, we held onto Lahore, and you know the rest. Peace with honour." He offered up his glass. Mike chinked his against it.

"Peace with honour," he said.

Mike shuffled in his seat and studied the drinks behind the bar as if he had never seen them before. "You know," he said, "I'm a bit of a history buff. Military history, that sort of thing." Bobby looked at him quizzically. Mike continued. "That's what I read, mostly. I've read hundreds of books about that stuff, especially the world wars, one, two and three. And of course I've been following this one, your one, in the news. Different to being there, I guess. How about you? Do you read that stuff?" he asked.

"Not really," said Bobby. "We did a little in training, studying tactics, strategy and so forth, but I'm not much of one for history."

"It's really interesting," said Mike. "It fascinates me."

Bobby sipped his drink.

"I was a big supporter of the Commander Program, you know? A lot of people didn't like it but I knew it would be good, I knew it would work and I knew it would be worth it. I think we lost our way with the drones. We lost something, you know what I mean? It made war too easy. Everyone was far too willing to reach for the military option when there were no risks involved. It made war, somehow," he struggled to find the word, ". . . dishonourable. Apart from this last war, do you know when the last time the USAN, or even the old USA as it was then, last deployed human soldiers on the battlefield?" Bobby shook his head. "It was 2087, WWIII. That was the last time until this one, a hundred and fifty years without a single live soldier deployed on the field of battle. Even in the civil wars it was all drones on the battlefield. The Battle of Seville was actually fought in sheds in Kentucky." Bobby nodded. "So I take my hat off to you guys. That takes some balls, to do what you did."

"We just did what was asked of us," said Bobby. "I'd have been just as happy to have sat in an air conditioned shed in Kentucky than have had my ass shot off in Lahore. I just felt like I should give something back. The old country asked people to serve, so I did."

"What was it like in the Commander Program?" Mike asked.

"It was okay, I guess," Bobby replied. "We did all the standard training in the sims like regular soldiers, and then some field training on top. Training with the mechs suits was pretty rough."

Mike cut in, "Mech suits?"

"Yeah, the command drones. They're the same as the drones in your squad but with less ammo to allow space for you to be in."

"How many drones to a squad?" asked Mike, even though he knew the answer.

"Twelve, including the command drone. Each squad is eleven drones and one commander. The drones can all act autonomously, but can follow direct orders from the commander. If the commander is injured or incapacitated, control of the squad will fall back to remote pilots based outside the theatre of operations. But all the while you're in the field the squad commander has total operational control. The whole point of the program is that an operational commander there in the field, with direct personal experience of what is happening, is better placed to make situational judgements than someone sat maybe three thousand miles away. There's no substitution for actually being there on the ground."

"But the risks are," Mike paused, "unbelievable. And you volunteered. Incredible." Bobby smiled. "Someone had to do it."

Someone may have had to do it but it needn't have been Bobby. He was born a hundred and forty million miles away, and with his family connections he could easily have remained out of it. His father Jack had been mortified when Bobby told him he had volunteered, and had threatened to disown him. In truth Jack was terrified about what might become of his son, but he masked that feeling with anger, casting Bobby out of the House of Karjalainen and pulling his younger son Anthony even closer.

Bobby had always been the most difficult of the two boys, in trouble at school, in trouble with girls, in trouble with the police, but his easy smile and winning ways had always managed to get him through. When he was younger his sheepish grin and 'what the hell' shrug worked on his father too, but as he got older Jack Karjalainen became increasingly immune. He still loved Bobby but found it harder and harder to let him know it. Maybe that's why Bobby volunteered; to get a reaction out of his father. And maybe it worked, but Jack Karjalainen would never admit to it.

"Incredible," Mike said to himself. "Can I get you another drink?"

"I don't think you can," Bobby said, and then to the machine, "Hey, barkeep. Same again here." The robot arm performed its whirring magic, finishing with its weary message about drinking responsibly.

Mike grabbed his new beer and took a sip. "What did it feel like?" he said.

"Feel like?"

"Yeah, what did it feel like, the fighting?"

"It felt like the sims. You've played the sims right? *Mech Azimuth 4* and all those? It feels just like that, but with hard work and no resets."

"Yeah, but, I mean . . ."

"What?"

Mike took a breath and searched for the words. "I mean in an actual battle, firing actual weapons at actual people?"

"Yeah? Well," said Bobby, "they were trying to kill me, and they had volunteered to be there just like I had. They knew the risks; so did I. I guess it felt good."

Mike laughed. At first a nervous giggle, but then a full-throated belly laugh. "You hard-hearted son of a bitch," he said. "You're a cold-blooded killer!" He laughed again. Bobby laughed a little too. It wasn't quite true, what he had said, but it sounded good to the fans and the war buffs, and it put them off the scent of how he really felt.

"I guess so," Bobby said, "I guess that's what made me an effective soldier."

"I guess it did," Mike replied.

Bobby downed his remaining whisky. "I'm turning in now, Mike. It was good to meet you."

"Well," Mike said, "before you go I'd like to make a toast to the returning hero." He raised his glass. "To . . ." He paused blankly. "I'm so sorry, what was your name again?"

"Karjalainen. Bobby Karjalainen."

"Yes! Yes, I knew I knew your face. Goddamn! Great book. *Great* book." Mike grabbed Bobby's hand, shaking it vigorously as he continued. "To Bobby Karjalainen, and all those like him, to whom we owe our freedom, and because of whom we can sleep safely in our beds at night. Chin chin!" Bobby clinked glasses with him, though his own was empty. Bobby slipped from his stool and made to leave but Mike grabbed his shoulder. Bleary-eyed, Mike looked straight at Bobby and said, with all the sincerity he could muster, "Welcome home, Bobby. Welcome back to Mars."

The port was sparsely populated. Flights from Earth arrived only every two years. For most of the time the space was used for warehousing and the staff on duty today were security personnel from the main USAN base at Marineris. They knew exactly who was coming and they knew exactly what they were bringing with them. Every milligram had to be accounted for on the flight and, in addition to the exorbitant cost, a thorough medical and psych exam was necessary before anyone could be cleared for interplanetary flight. The cost would have made the trip off-limits to Bobby but the army picked up the tab both ways; as a volunteer for the military on the way out and as a war-hero on the way back.

On finishing his final tour Bobby had been paraded as something of a poster boy back in the USAN. His easy smile looked as good on the bulletins as it did on the posters, and he maintained enough gravity to make his flip and scripted answers to the tougher questions (tougher, but not tough. No one in the media would be dumb enough to ask an actual tough question) seem weighty and considered. He had consented to a ghost-written book, *Return of the Warrior*, about his experience in the Commander Program. The only part people were interested in was the Battle of Lahore. Bobby signed off on the book, even though it bore scant relation to the events it depicted. It had been jazzed up into an adventure story with just enough true horror and grit left in to make it seem serious and worthy. In reality it was a trashy and jingoistic thriller to be chosen above others because of the words 'true story' (in fact, '*The Explosive True Story!*') and the picture of Bobby looking suitably determined and heroic on the cover.

Bobby had ridden his fifteen minutes expertly and had enjoyed every moment. He'd been on seven different chat shows across four countries and had spoken at two prestigious universities. The rock star life had been great, but the travelling and the easy availability of admiring women had eventually come between him and Askel.

After initial training Bobby had served two outstanding virtual tours out of the famed 'Kentucky Sheds'. It appeared he was preternaturally gifted at remotely piloting attack mechs and drones, and he had an unusually well-developed sense of tactics and strategy.

His prodigious skills had not gone unnoticed and when he volunteered for the newly announced Commander Program he had been snapped up immediately.

As one of the first volunteers Bobby had been in the Commander Program more or less from the very beginning. His training group had worked closely with Helios Matériel Corporation, one of the top military contractors, in developing the command drones. Initially these had been adapted standard drones with little or no ammo. Important systems had been moved about the chassis in order to make room for someone to sit inside. This worked out okay in initial VR training but in field trials the problems became more and more apparent. The command drones were underpowered, under armed and under armoured. When it became clear that no amount of rejigging was going to solve the problems, Helios brought in their second most senior designer and briefed her to rebuild the design for the command drones from scratch. Her name was Askel Lund.

Bobby worked closely with Askel. He knew what was needed and he was always keen to test prototypes on the training grounds. Bobby was a passionate advocate for the command drones to be armed. Initially it had been thought that with the firepower of eleven battle drones at his or her disposal there would be no need for the command drone itself to be fully armed. Bobby knew that in a tight-spot the command drone would need to defend itself, maybe even using manual controls.

He knew too the value of armour. The Commander Program had been sold as a glorious return to the days of ancient warriors, risking their lives in honourable battle for the greater good. Some of that made sense to Bobby, but he didn't think solders should be throwing their lives away as a sop to some crazy ideas about honour and valour that were centuries out of date. Death on the battlefield was a possibility; it didn't have to be a duty.

Askel worked at the design and refined it with Bobby's input until she had honed it down to something usable and effective. The command drones stood four metres high and looked very similar to the humanoid mech drones they commanded. This was important, as it prevented the enemy easily identifying and picking off the commanders. The command drones had space in the body cavity from where the commanders piloted them. The commander's head was exposed to the front to allow the situational awareness that was at the heart of the program, but could be sealed off in a split second. A Plexiglas screen would instantly deploy to protect the pilot from any incoming threat. Once, in the training field, Bobby's visor deployed when a bee harmlessly bumbled past at a distance of five metres.

The headsets the pilots wore relayed live information to them via audio coms and a head-up display. Advanced algorithms processed all available data and, based on the situational scenario, mission objectives and a detailed analysis of the pilots previous actions, would only display information deemed likely to be useful. Commands could be issued to the commander's drones visually, verbally or via predetermined 'situational' responses. The drones had a huge array of fully customisable routines in addition to their independent heuristic evaluation techniques and constantly adapting AI.

Askel and Bobby had kept their relationship secret, fearing it would jeopardise their respective positions. They thought it might be perceived as unprofessional. The clandestine nature of their liaisons just added to the fun for Bobby but Askel had found it difficult. She took her job seriously and she hated the idea of the cliché that their relationship was; the serious professional woman bowled over by the rugged, handsome and rough-round-the-edges man in a uniform. To her there was more to it than that. She felt that she understood Bobby, having come from a well-known and wealthy family herself, and she knew that she saw a different side to him than he showed to the rest of the world. Bobby was the easy-going, up-for-anything guy, modest with it even though he knew how easily he fell to almost any task at hand, and he projected a what-the-hell, devil-may-care roguishness that the people around him loved. He was dependable, smart, just-a-bit-crazy-but-not-too-crazy and above all, something of a bad-boy. Crucially, not so bad that he was dangerous to know, but just bad enough that hanging out with him felt very slightly naughty. When you were with Bobby it felt like you might get caught and told off at any moment, and that was a *good* feeling. Askel knew that feeling; all those who knew Bobby experienced it at one time or another. But Askel felt she knew something that few if any others did; the real Bobby, the man at the core. That Bobby was sensitive, thoughtful and filled with a restless, searching melancholy. That was the true Bobby. Askel's Bobby.

Bobby shuffled along the check-in line, observing his surroundings. The building was large and like most buildings on Mars was mostly underground. It was pressurised against the unbreathable and low pressure Martian atmosphere, with a minimum of the structure above the surface. The entrance bays were served by ramps sunk into the ground. Thick reinforced Plexiglas skylights made up the bulk of the above ground parts of the structure. The skylights were bordered by rails on which were mounted brushes and power-jets which periodically whooshed up and down them, clearing the ever-present Martian dust which accumulated whenever the wind got up, which was often.

They had transferred from the landing vehicle through an airlock into what was, in effect, a large coach. They were then driven the few short kilometres to the warehouse terminal. Another trip through an airlock and they were ushered through to this larger area.

Bobby was relishing the luxury of space as he moved slowly up the line. The journey from Earth had taken six months. Since he had stepped into the 'bone-shaker' HLV back in Ontario half a year ago this was the largest space he had been in. From the HLV he had transferred to an HEO shuttle which had taken him out to the interplanetary craft, where he had spent the bulk of the journey. That ship never landed; it was on a permanent elliptical orbit around the sun. Once every two years you could hop on near Earth, and hop off six months later at Mars. The eighteen month return trip was unmanned and used primarily to transport freight, the most precious of which was the deuterium on which the early Martian economy had been founded. A second interplanetary solar orbiter was on a different orbit; Mars to Earth in six months with the eighteen month journey on the return.

The solar orbiters were functional but, necessarily, minimal. Space was at a premium. The ships had been designed so as to *feel* as big as possible to their inhabitants. The crew was limited to one doctor and one engineer, all other roles being fully automated or seen to by service drones. There was a gym, use of which was highly encouraged, and a combined refectory and day area in addition to the cabins. Cabins were equipped with entertainment centres, Immersive Virtual Reality (IVR) units and other home comforts. Customers could also opt for 'Enhanced Sleep' where, by means of drug therapy and careful electromagnetic manipulations of the subject's brain, the user could sleep for extended periods of up to three or four days at a time. This was a good option where there was, essentially, nothing to do for six months, but too much ES could lead to extended feelings of fatigue and headaches.

When the solar orbiter was close enough to Mars the passengers transferred to an HMO vehicle which took them down the landing craft in Low Mars Orbit. From there it was a mildly hair-raising trip down to the landing site.

Bobby was now two people away from being processed. He could hear the two security personnel in front of him processing the line. It was standard stuff; name, occupation, purpose of visit. It was, he thought, largely pointless. No one gets to stowaway on an interplanetary space craft. Every person is checked and rechecked and monitored constantly through all stages of the flight and every transfer. If a passenger caught a cold the security services would know it before they did. This was just a hangover from an earlier way of doing things. It felt like this was how you *should* run a terminal, so this was how they did run a terminal.

Bobby stepped up to the first border guard, who did not look up. "Hold out your comdev and state your name, nationality and purpose of visit."

Bobby moved his weight from one leg to the other. "Robert Harvey Karjalainen, USAN, I live here."

The guard looked up, acting for all the world as if Bobby's identity had come as a surprise to her. "*Bobby Karjalainen?*" she said.

Bobby looked her in the eye. "That's right," he said.

"Bobby Karjalainen the war hero?" The guard squinted at him.

"I served," Bobby allowed.

The guard exaggeratedly gestured to her colleague. "Hey! We've got us a war hero here. How about that?" she said.

Bobby looked away. The guard said, "Mr Karjalainen, could you please turn your face toward me as I have to positively identify you." It was nonsense. Bobby's comdev, like everyone else's, was biometrically encoded to him only and facial recognition at all points on the journey confirmed his identity. Whether a border guard thought Bobby looked like his most recent picture on file was neither here nor there. Any imposter would have been picked up on the ground at Ontario, and ever since then the system had had a lock on him.

Bobby continued to stare at a particularly uninteresting crate he had spotted halfway down the warehouse. The guard spoke, slowly and deliberately with ice on her words. "Hey. War hero. I'm talking to you."

Bobby flicked his eyes in her direction without moving his head.

"Please turn your face full onto me so I can positively identify you," she said, adding with venom, "Mr Karjalainen."

"Can I please go?" said Bobby. "It's been a long journey and I want to get home and rest."

The guard nodded a gesture at her colleague, who followed her around the desk and stood behind her as she took up a position side on to Bobby. "Sir," she said, with as little respect as she could give that word, "please place both hands palm down on the desk."

Bobby eyeballed her. "Really?"

"Hands on the desk, sir."

Bobby stepped to the desk and placed both hands on it as requested. The desk was low so he was slightly bent over. The guard walked behind him, kicking his legs apart. "You might think you're a big deal, but you ain't. Killing all those Asians? Big, tough character, huh? You don't impress me. Anything in your pockets that shouldn't be there?" She started patting him down without waiting for an answer. "I read your book. You come over like an asshole," she said.

"Thanks for the review," Bobby replied, "I'll pass it on to the writer."

The guard squatted down and started patting up Bobby's legs. As she got to the top of his left leg he glanced down and winked at her. "Why, thank you Miss," he said. The guard quickly span her hand around and grabbed Bobby's balls, squeezing hard. Bobby grimaced, but was determined not to react further.

"Think you're funny? You might be Charlie-Big-Potatoes back there, mowing down third-worlders and tellin' everyone how great it was, but you're in my world now. I'm gonna put a flag on you, and you'd better keep in line." She let go and stood up. "If you spit on the sidewalk we're gonna pull you in, and we're gonna see how you were aggressive and uncooperative at Immigration, and we're gonna think that maybe you need to be incentivised to get your shit right. You understand me?"

Bobby looked at her blankly. "Think so," he said.

EPHIALTES

The guard strode back around the desk. "On your way," she said. Bobby smiled at her and nodded to her colleague. He turned, walking toward the sign that said 'Exit.' The guard called after him.

"Welcome to Mars. War hero."

Bobby stepped into a driverless cab just outside the port. He had ordered it from his comdev while he was in the queue at immigration. Immediately it set off down the tunnel-like roads, which were darkening now as evening fell. Looking through the clear roof of the cab and the Plexiglas ceiling of the road-tunnel he could make out the first few stars visible that night. He saw a particularly bright one and wondered if it might be Earth. The day he left he had come to the port in a cab very like this one, but on that day there had been a dust storm. The only thing visible then had been a wall of that muted bloodstain red colour the planet was famous for.

The Karjalainen's family seat, as his father jokingly had it, was a few kilometres from the port. Bobby switched on the cab's built in comdev. He flicked through a few news channels and was surprised at the amount of local coverage. From his earliest memories right up to when he left the news had always been predominantly about Earth, and mostly about the USAN. He felt he knew Earth. That had been one of the reasons he had found it so easy to leave his home to go there. The stories he was flicking past now were as likely to be about Mars as they were the home planet. Hospital staff were considering a strike at St Mary's and Venkdt Mars Corp were due to make an announcement about their plans to start exploiting the asteroid belt.

Bobby had been following home planet bulletins on the trip out. Watching the news here in this cab he felt, for the first time in seven years, a very long way from Earth.

The cab slowed to a halt outside the house where Bobby grew up and he stepped out from it. The Karjalainens, being one of the pre-eminent families on Mars, had a dome fronting house in Central Marineris. Domes on Mars were expensive and generally only used for public spaces, but in some very exclusive neighbourhoods a dome would be the centre piece of a residential area with private housing about the perimeter. Bobby's family's house, like the others in this swanky burg, was mostly underground, extending back beyond the edge of the dome. A portion of the front, though, including the entrance hall, was above ground inside the circumference of the dome. The dome itself was eighty metres across and had been built by Hjälp Teknik, the Karjalainens' company. Six other houses shared the luxury of the dome, but the Karjalainens' was by far the biggest. The land in the centre of the dome was grassed and landscaped, and Bobby remembered climbing the trees there when he was a small boy. They were good memories.

Bobby tapped his comdev to pay the cab and slung his duffle bag over his shoulder, turning to walk up the path to his old home. As he reached the front door he noticed that it was already open and a slender figure was slouched in the doorway, in shadow from the light behind it.

"You're back," the voice from the shadow said, redundantly.

"Hey, Anthony," said Bobby, breaking into a smile and offering his hand.

Anthony grasped the hand reluctantly and said, "Dad's not here."

"He's not?" said Bobby.

Anthony shook his head. "At the hospital. Again."

"Oh," Bobby said, and took his hand back from Anthony. "Is it bad?"

Anthony turned into the house and Bobby followed him inside. Anthony half-turned and spoke over his shoulder, "Well, not good. Like the last time, I guess. I hope."

They walked down the hall to the kitchen where Anthony decided he should, at least for appearances sake, play the role of a gracious host.

"Can I get you anything to drink? Have you eaten?" he said.

"I'm beat, Tony, I'm gonna turn in in a bit. Cola?"

"Sure," said Tony. He took a cold can from the fridge and handed it to Bobby. Bobby cracked it open and took a swig.

"I saw you had a book out," said Anthony.

"Yeah? Did you read it?" Bobby asked.

"I don't like books about the military," Anthony replied.

"It's not such a great book, anyways," said Bobby. "Which hospital is Dad at?"

"St. Joseph's. We can visit tomorrow, if you like."

"I would. I'd like to see him. D'you think he'd be okay with that?"

Anthony shrugged. "He's dying. You're his oldest son. I guess he would."

Bobby nodded. "I've sent him the odd message over the last few months. I think he's thawing a bit."

"Yeah, maybe," said Anthony, uncommitted.

Bobby finished his cola, crumpled the can and threw it across the room into the bin, where it landed dead centre without touching the sides. He grinned and mock-shouted, "Score!" He wanted to think that he and Anthony were fourteen and twelve again. Anthony wasn't having it.

"It's good to be back, Tony," said Bobby.

Anthony Karjalainen half-heartedly suppressed a sneer. "Is it?"

Bobby slung his kit bag into the corner and crashed onto his bed. He closed his eyes and thought about the day. Images from the exhilarating trip on the landing craft, the incident with the up-tight border guard and his uneasy reunion with Anthony floated about his head. He thought about his father and the illness that was slowly dragging him down. He tried to sleep - he was tired enough - but he just couldn't do it. Opening his eyes he looked about the room, *his* room, or rather his twenty-one-year-old self's room. The posters seemed a little silly now, but still bought a smile to his face.

He swung his legs around and sat up on the bed, reaching into his pocket to pull out his comdev. He scrolled through the contacts, stopping on one and tapping the screen. He held the comdev up to his ear and walked over to his old desk, listening to the dial tone. He flipped through an old notepad on the desk absentmindedly. The dial tone stopped and he heard a woman's voice.

"Hey, this is Christina. I'm busy just now, leave a message. Buyee!" The recording stopped. Bobby coughed and paused a second, thinking.

"Hey, Christina, it's me, Bobby." He paused, searching for words again. "I'm back. Call me."

He ended the call and lay back on the bed. This time, he was asleep in seconds.

CHAPTER 04

Rumbles

Two Secret Service men with dark suits, dark glasses and concealed coms furtively stepped inside the door, one taking a position either side, both scanning the room and turning their heads slightly as they spoke into their concealed mics. They nodded to each other in agreement and pulled the door open. Two further agents, a man and a woman, strode briskly into the room. Having analysed the layout two days in advance they knew exactly where they were going. The man moved directly to the far corner, where he stood with his back to the wall, surveying the customers and waiting staff as the early evening clientèle went about their meals. The woman went to a discreet opening at the back of the restaurant where, just out of view of the customers, was a tastefully designed and tastefully small sign reading 'Staff Only.' She took up a stance, side on to the kitchen and side on to the restaurant floor, with legs apart and hands loosely behind her back. She too whispered something into her mic.

A few seconds later Vice President Gerard White entered. He smiled and shared a joke with the maître d'hôtel, clasping one of his hands in two of his. The maître d'hôtel gestured to a table on the restaurant floor, and White thanked him and moved toward it.

White sat down at the table as another Secret Service woman slipped into position at the table opposite.

"Hello, Mr Vice President," said Madeline Zelman.

"Hello, Ms Zelman," White grinned.

Madeline flung her hand about the room, gesturing to the agents. "Do you ever get tired of all this rock-star nonsense?" she asked, smiling.

White smiled back, "No, never." They laughed gently and easily.

"I know you don't have much time so I've already ordered," said Madeline.

"Good, good," White replied, quickly adding, "Not the fish?"

"Not the fish," Madeline echoed. "I thought we'd start with Pan-Seared Crab Cakes with Cajun Remoulade and have the Jambonneau of Duck with Wild Rice and Pine Nuts for the main."

"Crabs and Ducks?" said White. "So you're dragging me as near to fish as you can, huh?" He smiled at Madeline and she smiled back as she took a sip from her glass.

"Wine?" Madeline offered.

"I'd better not. I have a committee later." White reached for the carafe of water in the centre of the table and poured himself a glass.

"Great news about the war," said Madeline.

White nodded. "Not so great from a business point of view," he said.

Madeline frowned at the remark. "Come on, that's low. We're not in the war game, we're in the armaments game. Different thing."

"Is it?" asked White. He was hoping to pull the subject back to something lighter as soon as possible. He only had one hour with Madeline and he didn't want to spend it arguing about the morality of her portfolio.

Madeline was the majority owner of Helios Matériel Corporation, the number one USAN defence contractor. She had long held that in her line war was bad for business. If it came to an actual shooting war then her products had not served their true purpose; deterrence, or 'Peace Through Superior Firepower,' as the t-shirt had it. Madeline preferred Teddy Roosevelt's 'Speak softly, and carry a big stick.' All Helios did was provide big sticks. The best big sticks in the business, she thought.

"What are you going to do with those carriers now?" asked White as the waiter served the entrée.

Madeline thanked the waiter. "Deliver them to the client as planned," she said. "Like we were always going to. And the client is . . ." She pretended to search for the name, like she was solving a difficult riddle. ". . . the USAN Government, I think. Heard of them?"

White chuckled. "I surely have," he said. "We'll be paying for those damned things until my grandkids have retired," he said, gently shaking his head.

The two carriers, known together as the *Aloadae*, were to have been the crowning glory of the USAN Army Commander Program. The two ships - the biggest spacecraft ever built - had been designed to provide an extremely rapid response to any perceived threat, in any theatre at any time, on the surface of the Earth.

The carrier ships carried twelve dropships each and were to be stationed in permanent low Earth orbit, able to move around the globe as and when necessary. Each dropship could deliver a Commander Program squad to the surface of the Earth within twenty minutes of the order being given. Each dropship was fully automated but nominally piloted by the human commander of the squad. Eleven humanoid-shaped mech drones hung in the bays behind the pilot. Once the squad had been dispatched the dropship would then act as an aerial drone. The dropships had limited but useful firepower and were a huge asset in terms of reconnaissance.

The first carrier, *Ephialtes*, had been delivered three months ago. The peace talks were well under way at that time so, despite some skirmishes along the most bitterly contested borders, there had been no deployments made from it. Delivery of the second carrier, *Otus*, was scheduled for two months' time. The great warship was to be borne into the heavens two months after the war it was designed to fight had ended. White was sanguine about that. Maybe Madeline was right after all. Maybe the carriers had added to the deterrence element of the USAN's military might. Maybe that had played a role in the negotiations and therefore, maybe, *just maybe*, the carriers did help to bring about the end of the war, just as they had been designed to. Still, he'd rather not be paying for the damned things. Winning the war was one thing. White's focus now was on winning the peace and for that he, or rather the USAN government he represented, would need every spare cent there was.

The meal was agreeable and they ate together. As White had hoped, the conversation turned more convivial. They chatted about their kids and their day to day lives. Madeline's daughter Melissa had just got engaged to a realtor, and Madeline wasn't convinced it was a great match. For a short period White was far away from the jungle of government.

Presently, he looked at his watch and patted the sides of his mouth with a napkin. "Look, this has been great, Madeline," he said.

"You're not staying for dessert?" Madeline replied.

"I'd love to, but," he shrugged, "I've got to run."

White stood up and leaned across the table to kiss Madeline on the cheek. "I love ya, babe," he said into her ear and, winking, he straightened his tie and left.

Audrey Andrews sat in the biggest chair in the room. It was premium ethically grown leather, very comfortable, and higher than the other chairs. In front of her were to two long, short coffee tables end to end, with two rows of slightly less comfortable chairs surrounding them. On the tables were bottled water and bowls of fruit, which no one was eating. In the chairs were the brightest and the best of the defence department, or at least the most senior, and Andrews was their leader.

Andrews leaned forward. "What have we got?"

"Domestic terrorism is at a nine year low," said a man to Andrews' left. "There have been no major incidents in the mainland this year and only one last year in the entire USAN, where the perpetrators were quickly apprehended and their cell closed down. The powers granted us under the Restrictive War Measures have proved invaluable in intercepting terrorist communications. There'll always be a few loopy-loos with a cause picked up from the internet, and there's not much we can do about them, but the traditional domestic terror groups have all but been eradicated."

"Overseas?" said Andrews

A woman to Andrews' right, seated a little way down from her, responded. "The Asian Bloc poses no immediate threat. We are continuing to monitor communications and it seems they're as relieved as we are that the war has come to an end. There are some dissenters near the top of the regime - we've always known about them, of course - but even they recognise that the terms of the armistice were a necessary compromise. They would have been unable to sustain their casualty rates into the future and they knew that we had the upper hand in all areas - military, economic and logistic. Great wars always come down to battles of attrition, I guess, and in the end we managed to grind them down. The war has done lasting damage to their economies and infrastructure. They currently pose the weakest of threats, but their capacity to act against us in the short and medium term has been neutralized.

"Of the unaligned countries, none have the necessary economic or military power to pose a significant threat, nor the inclination, either. The greater USAN is probably now in the most secure position it has been in for the last hundred years."

Audrey smiled. "That's good," she said, "thank you." She glanced down at her papers. "We find ourselves in the happy position of not having a war to fight. Of course, that doesn't mean there's nothing for us to do. I expect that in the next few months we'll be hearing about cuts to our budgets, so I'd like you to start thinking about that now. I'd also like to ask you to consider how we should be rethinking our force deployment to best support the new peace and guard against any flare-ups in the more contested regions.

"Before the end of the summer I'd like a series of reports prepared. Budget reviews, analyses of our most problematic borders, and a deep overview of the geopolitical landscape we will be dealing with for the next five to ten years. A major war like the one we've just been through comes along maybe once every few generations, and thank God it's over, but peace tends to be fleeting, so very soon it's going to be back to pre-war business as usual for us. Our nation spans the globe and you can bet that someone, somewhere, is grinding an axe even as we speak. Tin-pot generals and wannabe revolutionaries bringing a little local misery into the world are likely to be the crux of our business for the foreseeable future."

At the far end of the tables a woman timidly raised her hand. "Ms Andrews?" she said. Heads turned to look at the woman, who half lowered her hand and shrank back a little. Andrews leant forward, better to look at the woman.

"Yes?" said Andrews.

The woman steadied herself. "You know there has been some seditious talk coming from Mars?"

Audrey looked at the woman. "There has? Well, get that into the report on geopolitics if you must, but I'd rather we focused on plausible areas of contention."

"One of our monitoring stations on Mare Orientale has recently picked up some conversations, believed to be from inside Venkdt Corp, with a decidedly unpatriotic bent."

Audrey looked at the woman. "Believed to be?" she said. "Honey, two PAs talking shit in their lunch break does not make for a revolution."

The woman hesitated. "We think the conversation was between a high ranking officer at Venkdt Mars and an equally high ranking Venkdt official here in the USAN."

"I think the hazard level will be minimal. Mars is no threat to national security – it's a hundred and forty million miles away, for one thing. And they don't have a military."

"They have deuterium," the woman said. "They could harm us as much by omission as commission."

Audrey's temperature was rising. "Maybe we'll leave this one to the foreign office. We're looking for military threats, and this isn't one. But thank you for your contribution."

Audrey spoke to the room. "In summary, the war's over. Get ready for change. We're currently geared up for a large scale global conflict that has now ended. We have to prepare ourselves for smaller, maybe more widely distributed hostilities in the future, and as part of that we need to be thinking about where those might arise.

"Go back to your desks, find the next potential crises and think about how we can stop them before they get started." She stood and left.

The old barracks was a no frills operation. There were no home comforts to speak of and it comprised of what were more or less sheds. The doors were draughty, and on a cold winter's night the windows would rattle in their frames. The living quarters were sheds with rows of double bunks down either side, with a red painted concrete floor shined to a mirror finish by generations of marines. The Commander Program, with its emphasis on the physical, embraced all that was old-school and hard and outdoors. For the commanders the air conditioned stations of the regular soldiers, with their IVR get-ups and their well-appointed living spaces, reeked of decadence. A real soldier - a Warrior - had to be in touch with the earth. He or she had to know the pain of hunger in their belly; know the chill of the cold against their inner core; know the weakness and the tiredness of days in the unforgiving wilderness, and by that know themselves. The commanders, willing to stride onto the field of battle and kill or be killed, could live and sleep in an unheated, wind-rattled shed and know it was luxury, never once thinking of complaining.

A group of commanders was coming home. From air conditioned hotels or the centrally heated houses of their families they returned from leave, coming back to their true home.

When Sebastian Foley reached hut thirteen Steiner and Johnson were already there. Steiner and Johnson shared a set of bunks, with Steiner in the lower bunk. 'I like to be on top,' Johnson liked to say. Foley greeted them with his customary long, 'Heeeey!' and they bumped fists and slapped backs like the jocks they were. Steiner had swung his feet around, sat up and got out of his bunk the moment he saw Foley approach. Johnson, who was sat on the top bunk, took a more laconic approach. He remained seated, a huge grin on his broad face, as he reached down to grab Foley by the shoulder. "What's up, man?" he said.

"What's up?" Foley replied, grinning back and nodding at Johnson as he took Steiner's offered hand and shook it firmly, pat-slapping him on the shoulder as he let go. "Steiner, my man!" he said, "Look at you. You look different, all cleaned up and filled out."

"Four weeks of home cooking will do that for you," said Steiner. "How've you been?"

"I've been good," Foley replied, "I'm rested, recuperated and ready to go."

"That's good," Steiner smiled, "that's good."

"How're you doin', big fella?" Foley said to Johnson. "How was your leave?"

Johnson slid from the bunk to the floor. "It was good. Caught up with Stone, done some fishin'."

Foley pushed his kit bag into his locker and hopped up on his bunk. "So we won the war," he said, "and now we're sad, for there are no more enemy to kill." He lay on his back. "What do you think this is about?" he asked himself as much as anyone else.

"It's Dubai. It's not happening, I reckon," offered Johnson.

"Investigation," said Steiner. "I've seen footage on the bulletins of Mombasa - great stuff, I might add - and I'll bet some whiny bedroom activist has spotted something in there or in the off-line feeds and raised shit about it."

"I don't care if they do," said Foley. "My conscience is clear. I didn't see anything that wasn't Marquis of Queensberry or Geneva Convention or whatever the hell it is. We did a good job and we did it right. If anyone's complaining about anything they should be complaining about what happened to Hughes."

"That's right," said Johnson.

Steiner stared at the floor.

"That's just savage," continued Johnson, "and they should be called to account for that. That was some bad juju." Johnson clapped one of his enormous hands on Steiner's back.

When Commander Sam Hughes' command drone had been taken out at Mombasa Steiner had taken his squad over to defend the wrecked drone while assistance could be organised and dispatched. He had ascertained that Hughes had survived the GRPG attack that had felled his drone but was trapped inside, badly injured. What he hadn't ascertained was that, in the few short minutes it had taken him to reach the area, Hughes' drone had been booby-trapped. When Steiner had used his huge mechanical arm to lift some of the wreckage from Hughes' fallen drone the blast had knocked his own drone clear over. Hughes was killed and Steiner suffered multiple injuries. He was out cold for several minutes. His head was superficially but bloodily cut. When he was picked up the med crew at first assumed him to be dead. His vital sign monitors had all failed in the blast and he was unconscious and covered in blood. The last thing he remembered was seeing Hughes turning to look at him, struggling to mask his pain with a weak smile and his thumb raised in the time honoured gesture of thanks. That image had stayed with him.

There was a whisper from over near one of the windows, "Captain's coming," and commanders scattered about and leapt from their bunks.

"Captain's coming," Johnson echoed as he, Steiner and Foley came to the front of their bunks, standing bolt upright with their arms straight at their sides, looking forward.

Captain Brian Connor entered the hut at a fair clip and strode immediately to the front centre, equidistant from the two rows of bunks which ran away from him up the sides of the hut. Without stopping to pause or even acknowledge any of the commanders he began to talk.

"At ease people, and gather 'round me here." The commanders moved at a quick saunter to form a semi-circle around Connor at the head of the hut.

Captain Connor was, at twenty-eight years, at least five years older than the oldest commander under his command. He was a born soldier and had jumped at the opportunity to become involved in the USAN Army Commander Program. He had finessed the original plans for the program and tested them on the training grounds. Having been in at the very beginning he had overseen the training of the instructors and after three long years had finally, at the second request, been given command of company slated for deployment in the Asian theatre, fourteen months before the end of the war.

As captain of the company Connor, while at least not some REMF controlling drones from a shed in Kentucky, was still not quite in the thick of it like his men. His role of comcon was best fulfilled from a semi-automated aerial drone, directing missions from above. Lucky for him, then, that he had been injured in a training exercise, for the scar it left him with on the right side of his face seemed to show to the world that he was a Physical Soldier.

He had been bawling out a rookie commander who was having trouble adjusting from IVR training simulations to being in an actual command drone. Connor was stood on the tarmac in front of him, dwarfed by the four metre tower of metal and ammo in front of him, shouting up at the pilot like he was training a poodle. It said something to the quality of the man that a trained soldier, encased in the frame of a metal giant with enough firepower to level a small town, was intimidated by a five foot five inch captain wearing nothing more than the olive-drab uniform of the USANMC and a cap. The jittery would-be commander, anxious to do the right thing under the tirade from Connor, proceeded to miscontrol his mech and a sixteen tonne metal arm wooshed around, smacking Connor in the face.

Connor was intensely proud of the scar, though he affected to not give it a moment's thought. He had received it doing his duty, and that was good enough for him. His service injury had marked him for life and was there on his face for all to see. He would have been ashamed to report to the MO with RSI like some of these rear echelon drone operators, for whom a paper cut would lead to at least a day off sick, or maybe even litigation. No so for Captain Conner. He had taken one to the face in the line of duty and got up and carried on.

Conner stood with his hands behind his back and his feet about sixty centimetres apart. His head was held high and he appeared to be addressing someone floating a metre or two above the people circled about him. His speech was deliberate, measured and loud.

"You people acquitted yourselves well in the war that has just passed. The corps is proud of you. I am proud of you. That war is now ended. What does the warrior do when there is no war?" He waited. "The warrior prepares for war. You will remain here on a training and preparedness detail, and you will remain sharp, and you will remain frosty."

The group shuffled just a little and a commander near the front offered a very pensive, "Sir?"

Connor snapped his head in the commander's direction. "What is it, Commander?"

"Does this mean we're not going to Dubai?"

Connor returned his address to the floating phantom. "The end of hostilities has rendered some of our planned postings obsolete. We are no longer required in Dubai, that detail is scratched. The corps requires you here until further notice, sharp and frosty. That is all." He turned on his heel and left.

Shoulders slumped all round and the soldiers slouched back to their bunks, the low murmur of their grumbling punctuated by a fist punching a locker.

"I knew it," Johnson said, "I knew we'd never get to Dubai. Goddamn, why'd they have to end the damn war just when we was being sent someplace good?"

"At least we got a thank you for winning the war," Foley offered.

"Tell that to Hughes," said Steiner.

In the mess hall Foley was chowing down with Steiner and Johnson. Foley was a slow eater and Johnson, for all his bulk, ate as daintily as a vicar's wife. Steiner, the smallest of the three, ate like someone was going to steal his food. Or at least he used to.

"Where's your appetite, Steiner?" said Foley.

Steiner shrugged, "I'm just not too hungry, I guess." He pushed some food around his plate and took a small forkful.

"You need to eat. *The corps needs you sharp and frosty*, amiright?"

Steiner rolled his eyes.

"*I need you sharp and frosty*," Foley continued his mocking impression of Connor.

"*Mrs Connor needs you sharp and frosty.*"

Johnson laughed. "Goddamn that son of a bitch," he said. "He thinks he's a hard-ass with that stupid shaving cut on his face. He should have spent some time with us on the ground, getting shot at."

"*I thank you for winning the war for me,*" Foley continued in the too loud voice. "*Mrs Connor thanks you for winning the war for me.*"

The three of them cracked up at the line.

"At least he had the good grace to thank us," said Foley. "I wanted to thank him for taking aerial pleasure trips eight klicks back from where the action was and staying the hell out of my way while I won the war for him," he sputtered between laughs.

Steiner pushed his plate away.

"Seriously, you need to eat, man. Are you okay?" said Johnson.

Steiner held his hands up. "I'm fine, I'm fine. Just not hungry today," he said.

Johnson and Foley exchanged glances. "You need to eat, buddy. Your body needs it," Johnson said, but Steiner just shrugged and shook his head.

Foley and Johnson had been concerned about Steiner since he returned to the company following the incident with Hughes. He had spent a week in a field hospital and had then been rotated back home for three weeks of rest and recuperation. When he returned he seemed to be a changed man. He wasn't the same Steiner who had left. It was little things. He didn't pick up on any of the running jokes they shared, and he didn't seem to remember some of the things they had experienced together. When Foley asked him, "Hey, buddy, have you got that fifty bucks you owe me?" Steiner had paid up on the spot, rather than making the customary reply, "No, I gave it to your mum last night. I gave her the fifty bucks, too." Foley and Johnson had been concerned that the brain injury Steiner had received had been more serious than had first been suspected, or that he was depressed or had PTSD or something similar. He had been passed fit for duty, though by the time he was back in the unit they never saw another shot fired in anger. Still, they worried about him. He was one of their own.

"So the glorious warriors of the last great war find themselves right back where they started, while the politicians and the generals take all the credit," said Foley. "I guess some things never change."

"I wouldn't knock it," said Steiner. "You've got a job, and a pension, and a bucketful of stories to tell the grandkids."

"And the scars to prove it," added Foley.

"I was sure lookin' forward to Dubai, though," Johnson said wistfully.

"Aw," said Foley, "I'm sure we'll have a great time, right here."

The bright late afternoon sunlight streamed through the large floor to ceiling windows, framing Secretary of Defence Audrey Andrews and holding her in shadow. Her dark hair was pulled back severely and rolled into a tight bun on top of her head. She leaned into her desk, signing papers which she examined through glasses perched at the tip of her nose. There was a knock on the door and Andrews looked up. It was the timid woman.

"Ms Andrews?" the timid woman said.

"Yes?" Andrews snapped. She liked to appear officious and irritable. She thought it stopped people from bothering her unnecessarily and deterred people from asking stupid questions.

"Do you have just a moment?" the woman asked.

Audrey slipped the glasses off and gestured into the room. "Come in," she said. "What is it?"

The woman walked into the office and stood across from Andrews on the other side of the desk. She held a manila folder across her chest like a child might hold a favoured cuddly toy. It seemed defensive, but despite her timidity at her core she had a steely resolve. She had something she thought the secretary of defence should know about and she was going to make sure she told her.

"My name is Colleen Acevedo. I'm an analyst in intelligence." Acevedo had always been modest. She was, in fact, a senior intelligence analyst, reporting directly to the Joint Chiefs of Staff.

"I know who you are, Ms Acevedo," said Andrews. She was vaguely aware of Acevedo and her work, but nothing more.

"I thought you might just want to look at the transcripts of the conversations coming out of Venkdt."

"Leave them on my desk; I'll have someone take a look." Andrews went back to her next piece of paper. Acevedo stepped forward.

"I really do think it's worthy of your time, Ms Andrews. We've done some further analysis on the conversations and we're pretty sure they're between Charles Venkdt and Michael Summers, the CEO of Venkdt Corp here on Earth. There are some other conversations within Venkdt Mars that suggest that Charles Venkdt is very serious about what he's discussing. He's had senior members of Venkdt making feasibility studies, costings, etcetera, and he's gone out of his way to keep it all under the radar."

Audrey Andrews sat back in her chair and bit gently on the arm of her glasses. She observed Acevedo, and squinted almost imperceptibly. "Feasibility of what?" she asked.

Acevedo took a second to process the question. To her, the answer was so obvious she thought she might have misunderstood the question. "Martian independence," she said.

Andrews thought. "Do you have the feasibility studies?" she asked.

"I do," Acevedo replied, holding up the folder.

"And what do they say?"

Acevedo took a breath. "Essentially, they say that independence is feasible, desirable and even necessary."

"Necessary?"

"Yes, Ms Andrews. Necessary for Mars to grow, economically. The arguments are essentially the same as in the Kasugai study, of which I'm sure you are aware."

"Yes, yes, of course," said Andrews. She had never heard of the Kasugai study. "So this is something they're discussing seriously at Venkdt?"

"At Venkdt Mars, Ms Andrews, yes. Michael Summers is bitterly opposed. He gets quite angry in the transcripts." Acevedo once again held up the manila folder.

"Show me," said Andrews.

Acevedo made her way around the unnecessarily large desk and opened the folder, searching through it and pulling out sheets that were variously stapled or paper clipped together. She laid them out in front of Andrews, explaining as she went.

"These are the feasibility plans, called Feasibility B and Feasibility F - don't ask what happened to A and C through E, we don't know - and these are four message conversations between Summers and Venkdt over a period of two weeks. They get interesting here." Acevedo pointed at one of pages. Andrews read it, turning over to the next page with deepening lines of concentration appearing on her forehead. Acevedo pointed to another sheet. "This is where Summers starts to lose his rag," she said.

Andrews read aloud:

> "Summers: The shareholders own Venkdt, and we both
> work for them. I'll be bringing this up at the AGM and
> we'll have your ass out of there before you even know it.
> Venkdt: I feel my position here is secure.
> Summers: You cannot break up Venkdt without a
> two-thirds majority of the board.
> Venkdt: Well, that might be true, strictly, but these are
> exceptional circumstances. We might have to bend the
> rules, just this one time.
> Summers: We do things legally here at Venkdt.
> Venkdt: I respect the law. But sometimes what's right
> and what's legal stray from each other, just a little.
> Summers: Don't do it Charles. I've got an army of law-
> yers here, just waiting to go.
> Venkdt: And where is 'here' exactly? You're a long way
> from where I am, and you can't see what I can. This has
> to happen. It's our destiny.
> Summers: It might be your destiny but it's sure as shit
> not your goddamned company. You have no right to go

through with this. I'll see you rot in jail for this if you try it, you son of a bitch."

Andrews looked at Acevedo. "He's going to break up Venkdt?"

"He proposes Venkdt Mars breaks away from the rest of Venkdt Corp. Given that Mars virtually is Venkdt Mars -"

Andrews cut in, "And Hjälp Teknik."

"The Hjälp Teknik operation on Mars is less than a tenth of the size of Venkdt's. Mars belongs to Venkdt, and Charles Venkdt wants out from the rest of the company. He has the means to do it, too."

"What about the garrison?"

"Less than two hundred of them. And they're more of a police force than an army."

Andrews thought. "So what are the security implications for us?"

"Practically none, as you pointed out before. They're a hundred and forty million miles away and they don't have a military. But they do supply the bulk of our deuterium, and they're a reasonably big player economically. The biggest threat to us is political. To lose our first - the world's first - off-world colony would make us look weak, particularly in light of some of the compromises we had to make to get the peace accords to work. We're already widely perceived as having caved into our enemies' demands at the negotiation table. If we then sit by and let our colonists secede from the union against our wishes we will look weak. And that can only be destabilising."

Andrews stood up and held out a hand to Acevedo. "Thank you for bringing this to my attention. This is good work, exactly the sort of thing we need to be looking at."

"Thank you, Ms Andrews," said Acevedo.

"Can you type all this up into a full report and get it to me by the end of the day?"

"Yes, Ms Andrews."

"Good. That's all"

"Thank you, Ms Andrews."

Acevedo made toward the door as Andrews returned to her seat. Just as she got there Andrews called out, "Ms Acevedo?"

Acevedo stopped and turned back toward her. "Yes, Ms Andrews?"

"Your report - let's just keep it between us at the moment."

"Yes, Ms Andrews."

CHAPTER 05

A New Order

Sat plumb in the middle of its own private hundred and twenty metre dome, Charles Venkdt's house looked like something from the home planet. Surrounded by lawns and even trees, here was a little bit of Earth on Mars. The house itself was large but functional. Venkdt didn't have time for ostentation. He was about doing things, achieving goals and finding solutions. It showed in the design of his house and it showed in his work.

Venkdt was of the fifth generation of his family working at the top of the company which bore his name. His great-great-grandfather, Alexander Venkdt, had founded the company in 2094 and marshalled it into one of the great global players. His grandfather's stewardship of the family business had been awarded to him for his involvement in the company's biggest and boldest gamble; the commercial exploitation of Mars. In 2143 Venkdt Corp was the first company to send a human expedition to Mars, and within five years of that Venkdt had a permanent base on the planet which had been growing ever since. In the first few years growth was slow and interdependent with the USAN Research Center, which had been established twenty-two years before and had a permanent but rotating staff of around thirty people.

Around twenty years after the base was established expansion really started to take off. Deuterium and other precious minerals were being extracted in ever-larger amounts and sent back to the home planet. The early camps were expanding into something much more comfortable than the original squat cylinders connected by tubes. The new buildings by that time were totally fabricated on Mars, made with Martian bricks and built largely below surface level as protection against the low atmospheric pressure and cold. All buildings had to be sealed against the exterior low pressure of seven or so millibars, not much more than an absolute vacuum for practical purposes. Being mostly underground helped with this and the extreme cold of a Martian night-time or winter. Once bricks and Plexiglas could be manufactured locally there was something of a building boom. Within twenty-five years the original Venkdt prefabs were abandoned and given the status of 'historic site'. They had gone from being cutting edge, wave of the future habitation to museum pieces in less than a quarter of a century.

By 2180 Venkdt's Martian operation dwarfed the USAN Research Center and expansion was continuing apace. In the first few decades of operation all Venkdt personnel eventually returned to Earth after serving terms of two, four, six or eight years. Their pay was very good and there was little opportunity to spend it on a frontier planet. Business was booming and Venkdt Mars was one of Venkdt Corp's most profitable divisions. As the operation expanded in terms of people and buildings some personnel chose to stay beyond even eight years.

The first humans born on Mars had come in the early days, but they had quickly returned to Earth with their parents soon after. Mars, it seemed, was no place to raise a kid. Over time this returning to the home planet became less of an obvious choice. Starting in the 2170s, when the total population was around fifteen thousand, some families opted to stay on Mars. There were building projects for homes that, unlike the previous Venkdt billets, could be bought by their occupants. Soon the ratio of natural born Martians to transients started to shift, ever so slightly at first but accelerating over time. By the end of the century more than half of the population was Martian born, with some of them being second or third generation.

Charles Venkdt himself had shipped out to Mars at the age of eighteen in 2185, and had never been back to Earth since. He had always been fascinated with the planet and his family's interest in it. And, in truth, he had wanted to get out from the shadow of his father. This didn't, of course, extend to striking out completely on his own. Given his good fortune to have been born into one of the richest families in the USAN, that would have just been foolish. Charles knew that he could make a name for himself working from within. If he worked hard and demonstrated competency he would soon rise up in the furthest outpost of the family firm. That he did.

Venkdt had been the managing operational director of Venkdt Mars for over thirty-five years. When he had first reached that lofty position the Martian population had been around thirty thousand; now it was close to one hundred thousand. He had overseen expansion from the exportation of raw minerals to the production of high quality finished goods. He had expanded the fledgling R&D Department to something of a fiefdom for its director. He understood that in their hostile environment Martians had to innovate, meeting every challenge with creative solutions.

Within the last thirty years or so he had seen the arrival of Hjälp Teknik, a comparatively upstart company who had arrived on Mars as a direct competitor to Venkdt. Charles viewed them with a mild contempt, but conceded that competition was good as it would drive efficiency and innovation. Despite that he couldn't help thinking, deep down, that Hjälp Teknik had it easy. The knowhow, the knowledge, the risk had all been borne by the pioneers of Venkdt, who had also supplied, latterly, much of the transport and coms infrastructure. These Johnny-come-latelies were sailing in on Venkdt's coat tails when all the hard work had been done, and taking the easy pickings.

Things were changing now, and rapidly. It wasn't just Hjälp Teknik who were the rivals any more. Mars had expanded at such a rate that, even with the exception of Hjälp Teknik, it was no longer a company town. Two Venkdt employees might get together and start a family, buying a house with their wages and becoming true stakeholders in the Martian adventure. What about their kids? Venkdt didn't necessarily owe them a living, and they didn't necessarily want to work for Venkdt. With some capital from their parents' savings, or even a loan, some of these natural born Martians could set up their own businesses. Venkdt's Martians craved entertainment and other fripperies to spend their hard-earned money on, and small businesses sprang up to provide it to them. In time, other services were provided too, leading to growth in the Martian banking sector. Initially most goods were imported - there was money to be made undercutting the official Venkdt Stores in this area - but in time demand drove local production. The Martian economy was fizzing, and the population was expanding. All of this made Charles Venkdt immensely proud. Though in truth it was his forefathers and their associates who had put in the *really* hard graft in the early days, Charles felt, with not a total absence of justification, that Mars was an ongoing project that he had built.

From his position on the veranda Charles watched the cab arrive, slowly winding its way up his short drive before coming to a halt in front of the house. His daughter stepped from the vehicle and reached back in, collecting her bag. She closed the door and looked up. "Hi, Dad," she said.

"Hey, gorgeous," Venkdt replied, a warm and genuine smile on his face. He walked to the top of the steps and greeted her with a hug and a kiss. They walked inside.

"I hope you haven't eaten," said Venkdt.

"I thought we were eating here?" replied Christina.

"Yes, yes, we are," said Venkdt. "Go through." He gestured to the dining room.

They entered the room and sat at places laid out for them. "How've you been, Dad?" said Christina. "Everything okay?"

"Everything's just fine," said Venkdt. "Drink?"

"You know, I think I will. Do you have any wine?"

Venkdt spoke to no one, "Can we have some wine in here please? And we're ready to eat." He turned to Christina. "How're things with you?"

"They're good, Dad. Work's good, the apartment's going well,"

"Have they finished yet?"

"There's a little left to do on the bathroom, but it's looking great. Thank you for all your help."

Venkdt waved a hand, "Don't worry about it, it's nothing."

A small drone entered the room and rolled up to Venkdt. "To my daughter, please," said Venkdt and the drone moved to Christina. The top opened and a plinth rose up with a bottle of wine on it and two glasses. Christina took the bottle and a glass. She lifted the second glass, gesturing to her father, but he shook his head and she returned it to the drone, which whirred away. It stopped by the doorway to allow in a second, slightly larger drone. This one approached Venkdt and opened to reveal two plated meals, steaming and smelling good. Venkdt took a plate and the drone moved on to Christina, who had just poured her wine.

"This looks good," she said.

Venkdt had already started eating. "It is," he said. "Tuck in."

They ate and intermittently chatted about mundane day-to-day family things, and the odd little stories from their lives. Picking his time Venkdt brought the conversation round to what he really wanted to discuss. "You like the salmon?" he said.

"Is that what it is? It's delicious," Christina said through mouthfuls.

"It's local, you know."

"Fabbed around here?"

"Not fabbed. Grown."

Christina looked at him, impressed.

"A couple of guys that used to work for us. They've got a place up in Dog Sur. Imported some eggs, built a pool and now they farm salmon."

"Amazing," said Christina.

"The wine too. Local, I mean. There's a dome in Eastside that's just filled with vines, and they press their own wines there. It's very expensive now, but as they expand costs will come down."

"I've heard about them," said Christina. "A guy at work is a wine nut. I can't tell the difference between this and the fabbed stuff, to be honest, but he was raving about them."

"Did you know around two new businesses are starting each month at the moment?"

Christina raised her eyebrows in acknowledgement. "I didn't know that," she said.

"The Martian economy is growing at a rate of four percent."

"That's great," said Christina. "Isn't it?"

"It is great," said Venkdt. "I think we should be a bigger part of it."

Christina looked at him, feeling a speech coming on.

"Venkdt is the biggest player in the Martian economy by far. For now. We dwarf our closest rival, Hjälp Teknik, and all the rest are just minnows. But to compete in the long term we need to be independent. And I'm not just talking about the Martian arm of Venkdt, I'm talking about Mars itself."

Christina did not quite follow, and Venkdt read it in her face. "At the moment Venkdt Mars generates huge profits. Most of those profits go back to Venkdt Corp on Earth. Our endeavours benefit the parent company and its shareholders, and not us. I propose that Venkdt Mars breaks away from the parent company and goes its own way. We should be trading with them, not working for them. As an independent corporation we can be at the heart of the new Martian economy."

Christina looked at him. "You'll never get that past the board. They're not going to sell off their biggest cash cow."

"Well, no," Venkdt allowed, "not if we give them the choice." Christina raised her eyebrows again, higher this time. "But what if we don't?"

Christina put her fork down, chewing and swallowing her remaining food. Venkdt had gone back to eating. Christina spoke cautiously. "If you don't *what*?"

Venkdt looked up, startled. "Give them the choice. We can buy out their shares at the market rate, and that's that. What are they going to do? Send an army?"

Christina frowned. "It would be illegal. Giving them the money for what you take from them doesn't make it right, if they don't want you to take it."

"We've made huge profits for them over the years. We've earned them trillions, and we've been out here taking the risks and building this thing and sending all the money back to them. I say we've paid our dues, and we should take what's rightfully ours. This can be a new nation here, hell, a new planet. It belongs to us."

Venkdt was smiling. 'Sheesh', thought Christina, 'he's really going to do it.'

"So you're going to go ahead with this?" said Christina.

"I think so. In a month or two the hundred thousandth Martian will be born. We'll make an announcement then."

"You've spoken to the board?"

"No. I've sounded out Mike Summers. He's not happy."

"You should take this to the board."

"I know what they'd say. I'm going to take it to the people."

Christina looked at him blank-facedly. "What?"

"I think we should run a plebiscite to ask the people of Mars what they think. I've got a pretty good idea what they'd say, too."

"This is crazy. None of this is legitimate. What about the garrison? The USAN will have you thrown in a cell before you get anywhere with this."

Venkdt lay his cutlery down. "Firstly, I don't think they'd dare. And secondly, we have our own security division to prevent that from happening."

Christina shook her head, her shoulders slumping. "Are you serious? People could get hurt, things could turn nasty. This is nuts."

"A little nuts, maybe, but necessary."

Venkdt patted his face with a napkin while Christina drained her wine glass, quickly pouring another. "Nuts," she said again, under her breath.

Charles Venkdt was beaming. "Dessert?" he said.

There was only one non-disclosure agreement prepared. It was a silly oversight. Although only Jack Karjalainen had been invited to the meeting it was well understood that he would be too ill to attend. For a number of months his legal team of Oatridge, Strich and Philips had been acting on his behalf. Their daily briefings at his hospital bed had become something of an irritant to the hospital staff.

"I'm so sorry, could you just wait here a moment while I sort this out?" said Venkdt's assistant.

The lawyers nodded politely as the PA left the room, embarrassedly pointing out the refreshments available and making further apologies.

"What do you think?" said Strich.

"I don't know. A buyout, maybe?"

"No," said Oatridge. "He'd wait for the old man's passing before trying that trick. And there'd be no need for the NDAs."

"It's probably just some new tech. Maybe he's willing to license it to us. Something to do with mining in the asteroid belt, or something like that," offered Philips.

"Whatever it is, we just nod and smile. We take it back to the old man before we do anything else," said Oatridge.

Philips twitched. "Can you please not call him 'the old man'? He's our employer and I think he deserves our respect," she said.

"I'm sorry, Toni," said Oatridge. "I meant it affectionately, that's all."

Philips pulled a quick tight smile and nodded in acknowledgement.

"Here we are," said Venkdt's PA, slightly breathlessly. She placed two additional sheets on her desk and, quickly moving to her side of it, she grabbed pens and offered them to the lawyers. "If you could just sign and date here," she said, pointing.

Oatridge, Strich and Philips dutifully signed their agreement not to disclose any details of the meeting to any third parties. "Of course," said Philips, "we will have to discuss this with Mr Karjalainen. We're only here today as his proxies."

"I'm sure Mr Venkdt understands your position, legally. Under any other circumstances Mr Venkdt would be meeting with Mr Karjalainen directly. All this would be dealt with by a handshake or somesuch, but we have to protect ourselves. I hope you understand."

"We understand," said Oatridge.

EPHIALTES

The PA ushered them into the boardroom.

Venkdt was seated at the head of the conference table. He was working on some notes. When the delegates entered he cheerily acknowledged them. "I'll be with you in just a minute, I'm just finishing up on this," he said.

To Philips this was perfectly reasonable. Venkdt was just putting the finishing touches to his presentation. To Oatridge and Strich there remained the possibility of a premeditated slight. The lawyers sat down at various places either side of the conference table. They prepared their devices and note-taking equipment as Venkdt finished what he was doing. Presently, Venkdt placed his pen at the side of the document he had been working on and waited for the others to settle before he began.

"Gentlemen, Ms Philips, first of all thank you for coming. I guess you're all aware of the upcoming hundred thousandth live birth on Mars, which we expect to take place sometime within the next two months. This is as good an occasion as any, I feel, to proceed with a plan that may have momentous impact on all of our futures, and the future of the colony that we, and our forebears, have established here at great cost and effort."

None of the lawyers had a clue where he might be going with this, but they kept their best courtroom poker faces on.

"I intend to propose a plebiscite be held, within six months of this day, asking the people of Mars if they would like to proclaim independence from the USAN and, thereby, independence from Earth itself."

'*What's a plebiscite?*' Strich discreetly messaged to Oatridge.

'*An election. For plebs,*' Oatridge replied.

Venkdt continued, "If the plebiscite returns a positive vote for independence, with more than a two-thirds majority, I will propose that we secede from the USAN and adopt our own constitution, written from the ground up to serve Martian needs and ideals. I've had plans for such a constitution drawn up, and in the event of a vote for independence we would run further elections to our own senate and presidency which would go on to provide the governance for an independent Mars."

Strich and Oatridges' message conversation had continued as Venkdt had been speaking.

'*Is he nuts?*' messaged Strich.

'*Probably,*' Oatridge replied.

'*What do we do?*'

'*Nod and smile.*'

"On whose authority would this plebiscite be held?" said Philips.

"It would be run under no particular authority," shrugged Venkdt. "It would be a grand survey of opinion, nothing more. And the two-thirds majority would be absolute to the population, not to votes cast. Anyone opposed just has to get out and vote."

"But where is the legal basis?"

"As an independent planet we'd make our own laws."

"But we're not an independent planet *now*."

"Not now. But if the people vote for it we'll secede quietly and honourably and start out anew." He smiled broadly at his last remark. "Any more questions?"

Strich was receiving another message from Oatridge. It read, '*Illegal and immoral*', and ended with a frowny face.

"What you're proposing is illegal and immoral. It just won't work," said Strich, smiling apologetically.

'*Don't antagonise him!*' came Oatridge's instant message, instantly. Strich couldn't help the smirking glance he shot across the table to Oatridge.

Venkdt shrugged. "Illegal, maybe. But it is moral. And it will work," he said. "Why wouldn't it?"

"Because no one is above the law, Mr Venkdt. I would strongly advise you against taking this course of action," said Philips. "You're a respected businessman of good standing. Why throw all that away? Even with the support of the Martian population the USAN could never let this stand. What you're suggesting is, after all, tantamount to treason."

Venkdt took a few seconds before replying. "Ms Philips, what I'm talking about here is bigger than the law. Out here on Mars we're way beyond the reach of the greater USAN. Of course, that doesn't give us license to act as we please. But Mars' destiny is as an independent state, and I feel the whole planet is behind me on this. We have the opportunity here and now to make a clean break. In order to do that we have to forego the niceties of law in the strictest sense, just temporarily on this one important issue. Don't get me wrong; I appreciate that the rule of law is essential. If I lose the plebiscite I will hand myself over to the courts. But I - we - have to do this. Our destiny is calling us."

"What does any of this have to do with Hjälp Teknik?" said Oatridge.

"I was hoping to talk with Jack Karjalainen directly. This will have a major impact on Hjälp Teknik, however it pans out. I guess in some ways I just wanted Jack to know. We're both old. I feel a kinship with him, despite our history."

"We'll relay your thoughts to him. Is there anything else?"

"No," said Venkdt. "The announcement will be soon, in the next few weeks, I hope."

"Thank you, Mr Venkdt," said Oatridge, standing. "I'd like to wish you good luck in your endeavours, but I'm afraid my conscience won't allow me."

"I understand," said Venkdt.

The Hjälp Teknik representatives left the meeting in amused shock.

"We should go straight to the garrison," said Oatridge, melodramatically.

"He's insane," said Strich.

Philips simply grimaced.

"This is treason, plain and simple," said Oatridge. "He should be locked up for it. Hell, they could lock us up just for having been a part of that meeting," he said, unsure if he was joking or deadly serious.

"It won't fly," said Strich. "It's just some crazy stunt. No one will take it seriously. I doubt if even he takes it seriously."

"He's serious alright," said Philips, "and he will do it. So we're going to be dragged into this whether we like it or not."

The other two thought about that. The three of them made their way from the building to the car park, where they walked the short distance to their driverless car. At the car they stopped and Philips spoke again.

"Venkdt is going to run this plebiscite and he's probably going to win. That's going to leave us in a very difficult position." They got in.

"I want you to look at all of our options, legal and practical, if this goes ahead," Philips said to Strich. "And I need you to look into every damn way possible we can make it not happen," she said to Oatridge.

The more Oatridge thought about it the less amusing it seemed. He noticed that the smiles had left Strich, too.

They sat in silence on the drive back to Hjälp Teknik.

St Joseph's Hospital was situated in the heart of Marineris. Like the majority of Martian buildings it was mostly underground. It covered three floors. The lowest was for maintenance and services. The next floor up was theatres, clinics and treatment rooms, catering and the transport hub. At the surface were the wards and private rooms. They had the luxury of daylight, which was seen as a therapeutic plus.

Jack Karjalainen was in one of the largest private rooms at the furthest end of the hospital. He had been one of the hospital's greatest benefactors and had personally paid for scholarships and bursaries to encourage bright young doctors from Earth, as well as Mars, to come to the hospital. He had used his waning influence on Earth, earned through Hjälp Teknik's respected medical division, to form solid links with one of the major teaching hospitals on the home planet at Calcutta.

Jack was proud of his philanthropic endeavours. He had always thought of himself as a moral being who had deep respect for other people and the rule of law, and he served them equally.

In his youth Jack had worked for voluntary organisations in the non-aligned countries. He had seen for himself the terrible conditions that some people lived in, and experienced at first-hand the folly of the fools who perpetuated such misery. It had forged in him a steely resolve to always do the right thing. To stand up and give a voice to the oppressed. To talk back to the pompous and the belligerent.

He had formed Hjälp Teknik on his return with the idea of developing effective and cheap solutions to problems affecting the poorest sectors of society, both at home and abroad. Nutrition, coms, education and transport were all areas where Hjälp Teknik had an interest. Products aimed at the poor had small margins but large client bases, and Hjälp Teknik worked that angle.

Karjalainen moved the entire operation to Mars based on one simple idea. The idea was this: to make the new world on Mars better than the old world of Earth. Earth was riven with factions and irrational belief systems, ingrained over centuries or even millennia, and these caused untold misery and unnecessary problems. On the new world these issues could be headed off at the pass, snuffed out at the very beginning, before they grew into something dark and destructive.

The move was funded by selling off the parts of the company that wouldn't work off-Earth, with the remainder being moved or torn down and replaced at the new location. Hjälp Teknik's most valuable assets were intellectual property and personnel, more than a quarter of whom signed up for the move.

Karjalainen had headed to the new world with his young family and re-established Hjälp Teknik there partly as a business decision. More importantly it was a mission, in every sense, to make sure that humankind, in that most unforgiving place, could be all that it could be. That it could rise above the petty squabbles of the old world and look forward to the new world in which people cooperated, interacted rationally and forged a bright new chapter in the history of mankind.

The business had faired so-so. It was not a resounding success due mainly to its dependence on manufactured goods. The real money (just ask Venkdt) was in raw exports. Mars was rich in minerals like silver, iridium, palladium and most importantly deuterium. Venkdt extracted these and shipped them off to Earth, making huge profits. Over time it became clear that Hjälp Teknik, despite its reticence, had to get into the minerals game if it was going to survive, but it found it difficult to compete with the mighty Venkdt Mars Corp.

Hjälp Teknik had gone into the deuterium market. Deuterium was five times more abundant on Mars than it was on Earth, and far more than five times easier to extract. Deuterium, a heavy isotope of hydrogen, was essential fuel for the nuclear fusion reactors which generated the great bulk of the power used on Earth, particularly in the USAN. It underpinned the whole of USAN society and was essential to it. As such it was literally worth more than gold and had been a key driver in the early settlement of Mars.

Hjälp Teknik diversified, moved into minerals and expanded a little, but was always in the shadow of Venkdt. Venkdt had been the only game in town for almost a hundred years and, despite some jitters when Hjälp Teknik first arrived, happily remained so. The research station, latterly the garrison, had not been in competition with Venkdt and benefited greatly from the improved facilities that came in their wake. Once it was clear that Hjälp Teknik was not a major threat Charles Venkdt was happy to affect a collegiate stance, proclaiming that everyone had to stand together in the great adventure of the new frontier. In private, he was more reticent. Venkdt was a little rattled that there was competition in his backyard and, although he was always very polite in public, deep in his heart he knew that he hated Jack Karjalainen. He hated the hippy-drippy attitude. He hated the lofty high moral stance, which he thought was a sham, and he hated the way Jack Karjalainen just knew he was right. Right, with moral certainty, about his beliefs. Right about his business decisions. Right about every damn thing he ever did. It rankled with Venkdt, who knew that he himself was filled with flaws. That was true honesty; looking in the mirror and knowing what an ass you could be. Looking at your customers, and knowing what asses they could be. And standing back, looking at the whole goddamned big picture and knowing that it was all a huge, juddering, wrong-headed mess. To see the world as it is, faults and all, and to make practical steps at working with all the inefficiencies, the greed, the malice and the sheer stupidity, and get it to somehow work - that, to Charles Venkdt, was truly noble. Pretending that everything was perfectible and that the good people were being held back by the bad people, who just needed to be understood and helped to become all they could be, seemed naive and irritating.

Karjalainen, with his unshakeable belief in his own rightness, had always seemed taller than he was. No longer. He was now a shrunken husk of the man he used to be. If he had been able to stand he would have appeared even shorter than his hundred and seventy six centimetres. He was propped up in his bed with pillows, and the bed was surrounded by monitoring machinery, some of which was connected to him by thin cables but others of which were working remotely. He was sleepy, by this late afternoon, and his eyelids hung heavily over his slow moving eyes. A breathing tube was taped to his face, running from his nostril over an ear and out of sight. A shaft of light from the Plexiglas skylight lay on the lower half of the bed and the reflection from the stark white sheets filled the room with a low glow. Distantly, Karjalainen heard a muffled discussion between two voices coming from outside the room. One voice was a nurse. The other was one of his legal advisers. He couldn't make out the words, but the rhythms and tone were clear. His rep was asking and becoming insistent while the nurse was denying, but her resolve was fading away. There were two final syllables from the adviser character, delivered staccato like a one-two punch, followed by short pause and one syllable from the nurse. After that, the door opened and three figures quietly and slowly slipped into the room.

Oatridge came to the head of the bed while the other two remained at the foot. They stood in silence, heads slightly bowed, as if Karjalainen were already dead and they had come to pay their respects. Oatridge coughed, very quietly and deliberately. Karjalainen lifted his heavy eyelids and swivelled his eyes toward Oatridge without moving his head. He swallowed, using a great deal of concentration to do so, and spoke.

"Well?"

"Mr Venkdt informed the meeting that he was going to hold a plebiscite, asking the entire Martian population whether they would like to secede from the USAN," replied Oatridge.

Karjalainen frowned and turned his head away to the side. "On whose authority does he think he's acting?"

"No one's. He's decided to do it independently."

Karjalainen thought. "And what are we going to do about it? Have you informed the garrison?"

"I'm not sure what the garrison would be able to do, sir. Venkdt's own security division more than outmatches them."

"So he holds his election, gets his result. What then?"

Oatridge took a breath. "I guess he would announce the secession and that would be that."

"Where would that leave us?"

Philips piped up. "That would leave us in a very tricky position indeed. We'd be forced to join a - I don't think I'm being melodramatic here - a revolution that we want no part of, or we'd be left sharing an inhospitable planet with an opposing force - I'm sorry about the language, but . . ." she shrugged and pulled a 'what can you do?' face, ". . . an opposing force who, frankly, we are no match for."

Karjalainen thought. "Venkdt wouldn't give us any trouble. But our position would be very difficult." His remark hung in the air. "What are we going to do about it?"

"We're already looking into what we can do to stop the plebiscite ever happening. Legal, practical, those sorts of things," said Oatridge. "And if we can't stop it we'll campaign rigorously for a 'no' vote."

Even at his advanced age, and at the extreme end of his ill health, it was still possible to pick up the 'what am I paying these people for' vibe that was flowing from Karjalainen into the room. With great effort he moved his head again to look at Oatridge. He shaped his words deliberately. "If you campaign, you legitimise the election. And you make us look like damned fools, because the result will be 'yes' and anyone can see that. I'll ask again: what are we going to do about it?"

Strich and Philips exchanged glances, glad that Karjalainen was locked onto Oatridge and wouldn't have the energy to turn his head toward them. Oatridge was too professional to panic but he did not have an answer. He looked into Karjalainen's old and watery eyes. "I don't know, sir. I think we'll have to play this one by ear."

Karjalainen closed his eyes. Whether it was tiredness or exasperation the three did not know, but after a quick and wordless conference they took it as their cue and left the room in silence.

Maya Foveaux was watching the sunset from her window. Unusually for a Martian building the headquarters of Venkdt Security was mostly above ground. It had been expensive to build and was difficult to maintain but the architect thought, and persuaded her client, that it was important that a security division should be able to literally oversee that which it was protecting, and that the protected be able to look up to see their protector.

The window in Foveaux's office was short but very wide, and it framed the Martian sunsets beautifully. When her workload allowed it Foveaux would take a few minutes to stand and watch. It calmed her and gave her some time to think and reflect.

With the light fading she turned away from the window and returned to her desk. Glancing at her terminal she noticed three new emails had arrived in the short time she had been away. One was an addition to a tedious chain that had been going back and forth all day. She didn't really know why she was copied into that one. Some officious type probably thought their dubious argument would somehow carry more weight if the boss was copied in. They were wrong. At the back of her mind Foveaux had marked them down sycophantic, indecisive and unconfident. The other two emails were from her ex-partner and Charles Venkdt.

Maya opened the one from the ex first, partly to get it out of the way and partly because it would be trivial, where the one from Venkdt was more likely to be important. Venkdt had only contacted her directly a handful of times before. At the moment the ex, despite her best efforts, was contacting her daily.

She glanced over the salutation and the first line and immediately got a sense of what the email was about. It was the same self-pitying, pleading begging for forgiveness and reconciliation that she had seen in previous emails. She stopped reading and quickly composed her reply:

"Please do not contact me again."

She hit 'Send' and immediately forgot about it as she opened the last email, the one from Venkdt.

Ms Foveaux

I would like to meet at the earliest opportunity to discuss matters arising from a proposed plebiscite taking place within the next few months. The plebiscite exists in something of a legal grey area, which may lead to some unrest. I would like to brief you in full on our plans, and provide you with any additional resources you may need to ensure that the operation runs smoothly and with any disruptions held to a minimum.
Please liaise with my assistant to arrange a time. I look forward to seeing you soon.

Charles Venkdt

Maya closed the email and fired off one to her assistant, asking that the meeting be set up as soon as possible. Any prior arrangements were to be shifted to make way for the meeting with Venkdt. That was to be the number one priority.

She shot a look back over her shoulder. The sun had disappeared below the horizon.

CHAPTER 06

The Old Order

It was early evening at the hospital. The outpatients and admin staff had left for the day and the clinics were over. It was calmer and quieter than the bustling day shift. Bobby had come through the transport bay, where he'd left his cab, and he was approaching reception. When he got there no one was at the desk, though he could hear a voice coming from the back office talking on a comdev.

As he waited he looked around. The reception area was clean and mostly white. The lighting was tastefully subdued and he could hear, just around the corner, a machine busily polishing the floor. He looked at the floor in reception; spotlessly clean. He wondered if this area was deliberately kept to a high standard in order to create a good impression on people just like him, or if it genuinely reflected a commitment to high standards throughout the hospital.

The receptionist appeared. "Hello, sorry about that, can I help you?" she said.

"I'm here to see Jack Karjalainen," said Bobby.

The receptionist scanned her terminal. "Is he expecting you?" she asked as her eyes moved down the screen.

"I don't have an appointment, if that's what you mean," said Bobby.

The receptionist looked up. "Mr Karjalainen only takes visitors by appointment, I'm afraid. If you want to leave your details I can let his people know, and we can maybe arrange something for another day?"

"I'm his son."

The receptionist took a closer look at Bobby's face. She half-recalled him from somewhere but couldn't quite place him. "Is this the first time you've visited?"

"Yes, it is. I've been away."

She gestured to an area on the reception desk. "Could you just hold your comdev over here for me, please?"

Bobby complied and the receptionist read from her screen. "Robert Harvey Karjalainen." She scanned further down the screen. "And you are indeed Mr Karjalainen's son." She let out a low hum as she thought to herself. "Well, Mr Karjalainen' other son Anthony, your brother, is the only person allowed to visit Mr Karjalainen unannounced so," she thought, "I guess it would be alright for you, too?" It was phrased like a question, but Bobby decided to hear it as a statement.

"That's great," he said. "Thank you so much. Which way is it?"

The receptionist hesitated, then pressed a key on her terminal. "Your comdev will take you right to it." Bobby thanked her and started to walk away. The receptionist muttered 'Robert Harvey Karjalainen' to herself, and only then did the connection click into place. "Are you Bobby Karjalainen; *the* Bobby Karjalainen? The commander?" she excitedly called after him.

Bobby turned and shrugged with an easy smile. "I guess I am," he said.

"Very pleased to meet you, sir," the receptionist said as he turned back and continued walking.

Jack Karjalainen was sleeping when Bobby entered the room. He approached his father taking slow, measured steps and took a seat by the head of the bed. He listened to his father's slow and shallow breathing as he looked at the man he had for so long despised. Beneath his hatred there remained the stubborn stump of love. He was saddened to see his father reduced to this. As a teenager he had often fantasized about his father being in this sort of position; weak and helpless, and close to death. In those fantasies he would tell his father what he really thought of him. He would use the most cutting words he could, and he would attack at what he thought were the weakest points in his father's emotional armour. He would *hurt* the man, the way he felt he had been hurt by him. Now he just felt sorry. Sorry that he was old, sorry that he was suffering and sorry that he was going to die. Most of all, he was sorry that the old man had been such an asshole that he had managed to alienate his own son in the last few years of his life. He was sorry, too, that due simply to his intransigent personality he had not been able to allow for his son being of a radically different disposition to his own. They were very dissimilar people. He should have just accepted that. Instead, he clashed with Bobby at every turn and made things miserable for both of them.

And now here they were.

Karjalainen's head was facing Bobby. He coughed and rolled his tongue around his dry mouth like he was searching for something. After a few minutes he opened his eyes and fixed them on Bobby. Bobby stared back, and smiled.

"How did you get in here?" said Karjalainen.

"I'm family," Bobby replied.

Karjalainen closed his eyes. "You shouldn't be here," he said.

"I am here, Dad. I couldn't not come. You know that."

Karjalainen waited. "I know that, do I? So you still know what I think?"

Bobby let it go. "How've you been? You're not looking so good."

"I've been better. I'm comfortable."

Bobby nodded.

"You've seen Anthony?"

"Yes. I'm staying at the house."

"He's happy with that?"

"I don't know about happy, but that's where I am."

Karjalainen grunted and opened his eyes again. "You shouldn't have gone over there, Bobby," he said.

"To the house?"

"You know what I mean. Always the wise guy. You shouldn't have gone to war. You let us all down."

Bobby nodded. It was what he had expected. "It's done now. Didn't you do a few things you shouldn't have, in your time?"

"Not the same."

"It's all over now. I'm back, and I wanted to see you."

"You're not in the will if that's what you mean."

Bobby shrugged. "That's not what I mean. You know it, too."

Karjalainen stared at him, then closed his eyes again.

"I just wanted to see you again, Dad. That's all."

Bobby couldn't tell if his father had heard the last remark, or if he had drifted off to sleep. Maybe he was just faking it to avoid dealing with the situation. The truth was that Karjalainen, in spite of everything, loved his son and Bobby, in spite of everything, loved his father. They were both too bloody minded to admit it.

Eventually it seemed that Jack Karjalainen actually was asleep. His breathing was once again slow and shallow and his mouth hung open, his dry old tongue lolling out of it. Bobby sat with him for another hour, and kissed him on the forehead before leaving.

Bobby had never liked the Hjälp Teknik Building, even when he was a child. As he strolled down the over-lit corridors he remembered countless occasions when he had come to work with his father and had to wait around in bright, airless rooms while the adult world went about its occult business.

He found the conference room easily, though it had been more than ten years since he had last been there. It seemed much smaller than he remembered it. On entering he saw Anthony seated at the far corner of the tables that were pushed together in the centre of the room. He was deep in conversation with a late middle-aged woman. As they noticed Bobby they immediately stopped talking and drew slightly apart, and a ripple of paranoia planed across Bobby's consciousness. As if to cover, the woman quickly stood and held out a hand. "Bobby!" she said. "It's so good to meet you again!" She was full of smiles and firm handshakes.

Bobby looked to Anthony and said, "Hello," then back to the woman, who was finally letting go of his hand.

"I'm sure you don't remember me," the woman continued. "The last time we met you were about," she gestured, "this high!"

Bobby tilted his head quizzically.

"My name's Toni Philips, Toni with an 'I'," she said. "I'm one of your father's legal team. Well, I'm the head of your father's legal team." She glanced at Anthony. "It still feels weird saying that! You used to play in my office, from time to time, when you were little. Do you remember?"

Bobby thought. "I don't think I do," he said, "but it sounds like a lot of fun." He didn't remember ever having fun at Hjälp Teknik.

"I used to take you to the refectory and get you ice-cream. Look at you now!"

"Well, I'm pleased to meet you," said Bobby, "again."

Bobby took a seat across the tables from Anthony and Toni. Anthony affected to be busily studying some of the papers in front of him. Toni sat with her elbows on the table, her hands together, fingers interlocked with her chin resting on them. "Okay. Down to business, then," she said. She addressed her spiel to Bobby. He assumed that she had already gone through a lot of it with Anthony, or that Anthony was so close to the operation that he didn't need to be briefed. "Your father, Jack Karjalainen, is nearing the end of his life. The nature of his illness has afforded him time to consider his legacy, and to formulate a plan for Hjälp Teknik moving into the future. As his representative, he has asked me to explain that plan to you." She paused, and moved some papers. She found her place on the next sheet and continued. "On his death, Mr Karjalainen's entire portfolio, including his majority shares in Hjälp Teknik, will pass to Anthony. The house in Allentown will also pass to Anthony. Mr Karjalainen's secondary residence in Dog Sur," she leant into Bobby, explaining unnecessarily, "*the flat*," before continuing, "shall pass to Robert." She paused for breath. "The position of Chief Executive Officer of Hjälp Teknik shall be given to Anthony, subject to ratification by the board." This last point was academic, Bobby noted. With a controlling interest in the company Anthony would be able to overrule any decisions made by the board.

Toni Philips quickly looked up at the two men. "Your father writes," she said, and read to them:

> *"It is my hope and belief that, under Anthony's stewardship, Hjälp Teknik will prosper and continue to build upon the good works started in my lifetime. Hjälp Teknik was founded on the belief that things can, and should, be better. We have always sought to provide goods and services that help the maximum number of people for the minimum cost. The bright new frontiers of Mars and the asteroid belt beyond can provide potentially limitless resources to a forward-looking organisation with faith in the people it serves. It can allow them to look toward a future filled with hope, and away from a past too often filled with despair. My son, Anthony Karjalainen, will guide Hjälp Teknik toward this future."*

Bobby thought about clapping, but knew sarcasm wouldn't go down too well. "Congratulations, Anthony," he said.

"I've been working very closely with Dad for the past few years," Anthony replied. "He wants the change to be as seamless as possible. I'm running most of the day to day stuff now anyway."

Bobby nodded.

"You understand -" Toni started, but Bobby cut in.

"I understand. Anthony gets the business, I get an apartment." He shrugged. "It's about what I expected."

Toni turned to Anthony. "Your father is placing a great deal of trust in you. He believes in you, Anthony." She reached out and patted Anthony's arm, her brow furrowed in pity. "I know these are difficult times, difficult for us all, but we have to think about the future. Your father is being very brave about all this."

Bobby shifted in his seat. "Is there anything we should be doing?"

"For your father?" asked Toni.

EPHIALTES

"For anyone."

Toni thought. "There is nothing that needs to be done at this time. If I were you two I would be spending as much time as I could with my father. There isn't long to go now, and," she caught herself before continuing, "the time we have with our loved ones is so precious." Toni, for the first time, looked sad.

Anthony looked across the table at Bobby. "Stay at the house for now. If you want to move out to the apartment you can. It needs remodelling, really. Stay at the house while we sort the apartment out for you. Stay as long as you like."

"Thank you," said Bobby. It rankled that Anthony made giving him comparatively nothing sound like a grand gesture, but Bobby knew this was not the time to get into that. He did not mind being largely frozen out of the will. He had expected it. Maybe he was being paranoid but the line 'My son, Anthony' had really stuck in his craw. He felt his dad was, even at this late stage, having a pop at him.

Bobby stood and shook Toni's hand again. "Thank you very much," he said.

"Thank you," said Toni. "If there's anything you need, either of you, just get in touch. Your father is a wonderful man. I'm so sorry for both of you."

Earlier in the week Toni Philips had visited Jack Karjalainen at the hospital. He had been very specific. "Anthony gets Hjälp Teknik. The board will have to ratify, but they will, if they know what's good for them. He knows it already, we've been through it a thousand times. I need you to write it all up and make it proper. Tie it all up legally, and don't leave any holes. Make sure Anthony's tied in. Lock his shares down for two years. Have letters written up to the board informing them of my decision. I'll sign them."

As an afterthought he added, "I've got an apartment in Dog Sur. It's Bobby's."

Toni had hesitated. "Nothing for Bobby but the apartment?" It was a nice apartment, to be sure, but in light of Karjalainen's accumulated wealth it was as nothing compared the share of the empire left to Anthony.

"My first born son has been a grave disappointment. I came here to get away from the bullshit and the squalor and the fighting. We were looking to the future. He always wanted to spite me. Even when he was a kid. And the first chance he got he went back there. To fight in their wars, to kill people. He made me ashamed to be his father. He deserves a place to live. Nothing more."

He had waved her away after that.

Toni felt that at this point, at the end of his life, Jack Karjalainen should be thinking about forgiveness.

Jack disagreed.

Leaving the room Bobby heard Toni calling after him. He paused as she caught up. "Bobby, I'm sorry your father feels this way. I tried to talk with him, but . . ."

"It's okay. I know what my dad's like. Stubborn as a mule. I don't need the money, anyways."

They walked together.

"It's so sad when families fight," Toni said. "No good ever comes of it."

"Hey," said Bobby, "my dad is my dad. He achieved everything he did by being a stubborn asshole. Why would he stop now? Admitting he was wrong about anything would kill him as surely as any cancer."

"I'll speak to him again."

They walked on.

"I've been to see him," said Bobby.

"You have?"

"He was okay with it."

"That's great."

CHAPTER 07

The Rumour

Audrey Andrews read Colleen Acevedo's report in bed the night she received it. There was a case there, and everyone had overlooked it. The crux of it was this: Mars was a long, long way away. It had been assumed, to the degree that no one had ever considered otherwise, that the colony on Mars was wholly dependent on Earth. Why wouldn't it be? It was so small and so distant that it seemed it had to be constantly looking back to the bountiful mother for support and reassurance. For these reasons, no one had ever considered Mars as a separate entity. For many years the Martians had held the same view from the reverse perspective. Like an old habit, they had routinely assumed that Mars was second best, out on a limb, dangerous and desolate.

It had been a slow realisation that once the Martian colony had developed beyond a certain point the relationship ceased to make sense. Venkdt Corp made huge profits on Martian deuterium and other minerals that went to its shareholders on Earth. What did Venkdt Mars get in return? It didn't need the protection of an army; it had no enemies. It didn't need any other services from Earth; it was too costly in time and money to go back there for anything. In short, it got nothing in return that it couldn't, with some minor development, provide for itself. Why wasn't Venkdt Mars trading *with* Earth rather than mining *for* it?

Once this idea had been grasped it was impossible to see things the old way. Mars needed Earth solely as a trading partner. But Earth absolutely relied on Mars as a source of increasingly scarce minerals, and would have to trade for them come what may. In this new paradigm Mars held the upper hand.

Despite not having or needing a military Mars held a strategic advantage, too. It was just too far away to threaten with a big stick. If they wanted to pull away, who was going to stop them?

Laying down to sleep Audrey mulled these ideas through her mind. As she sunk into progressively lower levels of consciousness something occurred to her. It was bold and radical, but it just might work. She slept like a baby.

Peter Brennan disliked having his routine disturbed.

"This better be about something. I've cancelled two meetings and a teleconference. The president can't make it, but he wants me to report back to him directly. We've got twenty minutes. What is it?"

Andrews spoke. "We have reliable intelligence coming out of Mars that Charles Venkdt is going to run a plebiscite asking the entire population of Mars whether Venkdt Mars should break away from the parent company. Since more than eighty-five percent of the Martian population work for Venkdt this would be tantamount to Mars declaring independence from Earth."

Brennan grunted, and noted something down.

"Should this come to pass it would present us with a number of problems. First, it would be a criminal act on a huge scale. Venkdt Mars is worth vast sums and would be, in effect, 'stolen' from its rightful owners. And that would be happening on the other side of the solar system, where we cannot police it.

"Secondly, it would damage us strategically and economically. Our whole society is underpinned by the power provided by nuclear fusion reactors and they run on deuterium which comes, in large part, from Mars. An independent Mars would mean the USAN were no longer energy independent. We would be hostage to the prices Mars could set for deuterium as well as other minerals which, at present, are more cost-efficiently gathered and transported from Mars than they are gathered here on Earth. We could see energy prices double, triple, quadruple; who knows?

"Thirdly, we would look weak politically. A major source of our energy and a major technical and social achievement in its own right - a source of national pride, no less - would be seen to walk away from us with utter impunity.

"And fourthly, we would lose our frontier outpost. Mars is our forward base, right out near the asteroid belt, which is ripe for exploitation. Ten, twenty years down the line we want to be out there mining those asteroids and looking out to the further reaches of the solar system. If we lose Mars, we're pushed a hundred and forty million miles backward, and that can't happen."

Brennan turned to Farrell. "What do you say?"

"Our analysis is largely the same, senator," said Farrell.

"What do we do?" said Brennan.

"Well," started Farrell, "certain actions are being prepared already. We can't move yet because Venkdt hasn't made a formal announcement, but we're expecting that soon. When he does, we'll be ready. We have a statement ready for the president, condemning the action in the strongest terms, and we have a team working now on all diplomatic avenues that we might want to pursue."

"Which are?"

Farrell shuffled his notes. "We can assure the Venkdt Mars hierarchy that we will pursue all legal means to prevent this from happening. We can pressure them into seeing the folly of taking this path. We can co-opt the Venkdt shareholders on Earth, and other stakeholders, to bring pressure on them to see sense. And we're looking at the practicalities of freezing their assets, should it come to it."

"Would any of that have any effect?"

Farrell seemed momentarily startled. "I would hope so, senator."

Brennan turned back to Andrews. "What have you got? There's a garrison up there, isn't there?"

"There is senator, but its role is very limited. Venkdt have their own security service and mostly police themselves. In terms of physical force they outnumber us ten to one. We couldn't jump to that at this stage, anyway."

"So we have an inadequate and outnumbered force that we can't afford to use, and persuasion? That's it?"

"At the present time that's it, sir," said Farrell. "I have a team working on this right now, and we hope to have something much firmer in the next few days. We have until Venkdt announces, too."

"What would we do if this was, say, Sri Lanka?" Brennan said to Andrews. It was what she had been waiting for.

"We'd do just what we're doing now, sir. Monitor communications, pursue diplomatic channels, play the media. But if it was Sri Lanka, sir, we'd park a carrier group off-shore, just for emphasis."

Brennan raised an eyebrow. "Ms Andrews, I take it we don't have any carriers in the vicinity of Mars?"

"No, sir, we don't."

"Nor do we have any such vessels in space at all, do we?"

Andrews didn't hesitate. "That's not quite true, sir. We do have the two LEO carriers. They're the most expensive ships ever commissioned by the USAN, and they're brand new and ready for service."

"LEO. That's Low Earth Orbit, isn't it, Ms Andrews?"

"Yes, sir, it is."

"So that's not going to help with Mars, is it?"

"Well, sir, if we could get them to Mars they would be exactly the thing to show we mean business. Their strike capability is enormous and highly configurable. They were made for policing the world. They could just as easily police another world."

Brennan thought. "Could we get them to Mars?"

"I don't know. The hard work was getting them built in the first place. If we could refit them in some way for interplanetary flight we could police our frontier."

"Is that even feasible?"

"I'll talk to Helios."

"Financially feasible?"

"I'll talk to Helios. Time is the issue. Even if it can be done it will take time, then we have to wait for a launch window. It'll take two years at a bare minimum."

Brennan shook his head. "It'll all be over by then. Too late."

"It's all we have. And it won't be over, legally. And they'll know we're coming from the minute we make the announcement."

Farrell called ahead from his car and had his people waiting for him on his return. He entered the room at pace, walking to his desk and planting his briefcase down on it as he said, "What have we got, people?" A handful of his top advisers were seated on plastic chairs in front of his desk. As he took his seat he looked at them expectantly.

"A special envoy is out," one of them offered. "The next launch window isn't for eighteen months."

"Who do we have on the ground?"

"No one," another adviser answered.

"Who's senior at the garrison?"

"That would be Colonel Katrina Shaw," another said. "I'm squaring it with defence that she can assume diplomatic responsibility for us."

"That's good. As soon as that's cleared I want her fully briefed on the situation and ready to meet with Venkdt the moment he announces."

"Yes, sir."

"What about legal?"

"Without the specifics of the plan we're guessing against certain likely scenarios. For each scenario we're working through the legal issues; which laws are being broken, who by, potential remedies etcetera," said an adviser.

"That's good," said Farrell. "As soon as Venkdt goes public I want to know what laws he's breaking and what laws he's proposing to break. And I want a warrant for his arrest in Colonel Shaw's hands five minutes after that."

"You want to arrest him?"

Farrell shook his head, "No, we can't arrest him. But I want him to know there's a warrant."

Audrey Andrews had already scheduled a call to Lewis J Rawls before the meeting with Brennan had begun. As her car pulled away she barked instructions to it. "Get me Rawls, put it on the wall."

Presently, the chest and head of Lewis Rawls appeared opposite Andrews. The image was slightly distorted initially, as it fell over the opposing cream white seats. The projector quickly recalibrated the image to allow for the uneven surface so what Andrews saw resembled the man in the flesh. A subtle but definite 3D effect helped, too.

"Make him smaller," said Andrews.

"Make him what?" came muffledly over Andrews' speakers. The image shrank a little.

"That's good," said Andrews. "I was just resizing you, Lewis. You were bearing down on me like some huge ape."

Rawls laughed. "That's just how I like it. What can I do for you Audrey?"

Audrey looked at the image of Rawls. Approximately life-sized now it felt disconcertingly like he was sat there in the car with her. She looked into his eyes as she spoke. "You've done a lot of work for us over the years, Lewis. Right now we need you to really pull something special out of the bag."

Rawls leaned into the camera. "I'm intrigued. And I'm excited, on behalf of billing."

"We're in the process of taking delivery of the second carrier. As you know, they're arriving too late for the war. We may have another use for them, but they would need some modifications. Is this all sounding plausible?"

"It sounds great so far, but you haven't got to the modifications yet."

"Well, it's this Lewis. We need the carriers to do exactly what they're designed to do, but we need them to do it someplace else."

Rawls didn't have a comeback for that. "Go on," he said.

"We need to get them to Mars," said Andrews. "Can that be done?"

Rawls sat back in his chair and was silent for a moment. "It," he paused for a long time, ". . . could be done, yes."

Audrey waited for more but there was none. "Talk to me Rawls. How could we do it?"

Rawls pushed the tips of his fingers together, with his elbows rested on the arms of his chair, and looked at them in concentration as he spoke.

"The carriers have ion drives for manoeuvrability. Their main engines are standard chemical rocket engines. They're for pushing them quickly around the world. There's not enough power in those for interplanetary flight, and there's not enough space for the necessary fuel."

Andrews pursed her lips.

"But. If we could replace the main chemical engines with nuclear fusion jet engines that would give us the necessary thrust, within the limited space available, to kick off into the void. So theoretically, yes, it could be done."

"How fast?"

"You're really talking seriously about doing this?"

"How fast could you do it, how much would it cost?"

Rawls thought. "I can't give you a price, but not cheap. And fast will at least double the price, whatever it is. In all of our projects we try to keep to standardised specifications, and we keep everything as modular as possible to simplify maintenance. That would mean that ripping out the current engines would be relatively painless. We could do that in, say, a week or less. The difficulty would come with the NFJ engines."

"What difficulty?

"They don't exist."

"Goddammit, why didn't you just say that!"

"Hold on. They don't exist *yet*, but one of my top engineers is working on NFJs right now. She has three prototypes, two full-sized, and is nearing the end of the testing phase as we speak."

"She has two? One for each carrier, that's great," Audrey was saying when Rawls cut back in.

"They are two *prototypes*. The work is extremely promising, but putting two untried engines in what I believe to be the most expensive vessels ever commissioned by the USAN would come with a high degree of uncertainty and risk."

"I know that Rawls. But this is a national emergency."

"It is? I haven't seen anything on the bulletins."

"Not yet. This is going to blow up in the next few days and we need to be ready for it." As an afterthought she added, "You understand this all falls under your confidentiality agreement?"

"Of course."

"These engines; if we sign off on the risk, you just fit them in and that's that?"

Rawls laughed. "Not quite that simple. As mentioned, we make all our stuff modular. Saves on costs, saves on headaches, keeps things simple. The prototype engines are the same form factor as the class of chemical engine that is currently in the carriers. Obviously, the NFJs don't need the huge fuel capacity of the chemical engines, but it's not a like-for-like swap. We'd have to look at that. And the control software would need to be overhauled, and we'd need to look at ramping up the power of the ion drives. Navigation and coms would need to be looked at, too. It could take months."

"We don't have months. If you had to do it fast, how fast could you do it?"

Rawls looked off to the side. "Audrey, bear this in mind. Everything takes at least four times as long as you think it will. That said, if everything goes without one single little hitch, and it won't, then I would say, maybe, six months?"

Audrey thought. "I need to take this to the president. I will strongly advise him that we should proceed with this course of action. We'll need the nod from him, and he'll have to find the money. Until then, can you proceed, with haste, to get this thing rolling?"

"I can start. You're confident the president will buy it?"

"He has to. There's no other course open to us."

"Okay. I'll put things in motion."

"Who's working on the engines?"

"You know her. She was second lead designer on the *Aloadae*, for a couple of years, anyway."

"I know her?"

"Sure, you must have seen her in design briefings and the like. Tall blonde woman, short hair."

Audrey thought, scanning through her internal archive but unable to locate an image of the tall, blonde engineer. "What's her name?" she said.

"Askel Lund."

Madeline Zelman patronised the arts. She could often be found floating through a private viewing, or holding court at the interval of a much anticipated première. She supported many prominent charities and occasionally travelled overseas to see first-hand the work that was being done with the monies she helped to raise. For a number of big-name NGOs she acted as a roving ambassador, hugging the poor here, opening a hydroelectric plant there. She smiled graciously for the cameras, gave good interview, looked good in pictures and was utterly unshakeable. A desperately ill (but still, give-or-take, photogenic) Haitian boy vomiting blood onto her virginal white designer dress couldn't phase her. She looked genuinely concerned for the boy and later shrugged a self-deprecating smile at the cameras as aides fussed over the bloody clothing.

She had had the colossal misfortune of having been born immensely rich. Her childhood had been happy and she had wanted for nothing. All of this had left her with a gnawing feeling that she should be doing something. What was she *for*? If she wasn't for patronising the arts and raising money and awareness for charity, at least it kept her busy.

As the majority owner of Helios Matériel Corporation she would often be met by protesters when she attended events. Chants, placards, eggs. But she was resolute. She knew that peace wasn't the natural state between people. She knew that not all people were good. And she believed, wholeheartedly, that the advanced weaponry that Helios made and sold was making the world a safer place.

She had met Gerard White through her fund-raising activities way back when he was just starting out in politics. She had contributed to his campaigns all the way through to when he was seeking the presidential candidacy. He hadn't quite made it that time, but he managed to get on the ticket as VP candidate. He balanced out Cortes. Cortes was swarthy, he was a WASP. Cortes was a hawk, he was a dove. Cortes was a hot-head, he was level-headed, always taking the long view.

Zelman hadn't contributed to their presidential campaign. She didn't trust Cortes. She'd been around the world, to the non-aligned countries, and had seen leaders like him there - generalissimos and tin-pots. There was something of that about him and she didn't like it.

When White's wife had died four years earlier he had drifted into a relationship with Zelman which, looking back, had always seemed inevitable. The relationship wasn't secret, as such, but it wasn't public either. They would meet for the occasional meal, or night, or weekend, and that suited them both. They were busy people.

On this occasion Zelman had booked a suite at a swanky downtown hotel. It was one they had used before and had been pre-approved by the Secret Service. They had additionally booked the entire floor, and strategic rooms above and below, and were in a position to maintain security from a discreet and low-key distance.

White arrived late. He closed the door behind him and crossed the large and minimally opulent living area to where Zelman was lounging on a sofa, reading a magazine. He lofted a bottle of champagne up in front of him and smiled. Zelman smiled back and nodded to the small table next the sofa. There was a bottle of the same champagne, their favourite Perrier-Jouët Belle Epoque, on ice in a bucket. White's face fell to mock sadness. "I wanted to surprise you. Well, I've had a two bottle kind of day, I guess." He took the chilled bottle and replaced it with his own. He poured two glasses, offering one to Zelman. He took a sip and sat at the other end of the sofa, Zelman lifting her legs to make space for him then laying them back on his lap. He stroked her calf and took another drink.

"I'm just finishing this article," said Zelman, distractedly.

White looked around the room. He could feel himself relaxing. It felt good.

"There!" Zelman exclaimed, half-dropping, half-throwing the magazine to the floor. "How are you, darling? A two bottle day, you say?"

White perked up. "Oh, maybe not that bad, I guess. Things are hotting up at foreign and defence. We're meeting with Cortes tomorrow."

Zelman was intrigued. "The Asian Bloc? Are they getting antsy again?"

"No, no. That's all going great. Bizarrely enough, there are storm clouds gathering over Mars."

"Mars?"

"Yup," White sighed. "With any luck it'll just be a storm in teacup but we have some intel - I shouldn't be telling you this - that Charles Venkdt is going to poll the Martian population on independence."

Zelman was genuinely baffled. "What do you mean, independence?"

"From Earth. Well, technically from the parent company but it amounts to the same thing."

"Ha!" Zelman couldn't help herself. The very idea seemed so ridiculous. "Is he mad? It's just some internal spat at Venkdt then, isn't it?"

"That's what we're all hoping. Because if anything crazy does go on up there there's not a damn thing we can do about it."

"What about the garrison?"

White snorted. "Two hundred guys gone soft. And what use would they be? Firepower is only useful if you have overwhelming superiority. The last seven years have taught us that. The greater your superiority the less likely your need to use it. Anyway, we can't be seen to be turning the military on USAN citizens. That could get *really* messy."

"Well," said Zelman, "let's hope it doesn't come to that."

"I don't think it will. But, you know, in our line we have to think the unthinkable."

Zelman smiled. "These things always seem important at the time. In two weeks this will all be over and forgotten about. Let's go to bed."

"You know, there could be a silver lining in this for you."

Zelman looked at him quizzically.

"Andrews is talking about refitting the carriers. Sending them to Mars, like some old colonial warships, to give the natives something to think about. Your stocks will go through the roof."

Zelman laughed. "That sounds like a grand idea! I've tried to tell you before, *peace through superior firepower*. That's the only foreign policy you need. They wouldn't really go through with it though, would they? The Martians?"

White rose from the sofa, reaching out for the champagne.

"Who knows what the hell they might do."

Rawls got off the phone to Andrews and lay back in his white chair, kicking his feet up on the desk. He closed his eyes and thought. Was what he had just told Andrews feasible? Probably. Realistic? Maybe. He felt a little scared. It was an exciting - as well as lucrative - project, and it was the risk of failure that made it exciting. His mind was racing a little. Had he oversold what Helios was capable of delivering? Even with twenty-third century production methods, refitting the two giant carriers was going to be a massive task. Intellectually, he reasoned that it could be done. But the fear was still there. It was good. And anyway, now they were committed.

He sat the chair back up and spoke to his terminal, "Get me Lund."

"Dr Lund is busy right now," the terminal replied.

"Can you let Dr Lund know it's me and that it's urgent," said Rawls.

He brought up some documents on his terminal and scanned through them. He looked at the plans for the carriers and at some of Askel's recent work on the engines. He looked at budgets and the project management records for the carriers' construction. He was sinking into the details of the engine fitting procedure when his terminal spoke again.

"Askel Lund for you."

"Great, put her on the wall."

The wall of his office sprang to life with the huge image of Askel's head and shoulders projected two metres high, and in incredible detail.

Her face was clean, honest and open, and her crystal blue eyes looked out vividly from the projection. "You wanted me?" she said.

"Hi, Askel. Got some ideas I want to run past you."

Askel's eyes narrowed almost imperceptibly. She couldn't say 'Can't you see I'm busy' to the boss, but her expression hinted at it. "Go on," she said.

"You worked on the carriers. The NFJs you're working on now, would they work in them?"

"No."

"Why not? They're the same form factor, aren't they?"

"They're not ready."

"No, but if they were ready they could be made to work in the carriers, right?"

Askel paused. "I guess. But there'd be no point. They'd be overkill for ships that just roam about the planet."

"I'm coming on to that. If you could get the NFJ engines into the carriers, there's no reason we couldn't get them to Mars, is there?"

Askel paused. "Well . . ."

"Could you do it?"

"It could be done, when the engines are ready, which they aren't, but it would take a lot of time and money and wouldn't be as effective as building ships from the ground up for interplanetary flight. That's where I'd start - with a new design."

"Askel, we don't have time for that. If we started right now, how long would this take?"

Askel shook her head gently in thought. "Six months, eight. If the engines were ready, which they aren't."

"If I gave you everything you needed, if we went at this day and night, could we do it in six months?"

Silence.

"Maybe. But the engines -"

Rawls cut her off. "I'm reading the test data right now. It all looks good to me. These engines are ready, aren't they? Really?"

"I'd like to do further tests. We're doing very advanced stuff here and I'd like to proceed with an abundance of caution."

"Can you think of a better test than putting them in working spacecraft?"

"Lewis, I . . ." Askel's voice trailed off.

"We can do this, can't we? And you said six months? That's great. I'll let the secretary of defence know."

Askel was already reluctantly thinking of the problems ahead. "I'll need more money. And I want it in writing that you're proceeding over my objections." Her mind was racing now. "And we'll need more production drones and an orbital laser lathe."

"You've got it, Askel. It's all billable. The client wants it and they want it fast."

"The client? The USAN? Why do they want to send the carriers to Mars?"

"They have their reasons. It's political, as far as I can tell. If you ask me it's a huge fuss over nothing, but they're asking for it and they're going to pay for it, so I say let's give it to them. Customer's always right, eh?"

"How much are we going to bill them for this?"

"Shitloads."

"Do I get a bonus?"

"Write your own cheque, Askel. Uncle Sam's paying."

Askel Lund, twenty-eight, pulled her chair up to her desk and prepared to concentrate. She sat in front of her terminal and grim-facedly set to work. She pulled files on the carriers; designs, redesigns and construction records. She pulled the project management data, where she could compare the plans for the builds, including projected milestones, against actual milestones. She looked at all the delays, their reasons and impacts. She hunted for short cuts; safety inspections that could be sped up; systems that could be worked in parallel. She maximised man and drone power to the point beyond which they would get in each other's way, which cut the time for some crucial tasks by as much as fifty percent.

EPHIALTES

She looked at the engines. Rawls had been right; they had been tested to exhaustion and Lund, ever thorough, had been delaying the sign off to make further tweaks and tests. Rawls had been right, too, in that the ultimate test would be to set the engines in spacecraft and put them to work. The engines were currently housed in a test facility in Winfrith, Dorset. They would have to be prepared for transport - five days - and then shipped by special lorries - need to organise that - to the spaceport at Foulness Island near Southend in Essex.

Lund was making lists as she went. There was a whole load of things that would have to be organised to make this thing move fast. Rawls would need to organise an HLV or two to get the engines into orbit. There were various tools and drones that would have to be in position against specific dates. There were work schedules and a huge shopping list of necessary supplies. Lund hammered away at the task without stopping, like a machine. The more she worked the clearer the whole project became in her mind, and she could see it as a reality. Initially, it had seemed something of a pipe dream but as she worked the numbers came clearer into view, and it did indeed seem like a plausible thing. A few hours later and in Askel's mind it was not only plausible, or possible, it was going to happen. Lund was gripped by the project. Every problem solved, every hour saved, every unnecessary system discarded was like a huge victory in service of the ultimate goal; to make this thing happen as soon - or even sooner - than she said she would. Rawls may baulk at some of the prices on her shopping list, but fast was never going to be cheap. And anyway, the bills would be passed on to the client with a twenty percent mark-up.

It was two hours after midnight when Lund finished. She had generated or copied, modified and amended a vast amount of documents and schematics by then. She kicked her chair back as she spoke to the terminal. "Check all of the documents I've produced in the last twelve hours. Check them for spelling, grammar, logical consistency. Check them with the highest grade AI for logic, and produce a report for any inconsistencies. Also, generate a report suggesting any improvements. Priorities are speed and efficiency. Let me know when you're done."

"Yes, Dr Lund," the terminal replied.

Askel rose from her desk and walked to the window. It was dark outside but looking up and to the west she could see what looked like a bright, slightly orange star.

Rawls picked Askel up early next morning. She had slept soundly and dreamlessly after finishing her work. The terminal had found a few minor inconsistencies and had made some very useful suggestions. She had quickly worked these into her documentation over breakfast and then showered. Her hair was still wet when Rawls commed through to tell her he was waiting downstairs. She buzzed him up.

"Good morning," said Rawls. "How's it going?"

"It's going great," said Askel, closing the door behind her.

"Everything's looking good?"

"I went through everything yesterday. I've got a full report, I just sent you a copy."

"I saw. I haven't had chance to look at it yet. We've got something to take to the secretary, though?"

"Yes, we have. It's all doable, provided they're willing to pick up the bill."

"That's great, Askel. I knew you could do it. Can you get it down to four months?"

"It's down to three. And of course, as I'm sure you're aware, there's a massive bonus with the NFJs."

"I thought so," Rawls grinned. "The poor defence secretary. She's just a dumb civilian. I bet she hasn't even thought about launch windows, which is a shame. She won't realise what an incredible thing it is that we will be providing to her. But maybe for the best. If she had known, she might never have come to us in the first place."

Askel looked out of the window as London slid by. "I wish they were going into a civilian transport. Rather than this."

"In the fullness of time, Askel. This is a major coup for us. This will be a news story around the world. You can't buy publicity like that. The whole world will be watching our ships, our engines."

Askel shook her head. "This is a hell of a job, Lewis. This only comes off if everything goes exactly to plan."

"I know. That's why I want you to oversee it personally. Lead designer and project manager. How's that sound?"

Askel turned away from the window. It sounded good and terrifying. "It sounds great. When do I start?"

"You already have."

They pulled into the Ministry of Defence local HQ at Whitehall, London and drove through the security checks down into the underground car park. They were escorted under military guard to the lifts, and were then whisked up to one of the higher floors. As the lift doors opened they were greeted by a huge bear of a man. He thrust a paw in their direction, beaming brightly. "General Terrence Cain, just call me Terry. Great to meet you, Mr Rawls, and you must be Dr Lund. Very excited to meet you, come this way. The teleconference will start in just over ten minutes. If there's anything you need just let me know."

They nodded their 'thank yous' and, after the handshaking and pleasantries, followed General Cain down a series of corridors until they came to a room labelled 'Conference Room A'. There were two armed soldiers guarding either side of the door. They snapped to attention and saluted General Cain as he approached. Cain returned the salute as automatically as he put one foot in front of the other when he walked. He held the door open and Rawls and Lund entered.

The room was large and low-lit with no windows. It was air conditioned cool and there was bottled water and glasses on the large table that dominated the room. The far wall was blank white. That was where the images would be shown when the teleconference started, Askel guessed.

"Please, take a seat," said Cain. "We should have the feed from Dallas up in the next few minutes." He seemed genuinely excited, like he had never done this sort of thing before. Maybe he hadn't.

Lund and Rawls took seats at the far end of the table near the screening wall. They sat on opposite sides. Cain took up a seat one down from Rawls.

"This line is fully secure, is it?" asked Lund.

"Oh, yes," replied Cain. "Military grade. Literally. We're sorry we couldn't do this over standard coms; the secretary requested the highest levels of security."

"Can you patch my comdev in? There are some files I'll need to show."

"Yes," said Cain. "Can you just pass it here?" He took the comdev and held it under his own, slid his fingers about the screen and handed it back.

"It's Conference Room A, Screen 1," he said.

"Thank you," said Lund. She fiddled with her comdev, her brow furrowed. Rawls seemed relaxed. He took a bottle of water and poured himself a glass. He took a few sips. He might have been sipping a G&T in some Mediterranean resort for all the stress he displayed.

"Ah!" said Cain as the screen flickered to life. The head and shoulders of a woman appeared, three metres high, filling the screen. "Hello, London," she said in a southern drawl.

"This is London," said Cain.

"Hi, there. I have the secretary of defence here for you, we'll be patching her through in just a few moments."

"Very good." Cain winked at Askel.

The screen cut to a conference room similar to the one they were seated in. The resolution was extremely high, and the three dimensional effect made it appear almost as an extension of the room they were in. Audrey Andrews was seated to the front and side of a similar conference table. About her were five or six senior staffers and assistants. A young, suited man was half leant over saying something to Andrews. She seemed to thank him as he left, walking across the screen and out of shot. Andrews looked at them. "Hello, Lewis. I see you have General Cain there."

"Hello, Ms Andrews!" said Cain.

"And this must be Askel Lund."

"Good morning, Secretary," said Askel.

Andrews cut straight to it. "Dr Lund, Lewis has assured me that Helios can refit our two orbiting carriers, with engines and other necessary equipment such that we can transport them to Mars, within six months. Is that reasonable, in your opinion?"

Askel glanced at Rawls. "I've looked at the figures and have come up with a preliminary plan. The plan is dependent on many factors - I'm sending you all the documentation now - but if we get all those in place I think we can deliver the modifications in three months."

"*Three months*!?"

Askel beamed, just a little. "Yes, I think so. As mentioned, that would depend on many things. We would need some assistance cutting through some red tape and it would not be cheap. I mean, it would not be cheap anyway, but to do it quickly and safely will require a big financial commitment."

Andrews looked invigorated. "But in three months' time we could set our two carriers off to Mars, if we had the will and the money to do it?"

"That's correct. And that's only possible with NFJ engines."

"I'm sorry, what's only possible with these engines?"

"There are a number of papers in the tranche of documents I've sent over explaining it in detail, but with these engines we don't have to wait for a launch window. As you know, with conventional chemical engines we can only launch about once every two years, during a very specific launch window." Andrews nodded. "That is because the cost, in terms of weight of fuel, is too high at any other time. When the orbits of Earth and Mars are at just the right relative positions we can jump off the Earth, which is already moving around the Sun at about 108,000km/h, and accelerate up to a speed where we can travel to Mars within six months. We're limited in how fast we can go by two factors. One is the weight of necessary chemical fuel and the other is our speed at arrival. If we're going too fast the gravity of Mars won't be strong enough to catch us when we get there. For every kilo of fuel we need to accelerate we need the same amount to brake at the other end. With conventional fuels the cost is just too high. To go fast *and* stop at the other end, or rather slow down to the speed necessary for orbital capture, the fuel tanks would have to be enormous - far beyond what is practical."

Andrews was nodding her head in all the right places, her brow furrowed with concentration. Rawls was looking content, like a proud father, and Cain was beaming like he'd just received the best birthday present ever. Lund continued. "The ratio of thrust to fuel weight with a nuclear fusion jet engine is simply enormous. That means that for a trip to Mars we can accelerate to a speed far beyond what has been used up to now, because the cost in fuel weight is so low. It also means we don't have to wait for a window when Earth and Mars are at their closest. We can go whenever we want, because we'll have more than enough fuel left to decelerate to the necessary speed when we arrive at Mars."

"So three months from now, we could send the carriers off?"

"Yes."

"And how long would it take them to reach Mars?"

Askel frowned. "I think, given the current positions of the two planets, if we launched in three months' time it would take approximately six to eight weeks to arrive in Mars orbit."

Andrews looked impressed. She leaned back and spoke to one of the men behind her, nodding at him as she turned back to the screen. "If we can get the funds and other resources, smooth out some of the paperwork, you can get us two carriers in orbit around Mars within five months. I've understood you correctly, Dr Lund?"

"Yes, Secretary. If we start now."

"Thank you. And thank you for the documentation. I assume the costings are in there?"

Rawls cut in, "Audrey, that's the one on top of the pile."

Andrews smiled. "I'll be taking this to the president. In the meantime, can you assume you have approval? Get things going?"

Rawls puffed his cheeks.

"If for any reason this doesn't come off we'll reimburse you for any losses. But we need to hit the ground running."

"I wouldn't do this for anyone other than you, Audrey," Rawls said, and chuckled to himself.

"That's great. Thank you for your time, we'll speak again soon." Andrews stood up and the screen cut back to the head and shoulders of the woman. "Dallas here, were finishing the conference at 08.47, London time, is there anything else?"

"We're all fine here," said Cain. "Good morning to you, Dallas!"

"Good morning to you too, sir, have a great day, Dallas out." The image cut and the wall was a wall once again.

Rawls turned to Lund. "Need a ride home?"

"Sure. There's a million things I need to do."

Rawls nodded. "And you'll need to pack, too."

Askel gave him her quizzical glance.

"Your new position. It's based on *Ephialtes*."

Askel didn't like spaceflight. The prospect of spending the next few months on *Ephialtes* filled her with a mild dread. Still, at least she would be busy. She'd hurriedly packed some things and had asked a neighbour to keep an eye on the apartment; she would be gone about three months. She'd made a few calls to a few people, letting them know she'd be gone, cancelling the odd arrangement. Then she'd taken the ride out of town in one of Rawls' cars, which he'd sent over for her. She'd left London at dusk and now found herself heading out to Foulness Island in the growing darkness. She could see the port on the distant horizon, all glimmering lights and wisps of propellant venting off into the night.

She was met at the port by a no-nonsense sergeant, briefed to see her aboard the bone-shaker taking her up to orbit. He was thorough and impersonal, which suited Askel just fine. She was in no mood for small talk and pleasantries. Her mind was occupied with the low-level fear of launch, overlaid with the million and one things she needed to do, check or delegate at the next opportunity.

She had never been to *Ephialtes* before but it was practically the same ship as *Otus*, where she had spent some months soon after its float-out. She had contributed to the design of both ships, particularly in terms of their accommodation of dropships and drones. She knew the Commander Program well and she knew the dropship carrier system probably as well as anyone on the original design teams. Her AIs had done most of the design work and she had overseen the linking together of the two systems, carrier and dropship. The two great carrier ships, known together as the *Aloadae*, were the pinnacle of the Commander Program system. They could dispatch a fearsome fighting force anywhere in the world within hours, and with minimal notice.

She had been moved to the NFJ project just before *Ephialtes* began fitting-out. It was a great opportunity to raise her stock even higher within Helios. She knew she had impressed Rawls and that he had great faith in her. She had been determined to prove him right.

As well as the technical challenges of the NFJ project (designated *Aphrodite*) there were personal ones too. The project was based in Dorset, England and took Askel away from her settled home life in Kentucky. It took her away from Bobby Karjalainen. Initially, a long distance relationship seemed doable. Bobby was often posted overseas anyway. But it had put a huge strain on the relationship from the very moment Bobby had meekly responded 'Okay' to the proposal, rather than being taken aback like Askel had expected. Suborbital flight meant that the UK and North America were less than forty-five minutes apart, but the connecting journeys either end increased the length of the trip by a factor of ten. Over time the relationship faded and crumbled. Askel missed Bobby but she had no idea if he felt the same way. She'd noted that he hadn't mentioned her in his book. Whether that was due to his respect for her privacy or whether he had airbrushed her from history she did not know. But he was gone. The last she heard he was truly gone - headed back to Mars.

She checked her baggage with the sergeant and was fitted for a flight suit. She was given a medical scan, signed some papers and was then put on a bus with some other Helios personnel. She recognised some faces - many of the *Aphrodite* team were there, but there were some from other divisions who she did not know. One way or another they were there at her behest. She had detailed all the personnel she would need by skill and ability and here, less than forty-eight hours later, some of them were. Frantic dealing was still going on in the Helios HR and purchasing departments. It was an overtime bonanza as favours were called in, deals were struck and backs were scratched. There would be more flights like this, freight flights, too, over the coming weeks but, appropriately, Askel was at the vanguard.

The bus ferried them to the launchpad where they got out and ascended the tower by elevator. Askel attempted some small talk with her team members but, with her mind racing from the fear of the launch and the enormity of the task at hand, she kept falling back to talking shop. She was constantly making lists in her mind and delegating tasks here and there. They got out of the elevator and were ushered across a gangway into the craft itself.

The Heavy Lift Vehicle was a large SLSVII class rocket, the fundamental design of which had not changed in more than two hundred years, though it had been hugely refined. The cabin of the cylindrical spacecraft on top was divided into two floors. Each had around thirty seats, set out in rows and aisles like some sort of futuristic bus tipped up on its rear. The seats were large, with harnesses and ports for various life support, monitoring and coms systems. The passengers had to climb up a retractable ladder mounted in the aisle and then work their way along a small gantry above the rows to their seats. Askel worked her way to her seat in the front row on the top deck, plugged herself in, and waited.

Coms crackled over Askel's headset informing her that conditions were good and that launch was on schedule to proceed within fifty minutes. She was informed that a countdown was available should she wish to patch it through, but she declined. As she lay back into her chair she could feel it adjusting to accommodate every curve of her body. She absentmindedly thought about getting one for home - surely she could swing it with Rawls - but then her mind was racing again with a controlled anxiety about the project and about the flight.

The last five minutes were the longest. She kept trying to distract herself but it didn't work. She told herself it would be over in ten or fifteen minutes. She would be in orbit, and it would be over. Her colleague next to her tapped her on the arm and told her when it was T-1 minutes. She nodded and smiled weakly at him, closing her eyes.

When it began the first thing she felt was the rumble, which started powerfully and grew ever stronger. It felt and sounded like she was in a collapsing building, then there was a sudden kick in her back. It felt like one of those awful falling nightmares, except instead of falling she was rising ever faster and she didn't wake suddenly, as much as she longed to. The incredible force and roar could hardly fail to impress, but Askel's mind was in a place far away from such things. She was in a zone somewhere between serenity and panic, knowing that there was nothing she could do. She was committed to this and all she could do now was just *be*, until it was over.

Very soon - Askel couldn't tell if it was minutes or seconds - the violent shaking smoothed out and the incredible pressure she had felt on her body eased off. She felt the tension in her body relax a little and she started to feel light. She turned to her colleague and nodded a smile at him. He smiled back and gave her the thumbs up signal. A voice came over the com. "All passengers, following a successful launch we are now in orbit around the Earth and are due to dock with *Ephialtes* in approximately two hours. Please remain seated for the rest of the journey, if you have any problems we are right here for you. Thanks."

Askel let herself relax. It was going to be a tough three months and she thought she'd earned it.

It was dark when Andrews reached the New Oval Office. She spoke briefly to Cortes' personal assistant and let herself in. The lighting was low and Cortes was in his chair, turned away from the great desk of office, facing the window. At first she thought he might be asleep and she approached cautiously.

"Thanks for coming, Audrey," he said without turning. "Take a seat over on one of the sofas. I'll be over in a minute."

"Yes, Mr President," Andrews said, and she walked over to one of the sofas and sat down. She felt a little awkward, like she was intruding on some intensely personal moment. She was surprised when Cortes spoke again.

"You know, it's been quite a day," he said. "I got the intelligence briefing this morning. I guess that's what you're here to talk about."

"It is, Mr President."

"I thought so. You know, this job never ends. It's just one damn thing after another."

"I guess so, Mr President. I guess that's what our jobs are; dealing with issues, one after another."

Cortes chuckled. "Well, that's true enough," he said. He turned in the chair and stood up. As he walked over to Andrews he asked the question she had been preparing for all week. "What have you got for me, Audrey?" he said.

"Well, sir," Audrey replied, "I've spoken to Helios. They can refit the *Aloadae* for interplanetary flight. They have experimental nuclear fusion engines they can use. We can have the *Aloadae* in orbit around Mars within six months if we need it."

Cortes nodded, impressed. "I guess that wouldn't be cheap," he said.

"Well," said Andrews, "not financially, of course not. But it might be cheaper than losing a planet."

Cortes thought for a moment. "They can really do that? In six months?"

"They've assured me they can," said Andrews, "and I've no reason to disbelieve them."

Cortes paced. "How would that look, politically? Is it overkill?"

"Not at all," said Andrews. "We have these ships, more-or-less redundant now over Earth. Think how powerful we look if we can send them to Mars. Not just to the Martians but to the Asian Bloc, the non-aligned countries, even to our own country. It would be a great demonstration of our power. Reassuring to those at home and impressive and intimidating to those abroad."

Cortes stopped pacing. "What do you need from me?"

"I just need the executive order authorising the expenditure. You still have the elevated powers from the war. If you want to go ahead, let me know now and I'll tell Helios to proceed immediately."

"How much will this cost again?"

"I sent you the costings. It's a lot, but we can afford it."

Cortes paused. "Okay. Go ahead. The bigger the stick the less likely you'll need to use it, right? That's the principle we're following here, isn't it?"

"Of course, Mr President. We'll stop this thing before it's started."

"I like that," said Cortes. "The last thing we need right now is another war."

CHAPTER 08

Recruitment

"Is this a secure line?" White barked at one of his security team.

"Yes, sir. For all practical purposes it's undecryptable."

"Good," said White. "What about records? I don't want this call to have existed."

"We have an AI to wipe all records as soon as the call has ended, Mr Vice President," the security woman replied.

"Okay," said White. "Can I have a few minutes privacy?" He made a gesture ushering the security woman and some other assistants out of the room. When the large oak doors clunked shut he spoke into the phone.

"Sherman, is that you?"

"It's me, Mr Vice President," came the reply.

"Good," said White, "I hate to call you but I can assure you this line is one hundred percent secure. All records of this conversation will be wiped the moment the conversation is over."

"I understand, Mr Vice President."

"Listen," said White, "they're putting together a squad of commanders to send to Mars, if you can believe that. The goddamned president has just finished one war and it looks like he's hell-bent on starting another. We can't let that happen. The two carriers, the *Aloadae*, are being fitted to go off to Mars. We need one of ours to be going with them. Is that something you can do?"

The voice on the end of the line paused. "Yes, Mr Vice President, I think that's something we can do."

White didn't quite believe him. Sherman had fingers in many pies but getting an agent aboard a military ship filled with handpicked commanders seemed way too big of an ask, even for him. He had no choice but to go along with it.

"That's great. Can you get on to that as a matter of the utmost emergency? They're putting this team together now and we need to be right on top of it."

"I'll do what I can."

"I'll meet you in a few days at the burger joint. You can fill me in."

"Can I speak frankly?"

"Go ahead."

"Are you crossing a line here?"

"Crossing a line? Hell, I'm trying to pull everything back *over* the line. This country is the finest there has ever been on the face of this planet. When was the last time we had elections? Too long ago. The war's over now, at least the last war, and the people have a right to elections. That's the least we owe them. I'm scared for this country, Sherman. I'm scared of what it's becoming. We can pull it back from the brink if we act now, but if we don't who the hell knows where we'll be in six months' time."

"I understand, Mr Vice President. I'll get it done. Maybe in the future they'll give us medals for this."

"In the future, maybe," said White. "For now they could send us to the gallows for treason. Don't forget that."

"I'll try not to, Mr Vice President."

Steiner was on his fifth beer of the evening when the call came through on his comdev. At first he was going to ignore it. The bar was rough,

EPHIALTES

just how he liked it, but it was dull and he decided a call from Captain Soward may lend the evening some much-needed excitement.

Steiner was at the bar on his own. The place was a dive, with servicemembers and hangers on lolling about the place like underwear strewn around an unkempt bedroom. There were sports showing on TV in the corner but Steiner wasn't interested. A couple of people, one of them a reasonably good-looking woman, had tried to spark up conversations with him earlier, but he wasn't in the mood for talking. His plan for the evening, so far as he had a plan, was to keep on drinking then go back to the barracks to sleep it off. Maybe he'd stop by and pick up some Chinese food. He wasn't fussed. He was slowly and quietly drinking himself into a stupor when he felt the comdev buzz in his pocket. Initially he looked at the screen and, seeing it was Soward, put the device back in his pocket. When it rang the second time he gave in and answered.

"Steiner, is that you?" said the voice at the other end of the line.

"It's me, Captain," said Steiner, laconically.

"Good to hear you Steiner," said Soward. "Everything good with you?"

"I'm good here," said Steiner.

"Good, good, that's good to know. Listen, something's come up, and we need some guys like you for a special mission. What do you say Steiner, are you in?"

The four beers had dulled Steiner's senses enough that he took a second to process the information.

"What is it?" he said.

"I can't say at the moment, but it's classified, it's big and you'll want in."

Steiner took a swig from his beer. "Sounds interesting," he said. "What is it again?"

"Well, Steiner, you understand I can't go into details here, but I've been asked to put together a team of the best guys I've worked with, and your name was at the top of the list. I'll be calling some of the other guys but I want you, Foley and Johnson. This has come down from the very top. Listen, where are you?"

Steiner looked around the bar. "I'm in a very exclusive nightclub," he said. "It's members only, and I'm in the VIP lounge."

"That's great, Steiner," said Soward, "but where is it?"

"I'm at Joe's Bar," Steiner conceded.

"You are? That's great, I'm at The Ranch, it's only five minutes away. Come over."

Steiner glanced at the empty seats either side of him. "I'm kind of in the middle of something here," he said. "It might take me a while to wrap this up."

"Get over here Steiner, you bum," said Soward. "You're drinking alone and looking for trouble. I know you. That's why I want you on my team. Get your ass in a cab and get over here."

Stepping out into the cold night air reinvigorated Steiner somewhat. The cab was already waiting for him and he stepped inside. In the short journey to The Ranch he thought about the old days with Soward. They had had many crazy adventures during the war, both on and off the battlefield. They had never quite seen eye to eye but Steiner held a grudging respect for Soward, as Soward did for him.

Steiner entered The Ranch through a side exit. He scanned the blue neon-lit interior looking for Soward, but he couldn't see him. He needed to go to the bar first anyway so he headed off in that direction. He ordered his drink and turned to look back into the room. He scanned again and this time spotted Soward. He was sat in a booth off to Steiner's right, alone. Steiner collected his drink and walked across to the booth. He sat down, nodding at Soward. "Captain," he said.

"Thanks for coming," said Soward.

"Didn't feel like I had much of a choice," replied Steiner.

"Everyone always has a choice," said Soward, grinning. Steiner grinned too, though he didn't really get the joke.

Soward had a medium build with very broad shoulders and a well-weathered face. He looked like he had been left outside for a few years. He was one of the few men Steiner had ever seen who wore a moustache. Soward was big on military history. He'd seen pictures of soldiers from the past sporting huge moustaches and decided it was a good look.

It wasn't, but who was going to tell him? He was military through and through and carried with him an implied threat wherever he went.

"So what's the job?" said Steiner.

"Well," said Soward, "like I said already, I can't really talk about it in detail. Now we're off the com I guess I can tell you a little bit more."

Steiner couldn't help but look intrigued. "Go on," he said.

Soward had a beer clasped in his hands on the table in front of him. He stared intently at the beer as he spoke. "There's some stuff going on at the moment, secret top-level stuff, and the brass are worried that something is going to go down if we are not there to provide a show of strength. You know the *Aloadae*?"

"Of course," said Steiner.

"Well, we'll be working off them."

Steiner's ears pricked up at that. The *Aloadae* were the absolute pinnacle of the military, the most fearsome, most modern military implements in existence. Soward saw the subtle change in Steiner's attitude. "I thought that might interest you," he said. "We'll be training for a special mission, very hush-hush and happening soon. I have dispensation to pull you out of your current unit. I can have you on the bus tomorrow morning if you want in. What do you say?"

Steiner affected to be thinking it over. In fact, he was sold the moment Soward said *Aloadae*. "I need some time to think about it," he said.

"Bullshit," replied Soward.

Steiner grinned. "That's why I always liked you as a captain. That intuitive bond we have, the way we both know what the other's thinking, so we don't have to waste time talking aloud. Like players on a great football team, or something."

"Screw you," said Soward. "I know what you're thinking because you're such a simple-minded, predictable son of a bitch. You only wish you knew what I was thinking."

Steiner laughed. "Okay," he said. "Sign me up."

Steiner didn't finish the rest of the evening as he had planned. He didn't go back to Joe's Bar and drink himself into a stupor. After he finished with Soward (just one more drink each, and some catching up and talking over the old days) he had gone straight back to the barracks. He found Johnson and Foley there, both excited and conspiratorial. They looked at him suspiciously. "Did you get a call from Soward?" said Johnson.

"I did not," Steiner lied. "Why, did you?"

Johnson shot a glance at Foley. He didn't quite know what to do. "Ah," he said, "no?" It was much more of a question than a statement. Foley's eyes narrowed as he scrutinised Steiner's face. He figured out what was going on, as ever one step ahead of the reliable but not so quick-witted Johnson.

"I didn't get one either," said Foley. "In the one I didn't get the captain made me a really interesting proposition. How about you, Steiner?"

"Me too. In fact, in the one I didn't get, I wasn't invited to a personal audience with the great man, and he didn't spell out that we might be taking a trip . . ." He pointed skyward, and grinned.

"Son of a bitch," said Johnson, "you did get a call. Damn, we all got one too," he said, somewhat redundantly. "He didn't say nothing about no . . ." Johnson awkwardly made the pointing upward gesture.

"Well, that's the benefit of being the captain's favourite," said Steiner, laughing. He hopped up on his bunk.

"So we're leaving tomorrow," said Johnson. "All of us?"

"Looks that way," added Foley.

"Looks that way," echoed Steiner.

"Damn," said Johnson, mostly to himself. He scratched his head and wandered off to his bunk.

Steiner, Foley, Johnson and a number of others from their company rose early next morning before reveille and walked across the hard tarmac of the drill square to the transport depot. There, as promised, were two coaches. The men boarded in silence and were whisked away from the compound before sunrise.

Four hours later they arrived at another compound. This one was smaller, but had the same no-nonsense practicality. They were herded off the coaches and led to a large red brick building. They went down a series of dimly lit corridors, finally arriving at what appeared to be a large lecture theatre. They took their seats and, presently, Captains Soward and Connor took to the stage.

"Settle down people," Connor said with a quick hand gesture. He stood to the side fiddling with his comdev while Soward took centre stage. Soward cut straight to it.

"People, you all signed up to serve your country and most of you here have already served it on the field of battle. Well, your country has more to ask of you. You've all been handpicked for this mission as you are highly trained, battle hardened combat veterans, and for this mission we need the very best. Myself or Captain Connor have spoken to all of you in the last forty-eight hours, and as part of the high level of security around this assignment we were unable to give you the full details of what the mission entails. Well, now you're all here we can be a bit more forthcoming about the task we have at hand." He fiddled with his comdev and the screen behind him lit up with the image of one of the *Aloadae*.

"First thing you'll need to know," he said, "is that we'll be operating out of one of these." A ripple of excitement ran around the room. "Now, the fighting personnel currently stationed on these two ships have been highly trained for just that duty, but they have no combat experience. For this mission they can't afford to be sending greenhorns and that's why they're sending us."

Johnson elbowed Foley in the ribs. "It's China," he whispered. "They're sending us to goddamned China!"

Soward continued. "But as experienced as we are in the art of war, even we may not be fully prepared for the theatre in which we will be expected to operate." He let that sink in. "People, there is currently a diplomatic crisis brewing with our colony on Mars." That shot around the room like electricity, a low fast mumble of conversation audible from the stage.

"Quiet, you people," barked Connor. Soward grinned. He knew now he had the undivided attention of his audience.

"It's anticipated that this crisis will develop over the coming months and that we will be needed to lend emphasis to the ongoing diplomatic efforts of the USAN. As you know, for any threat to be effective it has to be plausible, achievable and credible. For us to meet those criteria we will train for a number of scenarios on the Martian surface, and from and in orbit around Mars." The room was silent. "At this stage we don't anticipate this will come down to an actual fighting war but, by God, we will train for it as if we know it's going to happen. If we are called upon to take military action against any Martian targets we will be ready to do just that."

Connor stepped forward. "Listen up," he said. "This is a highly classified mission, at this point. We have three months until we'll be heading out and until then we'll be training every day. The boys and girls over at Helios are working away now at the modified code for the sims and the drones. Mars represents a new challenge for us and it's one that we will meet and excel at. There's some preliminary work gone on already, so you can set your IVRs to Martian gravity and get to work on some virtual training exercises right away. Myself and Captain Soward will be developing more advanced and realistic training scenarios over the next few days and we'll get you into those sims as soon as possible. Practical training for this mission will not be possible. The only way we can replicate the 0.38 relative gravity of Mars is in the sims." He paused. "We're leaving in less than three months. We do not know how long we will be gone. Get your affairs in order and get your asses in the IVRs. Dismissed."

Steiner, Foley and Johnson left the meeting and headed straight to the compound's IVRs. They were housed in a large shed-like building across the drill square from the red brick building where they had just been briefed. Military IVRs were even more immersive than the commercial home versions. The shed had twenty down either side. They took the form of large pods with ladders up to the cockpits. Once inside the user would have been hard put to tell that they were not sat inside a commander combat mech. Very high-resolution screens played representations of the outside world and any movement by the user was reflected in the apparent movement of the virtual combat mech. It was a very convincing illusion.

"Goddamned Mars, can you believe that shit?" said Johnson. "I thought we were going to China, for sure."

"Mars, China, it's all the same to me," said Steiner, mockingly. "I'm a trained warrior, hungry for war and I'll go wherever there's a war for me."

"Shit," said Johnson. "Mars is so goddamned far away. We're not gonna get no R&R on Mars."

"I don't know," said Foley. "I joined the Army because I wanted to travel, so I guess I can't argue with it."

Steiner grinned. "That's right, travel the world, meet interesting people and kill them. That's what I signed up for, too."

"You think we'll be in the same company?" said Johnson.

"Sure," said Steiner. "We've been selected for our veteran status, so they'll want people who they'll know can work together. Don't worry, we'll have your back."

"That's right," said Foley. "We'll carry you just like we did last time."

"You didn't carry nothing, fool!" Johnson shouted, but he was secretly glad he would be with his old comrades.

They entered the hall of IVRs and spoke briefly with the sergeant in charge. He pointed down the left-hand side and Steiner, Johnston and Foley walked down to their pods.

"Let's hope the diplomats don't screw this up for us," said Steiner as he climbed up the ladder. "If I'm training for three months I want to be kicking some Martian ass at the end of it."

"Prepare for peace but pray for war," said Foley, as he slid into his IVR and closed the hatch. Johnson just grunted and shook his head.

Once he was inside the IVR Steiner put his headset on then slid his arms into the full-arm joysticks in front of him. He issued the command 'compress suit' and felt his body become engulfed by the IVR.

He spoke into the com, "Commander Foley, Commander Johnson, do you read?"

Foley came back, "I read you, Commander Steiner."

There was a delay and some quiet cursing before Johnson came over the com. "Reading you here, Commander Steiner."

Steiner spoke to his sim. "Give me a Martian scenario," he said.

The sim replied, "I'm sorry, we currently have no Martian scenarios."

Steiner frowned. "Okay, give me a scenario in Devon Island, Canada, do you have maps for that?"

"I do," the com replied.

"I want a medium-sized town, well defended with AA guns and guided missile towers. Patch Commanders Johnson and Foley into the sim. Set the temperature to -80°C."

"Setting temperature," said the sim.

"Are you ready, boys?" said Steiner.

"Ready, Commander."

"Ready, Commander."

"Set us down eight klicks southwest of the ville."

"Eight kilometres southwest of the ville," the sim echoed.

"Prepare to begin simulation," Steiner said, and then he remembered. "One more thing, simulation, please?"

"Yes, Commander?"

"Set the gravity to 0.38."

"Yes, Commander. Please be aware that a gravity setting of 0.38 is outside the bounds of a realistic simulation."

"I know that," said Steiner. "Can you please save these mission parameters to a new template?"

"Certainly, Commander. What would you like to call the template?"

Steiner did not give it a moment's thought. "Martian," he said.

Foley was lying on his bunk in the early evening when a call came through on his comdev. Steiner and Johnson, and most of the others, were off somewhere catching up and putting the world to rights but Foley was just lying there, awake and enjoying his own company. He reached into his pocket, grabbed the comdev and held it up to his ear. "Hello," he said.

"Commander Foley?" said the voice on the other end.

"Who is this?"

"I'm calling on behalf of a very powerful client. We have a job we'd like to offer you."

"I have a job," said Foley. "I'm a Marine Commander."

"We're aware of your résumé, Mr Foley, which is why we're interested in you for the job."

"Who did you say you were again?"

"We're a private military contractor, a PMC. We work for the most exclusive clients, and we have a job for which you have been highly recommended."

"Recommended by who?"

"It's a very sensitive job. If you choose to accept my client will be extremely grateful."

Foley thought it might be a test. He wasn't going to play ball.

"Listen pal, I ain't interested, okay?" he said.

"The pay is *very* good," the voice said, putting a huge stress on 'very.' "If you decide you want in just send an email in the next two days."

"Send an email? Who to?"

"Anyone. We'll pick it up." The voice was gone.

Foley looked at his comdev. He had an application on it called *OutHide*. It traced all coms, video, audio or data to their sources. Flicking through some screens he found it and pressed on a big red button marked 'Trace'. Some text and numbers shot up the screen, too fast to read, with larger text laid over the top that read 'Analysing . . .' The results screen appeared: Last Incoming Call 16:18, Steiner, Hayden. That had been a call from Steiner in the afternoon. The time now was 19:09. The caller had left no trace.

Foley rolled over on the bunk and pushed the comdev back into his pocket. He was intrigued by the call, but it seemed way too suspect to take at face value. He wondered if anyone had called Johnson or Steiner. Maybe he would ask them.

Rodney Sherman's eyes were small and close together. He didn't speak much and he moved in such a way as he never drew attention to himself. He lived in the background. He could circulate as easily amongst cons and gangsters as he could amongst senators and captains of industry. He could talk a lot without saying much when he needed to, or he could speak volumes with a single word. He possessed a quiet control which often seemed like contempt. But he got things done, and that was what Gerard White liked about him. He could fix things when they needed fixing and he didn't mind - in fact he seemed to positively enjoy - getting his hands dirty.

Sherman was sat in a booth at the back of an upmarket burger joint. It was midafternoon and relatively quiet. He had ordered a burger and a cola but had only taken a couple of bites from the burger, and had not touched the cola at all. He looked at his watch. It was 15:15. He disliked it intensely when people were late for meetings. He was considering leaving when White entered via the kitchen and strode quickly over to the booth. He'd managed to ditch his security detail and had an understanding with the burger joint's owner.

"I'm sorry I'm late," he said. "Had trouble getting out of a budget meeting. Have you eaten?"

"I'm not really hungry," said Sherman.

"I'm starving," said White, "but I don't really have time to eat."

Sherman pushed the burger across the table. "I've had a bite, that's all," he said. "Go ahead."

"Really?" said White. "Thank you, I haven't had chance to get a bite all day." He picked up the burger and bit into it. "Oh boy," he said, "this tastes so good."

EPHIALTES

As he bit and chewed Sherman studied him. Through a mouthful White said, "Is it done? Did you manage to get someone?"

Sherman waited a little. He felt powerful in that moment. "We have someone inside," he said.

"That's great," said White. "And he's contactable at all times?"

Sherman nodded. "He or she is contactable, yes."

"Good."

"How do you want to proceed?"

White chewed and swallowed another bite of burger. "For now, we don't need to do anything. This is a precaution against what might go down in future. If things start to get out of hand we need a way to stop it from the inside." He chewed more burger. "But I doubt it will ever get to that. Always good to have a fallback position, though, so I thank you for that. We get reports back if we need them, right?"

"If we need them. Every communication is a risk, though. I thought you wanted a sleeper, just in case, not a spy."

"Of course, of course. Let's leave it at that for now. As long as we have someone in place, in case we need them, I'd consider this a job well done. Thank you, Rodney." He held out a hand across the table.

Sherman couldn't help noticing the mustard and ketchup on one of the fingers but, despite himself, he took the hand and shook it. "Is there anything else?" he said.

"If anything comes up I'll let you know immediately," said White. "There's a lot of stuff going on at the moment. I think that mad bastard is getting crazier by the day. If there aren't elections by the end of the year I'm going to start getting seriously worried. But what can I do? I'm only the VP."

"If you need my help with anything, Mr Vice President, just ask."

"Of course," replied White. He felt uncomfortable as he often did in Sherman's presence. Sherman always liked to give the impression he was connected to everyone and everything, but the idea that he could help the vice president rein in the president seemed to go too far. Disturbingly, it carried a sliver of plausibility.

White dabbed his mouth with a napkin and stood up. "Thanks again, Rodney," he said. "I'll be in touch soon. This thing is moving way too fast and I appreciate all the help I get."

"No problem," said Sherman. He lifted a hand in gesture of salute at White, who was already heading for the exit.

CHAPTER 09
Moving Target

Twenty-third century media communications were chaotic. Every business, organisation, group and individual had their own media stream. They streamed video, audio and text, as much and as often as they wanted. Almost any information required was freely available. The issue for media consumers was finding a way to wade through the deluge of information to find that which was pertinent to them. Most people had an aggregator on their comdev or terminal. Via deliberately programmed preferences and highly tuned heuristic algorithms the aggregators would sift through vast oceans of information to provide individuals with news and information tailored to their interests. The newsgathering behemoths of old had become redundant two centuries earlier. Newsgathering now was scattered amongst the entire population. Every person was a potential journalist. Every person had a camera, a connection and a point of view. Whenever anything happened, from a war to a minor celebrity inadvertently exposing some underwear, there were plenty of 'journalists' there to record the event, comment on it, and send it around the world before it had even finished happening.

In a world where everyone was a journalist it didn't follow that everyone was a *good* journalist. A certain type of person loved the celebrity and attention they got from reporting and posting on events happening in the digital sphere around them. They would learn to develop sharp digital elbows to try to force their way to the top of the pack. They didn't even necessarily need to be where the action was. It was possible to follow the right feeds, have aggregators looking in the right places and have databases on hand to look up everything and anything necessary to embellish a story. When an event happened it could be quickly republished with additional comments and a sheen of the journalist's signature brand of zaniness, or seriousness, or sarcasm, or cynicism, in the hope that people would view the event through their feed rather than anyone else's. In this way it was possible become a minor celebrity in one's own right. Followers would bring in advertising revenue, so with a big enough audience it was possible to make a living from it. It wasn't journalism in the traditional sense. It was more like being the town gossip, but it was called journalism and it appealed to a certain type of person.

Elspeth J Ross was not that type of person. She was eighteen years old and had, she was often told, a very sensible head on her shoulders. Unlike the majority of her peers she wasn't particularly interested in the video, music and sports celebrities that were the bread-and-butter of most budding journalists. She was more interested in actual things. The way the world worked fascinated her. She could see the video, music and sports stars gliding across the surface of the world, having no actual impact on it. It seemed to Elspeth that the world was shaped by occult forces working far beneath the visible surface. That fascinated her and intrigued her. She wanted everyone else to find it as interesting as she did, and it was that that attracted her to the world of journalism.

She had studied economics, politics and the sciences at school. She had been one of the outsider kids. It made her slightly sad that the packs of kids at her school had rejected her simply because she had not been as shallow and foolish as they were. On one hand she wouldn't have wanted to hang out with such vacuous people. On the other, the rejection stung.

Happily, that period of her life was over now. She had finished school six months earlier and her plan, as far as she had one, was to become a successful journalist. Her streams had a few hundred followers, next to nothing she knew, but she was determined to battle on and build on that number.

Elspeth had been brought up by her mother. She was an only child. Her father had died before she ever knew him. Her mother worked for Hjälp Teknik in one of their production plants. They had lived in one of Venkdt's housing projects in Eastside. It had been a happy childhood, apart from the difficulties at school, and her mother had always been supportive. Elspeth was a shy child, but always inquisitive. She found it difficult to talk to people and she felt uncomfortable in unfamiliar situations. But she had a gritty determination that, tied to her inquisitiveness, drove her to overcome her inhibitions. She didn't like speaking to strangers but she knew that if she wanted to find out that little titbit of information she wanted to know she would have to ask.

Her proudest moment at school had been a journalistic presentation about Hjälp Teknik. She had interviewed her mother, some of her mother's co-workers and a media relations person at Hjälp Teknik and had made a potted history of the company. The presentation was fluid and polished. It held the attention of the viewer and also imparted some useful and interesting information. Her classmates had laughed at it but the teacher was full of effusive praise, and Elspeth knew it was good. That feeling touched something in her and she knew then that that was what she wanted to do.

In a game where your competition is more or less the entire world (strictly speaking, the entire *worlds*) it makes sense to have an angle, something unique to make you stand out from the pack. Elspeth thought she had it. She would *make* news. She wasn't going to throw old ladies under the bus and post videos of it - nothing as crude as that, though there was probably someone somewhere who was mulling over such a scheme. Elspeth's idea was far more subtle and sophisticated. She'd noticed it in the Hjälp Teknik presentation she did at school. The Hjälp Teknik PR person presented the company in a different light to the workers who worked there. By juxtaposing these two points of view Elspeth had created something new, interesting and worth hearing. She had created news by combining two separate elements. It was almost like chemistry. That, she thought, would be her angle. She would study the streams and make the connections that other people missed. She could dig out information, combine two apparently disparate elements and create a third thing, unique to her and worthwhile.

She had tried this a number of times so far, but with little success. She followed the streams diligently and had made some interesting connections, spinning new stories from them, but these had failed to set the world alight. The trouble was, so it seemed to Elspeth, that though the stories were interesting and of some minor import, they would never reach a large audience because what the large audience wanted to see was a cat falling off a hammock or a minor celebrity leaving another minor celebrity's apartment in the middle of the night. Elspeth wanted to do serious news. She also wanted a serious sized audience. The two things seemed exclusive until one day she hit on a big idea.

Bobby Karjalainen.

It was a perfect plan. If she could interview Bobby Karjalainen she would have a major news story. Not only that but she could use her alchemy to spin it even bigger. Bobby Karjalainen would be the perfect interview subject. He was a very minor celebrity in his own right, what with his book and war hero status. He looked good, so just a picture of him would attract interest. And unlike most minor celebrities he had actually done something interesting and significant. Elspeth thought she could sell the interview like this: come for the beefcake, stay for the harrowing war stories. There was another bit of magic she could add to the mix; Elspeth knew that Jack Karjalainen was dying. None of the celeb journalists would have given this a moment's thought. As an old man, a captain of industry and not in the least bit photogenic, who cared about Jack Karjalainen? Elspeth did. She followed the business streams. She had read Bobby's book and she knew that Bobby had a very strained relationship with his father. His father was now dying and Bobby had returned to Mars.

Why?

EPHIALTES

It seemed very likely to her that Bobby was seeking reconciliation with his father and that could be human interest dynamite. The celeb-junkie audience might not give a stuff who Jack Karjalainen was, but a story about a good-looking, semi-famous war hero tearfully reuniting with his dying father could be a blockbuster. It even had that sheen of seriousness that appealed so much to the shallow-minded. All she needed to do now was track Bobby down and arrange an interview.

There were two possible stumbling blocks. She might not be able to get hold of him, and if she did he might decline the offer of an interview with an eighteen-year-old girl who had no track record whatsoever. Elspeth figured if she was going to let things like that put her off she was in the wrong game. And she *knew* she wasn't in the wrong game.

Elspeth J Ross, journalist, was going to interview Bobby Karjalainen.

Elspeth thought that Bobby Karjalainen, the semi-famous war hero and one-time author, would be an easy person to track down, but it was not so. In the twenty-third century even minor celebrity was big enough that those afflicted with it took measures to avoid contact with the people who took such a prurient interest in their lives.

Elspeth thought she could reach Bobby directly through his mini-feed. It turned out his mini-feed was run by a pool of PR managers at his publishers on Earth. Even when she managed to contact an actual person they refused to divulge any of Bobby's personal details. They wouldn't even pass on a message.

Next Elspeth tried Hjälp Teknik. Hjälp Teknik told her that they couldn't discuss any details of their personnel without the express consent of the person involved. Elspeth suspected that Bobby had no official link to Hjälp Teknik anyway. They wouldn't even confirm that.

Elspeth didn't even try the military. She knew that would be a non-starter. All she knew for sure was that Bobby Karjalainen had recently returned to Mars and that his father was gravely ill in St Joseph's Hospital.

She trawled the streams for everything she could find about Hjälp Teknik and the Karjalainens. She found out where the Karjalainens' house was. That was useful. She guessed Bobby might be staying there, but she couldn't know for sure. In his book he'd spoken about his relationship with his family, which had broken down almost completely before he went off to war. If Bobby had come back to make peace, as she suspected, he may or may not be at the house. Maybe relations remained cold and Bobby was somewhere in the city. The only thing Elspeth had to go on was her hunch that Bobby had come back to see Jack Karjalainen. She knew where Jack was, so maybe she could find Bobby there. Reluctantly, she realised that she might have to do some old-fashioned journalistic legwork. She might have to physically leave the house, pound the streets and tell half-truths to strangers in order to elicit the information she needed. Half of her felt like this was going to be a huge pain. The other half was vaguely excited.

Elspeth got up early and took a cab to St Joseph's. She went to the refectory and had breakfast there while she thought about what her plan might be. It might be useful to know exactly where Jack Karjalainen's room was. It would be very useful to know who had visited him. She didn't know if the hospital kept such records. It probably did. Most large public buildings automatically scanned comdevs on the way in and out. If Bobby had been here recently it was almost certainly in a database somewhere. Accessing the database would be nearly impossible.

Elspeth thought.

She didn't have the first clue about electronic espionage but maybe she could have a crack at social engineering. One of the many obscure facts she knew from hour upon hour of voracious reading was that the weakest point in any security system was the human beings who operated it. Maybe there was a way she could fool a nurse or an administrator into divulging information from the hospital's database. It sounded like an exciting prospect. Elspeth smiled. It sounded, too, like it might be illegal. Elspeth frowned. As an eighteen-year-old girl who looked, if anything, younger than her age, Elspeth was often frustrated when people didn't take her seriously. But she was smart enough to play the hand she had been dealt. If she got caught she would play the ingénue. She would act gauche, young, dumb and innocent. "Oh my gosh," she would say, "I didn't accidentally crack your database and steal privileged information, did I? I'm *such* a ditz! I'm *so* sorry!"

Elspeth thought it over as she was finishing her croissant. It wasn't much of a plan, but she thought she'd give it a go. Steeling herself, she stood up and made her way to the reception desk.

Her heart was thudding in her chest when she said, as brightly as she could, "Hello! I'm here to see Jack Karjalainen."

The receptionist's response was automatic. "All of Mr Karjalainen's visits are by appointment only. Do you have an appointment?" The receptionist scanned his terminal.

"I don't have an appointment," said Elspeth, "but I'm family, though, sort of."

"Sort of family?" the receptionist said, with a hint of disdain in his voice.

"Well, *I'm* not," Elspeth said in her ditziest voice, "but my boyfriend Bobby is."

"Hold your comdev over there," the receptionist said, nodding to a pad on the desk. He continued looking at his terminal. Elspeth held her comdev out. With her arm outstretched it was all she could do to stop her hand shaking. She looked nervously at the receptionist and hoped he hadn't noticed. His concentration was focused on the terminal and as soon as the pad beeped Elspeth quickly withdrew the comdev.

"Elspeth J Ross," the receptionist said. "You're not on the list."

Elspeth frowned. "But I came the other day," she said, "with Bobby."

The receptionist was staring at the screen still. "We don't have any record of that," he said.

"It must be there," said Elspeth, leaning over the desk and trying to get a look at the terminal screen. The receptionist shot her the darkest of looks and tilted the screen away.

"Could you please remain behind the desk, Ms?" he said.

"I'm sorry," said Elspeth, "I thought I might be able to help if I could just see."

The receptionist stared at her with a concrete-hard look of officialdom. "I don't need your help, Ms," he said, "and this is confidential information. Please remain behind the desk."

"Of course," said Elspeth. "I'm so sorry." She tried to look as sweet as she possibly could. "I'm really, really sorry," she said again.

Elspeth thought as hard and as fast as she could. "It was just the other day," she said, "I think it was that day when my comdev was playing up. I'm almost certain of it. My comdev was playing up, and Bobby got us both in on his comdev."

The receptionist shook his head. Elspeth thought he might be becoming suspicious. She was feeling like everything she did or said was suspicious, but she knew that was just the pressure getting to her. She tried desperately to believe her own story.

"We wouldn't let two people in on one comdev. Just wouldn't happen," said the receptionist.

Elspeth shrugged. "It happened the other day," she said. "You know Bobby and his family practically own this place. I think it was that day when my comdev was playing up, and Bobby got us in. Which day was it?" She tried to say the last as casually and as off-hand as she could. She knew that was the steel-capped bullet she was here to deliver. She wanted it to come from nowhere while the receptionist was focused on the immediate issue of whether to let her in here and now. In her mind it sounded obvious and desperate. She hoped that to the receptionist it was an innocent enquiry from a dizzy young girl who didn't even have the sense to maintain her comdev properly.

The receptionist remained silent, his eyes flicking across the screen. Elspeth's heart was racing now.

"That was Tuesday," he said. "And I don't know who would have let you in without the proper clearance, Bobby Karjalainen or no Bobby Karjalainen, but I can't do that today."

Elspeth wanted to punch the air but she also wanted to keep selling the illusion, so she frowned and looked disappointed. "Really?" she said. "Not just for five minutes?"

"Not for five minutes, Ms. I have your details here on file now. I'll ask Mr Karjalainen if he's happy for you to go on the list, if you like, but I can't let you in now."

Elspeth slumped in theatrical disappointment, though inside she was doing a little dance. "Okay," she said, "how long will that take?"

"I'm putting the request through at this very moment," said the receptionist. "You could always just contact Bobby yourself and get him to give the okay? How about that?"

Elspeth felt cold ice run down her spine. She looked at her comdev, then back up at the receptionist.

"He's busy at the moment," she said, pleased with her quick thinking.

"Well," said the receptionist, "I've put the request in but until I get the okay I can't let you through. You could go and get a cup of coffee maybe and try back in half an hour?"

"Yes," said Elspeth, "I'll do that. Thank you." She turned from the desk and headed back towards the refectory.

"Have a good day," the receptionist called after her.

From the refectory she headed straight for the exit. This was the first time she had done any real on-the-ground, semi-illicit investigative journalism and it felt amazing. She felt like a rock star as she entered the cab and left the hospital. All she'd really found out was that Bobby had visited his father, which was not much really, but she'd found that information out herself, using her wit and ingenuity, and now she had a lead for tracking down the subject of the interview that was going to break her into the mainstream.

The minute Elspeth got home she fired up her terminal and looked for some retailers. She'd figured out the plan in the cab on the way home and had had a cursory look on her comdev. What she had so far was this: Bobby had returned to Mars and was reconciled or reconciling with his father. This meant that he spent some time, at least, at St Joseph's Hospital and that's where Elspeth was going to find him. She thought about setting up semi-permanent camp in the refectory, but that was just impractical as well as suspicious. How could she scope out the hospital without actually being there? She thought about hacking into the hospital's security systems but realised that having been successful dipping her toe into the world of digital espionage she had let it get to her head. She wouldn't have the first clue about hacking a security system and she didn't have any exciting, mysterious, tattooed hacker friends who would be able to do it for her, either. What she might be able to do, though, would be to set up a camera of her own and monitor that.

It was a risky plan. If the hospital's security did a sweep a commercially available wireless camera would easily get picked up. Elspeth thought she'd gamble on the hospital not sweeping the exterior regularly for covert surveillance devices. 'Why would they do that?' she reasoned to herself.

She had settled on a device that was reasonably good resolution and not too expensive. The camera was very small and could run for up to a week without needing to be recharged. It wirelessly connected to the nearest access point and fed its video back to anyone who knew how to connect securely to it. Elspeth's plan was to connect the feed to a facial recognition AI that in turn was set to contact her should the face of Bobby Karjalainen appear on-screen. She was pleased with the plan.

Later that day the camera arrived by shuttle post. After an hour or two fiddling with it in her apartment Elspeth was satisfied that she knew exactly how it worked, and she thought she knew of a good place to put it. She stuffed it in her pocket and for a second time that day called a cab for the hospital. Just as she left her apartment she grabbed a pair of dark glasses. She felt ridiculous and excited at the same time.

She got the cab to stop a short distance from the hospital, walking the last few hundred metres along the walkway. She put the glasses on, but wasn't sure if they made her more or less conspicuous. Arriving at the hospital she stopped and pretended to be absorbed in her comdev. Furtively, she looked over the top of her glasses and scanned the front of the hospital, looking for a place to mount the camera. She decided on a spot to the left of the main door. As a decorative feature on the wall there was a mosaic stripe. She thought the broken lines would help disguise the camera. It was less than two centimetres across and only a few millimetres deep. It would be very hard to see in the mosaic for anyone who was not actively looking for it. She put the comdev in her pocket and casually pulled out the camera. She peeled the paper from the self-adhesive backing and pushed the front of the camera into the palm of her right hand. She wanted to look about to see if anyone was watching her because she felt that everything she was doing was crashingly obvious. Anyone looking at her right now would know instantly she was about to covertly mount a surveillance camera on the hospital, she thought. She reminded herself of her brilliant performance earlier in the day, when she had assumed the role of a superspy with consummate ease. That's the person she was, she told herself, a brilliant undercover operator, below the radar and above suspicion. She was an unassuming teenage girl who could move through the world like a ghost. She was Elspeth J Ross, undercover journalist, and she was on a mission.

With that thought she strode purposefully toward the hospital. To the left of the main entrance there were two people, a man in a short sleeved shirt and tie and an older woman in a floral patterned dress. They were talking casually and the man was smoking. They seemed absorbed in their conversation and, so as far as Elspeth the superspy was concerned, they were no threat. As she neared the entrance she could see two men in green hospital uniforms who were walking toward the door. As she arrived they would be coming out. An insistent paranoia told her that they would grab her and wrestle her to the ground, but the more rational side of her mind reassured her that it was okay. They probably wouldn't even notice her.

She arrived at the door and the green-uniformed people came out and walked right by her. She stopped and decided to play the role of a person waiting to meet someone. She felt pretty sure that no one was watching her, but acting the part would make her feel better. Also, if anyone should review footage from the hospital's security cameras she would look less suspicious. She stood with her back to the hospital and pulled out her comdev. She acted like she was contacting someone, theatrically (but not, she thought, too theatrically) looking about to see if the person she was about to meet was on their way. She stood for a minute, then it was time for her big moment. She stretched her arm out and lent on the mosaic, like it was the most comfortable, natural thing in the world to do. She stayed like that for about thirty seconds, partly to make sure the camera had good contact with the wall and partly so it looked like she was just a normal girl leaning against the wall of a hospital. Presently, she pulled her comdev out of her pocket again and looked at it as if she was receiving a message. She put it back in her pocket and shook her head, instantly realising that was way over the top. 'What the hell,' she thought, 'I doubt anyone is looking anyway.' She wandered casually back to the walkway and called another cab. She was back home within twenty minutes.

Once inside she raced to her terminal and brought up the image from the camera. It looked great. It covered the whole entrance, enabling her to see everyone coming in through the main door to the hospital. She had already connected the feed to the facial recognition AI. All she had to do now was wait.

She pushed her chair back from her desk and thought about what a resourceful and clever journalist she was. Her comdev buzzed in her pocket. She grabbed it out.

"Hello?" she said.

"Hello, is that my girlfriend?" said the voice on the other end of the line.

"I don't think so," said Elspeth. "I think you must have a wrong number."

"No, this is the number," said the voice, "and I'm told it belongs to my girlfriend, so that must be you, Elspeth J Ross."

Elspeth felt her face reddening. "Mr Karjalainen?" she said.

"Hi, girlfriend," Bobby replied.

"Mr Karjalainen . . ."

"Please, just call me Bobby."

"Mr Karjalainen, Bobby, I'm so sorry, this must look *so* bad."

"Pretty bad," said Bobby, "but do go on."

"Mr Karjalainen, I'm a journalist and I really want to speak to you. I couldn't get hold of you but I thought I might find you at the hospital. I'm so sorry if you think I've invaded your privacy."

"Well you have, a little, I guess," said Bobby, "but I don't mind. What do you need to speak to me about?"

Elspeth had gathered her thoughts by now and sensed that Bobby was not angry with her. She sensed he was a nice guy and if she played this right she might be able to get the interview. "I'm just starting out in journalism," she said, "and I thought an interview with you could really help me establish myself. I'd really appreciate just a few minutes, if you can spare them."

"I see," said Bobby. "Anything in it for me?" Elspeth racked her brains quickly and, not finding an answer, thought she would have to go with disarming honesty.

"Not really," she said.

Bobby laughed. "Well in that case, how can I refuse?"

"Really?" said Elspeth. "You'll do it?"

"Sure, why not?" said Bobby.

Elspeth didn't quite know what to say. "Thank you so much. Can we arrange a time, place?"

"I'll let you know," said Bobby. "I have your details, I'll get back to you in a day or two."

"Thank you so much, Mr Karjalainen."

"It's Bobby, please just call me Bobby."

"Thanks, Bobby."

"No problem, Elspeth. Talk later, bye."

The comdev went silent.

Elspeth looked at the terminal screen in front of her. She saw a tubby little boy holding his mother's hand walk toward the camera then disappear right of screen as they entered the hospital. She wondered if she'd be able to get a refund on the camera.

Probably not.

CHAPTER 10

Countermove

Daniel Kostovich habitually monitored almost everything. He scanned all horizons - literal, digital and social. He liked to know what was going on lest he should need to counter it. There was a streak of paranoia in his personality that chimed well with his role at Vendkt. It was necessary that he knew what was going on in the world about him. The endless craving for information could be wearing at times, but at least he was good at his job.

The encryption used by the USAN was considered to be as good as undecipherable. That all information was held on secure networks which were constantly roamed by probing white-hat AIs was a second level of security. The third was that USAN Cyber Counterintelligence was continuously monitoring what was happening on networks outside of its own. The network was constantly trying to crack itself while monitoring what the outside world was up to. It wasn't a perfect system but it was active, constantly evolving and adapting. One of the biggest threats to security was complacency so the system had been designed to be internally non-complacent.

Kostovich was pleased when he found an in. It had taken many months to develop and was so complex that it was beyond even him to fully understand it. He had had the basic idea, but rather than develop it himself he set about creating very advanced AIs that could do the development for him.

The scheme needed to be robust. It had to have full access to all of the USAN network, and it had to be undetectable. It had to adapt with the ever-changing security protocols of the network and be able to negotiate its shortcomings. It had to be alive to the fact that not all of the network would be up to date at any one time. There would be parts of it that due to money, incompetence or necessary legacy compatibility would be using older protocols. The parasitical AI had to be aware of all of this and act accordingly.

Kostovich had injected his AI into the USAN system six months earlier. The system was so complex and vast that for the first few months all the AI could do was sit, watch and learn. Above all it had to remain undetected. For those months Kostovich left it to it. It was incommunicado.

It was a tense time. If anything had gone wrong he would have had no way of knowing. It was almost like old-school spying from the Middle Ages or the twentieth century. The agent would go off and ingratiate itself with the enemy, building false alliances and gaining favour until the moment it had achieved enough trust that it was in a position to betray it.

Just over four months in the AI had called home. It was in and undetected and it was hammering through the USAN security networks, starting from the edges but working its way inexorably toward the centre.

The first thing to go was low-level coms. Administrators, service personnel and some low-ranking military coms were opened up to Kostovich's scrutiny. There was nothing much of interest, but it showed the AI was working. Even the so-called 'low-level' security protocols applied to those on the bottom rung of the administration were extremely sophisticated. Kostovich's AI, once in a position to act, had eaten through them in days.

As the weeks went on the AI drilled further and further toward the centre of government and military communications. The secret world of the USAN's inner-core was opening up to Kostovich like a flower in the light of dawn.

EPHIALTES

The vast amount of information being pulled back to Mars could be seen, in some ways, as one more layer of security in and of itself; there was just so much of it. Here Kostovich employed several other AIs to plough through the mountain of information and zero in on that which was pertinent. That included such things as military R&D, procurement, finances, intelligence and such. The AIs would sort the information into clear and readable reports. Each concise report was sat atop of a pyramid of more and more detailed reports, going down as far as the reader wanted to go. And the reports could be dynamically reconfigured. The AI could be told, 'Give me the same report but with more detail about the dates and less about the finance,' or 'Merge this report with the other two and make the final one sixty percent shorter.'

There had been one final level to breach. The holy of holies; the top 'beyond top secret' level of the cabinet office and the Joint Chiefs of Staff. That had really been a tough one to crack, sitting as it did on its own network-within-a network with its own ever-changing, ever self-probing security mechanisms. Kostovich's AI had finally managed to break through two months after the original foothills of the basic administration levels had succumbed. Finally, he stood at the peak.

Kostovich thought he could reasonably be considered as the greatest spy in history. Not only had he availed himself of all the operating information of a state's political and military machinery, he had done it at up to a hundred and forty million miles distance.

There had been plenty of interest to read amongst all of the data collated, but what had really caught Kostovich's eye was the fact that Mars was being talked about in the uppermost circles of the USAN government. Defence and the foreign office were falling over themselves to file reports on 'The Martian Situation' and to suggest possible remedies for it. It had even made its way to the very top. Cortes himself was giving time to the issue.

Kostovich would have found this laughable - a classic case of an organisation misprioritising or chasing at phantoms - but for one thing. As recently as that very morning President Cortes had signed an executive order allowing funds be released to pay Helios Matériel Corporation an eye-watering amount of money to refit the *Aloadae*, the two massive dropship-carrying spacecraft currently orbiting the Earth with not much to do.

Cortes had acted in response to intelligence gathered by his foreign and defence ministries. They had the inside track that Charles Venkdt was going to announce some type of election, polling the people of Mars on Martian independence. Kostovich had known they were in the Martian systems, but he had trapped and isolated their AI and was letting it gather enough information that it seemed to be working, while holding back what he considered to be top-level strategic information. All of his own work was locked up watertight. Anything they could get to of his was fake, or rather an amalgam of real stuff that was unimportant, about ninety percent, and ten percent of what seemed like interesting and important work but which was bogus and heavily encrypted. He'd let them get to most of Venkdt's other information, which he'd considered of relatively low import. He'd noticed himself that Venkdt had been talking about a plebiscite, but he'd considered it inconsequential. The old man was getting a little crazy in his old age and Martian independence would surely mean little in practice. Nothing would change apart from notions of what was owned by whom. That was nothing to get excited about, was it? Cortes and the USAN certainly seemed to differ. To them it seemed to matter enough that they would send two huge men-of-war hundreds of millions of miles across the solar system to make a point.

Kostovich, who, until that point, thought that who owned what territory on which map was a matter for imbeciles and the feeble minded, suddenly felt affronted that a person or persons, many, many miles away, was sending warships toward him. For the first time in his life he felt the faintest stirring of patriotism.

"Prepare a report on the latest anti-aircraft, anti-spacecraft and anti-missile missile technologies for me, please," he said to his terminal. "The data set is the USAN military development dump. Keep the report fairly technical and I want to know how easily and quickly we could fabricate any of the systems in question here on Mars."

"Preparing report," the terminal replied.

Kostovich wasn't sure whether to go to Venkdt now with the information about the *Aloadae* or to wait for the report about missile technology. In his mind there was already an arms race developing. If the Earth was going to place a tank on his front lawn, as it were, he felt justified in stealing the Earth's plans for anti-tank missiles and building some in time for the tank's arrival.

Maybe he'd hold back on that plan, for now. The priority, it appeared, was to get this information to Venkdt. It seemed Earth was in a major strop with Venkdt before he had even announced that he was going to do anything. And what was he going to do, anyway? Hold an election? They were going to be held under the gun for holding an election? What kind of topsy-turvy world was this becoming? That was the sort of thing you read about in the Asian Bloc. He'd seen pictures on the bulletins; protesters with daisy chains and friendship bands, crushed under the wheels of tanks, pushed back with water cannon. Kostovich had never felt like a radical or an activist before but right now he felt annoyed. He felt like he was being pushed around, and he didn't want to be pushed around.

"Get me an appointment with Venkdt," said Kostovich.

"Christina Venkdt?" the AI replied.

"Can you stop with that? Whenever I say 'Venkdt' I mean Charles Venkdt, okay?" said Kostovich, struggling to keep the exasperation out of his tone. He knew the AI was a machine - he had programmed it, after all - but it was hard not to feel like it was mocking him.

"Mr Venkdt doesn't have any openings until next week. Would you like to proceed with booking the appointment?"

"No, don't bother. I'll sort it out myself."

For the most part Kostovich kept a low profile at Venkdt. Much of the time he'd stay in his office at the R&D Department, occasionally venturing out to the labs. That was on the days he came in. He often just worked from home. When he did come in he didn't keep to regular hours, oftentimes turning up late in the evening and disappearing again before the morning shift came in. As head of R&D he knew the security systems intimately and, of course, had a backdoor into everything. On the rare occasions when he was out and about he quite enjoyed being mistaken for a suspicious character. He'd show his security credentials on his comdev to whoever had stopped or challenged him and enjoy their confusion that such a young, dishevelled character was the head of a major department. Sometimes they would apologise profusely, other times grudgingly or suspiciously, like he couldn't possibly be who his ID said he was. He'd often check what the security guards or receptionists looked up immediately after they had left him, and frequently they would be interrogating personnel records, looking for a photo ID of Dr Daniel Kostovich, Head of R&D, Venkdt Mars Corp. It made Kostovich chuckle. As smart as he was, he still took enjoyment from being smarter than dumb people.

That particular morning Kostovich had only been stopped twice on his way to Charles Venkdt's office. It hadn't been so much fun as usual because he'd been in a rush. Arriving at the office he approached the desk of Venkdt's PA. "Hey, sweetness," he said, "is the big guy in?"

The PA didn't glance up from her terminal. "He is in, he's busy right now, and don't call me sweetness," she said.

"I have something really important I need to discuss with him," said Kostovich. "If I don't get in there right away I'll have to stay out here and chat with you."

The PA gave him a look of mock disapproval. "Threatening me won't help," she said, "he's busy."

Kostovich slumped into a leather sofa set across the way from the assistant's desk. "Just have to wait him out then, I guess," he said.

"Looks that way," said the PA. "How come you didn't make an appointment?"

Kostovich shrugged. "This only came up this morning and it's fairly important. I thought he'd want to know right away."

The PA thawed a little. "It might be quite a while. He asked not to be disturbed. Can I get you anything?"

"I'm fine," said Kostovich. "I might catch a few zees if that's okay with you?"

EPHIALTES

"Go right ahead," said the PA, "just don't make the place look untidy."

Kostovich had quickly fallen asleep on the luxurious sofa. He was woken by a scrunched up ball of paper hitting his forehead. He was just about awake in time to bat away a second paper ball before it landed. "He's free now," the PA said, grinning. "Do you need a little time to come round?"

Kostovich dragged himself to his feet. "I'm fine," he said, lumbering towards the office.

Venkdt was seated at his desk. He was in his early seventies, a little overweight and balding. He wore small round spectacles and had an air of jollity about him, like he was about to spring a surprise or was trying to keep an exciting secret. "Dr Kostovich!" he said, glancing up from his terminal. "What have you got for me today!" Perennially positive, Venkdt was probably hoping that Kostovich had made some exciting new breakthrough in product development, or had found a way to slash production costs. He'd come up good for the company so many times in the past, and he rarely if ever dropped by unannounced. "Take a seat, dear boy, take a seat!" Venkdt gestured to one of the two seats in front of his desk. Kostovich sat down.

"I've come across some information you might find interesting, Mr Venkdt," he said.

"Oh you have?" said Venkdt. "Do go on, please."

"Well," said Kostovich, settling into his chair, "as you know, I've been looking into the USAN's information systems. I've been in their system for the past few weeks, looking around, sifting through things."

Venkdt was glued to his seat, like this was story-time.

"I came upon some information this week that I think will be of great interest to you."

"Go on, go on," said Venkdt.

"It's like this," said Kostovich. "The USAN have been poking about in our information systems, too, and -"

"Ha! A quid pro quo there then!" Venkdt cut in.

"- and they seem to have picked up some chatter from you suggesting that you want to run an election -"

"It's a plebiscite, but do go on."

"Right, a plebiscite to see if Martians would like to be independent from Earth."

"That's not quite it," said Venkdt, "but I suppose that's broadly right."

Kostovich nodded. "Anyway, they're quite ruffled by the idea."

"Well," mused Venkdt, "I suppose they would be. But if it pans out, in the long run, not that much changes really. Jurisdictions, taxes and the like, but pretty much everything would carry on as before."

"I don't think they see it quite that way," said Kostovich.

"They don't?" said Venkdt. "What makes you think that?"

Kostovich took a breath. "Well," he said, "they're going to send two enormous carriers towards us."

Venkdt blinked. "Two what?" he said.

"You've heard of the *Aloadae*?" said Kostovich.

"The dropship carriers? Of course."

"Well, they're going to send them here."

Venkdt was silent. "Here? How?"

"They have some new engine technology. They're going to retrofit the engines and send those two ships over here to stare you down."

For once Venkdt's demeanour didn't seem so jolly. He was shocked and saddened.

"They'd do that?" he said, mostly to himself. "But . . ."

Kostovich wanted to say something to comfort the old man. "They haven't even started the refits, yet," he said. "It will take them months before they're ready."

Venkdt was thinking. "It's so unnecessary," he said, and fell silent.

"I've looked into countermeasures," Kostovich offered.

Venkdt looked up.

"Defence systems," said Kostovich, clarifying.

Venkdt shook his head. "Oh, we don't want to be getting into that, the escalation game."

"They would be purely defensive systems," Kostovich said, "based on the USAN's own technology. I have all the details. We could fabricate that stuff in a matter of months."

"No, no," said Venkdt, "it's too aggressive."

"It's not aggressive," said Kostovich. "It's defensive. These would be defence systems only. Sending carriers is aggressive."

Venkdt sat in silence, his brow furrowed, deep in thought. "Purely defensive?" he said.

"Purely defensive," echoed Kostovich.

Venkdt stared over Kostovich's shoulder and out of the skylight. "Could you build these systems discreetly, so we have them in our back pocket, but we're not flaunting them in anyone's faces?"

Kostovich nodded. "Of course."

"When are these ships coming?"

"They estimate they will be able to have them in Martian orbit within the next six months. Personally, I think they're overestimating but it looks to me, on paper at least, like they could have them here within a year."

"And what about your defence system?"

"What I have are all the details for the USAN's missile defence systems. I can customise them, rewrite the software and go into production in days. We could probably have something on the ground in a month or two. An orbiting defence platform may take a little longer but I think we could have one in place ready to meet the carriers when they arrive."

Venkdt placed an elbow on his desk and rested his chin in his hand, thinking.

"Listen, Kostovich," he said, "go ahead now and start developing these systems. Speed is of the essence, I suppose, but I'm going to continue thinking about this and I may well cancel this project when I've given it some deeper thought."

"Yes, Mr Venkdt," said Kostovich. "I'll get onto it right away."

"You do that," said Venkdt.

Kostovich got up to leave.

"Thanks for bringing this to me," said Venkdt. "Not the best news I could have had on a Tuesday morning, but thank you anyway. You're a good kid."

Kostovich smiled at Venkdt. "I'll get back to you soon with a progress report."

"Okay."

Kostovich hesitated a little. "When are you going to make the announcement? About the election, I mean?"

"It's a plebiscite. Probably in the next day or two."

"I hope it all goes well for you," Kostovich said over his shoulder as he walked towards the door.

"I'm sure it will," said Venkdt. "What could possibly go wrong?"

Kostovich had a call back from Venkdt just a few hours after he had left. Venkdt wanted to meet him and various other department heads and big cheeses that afternoon. Kostovich guessed that after giving it some thought he had decided not to cancel the missile plan. That was good. Bringing in more people, with more views, angles and axes to grind? Maybe not so good.

He had time to set a few things in motion before he returned to the executive level of Venkdt Mars Corp HQ early that afternoon. He set his AIs to merging advanced heuristic tracking algorithms into the guidance and monitoring software of the missiles system he had decided he was going to use as the basis for his defensive program. He had some ideas too about improving missile performance and alternative payloads. He inputted very precise parameters and set his AIs to work developing a much improved and, in some ways, scaled down version of a prototype missile system he had filched from the USAN's archives. The original design had been developed by Helios and tested and refined to a high standard. It looked now like it would not make it to production - well, not by Helios, anyway - since the war had ended and military priorities had changed. Kostovich thought it would have been a shame to let such thorough work fall to waste - particularly since, with a bit of tinkering here and there, it could be a good system.

One of Kostovich's first priorities was to scale the system down. Helios had been commissioned to design a system of missile batteries capable of defending coastlines or other long borders. They had done this by coming up with large batteries capable of defending a forty kilometre radius, meaning that, with redundancy, batteries could be placed along borders at distances of up to eighty kilometres apart.

Each battery consisted of six smaller sub-batteries, each with one hundred and twenty missiles available to it, and its own independent tracking system, capable of being supplemented with additional information from the other batteries and sub-batteries.

Given the relatively small size of the Martian colony, centred as it was on Marineris, Kostovich thought that four of the sub-batteries, stationed north, south, east and west of the city, would provide more than adequate cover for the populated areas, particularly since any threat would more than likely come from above. The cut-down size would also allow for the rapid production that was necessary.

That was part one of his planned system. Part two, which he was only making tentative steps on, was to mount two of the sub-batteries on an orbiting platform. This would truly give protection against external attack. The missiles' range through the vacuum of space would be greatly extended with the platform sited, as it were, at the far boundary post of Martian civilization.

The orbiting platform was at the back of his mind right now. It was desirable but not a necessity. The priority was to firm up the plans for the four planetside platforms and get them into production as fast as possible.

He had that thought in mind as he entered the board room. Venkdt was already there at the top of the table. Seated around it were the next tier of management below him. There was some low-level chit-chat as Kostovich found a seat, nodding to his unfamiliar colleagues as he sat down.

"I think that's everyone now," said Venkdt.

Venkdt generally didn't like to use the board room. He preferred to chat with people one on one, or at least in small groups. He thought that large formal meetings stopped people from expressing their true opinions and allowed the cocky and overbearing to ride roughshod over the more contemplative and withdrawn. For this occasion, though, he had made an exception. This was going to be a meeting of extraordinary import, and only the boardroom would do.

The conversation dropped off and Venkdt had the room's attention. He felt he was presiding over something that would live forever in the history books of the future, but he wanted to keep it simple and human. He coughed before beginning.

"First, I want to thank you all for coming at such short notice. I know you're busy so I appreciate it." He nodded his thanks about the room.

"What this is about may come as something of a shock to some of you. I'd appreciate it if you could keep what we talk about here today private, for the next few days at least. We've taken the liberty of blocking comdev transmission to and from this room, just for the duration of the meeting and purely as a precaution."

'Blocking *most* comdev transmissions,' thought Kostovich, with schoolboy relish.

Venkdt continued, his audience concentrating now on his every word.

"Some of you may be aware of my long-standing interest in jurisprudence as it relates to us here on Mars. I have long thought that as this small colony grows larger this matter will assume ever-greater importance. I've decided recently to pursue an idea I've been kicking around for a good number of years now. I intend to make an official announcement in the next few days but, due to some information I've recently come by, and which we'll get to later, I will let you in on it now."

He coughed, perhaps to underline the moment.

"I will be proposing a plebiscite, a poll of the people of Mars, asking whether they feel the time has come for Mars to be self-determining. A simple poll, that is all I propose. The issue at hand will be presented in the plainest of terms; should Mars become an autonomous state, or not?

"Should the people vote 'yes' I have a draught constitution and a proposed system for an elected government. There are details of the proposed constitution in the handout, and we will widely publicize them in the run up to the plebiscite. The constitution would allow that the first issues any Martian government dealt with would be pertaining to electoral wards, courts, and the constitution itself."

Venkdt paused.

"I would hope to achieve a 'yes' vote, and that any transition from the status quo to independence would run smoothly with very little effect on day-to-day affairs, much like a demerger."

He shuffled some papers.

"As mentioned, I will be announcing all this in a few days' time. I've asked you here today because of a slight wrinkle that's come up even before I've had the chance to announce. Daniel Kostovich," he indicated Kostovich at the end of the table, "has intercepted some USAN communications showing that they know about my proposals and," he paused, "are sending two very large warships our way to encourage me to reconsider.

"Now, I plan for this thing to be smooth, very bloodless and as civilized as possible. I expected it to ruffle some feathers and I realise that in a strict sense some of it will not be 'legal'. But I intend to play fair. Sending the heavies over before the other guy has even started talking? To me that is not fair. So in order to level the playing field back in our favour I've asked Dr Kostovich to build a missile defence system. This is a purely defensive system, you understand, and its purpose is to show the USAN that we will not be bullied, and that we are serious. I'd like you to all cooperate with Dr Kostovich in every way you possibly can to ensure that we have protection in place should we need it. I want that to be the top priority for everyone, superseding everything else. We will need production capability," he glanced at one of the managers present, "that's you, Bob, personnel, that's you Sally, and logistics and finance and everything else to get this working."

A hand rose near the head of the table. "What is it?" said Venkdt.

A man answered, his voice thin. "Isn't this . . . treason?" he said.

Venkdt pulled a weighing-things-up face. "Well, treason is all a question of dates, isn't it? I prefer to think of it as emancipation."

"I don't think that, in all good conscience -"

"Listen," said Venkdt, "if you don't want to be a part of this we can transfer you to another department, another role, and you can wait the whole thing out. And of course, you can vote 'no' when the time comes. But if the people vote 'yes', as I believe they will, by acting with us you will be serving their will. This is a tremendously exciting time to be a Martian. We will be forging a new nation. So no, it's not treason, far from it. In fact, the way I see it, it's a patriotic duty."

A flurry of questions followed. Most were positive and technical, with a few cool cynics in the mix.

"Who's paying for all this?" one sceptic asked.

Venkdt replied, "I, as you know, am not short for cash. And as Executive Officer of Venkdt here on Mars I have control of the local company funds. Since I believe that independence will be overwhelmingly beneficial to the company I think it's justifiable to invest now in securing that independence."

He similarly batted away other mild objections and in doing so seemed to bring people further and further on board. He had obviously thought the whole thing through with meticulous attention to detail. His plan - the elections and constitution - were prêt-à-porter and the funding, timings and a thousand other details appeared to have been considered and evaluated and accounted for. As Venkdt had it, it was more-or-less a demerger. Ownership would change, the company crest would change but the people on the factory floor would hardly notice the difference.

Mars, colony of Earth, would simply become Mars, independent state.

The meeting wound down and the managers filed away in little groups, talking excitedly amongst themselves, invigorated by the intriguing developments and change in routine.

Kostovich hung back, pretending to work on his comdev while he waited for the last straggler, who had button-holed Venkdt, to leave. Eventually the woman finished up and said a cheery goodbye to Venkdt as she left. Kostovich strode up to take her place.

"You won't be cancelling the missile system, then?"

Venkdt laughed. "No, I thought about it and it has to be done. As an independent nation we'll need defences anyway. We can't let them intimidate us."

Kostovich nodded.

EPHIALTES

"There's a provision for an army, a small one of course, in the draft constitution. I was going to have Maya split off half of Venkdt Security and donate it, as it were, to the new nation as the basis for an army. I guess they'll need weapons, so what the hell."

"You made the right choice," said Kostovich. "Igitur qui desiderat pacem, praeparet bellum."

Venkdt smiled. "That's Latin, isn't it, you clever bastard?"

Kostovich smiled too. "Yes, Mr Venkdt, it is."

"What is it?"

"It's from a treatise by Publius Flavius Vegetius Renatus on Roman military principles, written sometime around the fourth or fifth century."

Venkdt nodded along, impressed. "And what does it mean?"

Kostovich smiled again.

"If you want peace, prepare for war."

CHAPTER 11

Ship Building

Lund and her fellow passengers had to wait for half an hour after they had heard and felt the low *clunk* of their shuttle docking with *Ephialtes* before they were finally allowed to board. Releasing their harnesses and floating freely most experienced a giddy, childlike joy at the rare sensation of weightlessness.

"Well this is certainly easier than it was getting in," a colleague said to Lund, and she smiled politely in return. They pulled themselves along, making their way down - maybe it was up - to the airlock connecting them to *Ephialtes*.

Pulling herself through the lock Lund looked up and saw the face of Commodore Deborah G Lucero. Lucero held out a hand, grabbing Lund's and shaking it firmly. "Welcome aboard *Ephialtes*," she said. Lucero was a handsome woman. She was tough-looking, with a sparkle in her eye, and she looked like she could achieve anything she set her mind to. She let go of Lund's hand and was immediately shaking the hand of the next person. "Welcome aboard *Ephialtes*," she said again. A second officer behind Lucero guided Lund into to a position further into the room.

"Please just wait here," the woman said and went back to collect her next body. Lund waited until the room was filled and the hatch had been closed. Lucero floated herself into a position at the head of the room. "Welcome aboard everyone," she said. "Before we do anything we'll be bringing up the AG. This might feel a little weird, so we'll do it slow and you might need to manoeuvre a bit so you don't end up piled on somebody else, or even worse with somebody piled on top of you." Lucero nodded to one of her staff, who tapped at a comdev mounted on her arm. "Here we go," said Lucero.

Lund felt an odd sensation as she was gently pulled in one direction to a bare wall of the room. As instructed, she negotiated with her fellow passengers to find space for herself as the pulling sensation grew stronger and heavier. She lay with her back against the wall and felt a force pushing down on her. As she lay there soaking up the sensation she heard Lucero's voice once again. "And that's that," Lucero said, "you're back to 1G where you were a few short hours ago. You can stand up now."

Lund sat up. She had the feeling you might get coming out of a swimming pool after a long swim, or fully clothed. The pull of gravity, real or artificial, felt burdensome after just a few hours without it. Lund noticed clumps of people discussing it with each other. There were many smiles and animated expressions. It had the feel of a particularly exciting school trip.

"We'll see you to your quarters presently," Lucero said, "but before then just a few basic things you should know. Firstly, this is my ship. I am Commodore Deborah G Lucero and I am in absolute command here. This is a military vessel. We understand there will be a lot of work going on, and we will work closely with you and support you on that, but please understand that we retain ultimate control. I could bore you with safety regulations but none of you look stupid to me. I guess you're all here because you know what you're doing, so I'll summarise the safety regulations like this; don't do nothing stupid, okay?"

The room tittered, warming to the commodore. "I'll let you settle in and we'll meet up at the refectory in, say, an hour for some chow, and then I'll give you the tour of the ship." Lucero nodded to her subordinate. "Carry on," she said, and left the room.

EPHIALTES

The subordinate had shown them to their living quarters and Askel had unpacked her few things. Her room was small and functional with a bunk, terminal and a small seating area. She had lived on *Otus* before and had found the accommodation perfectly adequate. She wasn't planning on spending much time in her room anyway - she had far more important things to be doing. When she was in there she would either be sleeping or working at the terminal.

The chow was good - standard fare, no better or worse than what Askel was used to at the Helios refectories back on Earth. She had made small talk with the others at her table and had managed to put a few names to faces. Soon, Commodore Lucero appeared again, her back ramrod straight as she stood to one side of the refectory, feet apart and hands behind her. "Listen up, people," she said. "I am about to take you on a tour of this great vessel. I know some of you had a hand in designing and building this great ship, we all thank you for that, but that doesn't count for much anymore. You are civilians on a military vessel, so I'll thank you all to stay away from any restricted areas and to refrain from interfering with the crew and their operation of the ship. If you need any special access, if you need to interfere with standard daily operations, come to me and, of course, I will accommodate any reasonable requests. Now, if you'll follow me, the tour will begin."

The engineers, designers, software specialists and logistics experts from Helios stood and followed the commodore out of the room.

Ephialtes was enormous. It was shaped like a shallow shoebox. Four hundred and fifty-eight metres long, two hundred and fourteen metres wide and sixty-eight metres deep. Its purpose was to deliver the twenty-four dropships it carried in its lower deck to the surface of the planet below as quickly and accurately as possible, then offer support from above for the duration of the mission.

The lower deck held twenty-four chambers, known as bays, twelve on each side, which housed the dropships. There was room in the bays to maintain and loadout the dropships. Each dropship similarly had its own bays, six on each side. The dropships' bays each contained a drone mech except the twelfth bay, which contained a command drone. The commander operated the dropship either from within his command drone or from the cockpit. The dropships could be set to provide automatic flight plans and aerial support. The commander could simply dip in and add suggestions or requests to the AIs as and when necessary.

The mechs stood four metres tall and had a broadly humanoid shape; legs, torso, arms and head, though the head was fairly squat and close to the torso.

They were well defended and armed, with a selection of threat detection systems and countermeasures as well as pulse weapons and missiles. The mechs could act autonomously or, like the dropships themselves, with partial or total control from their commander.

The bays were serviced from a large open hangar deck running most of the length of the ship, stopping where it met the main engine housing two thirds of the way toward the rear. Here, the mechanics and mechanic droids could work on maintenance, weapons loadouts, fuelling and the like. It was a good space, available for multiple uses. The commanders were able to use it for some old-school fitness training and it had hosted the occasional football game.

Sitting above the lower, deep 'ship' deck were the upper decks. These were the main living and operational spaces on the ship. At the front was the bridge, which operated as the command and control centre for the whole operation, dealing with day-to-day management of the spacecraft and mission control should the dropships be deployed.

Further back from the bridge were various rooms and sections devoted to the military nature of the enterprise; intelligence, administration, coms and others.

Next came the living quarters, divided into sections each with a number of individual dorms arranged off it. It was next to the day area, which consisted of a series of interconnected open areas with various distractions; IVR booths, a bar, video screens and social areas.

Finally came the refectory, with the galley between it and the engines beyond.

EPHIALTES

The tour had started at the refectory and moved up along the top decks to the bridge. The bridge had impressed with its large forward facing widows and air of super-slick efficiency and order. The lower decks did not have the same gosh-darn awesome factor as the ones above but to Lund they were the most interesting. They were the guts of the ship, what it was all about. It was also where most of her alterations would need to take place. Internal access to the engine mountings could be gained at the far end of the hangar deck, and the deck itself would be used as a workshop for many of the physical alterations that would need to be made.

The dropship commanders on board would soon be sent home. The ship would not be operational for the duration of the refit and they would not be needed for the Mars mission. For that, a select group of combat veterans was being picked and trained back in the USAN. Some would be returned that very day on the ship that had bought the Helios staff to *Ephialtes*.

Lund waited until the tour had ended before she tried to snag Lucero. She had let others ask the obvious or unnecessary questions as they had been shown round the ship. Some seemed keen to demonstrate that they were intimate with excruciatingly fine details about the ship's construction or operation while others just abhorred silence and felt compelled to come up with something when asked the inevitable 'Any questions?'

Lund had kept quiet and refamiliarised herself with the ship. It was the same as *Otus*, with very minor differences, and Lund felt a childish excitement that she knew the ship without ever having been there before. She knew it too from the countless schematics and production documents she had studied from her time on *Otus* and which she had recently cribbed through again. Lund felt a sense of ownership that she grudgingly conceded to Lucero despite knowing, deep down, that *Ephialtes*, and what was to be the new and improved *Ephialtes*, was hers.

As the tour broke up back at the refectory Lucero made a quick exit, heading back toward the bridge. Lund had to duck and weave through the lingering crowd and then semi-sprint down a corridor to catch up with her. "Commodore Lucero!" she called after her. Lucero glanced over her shoulder, reluctantly slowing to a halt as Lund caught up. "Commodore, can I have a minute?" Lund said, panting slightly.

"Of course," said Lucero. "I'm on my way to the bridge, can we walk and talk?"

"Of course," said Lund, but Lucero had not even waited for the reply. She was striding briskly off and Lund had to make a little skip to keep pace. "I'm Askel Lund, I'm the chief engineer on this project." She held her hand out and Lucero shook it perfunctorily.

"I know who you are, Dr Lund. How can I help?"

Lund struggled to make eye contact with Lucero who, with her straight back, was semi-marching and making little effort to keep the conversation cordial.

"I was hoping," said Askel, "that we would be able to work together on this project, me from the civilian end and you from the military. I realise that it must be difficult for you, having so many civilians on a commissioned vessel, but it could be equally difficult for us. Usually we'd be doing work like this before we handed the vessel over, so we won't be used to having your people -"

"In the way?"

"No. I was going to say 'around'."

"But you think we'll be in your way, that's right, isn't it?"

"Commodore Lucero, I understand your security concerns, and I understand you have your ways of doing things that we may not appreciate, but I just want this to run as smoothly and efficiently as possible."

They reached the bridge.

"You do, do you?" said Lucero. "That's good, I think that's what we all want. The sooner we get this done the sooner you can go home and we can get on our way."

Lucero stepped into the bridge. Lund wasn't sure about the protocol; did she have to be invited? She stepped in anyway and hurried behind Lucero. "I was hoping we could get together, me and a few of my senior people and you and a few of yours, so we could get some of this sorted out."

Lucero paused before turning, perhaps sensing that Lund was not sure if she belonged on the bridge. Through an is-it-or-isn't-it-fake smile she said, "I think that's a great idea, Dr Lund. I'll have one of my people book one of the operations rooms and I'll let you know a time."

Lund faltered a second.

"You misunderstand me, Commodore Lucero." The bridge seemed unnaturally quiet. "I meant in the bar, now."

A definitely-not-fake grin spread across Lucero's face. She stepped forward to Lund, hand outstretched. "I like you, Lund. You seem like my kind of gal." She took Lund's hand and shook it firmly. "Did I shake your hand already?" she asked.

"Yes. Twice, actually," Lund replied.

Askel had put some credit behind the bar and Lucero and her senior officers had taken full advantage. The Helios personnel were more restrained but lubricated enough to form the beginnings of working friendships with some of the senior *Ephialtes* officers. There was still a lingering suspicion emanating from them - that would take weeks to subside - but they seemed a little more human and appeared, on the surface at least, to accept that the stowaways had a job of work to do, and that they had to help them get on with it. Lund lightened up a little, too. She had been intensely focused for the last few days and though she knew she would need that intensity in the coming months she was smart enough to realise that even she couldn't retain that level of focus and concentration indefinitely. It was important that she relax now and then.

Toward the end of the session, when most of the Helios people had drifted off, Lund found herself talking with Lucero. Lucero had started out as a drone pilot but had been offered officer training in light of her outstanding record. She'd found herself in some Indonesian backwater when the war had broken out, overseeing a drone base. The base eventually became as near as you could to get to being on the front line by the time the war ended, and had come under direct attack from manned ships and aircraft. Lucero lost people in the most ferocious attack, and would have received a citation for bravery under fire had her superior officer, three thousand miles away, not shot it down on the grounds that she should never have let the attack proceed as far as it did to necessitate such damn-fool heroics.

She lucked into the position on *Ephialtes*. Experienced senior commanders were thin on the ground and such a fearsome machine of war demanded a commanding officer who had field experience. She had been second choice but the first choice had become involved in some sort of incident that remained obscure. One minute he was going to be commodore of a flagship spacecraft, the next he resigned his commission and was bundled quietly out the back door. So be it. Lucero was only too happy to step up and take his place.

"You like this ship?" said Lund.

Lucero nodded. "You built us a fine vessel."

"We tried to."

"It's certainly impressive. I'm proud to serve here."

"How do you feel about Mars?"

Lucero thought. "I'm a service gal, Lund. I go where they send me. Milwaukee, Timbuktu, it's all the same to me."

"Mars is a little different, though, right?"

"It is? It's a sightseeing trip, it's not a mission. We go there, look scary, come back. I've had my war, Askel. This is all gravy to me."

"You got family?"

"Some, scattered around. Got a husband down there, somewhere," she gestured toward the Earth, just visible through one of the high-res virtual windows in the social area. Lund laughed.

"How about you?"

"I've got family," said Lund.

"Got a fella?" said Lucero, warming to the subject.

"No," said Lund. "There was someone a while back, but, you know. Work, the war . . ."

"Where is he now?" said Lucero, the slightest slur in her voice.

"I'm not sure," said Lund. "Last I heard he'd gone back to Mars."

EPHIALTES

"Shit the bed!" Lucero exclaimed. "We're heading out that way. Give me his address and we'll drop a tactical nuke on his head."

Lund laughed. "It's not like that, we just . . . I don't know. People change, I guess."

Lucero lifted her glass. "Well, if we're not going to kill him let's at least drink to the son of a bitch."

Lund clinked her glass against Lucero's. "To Bobby," she said.

"Bobby!" Lucero spluttered. "What kind of stupid-assed name is that!?" She reflected a little. "To Bobby," she said, in mock seriousness, and downed the drink.

When Lund got back to her quarters she was feeling a little woozy. She should have remembered from her time with the Commander Program, and when she was working on *Otus*, that it was foolish to try to match the military drink for drink. She would have been embarrassed to admit it but she had wanted to keep up with Lucero in order to impress her, or at least to give her the idea that she wasn't like the other white bread civilians she was going to have to be putting up with.

Askel crashed onto her bed and lay on her back. She looked up at the ceiling, checking for room spin, relieved to find there was none. She felt like she should sleep, but when she closed her eyes sleep would not come. Her mind was swimming with thoughts of past, present and future. A lot had happened in the last few years and a lot was happening very fast right now. Staying busy and focused had helped her to keep everything in perspective, but right now she was anything but focused. Her mind was a jumble of thoughts about what she needed to do to get the project up and running and on track; about whether Lucero and her people were going to be a problem; about her personal life - or lack of it - but she kept coming back to Bobby.

She hadn't thought about him much in the last few months but tonight with the drinking and with Lucero probing her about it he had been on her mind a lot. She guessed too that she was probably feeling lonely. She hadn't really thought, until tonight, about the fact that Bobby was on

Mars, where the *Aloadae* were headed. Lucero was joking about the nuke, but what if it came to that? Oh, that's just ridiculous, she told herself. Of course it won't come to that. Like Lucero had said, the mission was going to be more or less a pleasure cruise.

"But what if . . ."

The argument went round and round in her head, 'but what if . . .', followed by 'that's ridiculous', back to 'what if', and round and round again.

She thought about the first time she met Bobby. They were exciting times. She was young, on her first big assignment and Bobby and the other commander candidates were young and full of life and excitement too. The war built a feeling of comradeship and purpose amongst them, and they played as hard as they worked.

She was attracted to Bobby immediately. He was cocky and sure of himself like the others but there seemed to be a bit more depth to him. At times he seemed uncertain and he was more open than most about the limits to his abilities in the command drones. He still boasted, but his boasts were realistic compared to the others. He was sensitive to Lund, too. Where the others would rip the piss out of her when she screwed up, he would go easy, sensing her discomfort and offering reassurance. She knew he had taken risks to do that. The pack mentality of the commanders could easily have been turned on him, but he trod the line carefully, remaining one of the boys but supporting Askel when she needed it.

He could be cruel, too. They had had great times when they first got together, but sometimes he could be indifferent to Askel's emotional needs. He could seem cold and uncaring, but at other times he was a rock for Askel to lean on.

The long distance relationship had worked - just - for a while but when Bobby announced he was going back to Mars things fell apart. Askel could see that Bobby had not made any allowance for her in his plans. He said he had to go back because his dad was dying, with no mention about what that meant to their relationship. She knew he had hated his father, and his father had hated him, so it made no sense to her that he would leave her for a minimum of two years unless he thought the relationship was through. Maybe, she thought, something had happened to him in the war. In his book he had made the fighting seem like an exciting adventure, but she wondered if what he had gone through had had a profound but unseen effect on him. Whatever it was, he was going and it seemed like Askel didn't figure in his plans. He never even said goodbye.

As she lay on the bed Lund suddenly felt morose and sad. She could feel the tears welling up in her eyes as she relived the moment Bobby told her he was going home. She wished he was there with her now, though she didn't know whether she would slap him in the face or hug him until he couldn't breathe.

She tried to shake the feelings of sadness. 'It's just the drink,' she told herself, and even though she knew it *was* the drink, she also knew it wasn't *just* the drink.

She tried to think about the happier times with Bobby, but that just made it worse.

Askel woke with a throbbing head and an aching stomach. As bad as she felt, she felt in some way purged, as though some voodoo ritual had been performed on her and the bad juju had been cast out. She knew there was work ahead and that was where all her energies had to be focused from now on. She showered quickly and made her way to the refectory. While she rushed her breakfast she tapped her comdev, requesting the presence of her senior team members on the hangar deck within the next fifteen minutes. She had taken a pill for the headache but it wasn't having much effect. She downed her orange juice and headed for the hangar deck.

She waited for around five minutes and made some small talk with the few who had turned up in time. She couldn't bear tardiness, so as soon as the allotted time came around she began.

"This is a big project for Helios. We are against the clock. The client has specifically asked for this work to be carried out at the utmost haste. We have told the client we can deliver on that; I think we can."

A couple of latecomers rounded the corner and Askel fixed them with laser-beam eyes.

"In order to deliver this project on time we have to work fast, we have to work smart and we have to work honestly. If you're going to miss targets I need to know. If you don't think something is going to work, I need to know. This has to be a no bullshit operation. You are all being well compensated for this work so I expect you to work long hours and not complain about it. We have to trust each other and we have to trust our hosts. They may do things differently to us but we are their guests and we need their cooperation, so let's not rub anyone up the wrong way."

Another group of stragglers arrived. Lund looked at them. "Helios, above all else," she said, "is an engineering company. As engineers we demand precision. When I say the meeting starts at 08:15 I expect you to be there at 08:15." She fixed a stare at one of the latecomers. "What do you expect?"

The woman froze, unsure of how to respond. "I was in bed, Dr Lund," she offered hopefully.

"I gave you fifteen minutes' notice," said Lund. "Don't be late again." She turned back to the group.

"I've sent you all detailed work schedules. If you can see any problems bring them to me immediately. Let your teams know what's expected of them. Propulsion and Logistics stay behind. The rest of you get to work."

CHAPTER 12

Plebiscite

On 19 April 2241 by Earth's Gregorian calendar the hundred thousandth human being to have taken breath on Mars was born. St. Joseph's welcomed the little girl not long after midnight. Her mother was a software engineer at Venkdt. Her father worked there in one of the warehouses.

Charles Venkdt had had an app custom built for his comdev with a data feed from St. Joseph's. The app had a special dispensation to access sound, even after 10:00 at night when Venkdt usually preferred not to be disturbed. Shortly before 00:40 Martian time he was woken by from a deep and dreamless sleep. He grabbed the comdev from his bedside table and looked at it. At first he was too dozy to think about what he saw. As he reached for his glasses his head cleared enough that he remembered the app could disturb his sleep. He excitedly anticipated what he was going to see once he had his glasses on. He read the message twice and half chuckled, half grunted to himself. He thought about phoning Christina, but realised she would not thank him for it at that time of night.

He lay back down on the bed. He could feel history starting to move, like a freight train pulling out from a station - slowly, deliberately and unstoppable.

No one knew it yet but tomorrow he would kick a pebble from the mountain top that would spin and grow as it tumbled down the mountainside, eventually gaining enough material and speed and momentum that the roar from its sheer weight and heft would be heard clear across the solar system.

That was for tomorrow. He'd had the speech planned out for months, years in rough outline maybe, all he had to do tomorrow was deliver it. He rolled over in his bed and thought about it. Like a kid the night before Christmas, he had trouble getting back to sleep.

Christina had not been long out of the shower when she took the call from her father.

"I'm making my speech later today," he said.

Lost in the day-today of getting ready for work Christina didn't follow him. "What speech?" she said.

"I'm going to announce the plebiscite, live on my stream, later today."

"Okay. What does that mean?"

"Well, it means there might be some media interest, or some other fallout. It might pass without comment for all I know. But I'm very excited and I wanted to share it with you."

Christina stopped. "You know I don't think this is a good idea, don't you? I guess I hope it goes well if it's what you want."

"It'll be at four this afternoon, on my stream. I'll try to get Marsnet to restream it too."

"That's great, Dad. Have a great day."

"I will, sugar."

"Bye."

"Bye."

Venkdt trawled through his comdev to bring up the speech. He made some minor alterations then tried to get through to Marsnet.

Venkdt arrived at his office early. He could feel great moment in the day and he wanted to relish every minute of it. He had been at his desk for an hour or so, though it didn't feel half that long, when his PA appeared at the door.

"I thought I could hear you in here," she said.

Venkdt didn't look up from his terminal. "I have a busy day. Thought I'd get in early."

"This came," the PA said, striding toward his desk and placing an envelope upon it. "Is there anything you need?"

Venkdt glancingly noticed the envelope whilst looking up at the PA. "Yes," he said. "Can you clear the whole day for me? I don't think there was much booked in, but I need the whole day. Something's come up. And could you get someone from IT to bring one of those super-high resolution cameras by for this afternoon?"

"Yes," said the PA. "Clear the diary, arrange a camera."

She looked at Venkdt, hoping for an explanation. He obliged.

"I'm making an announcement this afternoon. On my stream. It's quite important, so I want it to look as good as possible. And I need the day to sort a few things out for it."

"I see," said the PA, though she didn't see.

"I'll get on to IT right away. Don't forget that letter. It was hand-delivered by courier so I think it's important or legal or something." She left.

Venkdt spent a few seconds finishing up what he was doing at the terminal before he picked up the letter. He was still reading from his terminal screen as he tore the envelope open.

The letter was headed 'Strich, Oatridge and Phillips'. He was familiar with them. They were the première law firm on Mars. He had recently met with all three senior partners in lieu of Jack Karjalainen. His eye fell to the bottom of the letter, where he saw the words 'on behalf of Hjälp Teknik Inc'. He half knew what to expect as he moved to the top of the page and started reading.

The letter was written in legalese and fundamentally didn't say anything. It expressed Jack Karjalainen's great displeasure and worry about Venkdt's proposed breakup. It alluded to various legal remedies that Hjälp Teknik may be forced to use if some vaguely defined events came to pass. It was bluster, piss and vinegar designed primarily to say 'we are annoyed with you and we have lawyers' and not much else. Venkdt felt disappointed. He cast the letter aside. He knew that the founding of the newly independent Mars would ruffle feathers and make enemies here and there. He was disappointed that the first enemy was someone so close by and someone so like himself, a captain of industry creating wealth on the new frontier. The letter also reminded him of the sad likelihood that Jack Karjalainen would not live to see the independent Mars.

Venkdt spent the rest of the morning working on emails. He would send them immediately he had finished his broadcast. He knew there would be some people who needed assurances, details and other calming words. He had been thinking about this project and this day for many years. He had worked it all out in very fine detail and he had masses of documentation regarding the constitution, the legal aspects, the economic impact and even the military angle, which was negligible. If anyone had any qualms or questions he had answers for them, oil to pour on the troubled waters of their minds.

He worked the rest of the morning in his office and took lunch on his own in an ante-room. After lunch he had a long snooze, not waking until after three. He had a few minutes to go over the speech one last time.

Charles Venkdt's personal stream was not, by any stretch of the imagination, oversubscribed. A good deal of his workforce were subscribers and there was a smattering of business and finance journalists. Some old school friends and long forgotten acquaintances made up the rest of the numbers. He had sent instructions to all his workers that they should tune in to the stream at 16:00. All managers were aware of this and where possible the stream was to be shown on the biggest screens available. Venkdt had also managed to get Marsnet to do a live restream of the announcement. Marsnet was one of the biggest information aggregators on Mars, the nearest thing it had to network television.

At 16:00 Venkdt sat in front of the camera he had ordered and made his speech.

"People of Mars," he began. "At a little after midnight this morning St Joseph's Hospital right here in Central Marineris witnessed the birth of the hundred thousandth human inhabitant of Mars. I believe this to have been a milestone in the founding of this great planet of ours. My forefathers and many of yours came to this seemingly barren planet with hope for a better future, and the strength and conviction to build that future. We follow today in their footsteps, and where they broke rocks and built basic homes and workplaces, we today need to break from the traditional hierarchy and build institutions and cultures that will see a strong Mars grow into everything it can be. To that end, I will be putting a plebiscite to you, the people of Mars, asking for your consent in the great adventure of building a new and independent planet. The plebiscite will make a simple statement; 'I believe that Mars should pursue a course independent of the USAN, with an independent financial apparatus, judiciary, legislature and executive'. Voters will be asked simply if they concur with that statement, 'yes' or 'no'. If the voters return 'yes', with a majority of more than two thirds, and with a turnout of more than eighty percent, I have a proposed constitution for an independent Mars - available for perusal - that we could implement in less than sixty days. The constitution allows for free and open elections to a senate. The very first matter of business for that senate would be to debate the constitution, and amend it accordingly."

He paused before carrying on.

"An independent Mars would have its own courts, its own laws, its own banks and it would represent itself democratically. We would have our own police force - I would personally donate officers from Venkdt Security to found this - and we would have our own military, as small as that might need to be.

"I understand that many of you will see this proposal as tantamount to treason or otherwise illegal. Let me assure you that if you vote 'no' your voices will be heard. If we arrive at a state of independence we will bear you no grudge. Our church will be a broad one. If any of you feel strongly that you cannot be a part of our new world we will do our utmost to help you resettle, if necessary, or to otherwise accommodate your exceptionalism. It is my hope that you will vote 'yes' on election day, and that the changing of Mars' status will happen smoothly and with very little effect on the day-to-day. Should a 'yes' majority not be achieved I would, of course, resign my position and submit myself to the mercy of the courts in the USAN.

"The plebiscite will take place in six weeks' time. There will be ample chance to debate the pros and cons of the issue and I hope we will have a lively and well-informed debate. I, of course, will be urging you all to vote 'yes'.

"This will be a crucial moment in the history of our planet and I put my trust in you, the people of Mars, to make the right decision.

"Finally, I would like to say that what I am proposing is not a radical departure from the lifestyle and culture that we enjoy now, but more of a reshaping of the underlying structure of our society here on this planet better to suit our development into the future. I would liken my proposal to something like a demerger. We would continue from much the same place we are now, but with ownership of our destiny. Thank you."

Venkdt Mars Corp retained the services of Christina Venkdt to oversee the organisation of the plebiscite. With a relatively small Martian population it wasn't a particularly complicated task, but it had to be seen as being fair and transparent. There was an open system for electronic elections that had been used for many years on Earth. Christina thought they would go with the same system and brought in Kostovich to take care of that end of things. Voter registration would be a little more complex; she had a small team for that. They would individually contact every person on Mars and have them register to vote or otherwise record their objections. Venkdt's initial proposal had called for a minimum eighty percent turnout. It was likely that some at the more extreme end of the 'no' camp, who were infuriated by what they saw as the illegitimacy of the plebiscite, would refuse to even register. Christina knew that it was therefore essential that registration refusals were kept to a bare minimum or the plebiscite would be lost before it had even been run. Working on the assumption that most Venkdt employees would go along with Venkdt's plebiscite, and

EPHIALTES

that most objectors would come from the Hjälp Teknik camp, gave them a probable nine to one ratio to start with. That meant that maximising the final ten percent of registrations was crucial to the success of the plebiscite.

Registration went well, far better than expected. To most people, it seemed, a plebiscite was the most reasonable thing in the world. The fact that Venkdt had no legitimate right to call a plebiscite, and that he was running it with no legal basis whatsoever, seemed of no import to most people. They seemed to see the plebiscite for what it was; a simple show of hands, a question innocently asked of the Martian populace - where did they see their future going? Venkdt had been smart enough to figure that from the off. To a legal mind it seemed crazy and against all reason. To the man or woman on the street it seemed like a reasonable question, and as such perfectly reasonable to ask it. Following from that logic it seemed perfectly reasonable to answer it.

There were some refuseniks, most feeling quietly dignified in their embrace with legal principles, but occasionally someone would pop up who wanted to make a big noise about it. Someone who would harangue the registrars over the phone, or who might take to the streams to tell anyone who would listen what a foul travesty of natural justice was being perpetrated upon the people. The people didn't seem to mind too much.

Senior management at Hjälp Teknik retained an air of aloof indifference as though they were above such coarse things. They went about their business like elderly women ignoring the skateboarders and glue sniffers they had to negotiate on their way to the shops. To deny the voter registration process any legitimacy they simply ignored it. As a policy it was hopeless, since most of the population didn't ignore it but positively embraced it. Those who denied the legitimacy of the plebiscite were simply left behind as its momentum and the public's interest in it surged past them. Within a few short weeks what had once seemed like a contentious issue simply became a fact, like the weather. A plebiscite was going to happen; the people were going to vote.

The date for the plebiscite was set for 6 June by the Gregorian Earth calendar, which many felt ill-suited to Martian requirements. Some of the more enthusiastic 'yes' campaigners were hoping that independence would mean a switch to a Martian calendar, which would make much more sense for Martians.

Kostovich had the necessary systems for the plebiscite in place within a few days. Hardware was not an issue, and from a software perspective it was a trivial task. Voter registration was mostly complete after two weeks, which left a further four weeks for campaigning.

Campaigning was mostly carried out via the streams. Aggregators could easily gather the most popular 'yes' or 'no' streams together for the interested viewer. 'Yes' streams massively outnumbered 'no' streams, and the popularity of 'yes' fed on itself. Not being a part of the 'yes' streams, consuming others' or adding your own, seemed somehow like being on the outside of the big party. 'No' streams often seemed dour, pompous, self-serving and backward-looking. 'Yes' streams appeared to be fun, dynamic, modern and forward-looking.

Charles Venkdt contributed a lot of his own 'yes' streams. His were mostly serious and detailed. He had thought the whole thing through in great detail and had masses of documentation to back himself up. He laid out his position clearly with very skilfully made arguments. He made a compelling case but was not the most popular 'yes' stream. That honour went to Independence Monkey - a monkey wearing a 'Vote Yes!' T-shirt who variously fell off a table, skateboarded, and flung his poo at the camera.

By the time plebiscite day came around it was looking like a done deal. Christina, Venkdt and Kostovich could all see potential for disaster. If everyone thought the die was cast there would be no incentive to vote. Though it seemed like there was an overwhelming 'yes' majority they would all have to turn out to vote in order that the necessary eighty percent turnout was reached. On the eve of the plebiscite ninety-four percent of the Martian population had registered to vote. The fourteen percent margin would be crucial to the whole thing. If fourteen percent or more of the Martian population didn't turn out then the 'noes' would have it. Despite riding the crest of a huge wave of popularity for the 'yes' campaign, for Charles Venkdt 6 June was going to be a very long day.

On the day of the plebiscite Venkdt rose at his usual time of 07:00. Voting started at 08:00. He went about his daily routine, arriving at Venkdt Mars Corp HQ shortly before 09:00. The security guard greeted him warmly as usual and he said cheery hellos to colleagues here and there on his way to the office. There was an extra spring in his step that day.

His PA greeted him warmly. "Good morning, Mr Venkdt," she said. "Lovely day for a plebiscite."

Venkdt smiled and nodded. "It is too," he said. Indeed, the skies were clear and the wind was low, though the living and working environments of the Martian population remained sealed off against the cold, low-pressure of the external atmosphere. "I'm expecting a good turnout," said Venkdt, employing the ancient electoral vocabulary. "I'll be in my office most of the day. I'm expecting Christina and Dr Kostovich to come by later, could you organise some lunch and drinks? Just sandwiches or something."

"Of course, Mr Venkdt."

Venkdt entered his office and sat at his terminal. He scanned through his messages and seeing nothing of note went to his aggregator, searching for any streams concerning the election. He quickly found one called *News Muncher*. It was quite a slick operation. The name seemed to ring a bell somewhere in the back of his mind, but he couldn't be quite sure if he had heard of them before. He didn't know if they were an ongoing organisation or if a couple of enterprising individuals had slung the thing together just to cover the election. Feeds ran across the bottom of the screen advertising books about politics, revolution and business - this was obviously where *News Muncher*'s revenue was coming from - but there were also many other advertisements and links for competing streams. Venkdt was happy enough with this one.

There were two anchors, discussing and commenting on events with at least some low-level insight. They constantly cut to other streams of people out and about, often little groups of people discussing how they had voted or what they expected the outcome to be, or how it might affect them. For every person who stated how they had voted a tracker in the top left corner of the screen kept tally. The anchors repeatedly mentioned how their tally 'was not scientific' but that the more people they canvassed the more accurate it was likely to be. By this early stage in the day they had caught on the streams one hundred and eighty-seven clearly voiced declarations, with one hundred and sixty-one claiming to have voted 'yes'. Next to the raw number was the 'yes' percentage: eighty-six percent, well over the sixty-seven percent needed for the two-thirds majority. This was what Venkdt had expected but it was no cause for celebration. The crucial number, he knew, was going to be turnout. If too few people voted they would not reach the eighty percent that he had stipulated in his proposal. He knew too that he really needed the turnout to be as high as possible. He needed the raw numbers to give any victory a natural legitimacy that it would not strictly have in law. He had known that all along, and knew it might be difficult, but it was absolutely necessary. For the plebiscite to represent the voice of the people it had to represent the voice of all of the people, or a good approximation thereof. It was, he knew, a numbers game.

He watched the show for the best part of an hour. By then it had become repetitive and its main point had been made many times over. The 'yes' vote was extremely strong, people were generally engaged in the debate and process, and there was something of a party atmosphere to the whole occasion. Venkdt had made the day a holiday; most of his employees had the day off. He had also laid on some special events such as election parties and cook-offs, complete with large screens showing election coverage.

Once his interest in the show had waned Venkdt thought it must be time for him to do the deed himself. He flipped the stream from his terminal up on to one of the walls and lowered the sound until it was only just audible. He brought out his comdev and ran the voting app.

It immediately asked him for his voter registration number. He brought that up on his terminal and sent it to the comdev, which dutifully told him it was a legitimate number belonging to Charles Venkdt. It gave his address and various other details and confirmed that the comdev it was running on was registered to the same Charles Venkdt as the registration number. It then requested an iris scan and a left thumb print. Venkdt held the comdev to his eye and then placed his thumb on the screen in the designated position. The comdev related the information back to the voter registration database and once again informed him he was eligible to vote, and would he like to proceed? He was about to answer 'yes' when he paused. He lay the comdev down on his desk and turned to the terminal. He fired up the built-in camera and fed it through to his stream. He spoke slightly awkwardly to the camera. "Hi, this is Charles Venkdt here and I'm about to vote in the plebiscite, and I hope you are too!"

He turned his attention back to the comdev. He pressed 'yes' that he would like to proceed. The screen changed. The independence statement was written across the top third of the screen in very clear lettering. Below it, in smaller letters, was a clock counting down from 00:59 surrounded by the works 'You have' and 'seconds remaining to cast your vote'. Below that the rest of the screen was taken up with two very large buttons; a green one, emblazoned with the word 'yes' and a red one with the word 'no'. Venkdt wanted to savour the moment but he was very aware of the counter, which had already reached 00:48 by the time he had carefully read the statement, which he knew to the letter anyway. He held the comdev up toward the camera and smiled for posterity then very deliberately pressed the green 'yes' button. The comdev spoke. "Thank you. Your vote has been recorded. You will be informed of the result when polling closes at 22:00 this evening."

Venkdt looked into the camera on his terminal. "That's all there is to it, folks. Make sure your vote counts! Enjoy the day!" He felt sheepish at his clumsy remarks and quickly cut his stream. He sat back in his chair and looked at the stream playing on the wall. Within minutes he was re-streamed on the show. The stream had been jazzed up a little - it froze on Venkdt's face while one of the commentators explained who he was and later it crashed-zoomed into Venkdt's finger pressing 'yes'. The anchors tried to joke that Venkdt's vote was shocking and unexpected. It wasn't particularly funny.

Venkdt ate lunch alone.

Christina arrived midafternoon. She had brought some work with her and she set herself up on the small conference table to the left of Venkdt's desk. They exchanged a few words, Christina turning down the offer of food. She had eaten before she left. "How does it seem to be going?" she said, nodding toward the screen.

"Good," said Venkdt. "The 'yes' vote is incredibly strong, we don't have any worries there. It all comes down to turnout."

"We've always known that, haven't we?" Christina said, adding absentmindedly, "Why is it called 'turnout'?"

Venkdt looked up from his screen. "In days of old - even now, I think, some places in the non-aligned countries where they're dirt poor - people would have to physically come to designated polling stations to cast a physical ballot. So people would have to - literally - 'turn out' to make their vote."

"Oh," said Christina. "You'll get the turnout, won't you? I mean, now that it's a simple matter of tapping into your comdev?"

"I hope so," said Venkdt, "but I wouldn't take anything for granted. I guess we've done all we can now. Now it's up to them." He gestured everywhere and nowhere.

By early evening *News Muncher* was showing their calculation for the percentage of voters voting 'yes' as eight-seven percent. It had varied throughout the day, but not by much. Venkdt and Christina shared a light evening meal around 19:00. Shortly after that Kostovich arrived. He had spent the day reworking USAN weapon designs. He now felt he had a good portfolio of well-designed and relatively easy to produce weapons and ancillary equipment with which to furnish a nascent army.

"I'm sorry I couldn't make it earlier," he said chirpily as he arrived. "I've been working on some very interesting stuff that I hope will come in useful later, if this thing goes the way we hope it does. Hello Christina."

EPHIALTES

Christina looked up from the papers scattered in front of her and made a thin smile. "Hi, Dan," she said, and went back to her work.

"You did a great job of organising all this. Tip-top, really," said Kostovich.

"It was pretty straight forward. Thanks for the voting system."

"Oh, it's standard stuff. It has to be. It's all open source code so everyone can see we're not fixing anything. I made some very minor changes. Trivial, really."

"Thanks anyway." Christina was engrossed in her work, or at least hiding in it.

Kostovich pulled a chair up to Venkdt's desk. "How're we doing?" he said.

"The vote is great, but it's the numbers we need. And we won't know them until it's over."

"Yes," said Kostovich, "about that."

"Yes?" said Venkdt cautiously.

"Well," said Kostovich, "you know all the information pertaining to the vote - votes cast, 'yeses', 'noes' etcetera - is strictly confidential until the vote is in?"

Christina perked up and she cut into the conversation. "Dan, please don't say what I think you're about to. You know I'm a lawyer. I can't get involved in anything untoward."

Kostovich cut back in himself. "Christina, I wouldn't suggest doing anything illegal. Of course not. But as the technical overseer I have to check that the system is working correctly. And provided no privileged information is allowed to influence any voting behaviour subsequent to it I may review that information as part of my duty to maintain that system."

"I think this is very dodgy," said Christina.

"Is it dodgy?" said Venkdt.

"I looked into this very carefully," said Kostovich. "I wouldn't want to jeopardise an entire election, and of course I wouldn't want to break the law. The articles of the election are very clear; I may have access to current voting information so long as I need that information to ensure the system is working correctly."

"Do you need it for that?" said Venkdt.

"Well, if I don't know what information is going in it, how do I know if it's the right information? Or if it's working properly at all? Look, I know it's all okay; this system has been around for years, it's as good as foolproof. But there's no harm in checking, right?"

Christina's brow was furrowed. "Do you know what you're doing? Really? You could screw this whole thing up."

"I checked the articles again and again. You must have a copy, check them yourself. As long as the information is not misused - as long as the information doesn't leave this room - I, as the returning software systems officer, am entitled to take a peek."

"I don't know," said Venkdt.

"Dad," said Christina, "as a lawyer I would strongly advise you against this. It might be kosher but if there's even a slight risk I would leave it well alone. What's to be gained, anyway? We'll know the result in a few hours."

Kostovich pulled out his comdev. "I know what I'm entitled to do. If you don't want to be involved, that's fine. I'm doing this by my own volition. It has nothing do with you." He started tapping.

"You dumb bastard. If we're in the room with you then of course it's to do with us. Put that thing away," said Venkdt.

"Oh!" said Kostovich. "Now that really *is* interesting."

"Put it away," said Christina.

"What's interesting?" said Venkdt.

"The turnout figures. Not what I expected."

"You could screw this up for all of us. Put that damned thing away!" said Christina.

"What are they?" said Venkdt.

"Well," started Kostovich.

"Fer Christsakes! Put 'em up on the damned wall!" shouted Venkdt.

Kostovich looked up at him tensely. He pressed and swiped the screen a few times and a bare console was overlaid on the election stream on the wall. There were two columns, labels on the right with numbers to the left. At the bottom was 'Turnout'. The number was seventy-eight percent. Venkdt clenched his jaw looking angry and worried. "It's twenty-past seven in the evening. Who wouldn't have voted by now, who was going to vote? Jesus, we're never going to make it."

"We've got nearly three hours, yet," assured Kostovich.

"I don't like it," said Venkdt, "I don't like it one little bit. We should be in the eighties by now."

"We'll get there."

"We will?"

"Sure. A couple of hours ago I extrapolated voting patterns through to ten o'clock. They'll continue to decline but, I predict, you should limp over the line sometime around 21:30."

Venkdt stared at him.

"I made the extrapolation extremely cautious, too. It's in the bag."

"In the bag," echoed Venkdt. "There are no certainties in this world, my friend. Have you eaten?"

Kostovich eyed the sandwiches and pastries on the conference table by Christina's elbow. "I could eat," he said. He went over and took a seat next to Christina, taking a pastry and pouring a glass of orange juice. "What are you working on there?" he said.

"It's nothing," Christina replied dismissively, "just some corporate stuff."

"Interesting?"

"Not really."

Kostovich chewed on the pastry. "You must be pretty smart to keep on top of all this legal stuff."

Christina stopped and looked up. "It's not interesting but it does require concentration. And you don't need to be smart - not smart like you are, anyway - you just need to be diligent, and not a moron. I'm trying to work, could you please be quiet?"

Kostovich nodded. "Okay, quiet it is." He finished the pastry. "Of course, I may let out a little shout around half-nine."

Christina glared at him and he moved back to his seat by Venkdt's desk. Kostovich fiddled with the console so it displayed the figures to two decimal places. Turnout was seventy-eight point nine six percent. It was a little over 20:00

They spent the next hour in near silence. Christina was wrapped up, or at least pretending to be wrapped up, in her work, Kostovich was fiddling on his comdev and Venkdt was variously sat at his desk, watching the stream or pacing the room. The turnout percentage crept up slowly over the hour:

20:15: seventy-nine point three two percent
20:30: seventy-nine point five one percent
20:45: seventy-nine point seven two percent
21:00: seventy-nine point eight four percent
21:15: seventy-nine point nine three percent

As Kostovich had predicted the number of votes cast per minute dropped and dropped as time went on but the eighty percent threshold inched ever closer. By 21:20 even Christina was interested. She pushed her papers to one side and looked at the screen. The terminal readout was laid over the *News Muncher* feed, which was currently showing a party somewhere. Revellers were being asked what they thought about the election. Most made idiotic half-shouted replies, too busy partying to take anything seriously. The 'yes' vote had it by a huge margin but many were ignoring the vital question of turnout. The partygoers were celebrating a victory they had not yet achieved. The *News Muncher* anchors were pushing the turnout question for all it was worth. It was the only angle that added drama to the result.

"We're going to do it," Christina said quietly and confidently.

The logical part of Venkdt's brain agreed but he felt too uneasy to go along with her, electing instead to remain with his eyes fixed to the screen.

It was 21:21. The turnout was seventy-nine point nine seven percent.

"I would expect a bit of late run," said Kostovich, "starting sometime around a quarter to ten or so. The last minute people, you know. People who have been putting it off but then suddenly panic."

Venkdt nodded silently as the turnout clicked over to seventy-nine point nine eight percent.

For the next five minutes nothing changed, then the turnout count flickered again: seventy-nine point nine nine percent.

Venkdt stood up. "Goddamn," he said, "how long now?" There was a clock in the corner of the huge screen they were watching but Kostovich answered anyway.

"The poll will close in approximately twenty-seven minutes."

Venkdt walked over to the conference table and poured himself a drink. He walked back and stood in front of the screen, taking sips from his glass and rocking back on his heels. He caught Kostovich's eye and smiled thinly at him.

"There'll be a surge at the end," said Kostovich.

"I know," said Venkdt distantly, his eyes fixed on that one tiny portion of the screen that said 'seventy-nine point nine nine percent.'

Eighty percent.

Venkdt breathed out heavily and, placing the glass on his desk, he walked to Kostovich who was rising from his chair and offering his hand. "Congratulations, Mr Venkdt," said Kostovich as Venkdt grasped the hand and shook it.

"Thank you, Dr Kostovich," Venkdt said, with genuine tenderness. Venkdt turned and Christina was already upon him. She flung her arms around him and spoke to the side of his head.

"Well, done, Dad. I know how much you wanted this." Venkdt hugged his daughter back and, disengaging, turned back to the screen. The turnout had already changed again, to eighty point zero one percent. The revellers didn't look quite so foolish now.

"I'd like to thank you two, both of you, for all the work you've done on this," said Venkdt. "I think this is a truly historic day for this planet and you've contributed to it immeasurably." He took his glasses off and cleaned the lenses on his shirt front. Kostovich thought he looked a little puffy around the eyes but he quickly put the glasses back on and it was difficult to tell.

"You know," said Venkdt, "this is just the beginning. There is so much work to do yet, and I'm glad to have you with me." He beamed at them both.

"This is going to be one hell of an adventure."

Maya Foveaux was working the late shift on plebiscite day. She wasn't expecting any more trouble than usual, and usual was pretty minimal. There were parties and other events sponsored by Venkdt scattered about and though she made sure there was a security presence at all of them they had turned out to be very good-natured, running without any hitches. She was due off duty at midnight and was in her office, running down the last few hours of her shift writing up some reports, when a junior knocked on the door. He stuck his head round and called out, "Results in soon, sir, we're watching it in the canteen if you'd care to join us." He'd gone before Maya had the chance to reply. She had been lost in what she was doing and hadn't kept track of time but she was, she realised now, interested in the result of the plebiscite. She finished up what she was doing and made her way to the canteen.

The canteen was way busier than it would usually have been at that time of night. An aggregator was playing streams on one of the walls. It was set to election coverage and was cutting between personal streams of revellers and some more highly structured pieces. Glancing around the room Maya noticed there was a mixture of on and off duty security personnel in attendance. It seemed Venkdt Security were having their own little election party. She felt slightly irked that she hadn't been notified, even more so that she hadn't been invited. She wondered if she might have cause to discipline someone over it but then she told herself to forget it; this wasn't any ordinary occasion.

EPHIALTES

An off duty officer bundled past her saying, "Drink, sir?" but before Maya had chance to turn it down the officer had melted back into the throng. Maya found herself a seat on the arm of a sofa with a good view of the screen. A security officer sat on the sofa next to her sheepishly offered his place but Maya graciously turned him down.

Soon enough it was like New Year's Eve. There was a countdown, starting from thirty and getting louder and more raucous as it got down to one. Where logically there should have been a zero there was instead an eruption of cheers and clapping. The stream flashed the words '22:00: Polling Closed' on the screen, quickly followed by the words 'Live Result:', but with nothing after them. A commentator on the stream informed her audience that, although the vote was electronic and as such did not need counting like an old-fashioned paper ballot, the result would need to be verified by the software systems returning officer. That might take anything up to one minute and only then could the result be officially announced.

There was a high-energy burbling hubbub in the room and a nervous excitement. Maya wondered if maybe she should have taken up the offer of that drink. She was looking away from the screen for a split second when the room erupted in cheers. She looked back to the screen for confirmation but her view was blocked now by standing, jumping, shouting people, hugging each other and punching the air. Even though she realised the result must have been 'yes', she still wanted to see the screen for absolute confirmation. Stepping to one side and craning her neck awkwardly there it was; 'Live Result: YES!!!' Someone suddenly grabbed hold of her, squeezing her tightly and rocking from side to side. The person reeked of beer, and Maya was relieved when he let go. She thought about disciplining him and again pushed the thought away in light of the momentous occasion. As the initial surge of cheering revelry rolled back the screen cut to Charles Venkdt's personal stream. He was beaming in his grandfatherly way and he looked tired but elated. He began to speak.

"People of Mars," he said, "you have voted today overwhelmingly to pursue a course of Martian independence. In full accordance with your wishes we will begin the process of disengaging our courts, security services, military and most importantly our business operations from their parent organisations on the old home planet. It is our hope and expectation that this process will proceed with the minimum of disruption here and back on Earth. We do not seek to antagonise our Earth-based brothers and sisters. We will fully compensate all Earth corporations, particularly my own company Venkdt, for the new fully independent operations that we will be demerging from them. We will pay the going market rate plus ten percent for all the businesses, stock and tangible assets that we will be taking over. Within the next month we will run full elections to the new Martian senate as set out in the proposed constitution, available for perusal on the Venkdt site and replicated on many others. I hope you will support those elections in the same enthusiastic and well-informed manner that you have supported this plebiscite."

He paused for breath.

"I would like, before I finish, to remind you all of what a brave and momentous choice you have made. I know it was not an easy choice; I wrestled with it myself. But we now set off into an exciting independent future, where the only limits are set by our imaginations. We are at the furthest frontier of mankind's progression across the solar system and into the galaxy beyond. Besides the many resources ripe for exploitation right here on Mars - our Mars - we are in a prime position to exploit the asteroid belt beyond. We can create huge wealth for ourselves, in terms both of treasure and experience. We do this for ourselves, and for generations yet unborn, of course, but ultimately we take these brave steps into the future for all mankind."

He paused one final time and only now did Maya notice that the canteen, from its previous boisterous maelstrom of noise, had fallen almost completely silent. Venkdt stared out from the screen and his voice seemed to catch in his throat as he signed off.

"Thank you, people of Mars," he said, "and good night."

Maya ambled slowly back to her office, at one point passing a couple snogging up against a wall. In her mind she was running over possible futures and wondering if anything would really change much. Probably not, she told herself. Like Venkdt, she thought that various names

EPHIALTES

on deeds and letterheads might change but the workaday routine would continue much as it ever had. Venkdt had asked her to make plans for a nascent independent police force should a 'yes' vote be returned. She had been told she could split the resources of Venkdt Security in half and form the new police service as she best saw fit. She had been flattered that he had put that much faith in her ability and she was confident she was up to the job. She had made rough, back-of-an-envelope plans but hadn't developed the ideas much beyond that. She decided as she walked that she would now have to flesh those plans out fast and put them into practice. She thought she would ask for volunteers and would try to forge an alliance with the soldiers stationed at the USAN garrison. Her guess was that the garrison would be resistant. They were not Martian and would feel much more traitorous than her own people, but she thought that co-opting them might help defuse any potential conflicts.

When she got back to her office she flicked through the streams, which were going crazy now. Her aggregator had trouble holding a single stream long enough for her to concentrate on it. She overrode it manually to stay on one stream that seemed to be a little more measured than some of the others. The presenter, a young girl in her teens, was restreaming one of the big news streams from Earth with her own additional commentary over it. The Earth reporter was jabbering seriously into the lens. Under the teen girl's commentary Maya caught him saying, 'This not going to go down well with the Cortes New White House, where sources are telling me the foreign secretary and the president himself are taking a very bullish stance on what they see as the Martian Rebels.' Maya snorted to herself. A bullish stance is all very well, she thought, but when you're a hundred and forty million miles away it loses much of its impact.

CHAPTER 13

Election

Kostovich deftly negotiated Venkdt's long-limbed secretary and slipped into the meeting late, as he almost always did. Venkdt was seated at the head of the table. To his side was Christina. There were two more people Kostovich didn't recognise, but they had an air of lawyerliness about them.

He took a seat opposite Christina. "Sorry I'm late," he said. "What have I missed?"

"Nothing much," said Christina, not looking up.

"We're just reviewing the documents," said Venkdt, "crossing every 'i', dotting every 't.' "

"Okay," said Kostovich. "Do you need me for this part?"

"I suppose not," said Venkdt, "but it's always useful to have another pair of ears, particularly someone who's not tied up in the legal profession. You know, someone with plain common sense who might catch something obvious that we've missed. I'd appreciate your sitting in."

"Okay," said Kostovich, covering his mild disappointment. He felt it was going to be a long day.

He was given a recap on everything that had been covered so far, then had to suffer the rest line by line. The lawyers, Christina included, went through the documentation of Venkdt's constitution almost a word at a time. They were careful to check, double check, and recheck every possible meaning of every sentence.

The constitution itself was short. Venkdt stipulated that one of the priorities for the new legislature should be to flesh out the framework of the constitution to meet Martian needs. The purpose of this first draft was to be a solid bedrock on which to build for the future.

Venkdt's constitution was fundamentally a 'lite' version of the constitution of the USAN. There would be a president, a legislature and a judiciary. The legislature would consist of one house only, the senate. There would be eight electoral wards, each returning two senators. Divvying up the planet into wards would be a job for Kostovich; they would discuss that later. The senate and the president would both have executive powers. Bills in the senate would require a two-thirds majority and presidential assent to reach the statute. The president could introduce bills and these would be subject to the same restrictions. The senate would check the power of the president and the president would check the power of the senate. The judiciary were to be appointed by the president, subject to approval by the senate, and three senior judges would be the absolute arbiters of the law. The president would be commander-in-chief of the military.

At its base it was a simple constitution, familiar in concept to anyone with even a passing interest in Mars or the USAN. Like any legal document it had to be framed with great precision. That's why the meeting seemed to be moving so slowly. Kostovich's main contribution would again be with the electoral process. He had his AIs split the planet - the occupied areas consisted of Marineris and a few far flung outposts - into the necessary wards such that, as far as possible, each ward would maintain geographic integrity but also represent a cross-section of Martian society; workers of different grades and, where possible, from different industries. Voters would have to register again for the new vote but since this would not be a new experience for them, or for the registrars, that should be a quick and easy process.

There were no parties on Mars as yet. All seats were available to be contested by all people. There would be crazies and attention seekers at first but it seemed likely that only serious contenders would be returned. Venkdt knew that in the long run politicians would inevitably coalesce into parties, and maybe that would work well in the future. Right now, individuals truly representing their electorate could only be a good thing. Venkdt saw the birth of the new Mars as a collegiate enterprise with everyone working together for the common good.

The voting date was set for early July. Plenty of time, thought Kostovich, to prepare everything for the election. The short timescale would actually work in their favour. Coming off the wave of euphoria generated by the 'yes' vote in the plebiscite, people would be likely to put themselves forward for election in the true spirit of public duty without having time to scheme and plot and deal. That, of course, might come later.

The meeting dragged on into the evening. Kostovich eventually got his chance to speak about the fine details of the electoral wards and the registration and voting systems. He was quizzed by the lawyers and gave them answers they seemed happy to accept.

Every person in the room knew that everything they did was essentially provisional. There was genuine excitement that they were breaking new ground. They had room to make mistakes, so long as the fundamentals of the constitution allowed for those mistakes to be corrected further down the line. They were satisfied that the checks and balances they had put in place between the executive, legislature and judiciary would protect against any abuses of power.

A little after 19:00 Venkdt signed off the document, designated MC05/1.5. It was the first official draft of the newly independent Mars' constitution. It would be put into full effect in a little over one month's time.

"Congratulations everyone," said Venkdt, "on a job well done."

"That wasn't as bad as it might have been," said Christina.

"I think we have a very robust document here, and a great basis to build on," said one of the other lawyers.

"Absolutely," another lawyer chimed in, "this is a very solid foundation. Thank you, Mr Venkdt, for your input, which helped a great deal."

"Not a problem," said Venkdt, "I was just stealing from the best; an exercise in summation, really."

"That may be so," said the lawyer, "but I think this is a rock solid base from which to build a nation."

"I hope so," said Venkdt, "that was always my intention." He stood and offered his hand to the two lawyers. "Thank you, gentlemen," he said. "It's been a great honour to work with you today." They shook hands and, exchanging further pleasantries, the lawyers gathered their things and left. Venkdt watched them go. He sat in his chair beaming. Christina looked at him.

"When are you going to announce?" she said.

Venkdt cocked his head to one side. He knew Christina was too smart to buy him playing dumb. "I don't know," he said. "I guess as soon as possible."

"Why not now?" said Christina, nodding to Venkdt's terminal.

Venkdt frowned. "I think I'll leave it a day or two," he said. "It might look a bit untoward announcing my intention to run for president only minutes after I finished framing the constitution."

"Will anyone care?" said Christina.

Venkdt thought. "Probably not. I care - a bit. I'll make an announcement the day after tomorrow."

Christina nodded.

"Would you like to be my campaign manager?" said Venkdt.

Christina gulped. "And what would that entail, exactly?"

"Well, getting the message out there, having a big presence on the streams." Venkdt struggled to think of anything else. "Shaking babies, kissing hands. That sort of thing, I suppose."

"I could do that, I guess," said Christina. "What is the message?"

Venkdt took deep breath and looked into the distance, focusing his thoughts. "The message is this: business as usual, stability and an orderly transfer of power. Openness and fairness. And in the longer term, the drive toward expansion. Greater wealth, greater participation and a dynamic and growing Martian economy. In the very long term - I'm talking maybe ten or twenty years - I think we should be expanding our area of operations out into the asteroid belt." He thought on that last part. "Maybe leave that for this campaign. Save that for the second term, eh?"

"Second term? Okay." Christina turned to Kostovich. "What do you think?"

"I think you'd be a great campaign manager," said Kostovich. "You'd get my vote." He smiled at her trying to appear cheeky and witty. It came off as slightly creepy. Christina quickly moved her attention back to her father.

"Okay," she said, "I'll do it. Send me your manifesto and any other documents you feel might be useful."

"Thank you," said Venkdt. "Dr Kostovich, as the returning officer I guess you will have to stay out of this. You'll need to be seen to be impartial."

"Yes, Mr Venkdt," said Kostovich.

"But I can always use a sharp mind like yours. If I win I'll have to resign my position here at Venkdt but I would need advisers. It would be great to have you along, Dan."

Venkdt had never called Kostovich 'Dan' before, and it sounded jarring to Kostovich's ears. He guessed Venkdt had used it deliberately, signifying a change in their relationship.

"I'd be happy to serve in your administration, Mr Venkdt," said Kostovich.

"Please," said Venkdt, "call me Charles. The spirit of change is in the air. I think we can lose some of the old formalities."

"Yes, Charles," said Kostovich. "I think you're right. Change is in the air."

There were few big open spaces on Mars. Space was at a premium. All buildings had to be immensely strong to withstand the necessary pressurisation they had to have. The Martian atmosphere outside was at a pressure of about seven or eight millibars. Inside the pressure was about four hundred millibars - far less than on the surface of the Earth but not so low that human beings couldn't cope with it. The lower pressure meant that buildings could be built to lower tolerances, but each building still had to be tough enough to resist exploding or even just leaking precious air to the outside.

In the previous forty years or so a number of large domes had been built. Mars by that time had the money, resources and technical know-how to build them. A few were private, such as the dome where Venkdt had his house, or the shared dome that the Karjalainen's were a party to, but most were public and took the form of parks. A large dome with diameter of eighty or ninety metres could house a small park with trees and maybe a pond or a sculpted seating area. These parks were the nearest thing Martians would ever get to an outdoor space on their cold, barren and thinly atmosphered planet.

The largest dome on Mars had only been open for two years. It had a diameter of one hundred and forty metres and used the most modern lightweight super-strength materials and some very clever engineering to support itself. It was called Central Park, a historical allusion that meant nothing to most people but seemed to tickle the architects somewhat.

Two weeks into his election campaign Venkdt held a rally in the dome. There was a stage toward one side and various stalls around the edges selling snack foods and T-shirts and hats. 'Vote Venkdt' flags were not for sale; they were free and everyone was encouraged to take one and wave it at every opportunity. Venkdt was due on stage at 17:00. Currently on stage was the comedian Oscar Mason, working the crowd like an expert. He was wearing a 'Vote Venkdt' T-shirt and pacing the stage with a microphone held closely to his mouth. His routine was largely observational; gentle digs at some of the more contentious work practices at Venkdt Corp and some mockery of prominent streamers. Oscar Mason's own stream was one of the most successful on Mars. He had a large following on Earth too, where his shtick of bumping into things and asking strangers random and confusing questions proved extremely popular.

At the rally he had the crowd in the palm of his hand. Every so often he'd make a few rambling but seemingly serious points about Martian independence and the upcoming presidential election, then he'd undercut his own seriousness with a gag at the end.

"How about that President Cortes?" he said, to whoops and hollers from the audience. "He's some guy, ain't he? Somebody told me he lost my dad's planet. I said no, no, no, he didn't lose my dad's planet but he did lose Ma's."

Venkdt was standing in the wings. "How do I look?" he said to Christina.

"You look fine," she said. "Do you have your speech?"

Venkdt pulled a wad of notes from his pocket and held them up. "I know it all anyway," he said. "When am I on?"

"Oscar's just finishing up," said Christina. "They're going wild for him. I don't suppose you have any jokes in your speech, do you?"

"Not really," said Venkdt. "If I think of one I'll drop it in."

"No, no, no!" said Christina in mock horror, "please don't improvise!"

Venkdt smiled. "Okay, campaign manager," he said.

Oscar Mason was finishing up. "Listen folks, you all know why we're here today," he was saying, "we're here in support of a man who can lead us into a bright new independent future, a man who is in a great position to do that, and a man who has for many years held most of our best interests close to his heart. I'd like to introduce you now to the man who is going to be the next -" he stopped and pulled a funny face, "next? first? whatever! the man who is going to be the president of Mars. Please, put your hands together and whoop it up for Mister. Charles. Veeeeeeeenkdt!!!!"

Oscar Mason gestured dramatically to the side of the stage and bowed down like a medieval serf. As Charles Venkdt ambled to the mic stand set centre-stage Oscar Mason moved backwards, remaining bowed, and disappeared off the other side of the stage. Venkdt stood before the microphone and waved at the crowds, soaking up the cheers. He pointed to a few individuals and appeared to mouth personal messages to them. Christina, at the side of the stage, couldn't tell if this was genuine or if her father was such a consummate politician already that he knew it would make him look good if it appeared he had genuine friends in the audience supporting him. He waited for the roar of the crowd to die down.

Just as it was starting to fall away he made a downward gesture with his outstretched hands, like he was a conductor.

"Thank you," he said into the mic, "thank you for such a warm welcome, and thank you to Oscar Mason, for such a warm warm-up." Venkdt clapped towards the side of the stage from which Oscar Mason had exited. Venkdt quipped to the mic, "By the way, that's not true about the Venkdt refectories." There was a ripple of laughter from the crowd. "I wanted to, but they wouldn't let me." Another ripple of laughter.

Venkdt let the laughter die away. He paused so the crowd would give him space to speak. He held the space well.

"I stand before you today seeking election to the great office of president of our new nation, indeed our new planet. Many of you will know me, in one way or another, as your employer. I hope you know I have always sought to do the best for our enterprise, and to do the best for the people who are the core of that enterprise. I will seek to continue in that vein if you elect me as your president.

"One of my first acts on assuming the presidency will be to continue the disentanglement of our affairs from those of our fellows on Earth. I will seek to do this amicably and with as little disruption as possible. Venkdt Mars Corp will compensate the parent company commensurate with the value of the Martian operation plus ten percent. I hope to do that by negotiation but if necessary we will pay the funds and take what is rightfully ours.

"I will form a police force. To that end I will personally donate approximately half of the personnel from what is currently Venkdt Security, and will continue that funding for the next five years while the new Martian police force finds its way. Similarly, I will form a small Martian military to fulfil a ceremonial role.

"I will encourage the development of new businesses and trade with Earth, as this will be at the core of our economic development and will provide us with great wealth as we expand and grow into the future.

"I will do all this with your help. It will not be easy. We are standing today at the furthest frontier of humanity. There are many challenges ahead. Our world is not a welcoming place, but through hard work, determination and industry our forebears have turned it into something great. If you elect me as your president I plan to build on that greatness. In time, I will ask you for hard work, commitment and the application of the strength I know you all have. For now, all I ask for is your vote. Thank you."

The crowd erupted, and Venkdt held two hands aloft in salute to them, turning from side to side, working the crowd. After a few minutes of accepting their cheers he walked back into the wings. Christina turned him around and pushed him back out. The crowd went wild as he walked back onto the stage, smiling and waving. He did the point and chat shtick again, but he was very careful to not overdo it. Eventually, the crowd let him leave.

"How was I?" he said to Christina as she handed him a towel to wipe his sweaty face.

"You did good," said Christina. "Listen to the crowd."

Venkdt listened to the crowd, and smiled.

Venkdt's opposition had all been minnows. His name, in truth, was the only one on the ballot that most people had heard of. In a way, for many years, he had been the unofficial mayor of Mars anyway. He had been a benevolent boss to most people at Venkdt and had presided over huge expansion of the company's operation on Mars. His closest rival had been a popular streamer whose manifesto was a teenager's fantasy and clearly not to be taken seriously.

When the result came in shortly after 22:00 on election day Christina bundled a reluctant Venkdt down to the transport bay of Venkdt Mars Corp and had him say a few words to the crowd there. He was gracious, thanking them as he always did and reiterating his immediate plans, the most significant of which was the buyout of the Martian arm of Venkdt.

As they were walking back to his office after the impromptu speech Christina said, "Great speech, Mr President," with a mile-wide grin.

"It was, too, wasn't it?" said Venkdt in return. He smiled at her and ruffled her hair.

Back at his office he slumped into his chair and rubbed his chin. "I guess there's work to be done," he said. He'd had his legal people working on the buyout, but they had made little headway. The parent company was resistant to any buyout, flatly refusing its legitimacy and threatening all sorts of legal actions. Venkdt had his legal people working on it round the clock but as a backup he also had Kostovich involved. Kostovich's knowledge of software systems and encryption could be put to use if necessary in forcing payment on the Venkdt parent company. As Venkdt saw it he could dump the money in their accounts and that would be the end of it, despite any complaints they might have. He'd rather do it the legal way, with mutual consent, but he knew it was worth having alternate strategies to fall back on. It was that sort of thinking which had made him an effective business leader and, he hoped, would make him an effective president.

The buyout was a priority. He had a mandate from the people and this had been one of the major planks of his manifesto. He decided it had to happen within the week. He fired off messages to his legal team requesting they make it happen. If necessary, they were to give the parent company an ultimatum. He sent a message to Kostovich, too. He was to prepare to pump the money into the Venkdt parent company's accounts using his software black magic should they refuse to accept the money by any other means. He was to liaise with Venkdt's legal team. Either way, with their agreement or without it, the Venkdt parent company was going to be paid off for their Martian operation within one week. Shortly after that Charles Venkdt would resign his position with immediate effect and take an oath swearing him in as the first president of Mars.

"If there's anything I can help you with just let me know," said Christina.

"I've taken up far too much of your valuable time already," said Venkdt, "and I'm incredibly grateful for it."

"It's okay, Dad," said Christina. "What are you going to do now?"

Venkdt leaned back in his chair. "I'm going to finish up a few loose ends here. Take maybe a week or so, then I'm going to resign and take up the presidency." He smiled at his words and enjoyed them so much he said them again. "Take up the presidency."

Christina smiled too. "That's good," she said. "You deserve it."

Venkdt beamed.

"You're going to buy Mars back from Earth, is that right?" said Christina.

"Well," said Venkdt, "we're going to buy all of Venkdt Mars from Venkdt Corp. The independent businesses are all Martian anyway. I guess Hjälp Teknik is a largely Martian enterprise, although they are traded on the New York Stock Exchange. What they do is their business. I guess foreign investment could be good for our new economy."

"And Venkdt are happy to sell?"

Venkdt frowned. "Probably not. But we'll be buying them out anyway, a sort of compulsory purchase. Ruffled feathers in the short term. In twenty years everyone will have forgotten about it."

"It's going to be good, Dad," said Christina.

"I think so," Venkdt replied.

Venkdt met with Foveaux in the morning.

"Congratulations, Mr President," said Foveaux.

"Thank you," said Venkdt. "Please, call me Charles for now. I wanted to speak to you today with both hats on. I'm still chief executive officer here at Venkdt at the moment and I want to go over these plans for setting up the police force and military. It kind of crosses over into my new role as president, so to avoid confusion and just for now, please call me Charles. Do you mind if I call you Maya?"

"Not at all."

"Good, good, then let's begin. Now, I asked you about splitting Venkdt Security. I know that you've been overstaffed, if anything, for the last few years so I guessed it wouldn't be a problem."

"It won't be," said Maya. "I sent you a copy of my proposals, did you read them?"

"I glanced through them. They looked good."

"They are good. When would you like to put them into effect?"

"Well," said Venkdt, "I'd say do it as soon as possible."

"Okay," said Maya, "I'll get onto it right away."

"You don't expect any difficulties?"

"I don't. I'll be taking volunteers from Venkdt Security and from the police service at the garrison. Man management may be an issue but I've got some very good people to soothe any bruised egos. It's change. Nobody likes change, but I'm sure we can get it done smoothly and quickly."

"That's good," said Venkdt, "I think you can too. I've been speaking to Daniel Kostovich - do you know him?"

"I've heard the name."

"He's been working on some equipment that might be of use to you. It's more military stuff than anything but if you introduce the new uniforms with body armour and the like it might distract your people from the changes going on. You know, the new uniforms being from necessity and not part of some clever psychological ruse to mould them into a new unit," said Venkdt, with a twinkle in his eye.

"I see. Does he have this equipment already?"

"I don't know. He's been working on it for the last few weeks. I'll send you his details. You two should get together and talk it over."

"I'm not sure what our needs are going to be. The policing role has to be the priority. I might hold back on the military part, initially. It's going to be symbolic anyway, right? Providing an honour guard at state occasions and that sort of thing. I think we need to concentrate on our immediate practical needs right now. It's not like we have any enemies, is it?"

"Well," said Venkdt, "yes and no. The main focus of your security force will be policing. That's what you will be doing, offering a police service to the Martian population when the garrison pulls out. But we do need a military, for psychological reasons if nothing else." He wasn't sure if he should mention the missile systems that Kostovich was building, and the reason he was building them. Since they would ultimately need some sort of military oversight and support he decided to come clean. "I guess you're right. It *would* make sense to just have one service initially but . . ."

"But what?" said Maya.

"The USAN are talking about sending ships here."

"Sending ships?" said Maya, genuinely thrown.

"Military ships," said Venkdt. "This is very highly classified information at this time. Don't worry, it's all for show. But we have to bluff them right back, so we need our military to be something a bit more substantial than we might have preferred."

"I see," said Maya. Her mind was whirring with the implications, but she kept a calm exterior.

"There will be courts soon, too," said Venkdt. "When the garrison goes we'll build some new courthouses. No more shipping the serious cases back to Earth."

"That's great," said Maya.

"About the garrison," said Venkdt.

"Yes?"

"We'll need to deal with them."

Foveaux looked into Venkdt's eyes for additional clues as to what he meant, but found none.

"*How* would you like me to deal with them?" she said, cautiously.

"Well," said Venkdt, "I guess that's down to you. But they're over there, disloyal to the new regime, and they have arms. I don't expect them to do anything but it would be good to have them thoroughly neutralized." Venkdt belatedly heard the words he was saying. "Oh! I don't mean anything like that. But surely you could use the building, couldn't you? And it would be good to have them separated from their firepower. There are plenty of places we could billet them for the next couple of years or so before we can get them shipped back home."

"I'll see what I can do," said Maya. Her mind was already forming strategies.

"And you can start all this now?" said Venkdt.

"We can," said Maya. "We've always had a good relationship with the garrison, I'm sure it won't be a problem"

Venkdt offered his hand. "That's great, Maya, I knew I could rely on you."

"Of course you can, Mr President."

CHAPTER 14

The Garrison

Since its inception the USAN garrison on Mars had taken the role of a de facto police force. There was no need for a military presence on Mars. There were no human enemies capable of reaching the planet and there were no alien races threatening the human outpost there. The purpose of the garrison was symbolic. A great nation had to show it was prepared to defend its territory. There were approximately two hundred USAN Army personnel stationed at the garrison. They had naturally fallen to the role of police force.

When the research station finally closed down and handed over to the military Venkdt Mars had only a few thousand employees, mostly hand-picked and highly trained. Police services were rarely needed. Petty crimes and minor complaints were dealt with internally. Most assaults and other violent crimes, serious thefts and burglaries were again subject to internal review. Where credible evidence could be gathered the accused would be sent back to Earth to be processed through the criminal courts there. With the advent of the military police it was possible to process all but the most serious crimes on Mars itself. The garrison housed a court and also had a stockade, where short and medium term sentences could be served. Any criminals facing sentences longer than two or three years were almost always sent back to Earth, depending on the proximity of launch windows.

Crime levels on Mars were remarkably low. The garrison kept order well but as the population had grown it had proved difficult for the garrison to keep pace with it. In truth, Mars had been under policed for a number of years and the judicial system applied there was shaky and provisional.

Maya's plan involved volunteers from her security division running the military-police force from the garrison. She hoped to co-opt as many members of the garrison's personnel as possible and meld the two groups into a new unit. She had permission and finances from Venkdt to expand the garrison, adding room for more personnel and a larger stockade. She also planned for there to be a second smaller base in Allentown West, away from the centre of the city. There was a Venkdt Security building there already. She would expand out of that.

One of Maya's great gifts was her ability to delegate. That would be crucial in overseeing a rapidly expanding service. She knew how to select people with leadership qualities; level-headed, unshakeable, determined good delegators like herself. She already had a few in mind, and hoped to pick up some more from the garrison.

Garrison personnel usually served terms in multiples of two Earth years. Rotation levels were high, multiple terms being served mostly by the higher ranking. Maya wasn't sure what their attitude would be towards Martian independence. They were the only people on Mars with a sworn allegiance to serve the USAN, and who took their pay cheques directly from the home planet. Accepting Martian independence was a far more complex issue for them. They were not Martians.

Maya was confident that the higher ranking officers at the garrison and their superiors on Earth wouldn't be so stupid as to try to use the power they had at their disposal to attempt to quell the independence movement by force of arms. They were unlikely to pose any difficulties from that angle. What they might do was sit tight and refuse to enter into any form of dialogue. That posed a problem for Maya in that she needed their building. If some of their number joined her new police force, helping to cement the broad coalition that Venkdt was trying to build into every element of Martian civil society, that would be a bonus, but she had to have the physical garrison complex.

As well as denying the rump of the USAN force home-field advantage she wanted them separated from their armoury and communications centre. She also wanted them away from the centre of the city. Left alone with their arms and coms, and with nothing to do for two years while they waited for the launch window that would take them back home, Maya worried that they might turn to suppressing the new Martian government out of sheer boredom.

At this early stage, with the disorienting shock of rapid change still in effect, Maya hoped to evict the USAN force by negotiated settlement rather than under duress. She had had some dealings with Colonel Shaw in the past and hoped they might be able to come to some sort of agreement.

Maya sat at her desk looking at her terminal. She could call Colonel Shaw now and put her proposal to her, even send over some of the documentation she had prepared. It seemed reasonable, but something was staying Maya's hand. She tried to rationalise what it might be. All she could come up with was this: Colonel Katrina Shaw was, like herself, a woman of action. Obviously, she hadn't joined the military to sit behind her desk answering messages from across town. What a woman like Shaw would respond to was a physical presence. Maya knew she would have to play this with caution - there was absolutely no point in needlessly antagonising someone who she needed as an ally, or at very least a neutral.

She decided, after thinking very carefully, that she would take three dozen of the volunteers for the new military-police force over to the garrison and chat with Colonel Shaw woman to woman. She was sure the colonel would not concede any ground whatsoever. She decided she would be blunt about her demands but courteous and understanding of the colonel's position. All the while she wanted the colonel to be aware that she too had a force of physically able people behind her.

In the spirit of immediacy that was current amongst the people of Mars Maya decided she would gather together the force of thirty-six personnel she thought she needed and head over to the garrison right then. She looked at her terminal. It was not long before 21:30. In her mind she ran over what she needed to do and how long it might take. Getting the word out to the people she needed, organising transport, briefing her people and taking the ride over there might take, in total, about two and a half hours. She gently chuckled to herself and shook her head. There was a good chance that by the time she was having her head-to-head with Colonel Katrina Shaw of the USAN Martian Garrison it would be close to midnight.

"Yes!?" The tone was exasperated, frustrated and irritated.

"It's Foveaux. I need three transports and arms for around forty officers. Can you do that?"

The voice at the other end of the line quickly changed and panickingly replied, "Ms Foveaux? Yes, we have three transports here. What arms do you need?"

"What do you have? Rifles maybe? Side arms?"

The voice paused in thought. "We can do the side arms, I don't think we have that many rifles. And we'll need authorisation."

"You have the authorisation, I'm sending it now. How many rifles do you have?"

"I think . . . sixteen, maybe?"

"Okay, we'll take them all. How about body armour, helmets?"

"We have some. We have the riot suits."

"Good. I'll be sending some officers down soon. I want them kitted out with as much riot gear as we have. Everyone gets a side arm, everyone who gets a rifle is assigned to the first transport. Second transport is the remaining rifles and the third is side arms only."

"Yes, sir."

"I want this to be ready when I get there. I'll be there within the hour."

Maya hung up and immediately made her next call. She worked her way through three senior officers, telling them essentially the same thing; they needed to gather a dozen or so of their people and meet her in the transport bay within the hour. Officers could be pulled off non-essential duties, given overtime or even be called at home. She needed the bodies and she needed them fast.

When she'd finished with the calls Maya made her way down to the quartermaster's office. It was located above the transport bay and shared many of its facilities. She approached the desk. "I want full body armour and a rifle. I need a tactical helmet, too. One of the newer ones with the flip-up fronts?"

The woman at the desk was servile and efficient. "Yes, sir," she said, and scampered away from the desk to find the items requested. Maya walked to the window overlooking the transport bay. Directly below her were three transports with a handful of officers mingling about them. As she watched more joined. Some were clambering into the armour they had just picked up, or were checking their rifles.

Two officers arrived at the quartermaster's desk behind her.

"Hello," one shouted, "we're supposed to pick up some kit? Special operation or something?"

The quartermaster's assistant returned with Maya's kit and placed it on the desk. "Hold your comdevs over here, please," she said to the two officers, "for sizes, etcetera."

Maya took her kit and strapped herself into the body armour. She slung the rifle over her shoulder and placed the tactical helmet on her head. It offered a head-up display, analysing whatever was picked up from the helmet mounted cameras and overlaying what its AI decided might be tactically useful information over the wearer's view. To test it Maya looked at the two officers who were now checking their weapons and putting on armour. The HUD immediately told her their names and ranks. It informed her that they had no criminal records, and that their weapons were registered to Venkdt Security.

She flipped the visor up so her face was fully visible and walked down to the transports waiting below. As she neared the transports a man and a woman approached her.

"Commissioner Foveaux," the man said, "we have fourteen officers here beside us and we're expecting the rest very soon."

"Good," said Foveaux. "I want the most heavily armed in the first transport with me, less heavily in the second and so on."

"Very good, Commissioner," said the woman. "Where are we going?"

Foveaux fixed her with a gentle stare. "I'll come to that in a minute. What's important is that we look scary and capable."

"Yes, Commissioner."

"Can you do that?"

"Yes, Commissioner."

Foveaux spoke to the man. "Let me know when the rest are here and I'll begin the briefing." As she was speaking another transport pulled into the bay. Two officers got out of the front and walked to the rear doors. They opened them and ushered out a group of worse-for-wear party-goers who appeared to be chained together. Behind them two more officers emerged from the transport. "Ind-dep-end-ent Maaars!" one of the party-goers bellowed. An officer prodded him in the ribs with a night-stick.

"Keep it down," he said, as they marched the revellers through the building for processing.

The stragglers seemed to arrive as one whole group. Maybe they'd met up at the refectory or had all just come off duty together. As they gathered by the transports, fiddling with their weapons and armour, Maya called out, "Listen up! Gather round me here." Officers duly congregated in a semi-circle about her. She waited for them to settle down.

"We are going over to the garrison. We are going there so I can negotiate with Colonel Shaw about the garrison's status now that Mars has gained independence. I expect Colonel Shaw will be resistant to any arguments I have to make. So be it. The reason we are going in force is twofold. Firstly, I want to show the colonel that we have force of arms and are a more than equal match for the forces under her command. Secondly, I want to deter the colonel from resisting the changes that have recently taken place by denying our authority. In short, I don't want her to try to arrest me.

"This will be a delicate operation. It will be a show of strength, not an attack. Realistically, I don't expect the colonel to accede to our demands. I do expect her to have plenty to think about once we have left. Questions?"

A hand was raised. "What do we do if they, you know, get rough?"

"Any sign of trouble we pull back. I'll say it again; this is not an attack. If things start to escalate we pull out immediately. But all the while we're there we need to look serious and we need to look plausible."

"When are we going?"

"Now."

The garrison was housed in a three storey building which was mostly underground. It was built into the rock, the rear side of it ending in a solid wall of Martian permafrost, but the front side facing an open area, like a standard office building on Earth. The open area served as a parade ground and training area, as well as a transport hub. Above this area was a huge vaulted Perspex ceiling, criss-crossed by the beams and struts supporting it. The technology was pre-dome, though the building was actually newer than that.

The garrison had two approaches, one from directly in front and one from the side. Foveaux's forces came from the tunnel to the side. Exiting the tunnel the three transports found themselves in a wider space with a perimeter wall and an entrance to the compound beyond guarded by two USAN troops.

Maya got out of the first transport and approached the guards. "Can we come in? I'd like to talk with Colonel Shaw."

"Do you have an appointment, Ms?" said one of the guards.

"I don't," said Maya, "but it's urgent. Could you get the colonel out here for me?"

The guards conferred, then one wandered away a short distance, mumbling into his comdev. The other spoke to Foveaux. "We're trying to get hold of the colonel for you now, Ms. Would you mind waiting back in the transport?"

"I would, actually," said Foveaux. She walked back to the lead transport and banged on the side. The back doors opened and officers spilled out. She repeated the operation on the other two transports until she was surrounded by armed officers. As planned, the most heavily armed were at the front. The guard now mumbled something into his comdev. He conferred a bit then put the comdev away.

He approached Foveaux. "Ms, could you please have your people wait in the transports?" he said. If he was nervous, he wasn't showing it.

"We're fine, thank you," said Foveaux.

The guard backed away without argument, once again speaking into his comdev. The other guard approached him and spoke quietly into his ear. He nodded, and the two guards went back to their positions either side of the gate. The second guard shouted to Foveaux, "The colonel will be with you presently." He went back to guarding, looking bored.

Ten minutes later Colonel Katrina Shaw left the garrison building and strode toward the gate. She was flanked by her subordinate officers, Majors Edley and Bowers. Behind them were at least a dozen armed soldiers of the USAN. They carried their sub machine guns in their hands, marching in step with their commanding officers.

Shaw was an unusually tall woman, and broad. She had swimmer's shoulders and her dark hair was closely cropped. She had strong features. Within a few seconds they were at the gate. Shaw gestured to the guards, who raised the barrier, and she walked through to meet Foveaux. Her phalanx of guards remained inside the compound, two deep across the entrance.

"Colonel Shaw," she said, "you must be Maya Foveaux. We've talked before, nice to meet you finally. What can we do for you?"

Maya had planned to offer Shaw her hand, but reacting to Shaw's tone, she felt disinclined to do so. "I'm here representing the new Martian Security Service. I'd like to discuss the handover of security operations."

"'Hand over of security operations,' well, well," said Shaw. "My commanding officer hasn't informed me of any such handover, so until I have a signed order from her there isn't much to discuss."

"Your commanding officer won't know about it because the decision came from me. We're taking over your operations. That's just how it is. I'd like it very much if you'd work with me. You and your people have a wealth of knowledge and other resources that could be of great benefit to our new service. We can work out terms and a timetable and do this in a civilized manner. I can offer a job to any of your people who want one."

Shaw shifted her weight from one leg to the other. "And on whose authority are you acting?"

"The authority of the people of Mars and President Elect Charles Venkdt."

Shaw nodded. "I'm an officer of the USAN Army. It says so right here on my shirt," she said, pointing to her shirt. "We swear an oath of allegiance to our country, and we answer to our commander-in-chief, President Cortes."

She took a step closer to Foveaux. "I do not recognise the authority of Charles Venkdt, so unless I hear otherwise from my superiors I will continue to run this garrison as the USAN has ordered me to."

She turned to walk away but Foveaux called after her. "How long have you been here? Nine years?"

Shaw stopped and turned back. "It'll be ten, next spring."

"You like it here, right? You're settled. What's back there for you? I know most of your men and women do a tour or two and rotate back, but not you. You're one of us, Katrina. A Martian. Help us build the new Mars."

Shaw eyed her suspiciously. "I'd prefer you to address me as Colonel Shaw," she said, "and I will not be able to assist you building a new country." She spat the words out contemptuously. "My loyalty is to the USAN, under whose president I serve. Until I receive the order I will not arrest you for treason, sedition or a hundred and one other things I could think of. Until then, get your goddamned tanks off my lawn.

Because I promise you this; if you want a real live shooting war I'll give you one." She turned and disappeared through her armed escort, who remained at the entryway staring out at Foveaux's Martian Security Service personnel, who stared back. There were maybe ten metres between the two groups, both carrying arms, both staring silently across the border between Martian soil and the one remaining vestige of the USAN's authority on the Martian surface.

Foveaux waited a while. She hadn't expected the meeting to go in her favour but she was disappointed with Shaw's entrenched attitude. Still, a point had been made. The garrison was contained. Shaw must know for sure now that she was outnumbered by the MSS and lacked popular support in the wider community. It would keep her at bay but Foveaux really needed the garrison to be totally neutralized. She would have liked to have Shaw on-side, and on a more prosaic level she wanted the garrison building itself. She could work on that later.

Foveaux banged the side of a transport with her fist. "Okay people, load up," she said. Her officers dutifully trudged to their transports and climbed aboard. Foveaux saw them all in before she took her place in the first one and led them back through the tunnel.

By the time she got back to her office it was late. The signing back in of all the kit and the debrief had taken longer than necessary. It was gone 02:00 in the morning when Foveaux sat back in her chair. She felt exhausted. Maybe it was the long day, or the adrenaline from the stand-off with Shaw. There was a slightly dreamlike quality to it all, like it maybe wasn't actually happening. It seemed too fast, too crazy.

She thought about what she would need to do next. Her first priority was to get the MSS fully established. Lacking the garrison building she would have to run it all from Venkdt Security for the time being. She worried about how that might look, what with the conflict of interests. She reasoned that she might get away with it for a few months. Everyone was so giddy with independence fever they would hardly notice. Maybe she could ask Venkdt for a new site. He

EPHIALTES

might have some warehouses or disused facilities that could do the job for a while.

She felt confident with her personnel. They had done well, doing exactly what had been asked of them. She had worked with them a long time and knew they could be trusted. The work ahead was going to be tough, but she felt assured. The only cloud on the horizon was Colonel Katrina Shaw and the USAN Garrison. She kept mulling over what her next move might be. Shaw would have to leave the garrison at some point. There were no flights back to Earth for nearly two years. Was she really going to sit it out for that long? Maybe she should have tried a more diplomatic approach. Shaw was the key. Maybe she would work on Shaw. She made a note on her terminal: 'Invite Colonel Shaw for dinner.' "Scratch that," she said aloud to the terminal. "Invite Colonel Shaw for breakfast." She then set to work on some documents and did not fall asleep until well into the night.

Katrina Shaw was a career soldier. She had signed up when she was twenty-one and fresh out of school. She had done officer training and risen quickly through the ranks, eventually attaining the position of colonel. She had been posted around the world and had requested to be considered for the Mars job should it become available. The stars aligned for her and, coming off a posting to Australia, she left for Mars in 2231.

She was well suited to the post. Though fascinated by military matters her strengths were man-management. The role on Mars was an odd one for the army. It was part symbolic and part police force. Shaw found it interesting, and she liked the smalltown feel of the place. The only thing she missed was the horses. There were some on Mars, but a trot around a dome was a poor substitute for the wild rides she had taken across the New Mexico deserts when she was a girl. She still rode occasionally, either in a dome or an IVR, but she sometimes longed for the open spaces.

Shaw arrived at Foveaux's HQ at 07:00 in the morning. Foveaux was asleep at her desk. She woke with a start and leapt up. "I'm so sorry, Colonel, I must've fallen asleep," she said.

"No apologies necessary," said Shaw. "What is it?"

"I just thought we should talk, woman to woman, without the theatrics."

"Okay. I'm listening."

Foveaux gestured to a sofa. "Please, sit down," she said. They sat on the sofa.

"I know you're in a tough position. I want to help you negotiate a path through it in a way that's best for you and best for us."

"I thought I was coming here for breakfast," said Shaw.

"Of course," said Foveaux. She spoke to her comdev. "Can we get some food in here, please? Two breakfasts and some coffee."

"Yes, sir," came the reply.

"You're in a tough situation. You have to hold your position as instructed, even though you know it's pointless and won't achieve anything. We will prevail, eventually, with you or without you."

Shaw had a quizzical smirk on her face. "I guess you're going to advise me on what I should do next?"

"Yes, I am. This doesn't have to be a fight. If you join with us you can bring all of your subordinates with you. They won't be committing treason, they'll just be following orders."

"I thought I made my position clear last night."

"You did, abundantly so. That was before you knew about this." Foveaux tapped her comdev and her terminal screen was displayed on the wall. A document there showed precise battle orders for an MSS attack on the garrison. There were diagrams, times and troop numbers. Shaw studied the plan carefully then turned to Foveaux.

"First of all, that's a terrible plan of attack. I can see you're a goddamned amateur at this and you're right about needing help. Secondly, this is obviously a bluff."

"Well," said Foveaux, "we can debate the first point, but you're right on the second. It's a bluff. But what if you decided to take it at face value? Surely capitulating in the face of such insurmountable odds would be the honourable thing to do. You would be able to justify surrendering your forces in order to save them from a massacre. They would be answerable to you and off the hook for any charges that might get thrown about at a later date. And you would be able to justify your actions as the only course you could take in order to avoid unnecessary loss of life."

Shaw thought. "I don't think I could convince a court martial that I found these bullshit plans in the least bit plausible."

A droid entered the room with the breakfast. Shaw poured herself a coffee. "And if I can't do that it leaves me on the hook for all of it. Treason, Commissioner Foveaux, and by a commanding officer no less."

"Surrendering isn't treasonous and I'd make sure there was plenty of evidence that you were acting under duress, with no other reasonable option open to you. In ten, fifteen years this will all be a distant memory. They'll forget all about it - maybe even give you a medal. Help me build the MSS. Don't stand in the way of history."

Shaw took a long draw from her coffee. "Thank you for breakfast, Commissioner Foveaux. I wish you the best of luck in all your endeavours." She held out her hand. Foveaux took it and shook it firmly. "I'll look forward to the attack," she said, and winked. She stood and went to leave the room. Maya stood too.

"What if we do attack?" she said.

"Now why on God's green Earth would you do that?" said Shaw.

"To make it look plausible," said Maya.

Shaw stopped in the doorway. "You'd do that? Bring two opposing forces together and risk a real live shooting war just to make it look like you mean business?"

"If I have to, yes," said Foveaux. "Do I have to?"

Shaw stepped back into the room, square on to Foveaux, eye to eye. She was close enough that Foveaux could see the fine downy hair on her cheeks. "Commissioner," she said, "I sure as hell hope you're a better reader of people than you are a military tactician. Do what you need to do, but make damn sure you do it right." She turned smartly on her heel and left.

Shaw's office was located on the second floor of the garrison building. She had a window overlooking the parade ground below. The window was open, allowing her to hear the bangs clearly.

She had been seated at her desk discussing procurements and leave provision with her two senior officers, Majors Bowers and Edley. The two issues were pressing since the disputed nature - disputed by them, anyway - of the planet threw up many concerns in these areas. Shaw had elected to presume that the garrison's personnel were effectively under house arrest. Venturing out of the compound and into the city seemed foolhardy. It could be read the wrong way by the MSS or lead to conflict with overzealous Martian citizens. All leave would have to be cancelled and reallocated later. Shaw was trying to figure some sort of additional compensation and distraction as she didn't want her charges going stir crazy.

Procurement was the other pressing issue. The garrison was in the habit of sending transports out to the ports and warehouses to collect goods as necessary. They would now need to arrange deliveries. It would also be worthwhile stockpiling as much as they could in case any developing situation demanded it. Could they do that without raising suspicion? And what about the funding? Payment was usually made directly from Earth. What was the situation with that? There was lots to discuss and the meeting had been dragging on for most of the afternoon.

Bowers was a no-nonsense Texan, old for his twenty-six years and by the book. He thought in clear, straight lines and had trouble with the idea of adaptation or flexibility. He was great at executing orders, getting things done. Less so at thinking problems through. Edley was the more thoughtful of the two. She could analyse and assess as well as act. They were of equal rank but Shaw thought of Edley as her number two. Bowers would follow an order like a dog would follow a thrown ball; excitedly and with tunnel vision concentration. Edley was much more useful as a sounding board. She could contribute to a discussion and suggest strategies and alternatives. She might notice an angle that Shaw had not, and because of that she was a great second to have around. Bowers' contribution that afternoon had mainly been to point out where the disruptions to their current systems were. Shaw and Edley had provided the possible workarounds.

The first bang had sounded suddenly and mysteriously, instantly superimposing the thought 'What was that?' over all others. Maybe it was something falling over in the stores, or an accidentally discharged weapon. The subsequent bangs came rapidly and immediately spoke of something unusual. Shaw had instantly snapped her head upright at the first sound, like a dog with its ears pricked up, and saw the subtle flashes illuminate the room from the window for a split second before each of the following reports. "What is it?" said Bowers. Shaw and Edley were already headed to the window. Shaw gestured to Edley to keep low, and together they cautiously peered out.

"Stay down," said Shaw.

Shaw's window afforded them a view almost directly down the main tunnel entrance at the front of the garrison. Like the side entrance, the tunnel opened out into a small patch of uncultivated land, beyond which was a guarded entry point to the parade ground and the garrison building itself. Shaw could see that the guards had been overcome and were not at their positions. She guessed they had been sneak attacked with flash-bang grenades, bundled over and tied up before they even knew what happened. Shaw craned a little to try to get a view of the side entrance. She couldn't see it clearly but guessed the same had happened there. She tried to think how many bangs she had heard. Five? Six? She couldn't recall.

"Get everyone together. Seal the doors. No one fires without an explicit command from me," said Shaw. "Open coms. Bowers, take two platoons to the third floor refectory. Cover the side tunnel. Do not open fire."

"Yes, sir," Bowers said smartly, and disappeared.

Shaw looked at Edley. "Take two more platoons to the entry hall. Await my command."

"Yes, sir," said Edley. "What about the admin offices?"

"Two guys per office, all along the front. No one is to shoot, okay?"

"Yes, sir," Edley said, then left.

Shaw peaked out of the window again. She could see the outline of a transport in the tunnel. She guessed there were more behind it. Foveaux's troops had streamed down the tunnel, neutralized the guards and were now massing behind the perimeter wall. Foveaux was putting her plan into effect. But that was madness. Would anyone really show their opposite number their plan of attack, then put that plan into effect hours later? Was it a bluff? If so, which part? Shaw could hear muffled sounds from behind the wall; soft footfalls and whispered commands. Louder were the shouts in her own building.

'You, yes you!'

'Keep moving!'

'Stay low.'

Distantly she heard Bowers and Edley issuing commands. Their voices carried authority. They did not sound panicked. Good. That placid concentration would be transferred to the soldiers they were commanding.

As Shaw watched the barrier at the main gate rose into the air. She first heard and then saw a small armoured transport rumble down the tunnel into the scrubland then continue through the gate. It moved slowly and came to a stop in the middle of the parade ground. The engine cut out and there was silence. Shaw looked on, waiting for the next play. She spoke to her comdev. "Major Edley, are you in position?"

"In position, Colonel."

"Major Bowers, are you in position?"

"Yes, Colonel."

"Hold you positions and await further orders."

There was a crackle and a short whine of feedback from the lonely transport on the parade ground. "This is Commissioner Maya Foveaux of the Martian Security Service. I would like to speak with Colonel Katrina Shaw."

Shaw stood. She thought about shouting from the window but quickly realised the moment called for something more dignified. She moved to the stairwell and rapidly descended to the ground floor lobby. The lobby was filled with silent troops. Some of them were not in uniform but all were bearing arms. Edley approached Shaw. "Are you going out there?"

"I am."

"We'll have you covered."

"Thank you, Major Edley."

Edley walked with Shaw and opened the door for her. Shaw stepped out and, turning back, said, "If they try anything cute let 'em have it."

"Yes, sir," said Edley, closing the door behind her.

Shaw walked at a deliberate pace to the armoured transport. She glanced right to confirm what she already guessed about the second entrance. There were no guards. She stopped in front of the transport. "Here I am," she said.

The door opened and Foveaux stepped down. She walked around to the front of the transport and held out her hand to Shaw. Shaw looked at the hand and then back up at Foveaux's face. "Commissioner," she said, "until yesterday we had only exchanged the occasional message. This is the third time in twenty-four hours you have approached me directly. Are you stalking me?"

Maya withdrew her hand and concealed her disappointment. "Just doing my job," she said. "Could we go inside? I have something I need to show you."

Shaw stared at her, not betraying any emotion. Without breaking her gaze she lifted her comdev to her face. "Major Edley, we're coming back inside."

"Yes, sir,"

Shaw gestured toward the garrison building and they set off towards it. Edley opened the door to let them in.

The heavy armoured door closed behind them with a solid clunk. They made their way through the crowded lobby. All heads followed them as they walked to the stairs.

"Would you please come with us, Major Edley?" said Shaw. Edley nodded and the three of them ascended the staircase to Shaw's office.

From the third floor refectory Bowers was listening in to the coms. "Listen," he said to his second in command, "you stay here and await my orders. I'm going to the colonel's office. Watch the perimeter."

Shaw took her place behind her desk. She gestured for Foveaux to sit.

"I prefer to stand," said Foveaux.

"What is it?" said Shaw.

Foveaux pulled a sheaf of papers from inside her body armour. "It's the articles of surrender." She placed them on Shaw's desk. "I'd like you to sign them and then address your troops explaining the surrender."

Shaw eyed her carefully, looking for any signs of weakness. "If I don't sign?"

"We can hold you under siege indefinitely. Don't make this difficult. Sign the papers and you and your officers can see out the next two years at a comfortable Venkdt secure facility waiting for the next flight home. It's the only reasonable option."

"Whoever told you I was reasonable?" grunted Shaw.

Bowers slid his body along the wall, stopping at the half-open door to Shaw's office. He craned his head over his left shoulder and looked sideways into the room. He could see Shaw, Edley and Foveaux. He'd missed the start of the conversation but managed to catch Shaw saying to Edley, "Hand me a pen, would you?" He drew his pistol and a bead of sweat ran down his temple.

Shaw had just taken the pen when Bowers turned into the room. Shaw looked up at him then down at the pistol in his hand. Foveaux saw the pistol too and instinctively put her hand on her own side arm.

"Stand easy, Major," said Shaw. Bowers glanced at Foveaux and, seeing her hand moving, swung his pistol toward her.

Edley moved toward Bowers and held her arm up across his chest, saying, "It's okay, stand down." In the moment it took Bowers to shake her off Foveaux's gun was pointing at him, and his at her.

"Put the weapon down, Major," said Shaw. Her voice carried a calm authority, but Bowers didn't waver.

"What's going on here?" he said.

"We're in discussions with the commissioner. Put the gun down, Major, that is an order."

"What's the pen for? What's she making you sign?" Bowers seemed panicked. Foveaux held her gun pointed precisely at Bowers' head. She could see he was wearing body armour. She could see he was nervous. She was waiting for the slightest sign he was going to act. She felt an intense concentration.

"Put the weapon down," said Shaw. Bowers just stared at her. He couldn't quite comprehend what he was seeing. The commissioner who was leading the attack on his garrison was now in the commanding officer's office. What was happening? Was Shaw a traitor? Did the commissioner have her acting under duress? What was happening?

Shaw flicked a look at Edley. She was well placed to wrestle Bowers to the ground, but it would be a huge risk. Foveaux to her right was an unknown quantity. Might she think the whole scene had been orchestrated? Would she think it was a trap? Or would a woman with balls big enough to assault a USAN barracks in broad daylight have the stone-cold level headedness to evaluate the situation correctly and do the right thing?

"Major Bowers," said Shaw, "Commissioner Foveaux has been asked by the new Martian president to take control of our garrison. Though she is prepared to do that by force she has offered us generous terms of surrender. Since we are in no position to resist, and to avoid needless violence, we will be taking her up on that offer. I am about to sign the instrument of surrender, so I'll thank you to put your weapon away, and we'll proceed."

"We can't surrender," said Bowers, with true panic in his eyes. He moved his gun now between Foveaux and Shaw. "What are you talking about? This woman attacked us."

"Put the gun down," said Shaw. At that moment Edley launched herself at Bowers, crashing him into the wall. There was a deafening bang as he discharged his weapon. Foveaux felt something hit her head but she maintained her aim on Bowers, who was half slumped against the wall.

He cracked Edley in the side of the head with his elbow and was semi-righting himself when Foveaux shouted, "Drop the gun now!" Even as her words faded he was re-extending his arm in her direction. She fired, the deafening sound filling the room and the 'smokeless' charge giving its distinctive smell. Bowers fell back, blood trickling from a single hole just below his right eye.

Foveaux kept him covered with her gun as he hit the floor and stopped moving, a small pool of blood spreading behind his head.

Edley was already shouting into her comdev, "We need a medic up here, now!" and moving to Bowers body. She quickly checked for vital signs and though he was still alive she knew he would be dead very soon.

Shaw spoke to Foveaux. "You can put that gun away now, Commissioner." Foveaux withdrew from her tunnel of concentration and was somehow back in the room. She lowered her gun and without even thinking about it raised her other hand to her head. She could feel a warm sticky liquid and pulling her hand away she could see it was blood.

"Let me look at that," said Shaw. She pulled Foveaux's head toward her and gave it a cursory examination. "Glancing blow," she said. "You're lucky. Couple of centimetres lower and you'd be going the same place as him. Are you okay?"

Foveaux blinked. "I'm fine. Where were we?"

"Well," said Shaw, "we need to get this sorted out first. Where's that medic?"

"Bowers is dead," said Edley.

Outside a group of troops had gathered at the top of the stairs. They had their rifles drawn and they looked serious and intense. A medic squeezed between them and ran to the office, where she squatted next to Bowers and began to work on him.

"Back to the lobby," said Shaw through the door. "It's all over here. The situation is under control."

Edley watched the medic work but she knew it was futile.

"Where's that pen?" said Shaw.

"I think it's still in your hand, Colonel," said Edley.

"Oh yes. It is," said Shaw. "Will you please come here and witness this for me?"

Edley moved to the desk and watched as Shaw signed the papers in two places as Foveaux pointed them out to her. Foveaux was clutching at her head with her other hand and blood was seeping between her fingers.

Shaw called to the medic, "When you've finished there I have an injured officer here." She looked at Foveaux. "So you didn't get your bloodless coup. Damn shame, you came pretty close." She offered her hand to Foveaux who shook it gratefully.

"I'm sorry it happened this way," she said.

"Me too," said Shaw. "Are you going to be taking me back with you?"

"There's no need. I'll leave a small deployment here. You can gather your things, speak to your troops, organise the handover."

"You trust me to do that?"

"I have your word."

"Thank you," said Shaw.

"I'll come back tomorrow for an official handover."

"Let me see you out," said Shaw, and she went to guide Foveaux around the medic and the body of Bowers, which had been stripped to the waist and was now staring lifelessly at the ceiling.

"You forgot this," Edley called after them. As Foveaux turned Edley handed her the articles of surrender. They were smeared with blood.

CHAPTER 15

Old Friends

Bobby picked Christina up around seven. They were at the restaurant by eight. They had stopped by at one of the older domes - Bobby wanted to reminisce about the times, many years before, when Christina had brought him there. There was a children's play area in the dome and Bobby, as a thirteen-year-old, was torn between rejecting it out of hand as a worldly teenager and showing off his physical prowess to his oh-so-sophisticated (as she seemed to him then) guardian.

Christina had started babysitting for the Karjalainens when she was around fifteen. Bobby was ten and Anthony was eight; she could just about handle them. She knew them vaguely from school. Being rich kids they had all gone to the exclusive Glenn Academy. While Venkdt and Karjalainen were business rivals their partners had met each other through the school and had quickly made friends. They and the kids were often in and out of each other's houses. Christina was too old to play with the boys as peers but she had a strong maternal streak and loved to spend time looking after them, helping them play together.

When Bobby was sixteen he had asked Christina out on a date. Not quite sure of the dynamics of such an interlude she had cautiously agreed. In truth, she was quite a young twenty-one-year-old. She had spent a lot of her adolescence wrapped up in books, either schoolwork or her adored fantasy novels. She was mildly shy and stood off from the world a little.

Bobby, on the other hand, wanted to grow up fast. Nothing ever fazed him or gave him pause and, like most teenagers, he knew everything. Why wouldn't you ask your babysitter on a date? She was kind of cute, and that reserved way she had immediately piqued one's interest. What was going on in that hinterland behind the coy smile and gentle flick of the hair? There you are, sixteen, a man or as good as. Ask the girl out. Why not?

As the waiter brought their drinks Christina looked around the room. "Remember the first time you brought me here?"

"I do," said Bobby. "It was the first date I ever had."

"Oh!" said Christina, "so it *was* a date."

"Of course. What did you think it was?"

"I just thought one of the kids I looked after was treating me as a thank you for the many times I had taken care of him, played with him, tucked him up in bed and read him stories."

Bobby smiled. "Maybe that too."

"And anyway, you never called afterwards," Christina smiled back.

"Well, you were a little intimidating, I guess."

"Intimidating! Me!"

"You know; sophisticated older woman."

"Ha!" said Christina. "You were so funny, so full of yourself."

Bobby nodded. "And I hope I haven't changed."

He had changed. The bright sparkle in his eyes had dimmed a little. The 'Let's do it here! Let's do it now!' enthusiasm had been dialled back a little, too. Christina wondered if it was the war, or if it was just that he was older now.

"What are you up to now?" said Christina.

"I'm just staying at my dad's place."

"No work?"

"No. I've got a combat pension and some money from the book. I guess I should figure out what I'm going to do next. No rush."

"How is your dad?"

"He's not great. I don't think he's got long left."

"I'm sorry. Have you seen him?"

"Yes. I've been going to the hospital."

"That's great."

"I don't think he's got the energy to argue anymore," Bobby shrugged.

"But it's great he's talking to you again."

"I guess. It's why I came back, I suppose."

"Family's the most important thing, Bobby. It's really good that you've made peace with your dad before . . ."

Bobby noticed her discomfort.

"I wouldn't go as far as 'making peace.' He can stand to have me in the room with him. Progress, I suppose. How about your dad?"

"Well, as it happens, he's the president of Mars. I always knew he'd make something of himself."

They laughed.

"How's that going," said Bobby.

"It's sort of ordinary, at the moment. He was always the unofficial Mayor of Mars Town anyway. I guess this just makes it official. Or not official, depending on your point of view. There was some dodgy business over at the garrison yesterday. Our security people were supposed to take the place over but something happened and someone got killed."

"I heard about that on the streams."

"It's awful that someone got hurt but I think it's all over now."

"How about you? How's the law?"

"It's good. I'm working mostly for my dad, taking on the odd thing here and there."

"And your personal life?"

Christina grimaced. "My *private* life? Private, I guess?" she offered.

"You can do better than that," Bobby teased.

"Well, I'm still a spinster, if that's what you mean. What about you? Still breaking hearts?"

"No, I'm a spinster too."

"I thought you were all partnered up. Back on Earth. It didn't work out?"

Bobby shrugged. "You know. The war. She had to travel a lot for her work. It kind of . . ." his sentence trailed off.

"What was her name?"

"Askel Lund. She's an engineer. One of the top development people at Helios, actually."

"Askel," said Christina. "It's a nice name."

"It is a nice name," said Bobby. "Shall we order?"

Christina was determined to find out about Askel. She thought of Bobby like a younger brother and instinctively wanted to look out for him. There had been rare occasions when she had imagined what it might be like if she and Bobby were a couple. He was a good man and certainly not hard to look at. But that was an idle daydream. Christina was too down-to-earth for a livewire like Bobby and besides, it would just be weird.

"So Askel travels a lot?" said Christina as they ate.

"She does," said Bobby, between mouthfuls.

"She sounds like just your type."

Bobby paused. "Do I have a type?"

Christina thought. "I guess not. What I mean is that you're a doer. You go places, you do things. It sounds like she is too, so it seems like it should have been a good match."

"Askel's a great gal, and we got on really well together. But we both had lots of work commitments and we were based in different countries. It was a strange time, with a war going on and all that."

Christina surveyed Bobby's face as he ate. He seemed rattled.

"So it was just the war that came between you, then?"

Bobby put his cutlery down. "Are you my mum?" he asked. He tried to make it sound playful but the underlying irritation seeped through.

"I just want you to be happy, Bobby. Am I prying?"

"You are, a little bit."

"I'm sorry." They carried on eating but Christina still couldn't let it go. After a few moments she said, "What about when the war was ending? You didn't think about getting back in touch with her?"

EPHIALTES

"Look," said Bobby, "Askel's great, right? She's terrific, she really is. She's a great person, she's incredibly talented, good at her job and she's beautiful too. War is a strange time. I'd finished my tours and was being let go from the army. My moment in the sun was over. Askel's star was rising higher and higher and I knew I just had to let her go. I always knew I was going to come back here and I couldn't see Askel in some backwater like Mars. It's just not where she belongs. I could see how it was going to end up so I had to walk away." He looked sad and thoughtful. "She was . . ." he began, but he didn't finish the sentence.

"I didn't mean to upset you," said Christina.

"It's okay," said Bobby. "I guess everything has a way of working out in the end so . . ." He paused. "I'm sure it was all for the best."

Christina looked at Bobby sympathetically, nodding. "If you love her, set her free," she said, absentmindedly.

Bobby looked at her with a screwed-up face. "*Did you just say that?*" he said.

Christina snapped upright and she caught herself. "No!" she said. "I absolutely did not. You just imagined it."

They carried on eating.

CHAPTER 16

Outrage

"If I offered you a million bucks would you sell me that skirt you're wearing right now?"

"For a million bucks, yes, I think I would."

"But I mean right now. You can't change or send out for a replacement. You take it off here, now, and hand it over."

"I think I still would for a million."

"Okay, here's the thing, it's not even that. For a start, it's not a million, it's cost plus ten percent. How much was the skirt?"

"I don't want to . . ."

"How much was the skirt, Lorene?"

"It was a hundred and twenty dollars. On sale."

"Okay, a hundred and twenty dollars plus ten per is a hundred and thirty-two dollars. Let's call it a hundred and forty. If I came to your office, ripped your skirt off and left a hundred and forty dollars on your desk, how would you feel?"

"And you'd love to do that, wouldn't you?"

Farrell smiled. "This isn't about me, it's about you. How would you feel?"

Lorene thought. "I don't know. Violated, I guess. Robbed?"

"Exactly!" Farrell jabbed the air with his finger. "Violated and robbed. It's not a trade unless both parties agree. Robbery. Exactly!"

"However, if you were going to take my skirt unannounced I'd rather you left a hundred and forty dollars than didn't."

"Not the point at all. It's a crime. A major crime."

"So what do we do?"

"We have to make it right. Not only is it criminal, causing huge distress and damage to Venkdt Corporation and their shareholders, it also affects national security. The world runs on deuterium. All the while we have control over its production we are energy independent. If we are forced to buy our deuterium from an independent state we are no longer energy independent; we are reliant on them. They could withhold supplies, raise prices on a whim, whatever. We would be totally beholden to them and that is not acceptable. Those deuterium processing facilities belong to the USAN. Their value is far beyond their dollar worth."

"You haven't answered the question."

"Not up to us. It's up to the big guy. It's up to us to *advise him*. We have to impress on him what is at stake.

"And we have to give him options.

"We can give him those; trade embargoes, diplomatic channels and all that. But it's bullshit. Any trade embargo is going to hurt us far more than it's going to hurt them. The clever bastards have waited until they didn't need us anymore. We need that deuterium. What do they need from us? Diplomacy is up the spout too. Our most senior person on that planet is the colonel from the garrison; she was put under house arrest yesterday. We're screwed - we have nothing to offer him. The only people who have anything they can put on the table are Andrews' merry band at defence. We've got nothing. Nothing."

"The meeting has been bumped forward to 14:00 this afternoon. I can get you a teleconference with Andrews before then. Would that be useful?"

Farrell thought, distractedly. "Yes, it would. Do that. If we present together it won't look so much like we have nothing to bring to the party. I'll get behind Andrews and back her up. She's got guns and shit - that's the only thing that's going to get this mess sorted out." Farrell stared out of the window. "I used to think politics was a noble calling. Debate, reason. People, nations even, talking things out instead of fighting. Finding common ground, compromising, building by common consent. But over the last seven years I've come to realise, and this is just demonstrating it all over again, that just being right doesn't count for shit. You don't win the argument by making your point better than the other guy, or by persuading people of their logical errors. At base, when it comes down to it, you prevail by punching the other guy harder than he can punch you. And first, if possible." He looked at Lorene. "We do all the arguing and persuading here, don't we? And it hasn't got us anywhere. Andrews is in charge of punching."

Lorene was fiddling with her comdev. "Andrews has a window at 12:15. Should I book you fifteen minutes?"

"Do it."

Directly in front of the president's huge oak desk in the New Oval Office, set back a way, were two leather sofas facing each other over a long coffee table. Adjacent to the sofas were two leather armchairs, at either end of the coffee table. The set up was not dissimilar to a small living room. Cortes liked to have meetings there if they were small enough to allow it. He liked to dispense with formality so people could express what was really on their minds. The sofas helped with that. Cortes sat in one of the armchairs with his back to the desk of office. He was framed by the flag of the USAN on one side and the flag of the President of the USAN on the other.

On one sofa were Farrell and White. Opposite them was Andrews. Cortes was flipping through the latest intelligence briefings. He looked up. "What can we do?"

White spoke. "Mr President, at this stage I think we should proceed very cautiously. The Martians, maybe I should just say Venkdt, have timed this very well. There is little here in our favour. Obviously, we have to condemn the Martian actions in the strongest terms now, but in the long run we can deal with them. They can be allies."

"So we suck it up?"

"No, Mr President, we tread carefully with our eyes on the long term. For now we make the right noises about justice and rest of it, but downstream our priority is a stable Mars that we can do business with."

"What about you?" Cortes asked Farrell.

"Mr President, we're very concerned about the situation. As you know, we are dependent on Martian deuterium. An independent Mars will have control over our ability to produce energy supplies - something which underpins everything we do."

"We have other sources of deuterium," said White.

"But not enough, and way more expensive. The financial ramifications alone are truly scary. If the Martians decided to push the price of deuterium up, or even withhold supply, it could destroy the economy. That planet is ours, that deuterium is ours. We simply cannot afford to have it under someone else's control. And this whole thing is illegal, anyway. None of the Venkdt shareholders have agreed to be bought out. We can't let that go."

"I agree, I agree," said White, "none of this is ideal. But we live in the real world, where it's messy and 'good enough' has to do. Ideally none of this would have happened, and the buyout is morally unsound, we all know that. But let's work with what we've got. Provided the Martian government is stable, and we currently have no reason to suspect it won't be, we can deal with them as allies. Have them inside the tent pissing out. As long as the deuterium keeps flowing I say let them fly their funny new flag."

"You think the most important energy producing region of the USAN should just be allowed to secede?" said Cortes.

"I would rather that didn't happen, of course," said White, "but it has, and we have no remedies open to us. Working with what we have I say we should let the initial impact blow over then work like hell to keep them onside. Get the diplomatic channels working, keep the deuterium flowing. Get an embassy, you know. Hold them close."

"No remedies," Cortes repeated. He jotted something down on his briefing notes. "I thought we were modifying the *Aloadae*? How's that coming along?"

"Work is progressing," said Andrews.

"It is?"

"Yes, Mr President. As you know, Helios are working on modifying the *Aloadae* for interplanetary travel right now. We could have them in Martian orbit within five months."

"What are we going to do, invade Mars?" said White.

Cortes lifted a hand and gestured for White to back off. "What would that do for us?"

"It would focus the minds of the Martians. It would demonstrate that we take this issue very seriously."

"It would needlessly escalate -"

Cortes cut White off. "What do you think, Farrell? Overkill?"

"Mr President, I think a prominent demonstration of USAN power would be very useful. If it's possible."

"It's very possible," said Andrews.

"Okay," said Cortes, "we have two of our most powerful ships in orbit around the planet. They know we mean business. What next?"

Farrell spoke. "Our most senior person on the planet, Colonel Katrina Shaw, can step up and negotiate on our behalf. The *Aloadae* will provide the big stick she needs when she's talking softly to them on our behalf."

"Shaw. What's she doing for us now?" said Cortes.

"She's under house arrest since they took control of the garrison on Monday."

"Goddammit!" said Cortes. "So who do we have up there, anyone?"

"At the moment, Mr President, no, we don't have anyone."

"Jeez," said the president. "Okay, so we bring our big guns in and somehow reactivate Colonel Shaw. What next? What if they don't play ball?"

"I think we all agree, Mr President," said Andrews, "any threat or deterrent has to be credible. There would be no point sending the *Aloa-*

dae to Mars if we didn't have a military strategy to go with them. If the provisional Martian government refused to accede to our demands we could take the deuterium processing plants and all other ancillary facilities by force. Remember, Mars has no military capability to speak of. They have a security service with a few lightly armed transports and a handful of small arms. It would be a simple matter to capture the vital areas and implement control over them."

"Okay," said the president, "so maybe we're bluffing, but it's a credible bluff. We could realistically, by force of arms, retake the planet quickly and with minimal casualties. That's what you're saying?"

"That's exactly what I'm saying, Mr President."

"Okay, let's continue with this train of thought. What next? We have all the vital facilities we need, we've taken control. What then? What about the population? The vote was emphatic. How would we maintain order when we have just crushed a hugely popular government? We could win the war with barely a shot being fired; how would we win the peace?"

"While the vote for independence was very strong," said Farrell, "it wasn't absolute. Some voted against it. Jack Karjalainen, the other leading industrialist on Mars, was opposed. There were others too, enough for us to form a government there."

"Karjalainen. Why do I know that name?"

"Probably from the oldest son, Mr President. He was something of a war hero. Wrote a book about it, too."

"That's right. I gave him a medal, didn't I?"

"I believe you did, Mr President," said White.

"So you're saying we could install Jack Karjalainen as a friendly president if we have to put boots on the ground?"

"Not him, Mr President," said Farrell, "he's ill. Dying, actually. His son Anthony is set to take over the family business. We could maybe do business with him."

"It's way too early to be talking about boots on the ground and installing governments and the rest of it," said White. "Unauthorised elections, compulsory buyouts, it's all illegal, we know that. But how's it going to look sending in the army to capture USAN territory? To have English-speaking soldiers firing on other English-speaking soldiers. Maybe even kids from the same home town, who knows? How's that going to look?"

"Relax," said Cortes, "it's never going to come to that. But we have to plan as if it might. Audrey's right; a threat with no credibility is no threat at all."

"We are sending the wrong message here," said White. "How can we complain about them running elections when we haven't had one here in nine years?"

Farrell and Andrews froze momentarily and looked to Cortes for his reaction. His eyes narrowed and he stared coolly at White, who was staring coldly back.

"You know, Gerard, that the introduction of the Restrictive War Measures here in the USAN was an absolute necessity given the unprecedented security issues which arose during the war. I took the step of suspending elections with the heaviest of hearts, and I did it in the best interests of this great nation that we all love. I would prefer it if you didn't compare the actions of a loyal and dedicated president with those of self-interested renegades who are threatening the very stability which we've strived so hard to protect over the last seven years."

Frost hung in the air.

"I apologise, Mr President."

Cortes held White's gaze for a few long seconds before returning to Farrell. "Anthony Karjalainen. He's someone we could work with, you think?"

"He's reasonably unknown but he was close with his father, and his father was very vocal in his opposition to independence. When Anthony takes control of the family business he will have a big stake in Mars. He has employees and other assets and he would be a credible political leader. I'll see if we can feel him out and get some further intelligence. But I think so, if it came to it."

"Good. So we have a worst case plan. Take back what is ours and install a local government. We give the Martians independence but on our terms. That's the credible threat and it gives us plenty of room to negotiate anything up to and including that. When the *Aloadae* are in orbit we have the upper hand and we can negotiate through Colonel Shaw. It sounds good to me, what do we think?"

"It sounds very good, Mr President," said Andrews. "Militarily all we are waiting for is for the *Aloadae* to be in shape to make the trip. Helios assured me they would be able to do it within four months. Let's call it six, plus another month and a half for the journey. We can start talking about it now. When you're condemning the Martian actions you can talk about the task force which will be setting off for Mars soon. As soon as they know we're coming they'll have pause for thought."

"Farrell?"

"It's good from our point of view. At the moment we have no purchase on this issue whatsoever. As soon as we have military in the area Colonel Shaw becomes a player again, and her words as well as ours will carry real weight. I'll look in to this Anthony Karjalainen, and we'll think about what sort of governmental structure we might be able to put in place."

"Mr Vice President?"

Gerard White drew a deep and deliberate breath. "You know what I think. This is over the top and provocative. This isn't foreign policy as I would run it. I don't know if maybe the last seven years have got us thinking about these things in the wrong way. If we've become too used to wielding our swords rather than our powers of persuasion. But if you think this is the right thing to do then you have my support."

"I do think it's the right thing to do and I think Secretary Andrews and Secretary Farrell agree with me. This is what we are going to do. Audrey, can you get me an update on how things are going with the *Aloadae*?"

"Yes, Mr President."

"And Charles, look in to this Anthony Karjalainen or any other suitable characters that we might need if it comes to it."

"Yes, Mr President."

"Mr Vice President, I appreciate your support, but if you want to keep your distance from this in public go ahead. It might be useful for us to have some doves on board when it comes down to the negotiations. Okay?"

"Thank you very much, Mr President," said White. "I guess that suits both of us."

"It does," said Cortes.

"Where are we at?"

"We're good."

"What's good? You know the president is about to launch a war against Mars. It better be good. It better be better than good." White walked beside Sherman as they ambled around the lake in Bachman Park. Two Secret Service personnel were keeping a discreet distance sixty metres behind them. Another two were sixty metres ahead.

"We have what you asked for. They're assembling the assault teams. All commanders, all combat vets. We have someone."

"Are they in?"

"I can't say yet. The teams are still being put together. But we have candidates."

"And these are reliable people? The candidates?"

"Very."

"What do they know about what's required?"

"Look, they're all current or former commanders, from the program. They've all been to war, they know what the score is better than you do. They're cynical about Cortes and the wars. They'd be onside even if they weren't being compensated. You can trust them."

"I wouldn't trust anybody who'd rat out their comrades for money. You haven't dealt with anyone directly? Deniability is central to this. If anything goes wrong, nothing touches me. Better yet nothing touches you. You're discreet, right?"

"Always."

"This thing that's happening needs to not happen. Now, a spanner in the works, food poisoning, whatever it takes. The more mundane the better. Failed health and safety checks, I don't care. We just need those refits to take as long as government commissions usually take, or even longer, and we need the budgets to spiral and we need everything to go wrong that can go wrong. All plausible, all untraceable. You understand that?"

"I understand. We're running interference."

"Exactly. Interference, delay. That's the mission, and nothing beyond. Helios have told defence they can have those ships ready in four months. In a pig's eye. We just need to help them be as inefficient as we know they can be."

"We can cover that."

"When are they making the final selections?"

"Soon. It's all hush-hush. We'll have someone." Sherman stopped walking and White was forced to stop too. He turned to face him. "I know this is all softly-softly delaying tactics. But what do you really want? These two machines are state of the art, cutting edge designs, now with experimental engines, too. There are a millions things that could go wrong with them. Just an enquiry into a serious failure could take months, years to complete. Even then it might not find anything, particularly if we're careful. That would heap on even more delays."

"I hope you're not saying what I think you are. That is off the table. Understand?"

"Mr Vice President," said Sherman, smiling for the first time that afternoon, "you misunderstand me. All I'm saying is we can throw popcorn from the back row and be a pain in the ass, and add the odd day or week here and there, or, with such highly technical, experimental machinery we might nudge something the right way and all of a sudden there's a major setback. That's what you want, isn't it?"

"I want those ships to stay right where they are. I want absolute distance from anything that happens up there. And I want it to happen simply, with minimal fuss. Goddammit, I'll bet this is the first time in their history that Helios will actually hit their deadlines on time." He started walking again and Sherman followed on just behind his shoulder.

"I'll see to it that that doesn't happen, Mr Vice President."

Sherman had always been a shady character. He revelled in it. Even his legitimate dealings, of which there were many, had dubious undertones. He liked operating at the margins. He liked late night meetings in dodgy bars. He liked stepping over the line. He was the sort of man who might win the lottery then steal a tin of beans from the local supermarket.

He liked to keep his contacts separate from each other. To all of them he had a murky background. Contacts, connections with others, no doubt, but names or faces? Who knew? You couldn't ask him, either. He was a master of obfuscation and evasion and if he ever sensed you were anywhere near figuring something out on him he would be gone. You'd be dropped - a security risk in the real or imagined world of Rodney Sherman.

Sherman pulled into a space on the deserted top floor of a parking garage at one of the out of town malls. He waited half an hour before getting out of his car and walking leisurely to one corner of the level. From there he could see the open car park and access roads beyond, and the mall itself off toward the left. It was 02:40.

As if it had melted from the darkness itself a figure appeared beside him. Sherman barely acknowledged the man as he reached into his jacket and pulled out a packet of cigarettes. He offered one to Sherman, who shook his head in refusal. The man lit his cigarette and inhaled from it deeply. He flicked his match over the side of the building, where it lost its flame and disappeared into the darkness.

"We're good," he said.

"We are?" said Sherman.

"Yes. The final selection has been made. They've been assigned to the assault teams. Assignments to each individual vessel will come later. But we're in."

"What about communications once they're aboard?"

"We have channels."

"Are you sure? Those are military ships. Security is going to be through the roof."

"Relax. We know what we're doing. And we're very discreet."

Sherman nodded. "What do you need from me?"

"Further instructions and money."

"The money comes when I know he's in. The instructions remain those we already agreed to. Disrupt the refit, stop the *Aloadae* from leaving for Mars any time soon."

"You think it's a he?"

"I don't give a shit. The less I know the better. When I know he - or she - is onboard and causing delays you get the money."

"How?"

"Same as before. That okay with you?"

"It's good."

"Don't contact me unless absolutely necessary."

"Of course. Anything else?"

Sherman shrugged. "You should think about quitting smoking. It's a disgusting habit."

The man took a deep drag from his cigarette. As he grinned back at Sherman plumes of smoke streamed between his teeth.

Askel worked diligently on the refit project. She had made three EVAs in eight weeks. The first was to inspect the ion drives that the ship needed for manoeuvrability. The second was to take delivery of the NFJ engine, delivered into orbit from Earth on a HLV boneshaker, just as she had been. This third time was to oversee the moving of the engine into place on *Ephialtes*.

The original engine had been removed early on. It was a simple yet time consuming reversal of the installation process. The ship could still manoeuvre with the ion drives. The main engine was for speed. They had been orbiting sans main engine for most of the time Askel had been aboard.

EPHIALTES

Askel had a three dimensional overlay of *Ephialtes*, the new engine and the construction drones manoeuvring it projected virtually in front of her. She studied it carefully and compared it to the actual events, which she could see by refocusing through the overlay and simply looking around. She could speak to the teams operating the drones through her com. She was untethered and could, with a few quick bursts from her jetpack, make her way to wherever she needed to be in the mix. The Earth turned lazily below her.

"Bring the rear end around a bit," she said into her com.

"Five degrees lower," came the reply.

"Five degrees. Make it seven?" said Askel.

"Affirmative, seven."

"*Ephialtes*, please prepare the mounts."

"The mounts are ready."

"Okay, please stand by." Askel moved herself until she was behind the engine. She could see it was lined up pretty well. "Drones one and two, please begin the approach to *Ephialtes* at no more than one metre per minute"

"Roger."

Askel used her jets to circle the engine, looking for any damage or other anomalies. She checked the alignment was good, or good enough, then moved back for a better overview. Behind her was the Earth, one of the most magnificent sights in the solar system, but she was fully immersed in what amounted to threading a very big needle.

"Cameras three, five and seven, how do we look?"

"Uh, this is camera seven, you need to move up by about eight centimetres."

"Camera five, we are within the tolerances here."

"Camera three, we're good here too."

Askel floated around to drone seven's position to check for herself, and seeing the problem said, "Drone one, just a two second burst, please."

"Roger."

She saw the small burst of gas from one of the jets on drone one. The movement it created was so small as to be imperceptible. "Camera seven, how are we looking now?" she said.

"Camera seven, looks good to me. In the zone."

Askel's eyes were fixed on the end of the engine as it approached the bay. It was smaller than the space it had to fit into but the margins were slight. "Cameras three and five, are we still good?"

"Three's good."

"Five. Good here."

"Drone team, give me your relative speeds, please."

"Drone super here, we have 0.83 metres per minute."

"Keep it there," said Askel. "Mount team, stand by."

"Copy, standing by."

The bulk of Askel's work on this particular job was now done. The engine was aligned and now slowly moving into position in the engine bay of *Ephialtes*. She spent an anxious ninety minutes checking and rechecking all the information coming into her headset and making verbal enquiries to the three major teams on the operation. When the engine was in place temporary mounts tightened around it. The clunks as the mounts fell into place reverberated around the huge vessel. Askel only heard them second hand through her com. When the eighth and final mount clunked into a locked position Askel heard the cheers too, and the clapping of hands.

"Askel, I think we have a new engine. Thanks very much, you can come on in now."

Askel smiled. "You have the engine. Now we just have to wire the damn thing up. Well done all of you, but we've a long way to go yet."

She stayed a while to look at the engine and hoped she would be able to deliver on all she had promised. She watched the construction drones make their way back to their bays and finally spun around for a view of the Earth.

"It's amazing, isn't it?" she said into her com, to no one in particular.

"It is amazing, Askel, but we need you back in here. Propulsion have a question about the mounts."

"Okay," said Askel as she made her way to the airlock and prepared to get back to work.

Askel's plans had been thorough and well thought out. They had gone mostly to schedule with only a few minor delays. There had been some personnel issues too, but that was behind them now. Once the work was under way Askel was busy every waking moment. She knew her plans were good, but they were only plans. The real world, and 'problems arising', were where the real skills came in. The world as it was and as it was represented in the plans, schematics and records diverged somewhat. Thinking on the fly and reacting was what Askel was good at. Improvising and making the best choices given the limitations and materials available.

Now the engine was in position she had some real meat to work with. Real world data to mix with her plans. The engine was mounted on temporary mounts. They would need to be replaced with stronger permanent mounts, which in themselves were a little miracle of design, accommodating the original specification of *Ephialtes* with the newer spec of the prototype NFJ engine, where the mounts were in a different position.

She set at the work with abandon, pulling extended shifts and often working long into the night. When she wasn't at her terminal she could be found in grimy overalls, deep in conversation with the engineers right there, getting literally hands on to any issues arising. Askel could solve problems and muck in with anyone from grease monkeys to senior project engineers.

Work was progressing. They had slipped behind their schedule but only by a couple of days. It was a huge project, involving manual labour, software design, cabling as well as man management, accounting and above all engineering.

Less than a week after the NFJ engine had been fitted it was fired up for the first time, albeit briefly, for some cursory testing. More real-world data for Askel to work with. She plugged the data into her models and refined here, re-jigged there then retested, then back round again. Test, process results, refine design, rework the system and back around to test.

Askel had enjoyed running marathons back on Earth. She applied the same mentality to the huge task in front of her. Head down, concentrate on the immediate task. Forget what's happened, don't think about what might happen, concentrate on now, make it work, move to the next task. She processed her work like a machine. She held her consciousness off to the side, like she was blocking out pain. Her mind was tightly focused on the task. The task was all that mattered. Each task was a sequence of small tasks. Take each task, break it down into smaller tasks, do the task, move to the next one, carry on. One foot in front of the other. It was tiring, oppressive but also strangely liberating.

Two weeks on from the installation of the engine the permanent mounts were finished. The major cabling to the new engine was complete and the overhauled software control systems were at beta stage two. They had caught up, as well. They were now just one day behind schedule. With the engine installation nearly complete Askel could spend more time working on the other systems. Life support, food, oxygen, waste processing and auxiliary power all had to be more resilient for interplanetary travel. From low Earth orbit it would be possible to, in effect, bailout to the Earth below. The dropships were designed to get to the surface of the Earth in minutes. In an emergency it would be possible to evacuate the mothership. A hundred and forty million miles away from home there had to be alternatives should things go wrong. The NFJ engine needed only a fraction of the fuel that the chemical engine needed. The extra space gained was utilised to make more resilient fallback systems for anything critical to the survival of the crew. Additional space was needed too for munitions; at such a long range there would be no opportunity to be restocked from a friendly bone-shaker. The ship was being made into a self-sufficient long-distance spacecraft carrier.

One evening Askel was working at her terminal when she received a call from Rawls. "How's it going?" he said.

"Good. There have been wrinkles - you heard about the spill duct - but we're on top of it now. I estimate we'll be done pretty much as estimated on the work schedule."

"That's incredible," said Rawls. "When we sold that to Andrews I thought you were kidding. I don't think we've ever brought a project in on time. I thought it would be twice as long as the estimate, minimum."

"Is that the extent of your faith in my abilities?"

"Well, I have to be honest, maybe it was, but it certainly isn't now. I knew you were good Lund, I just didn't realise you were this good. I guess I'm going to have to give you a raise. That or fire you; you've got me looking over my shoulder."

Askel smiled. "You don't have to worry about me, Rawls. Should it ever become necessary I'll stab you in the front, not the back."

She heard Rawls chuckle down the line. "That's good to know," he said. "Can I take this date to Andrews? I doubt she'll really believe it either. I'd love to see the look on her face."

"Well," said Askel, "it's still only an estimate, but go ahead. We've done all the heavy lifting, as it were, although we did do some actual heavy lifting. The next four weeks are really snagging and finishing off. I guess it might be Murphy's Law that some minor thing will hold us up for weeks, but it shouldn't, not on paper anyway. Take the date to Andrews."

"I'll do that. Anything you need from me?"

"Just your ongoing support."

"You always have that, and you know it."

"I do Lewis, good night."

"Good night Askel. I'm going to look out the window and see if I can see you. My own little star in the night sky."

Askel hung up.

While Askel had been working on *Ephialtes* Adam Speight had been overseeing the refits on *Otus*. *Otus* was a week ahead of *Ephialtes*. As lead designer Askel had been tied up making plans before she could leave. Speight had left for *Otus* almost immediately and had begun work on tearing down the chemical engines and the fuel store areas. *Otus* was the newer of the two ships and had only been in service for a matter of weeks. In some ways that made her easier to work on. There was still some snagging going on and the crew had yet to settle into their routines. They were easier to disrupt and didn't quite yet have the sense that it was their ship that Speight was messing with. He was fast, too. He lacked a little of Askel's imagination but he made up for it with ruthless application. Like a terrier he would worry away at any job and not let go until it was done.

Speight's data was mixed in to Askel's from *Ephialtes*. The two ships were virtually identical, with only minor differences. Small problems that came to light on *Otus* could be avoided on *Ephialtes*, where those systems had yet to be implemented.

Although Askel had never worked closely with Speight she knew of his high standing at Helios. He was known to be thorough and had something of a reputation for ruthlessness. Like Askel, he had risen rapidly at the company. Unlike Askel, he had left some bad feelings in his wake. To some it seemed he had climbed to the top over the bodies of those he'd used to get there.

Askel hadn't chosen Speight for the *Otus* job. He was Rawls' choice. Rawls was a good judge of character and although he disliked Speight on a personal level he knew that he was a great choice for this job, which required absolute attention, diligence and perseverance. Some feelings might get hurt along the way; so be it.

Askel had had daily briefings from Speight, mostly in the form of messages, but occasionally she would have to make contact via video link to discuss specific issues in depth. She didn't mind his curt manner and slightly aloof air. In fact, it made things easier for her. There was no time wasted on the social niceties; they could get straight down to discussing the important matters at hand. That suited Askel. For these few months she wasn't about making friends or sustaining relationships. She was strictly business, so Speight's manner was fine with her.

On this particular evening he had called early. They had scheduled the conversation to take place at 20:00 but he called at 19:40. Askel was sitting at her terminal tweaking a subsystem of the navigation software. She took the call.

"Askel, I've sent you the data from our test burn earlier today. All looks good to me, can you give it the once over and get it back to me?"

"I'm doing that right now, it should be back to you within the hour."

"Good. How about the navigation software? We might be in a position within the next ten days or so for a run out to the Moon. Would it be ready for that?"

"Maybe. I'm working on that now, too. If you need to go to the Moon just go. The current system will handle it just fine."

"But if we have the new software we can test that, as well as the engine."

"I know. But the engine is the priority."

"Anything else for me?"

"Will you be doing a full burn on the Moon trip?"

"Not a full burn, it would be too much. About point five for a free return."

"No braking?"

"Not yet. You think we should?"

"Maybe not. The data from a point five burn will be incredibly useful."

"It will. It will tell us everything we need to know. We can extrapolate the data to a virtual full burn."

"Okay."

"Speight out."

Askel didn't have time to say goodbye. As he spoke Speight had lent towards the terminal and tapped the screen to end the conversation.

Steiner, Foley and Johnson had been in the refectory watching the streams from Mars when news of Venkdt's election to the Martian presidency had come through. Johnson had immediately thrown a cupcake towards the screen. "Get off my damned planet," he had said, to laughter from the others.

"That fella needs an ass-whooping," said Foley, "and I mean to give it to him."

Steiner slapped Foley's back. "Politics by other means, my friend," he said, "and we are most certainly other means. In fact, we're one mean other means."

"What are you talking about, fool?" said Johnson.

"I'm talking about our upcoming debate with Mr Venkdt there," said Steiner. "He'll be using ten dollar words and we'll be using plasma rifles. Should be an interesting discussion."

"I'm not debating nothin' with that fool," said Johnson. "I just want to kick his ass for being un-American. I can't even stand to look at his face," he said as he launched another cake.

"You trying to feed him to death?" said Steiner.

"Can't stand to look at the fool," said Johnson, "that's all it is."

"I appreciate the sentiment," said Steiner, "but can you throw your own food instead of mine? I'm still hungry."

"Hungry? You should be honoured I'm throwing your food. It's your patriotic duty. You're always thinking of yourself, Steiner. How about giving something up for Uncle Sam?"

"I've given Uncle Sam plenty. The cakes are mine."

Johnson gave him a sideways look. "I never trusted you, man," he said in mock seriousness. "Anyone who puts his love of cakes over the love of his country is suspect to me. Maybe I should kick your ass before I kick his," he said, nodding towards the screen. The streams moved on to some other news and Steiner, Foley and Johnson went back to their eating.

They had been training now for weeks. They had spent hour upon hour in the IVRs and as much time again physically training in the gym. The Martian template for the IVRs had been massively useful. The lower gravity had many effects which they hadn't considered. The parabola of any ballistic weapon was a significantly different shape due to the lower gravity. It took a long time to get used to their munitions acting differently. Atmospheric pressure was much lower on the Martian surface too, again affecting their shells and missiles. They had to relearn the way they aimed. The command drones themselves were a little sprightlier in Martian simulation since, in effect, they were nearly two-thirds lighter than they would be on the surface of the Earth.

Though it seemed difficult at first (Johnson in particular was worried that he was unlearning many years' worth of highly commodifiable experience) they had settled in to the Martian training and now felt as comfortable fighting on the surface of the virtual Mars as they had on the battlefields of Earth. Venkdt Corporation had provided very detailed models of their facilities on Mars and their own brass had provided many scenarios for them to train in.

They had trained at capturing Venkdt facilities on the surface of the planet. Some of the remote facilities were comprised of just a few buildings. Capturing them consisted mostly of walking up to them and finding a way in. Threatening the personnel with massive armed violence and persuading them to allow access seemed to be a very successful tactic in these scenarios.

Venkdt facilities in the big conurbation of Marineris could be captured the same way. Here there was more scope for demonstrating firepower. They knew which facilities should be unmanned and they had scanners to help confirm empty buildings. Such buildings could then be spectacularly destroyed, concentrating the minds of the enemy.

At first they had run simulations as close to what they were expecting as possible, which was absolutely no armed resistance. There was a security service on Mars but their arms were limited to rifles and pistols. Compared to the armoury available to a commander that might as well have been no arms at all. After a few weeks of training the exercises all seemed to boil down to the same thing; wandering up to the target, being threatening, and then being let in the front door.

Part of the ethos of the Commander Program was to be ready for anything. Anticipating the unexpected and exploring every possible avenue the enemy may pursue against you was ingrained into every commander. As such, and at least in part to relieve the boredom, they had recently begun running simulations with a well-armed Martian resistance. These simulations had proved more of a challenge, but not by much. They had been useful because they had forced the commanders to think more tactically about their approaches and to focus more closely on the buildings and landscapes available to them. But the end result of these simulations had been the same; fast and total victory.

All the hours of training in the IVRs had taught them some fundamentals about what to expect on Mars when they arrived in theatre. It had taught them that the atmosphere and gravity on Mars were not the same as they were on Earth. It had taught them to adjust their aim to compensate for the limited resistance and weaker pull of gravity. It had given them intimate knowledge of the layout of some of the buildings they might be likely to attack. But most of all it had taught them that victory would be fast and total. That much they did not question.

Steiner was casually destroying a warehouse when his simulation was interrupted by a message from Soward.

"All commanders, please stop your simulations."

Steiner stopped immediately but Soward paused for a few seconds. He assumed others, perhaps at more complex moments in their simulations, had needed time to finish up.

"All commanders please be advised that we will be shipping out for *Ephialtes* and *Otus* this coming Saturday at 06:00 hours."

Steiner spoke into his com, which was patched through to Foley and Johnson. "Get some!" he said.

"Squads A through G are assigned to *Ephialtes*. Squads H through N are going to *Otus*. Make sure you have your shit squared away and are ready to pull out first thing Saturday morning. That is all." Soward's voice disappeared as quickly as it had arrived.

"Up and away," Foley's voice came over the com.

"Do we get a pass between now and then?" said Johnson. "Once we're up there a pass ain't gonna do us any good. And we're gonna be up there for months."

"Up to Connor, I guess," said Steiner.

"That's a no then," said Foley.

"Damn!" said Johnson. "I need my pass. I'm nearly stir crazy from being in this place. God knows what it's gonna be like up there. I need a pass. We all need a pass, any fool know that."

Steiner began to climb out of his IVR unit. "So we've got *Ephialtes*," he said, "and a free trip to Mars thrown in too." He had just finished climbing down the ladder when Foley opened his hatch.

"I heard it's pretty nice up there," he shouted down. "A friend of mine said it's like a five star hotel. Though I doubt he's ever actually been in a five star hotel. Anyways, he said it was pretty good."

"That's right," said Steiner, "it's a good gig, or it was. The guys we're replacing just had to float around the world playing pool and watching videos, waiting for the phone to ring, which it was never going to. It might be comfortable but we've got a very different mission. We're covering the best part of a billion miles and we might have to do some actual fighting somewhere along the way."

"Bullshit," said Foley. "This is just a policing action. Think of it like an ocean cruise. And anyway, we've just done the hard part." He slapped the side of his IVR twice. "From now on it will be piña coladas all the way to Mars and back. And on double pay, too."

Johnson was also clambering down. "You're a damn fool, you know that, don't you?" he said to Foley. "There ain't no easy jobs in the army. It wouldn't surprise me if this was some sort of a set up. Like they've got some other plan for us once we get there. No easy jobs in the army."

"It must be tiring being so jaundiced all the time," said Steiner. "You need to get into the party mood like me and Foley here. If you're just going to be grumpy the whole time we might not even take you with us."

"That's funny, fool," said Johnson, "but I'm telling you the army don't do nothing the easy way, and there ain't no easy jobs in the army. If you two think this is going to be an easy tour then I just about know for sure that's exactly what it ain't gonna to be. I need a pass."

They walked together towards the changing area.

"What would you do with a pass anyway," said Steiner, "meet up with the local crochet circle?"

"You know exactly what I'd do, friend," said Johnson, "and it don't involve no goddamned crochet."

"So, *Ephialtes*," said Foley, absentmindedly.

"*Ephialtes*," repeated Steiner. "That's going to be home for the next few months."

"I like the sound of it," said Foley. "It kind of rolls off the tongue, *Ephialtes*."

"Sounds like a bullshit name to me," said Johnson. "I like them proper names, like *Vengeance* or *Predator* or *Invincible*. That's the sort of thing a warship should be called."

"I don't know," said Steiner. "*Ephialtes*. Sounds good to me."

CHAPTER 17

Aggressive Expansion

Kostovich had incredible amounts of data relating to the USAN's military capability and equipment. He had taken their missile technology and adapted it into a system that was suitable for Mars and could be built quickly and cheaply. That system was well on the way to production. Parts were being fabricated and assembled already. Four designated sites had been selected north, east, south and west of the city and they were being prepared to accept the installations. Building contractors were laying the foundations to Kostovich's precise specifications. They would start taking the prefabricated units of the missile batteries as soon as they were ready. They would be ready soon.

The system was run remotely, controlled by software distributed around the Martian network. It was very resistant to cyber-attack. The physical system was somewhat resistant through redundancy; its four separate geographical locations covered widely overlapping areas. Each battery, to some degree, covered the others and they all covered the main Martian city of Marineris.

Unlike Askel Lund, Kostovich was hands off in his overseeing of the building of his great defence system. He made the plans, which were precise and exquisitely detailed, then fired them off to engineers, builders and subcontractors. He kept his mind very much in the theoretical space and left the real world to others.

As soon as plans were completed for the planetside missile batteries Kostovich turned his attention to the orbiting platform. The missile batteries on the planet were basically scaled down versions of plans stolen from the USAN. The orbiting platform, however, was different. For this one he had to design the platform from start to finish. He had set his AIs to the task and had overseen what they produced. He made tweaks and suggestions and read them back into the AIs and refined them again and again. The platform had to be designed such that the separate parts could be transported into orbit and assembled there. That made the task more difficult, but Kostovich and his AIs had found a way. The final design required more than six launches and major construction in orbit. For this Kostovich had adapted one of the USAN's designs for an advanced construction drone. Two of these would be charged with assembling the prefabricated parts.

Fabrication of the orbiting missile platform parts had taken many weeks and there were further delays due to the limited number of available flights into orbit. But it was coming together now. The orbiting platform was actually starting to look like an orbiting platform rather than disparate lumps of metal floating in roughly similar orbits. As ever, Kostovich observed from afar. He gave extensive notes to the contractors charged with making them a reality. Everything was proceeding well.

With the missile batteries project in hand Kostovich was able to turn his attention to the smaller items on his to-do list. He had been charged with arming a new army. Not only a new army, but a new army in a circumstance previously unknown to human warfare. He had picked through the USAN's designs and decided on a few fundamental pieces of equipment the army would need. Martian infantry would need a workhorse weapon that could be quickly and easily manufactured and used just as easily. For that, he selected the USAN plasma rifle. He made minimal tweaks, mainly due to the limited availability on Mars of some of the required precious metals. He found suitable substitutes. He thought a Martian army would need at least one form of armoured transport. By melding together two USAN designs he came

EPHIALTES

up with an armoured troop carrier with a mounted plasma cannon. He tweaked the design of the cannon such that he doubled its power, making it a truly formidable weapon. Again, he streamlined the production process to make it easier to manufacture on Mars, and got his design to the fabrication plants as soon as possible.

The uniform, he thought, needed to be light, practical and armoured. The USAN had very recently made some interesting advances in lightweight armour. He had looked at those and then integrated the armour design into a standard military battledress. He was working on the designs because of his technical knowledge and understood that the uniform, above all else, had to be a practical thing. However, as someone who had grown up playing IVR battle games he couldn't resist tinkering with some of the cosmetic aspects of the uniform design. He gave the Martian battledress a subtle desert camouflage. The colours were rusty brown and a lighter brown, similar to the colours found on most of the Martian surface. He chose what he thought were impressive crests for various ranks. The crests contained long distance RFID identification markers so that any Martian troops could be instantly identified on the field of battle.

His design for the Martian trooper's helmet included a head-up display which overlaid real-time information on the world. The LDRFIDs constantly fed back to a huge battlefield model, which in turn fed the information back from the model to the troops on the field. This meant that, for example, a trooper on the field would be able to see all of his comrades, whether he had line of sight or not. If they walked behind a building his head-up display would superimpose exactly where they were over his vision of the real world, just as if he could see them through the building. All friendly troops, and where possible friendly buildings and civilians, would be marked as such by means of a faint green glow. Enemy structures, transports and troops would conversely be marked with a glowing red outline.

Coms were similarly enhanced by tracking technology which transmitted any given communication to the comrade the trooper was looking at. Extremely sophisticated heuristic algorithms would analyse the content of the communication in its situational context, together with other battlefield variables, to decide whom the communication might be most useful to. It would then route it to them. If a trooper were to say, 'Look out for that sniper', for example, the algorithm would figure out, from where the trooper was on the battlefield and what direction she was looking, where the sniper was. It would then figure out what area the sniper was covering and compare that to where other troopers were moving. If it thought any troopers were likely to move into the area covered by the sniper it would route that particular communication to them. It would also send a visual cue to their head-up displays, showing where the sniper was and what areas he had covered.

The AI running the battle model was the great arbiter of who should know what, where and when. Too much information on the battlefield could be as dangerous as too little. The AI could filter out orders or information that was irrelevant. The battle model AI's job was to see that the troopers got the information they needed and no other distractions. It was something Kostovich was particularly proud of.

Plasma rifles, uniforms, light artillery and helmets had all recently gone into production. Kostovich had prototypes of the basic military kit in his office. He was expecting to take delivery of the first large production batches very soon.

Venkdt had given Kostovich a number of warehouse facilities to store the kit as it came off the production line. Warehouse 63 had previously been used for storing some of the goods the Martians had been selling to Earth. That hadn't been a great success. The huge cost of transportation to Earth had made the endeavour risky to start with. Though Venkdt Mars had been able to come up with some advanced designs for consumer goods it hadn't really made economic sense to produce them on the planet. Raw materials were the truly valuable commodity that Mars produced. That failure had worked out for Kostovich. It meant he had this huge warehouse and it was now being filled with equipment he'd designed and adapted. He was going to be the first, and best, quartermaster of the Martian army. It was a job he relished. He usually stayed away from any jobs that involved being around other people but he wanted to be there for this one.

He had called Maya a few days before and arranged a time. He knew that, strictly speaking, he should have involved Maya in the design process - that's what Venkdt had asked for - but he had managed to wriggle out of it. He thought that when you started asking people what they wanted they would overthink things and make them too complex. It was wise of him, he supposed, to simply go ahead and do what he thought was best. It made sense to him. After all, this new equipment was at least equivalent to what the USAN Army had and at the moment it looked like they were the only plausible enemies Mars might have. Even that seemed fanciful but it would be good, if the USAN Army did make it across the hundred and forty million miles of space between them, to be able to match them with a force equipped to the same standard.

He had asked Maya to come to the warehouse bringing as many of her MSS personnel with her as possible. He planned to kit them out there and then.

He sat in the control room and watched as four forklift drones unloaded containers from transports and piled them up to one side of the warehouse. These were the plasma rifles. Other sections of the warehouse already had their boxes of uniforms, body armour, advanced communication equipment and helmets. He felt at that moment like a martial Father Christmas.

He had spoken to Maya a few times on his comdev but had yet to meet her in person. He was looking forward to it. Her strength and directness appealed to him and he hoped that she might be impressed with everything he had done for her.

A few minutes before the agreed time he went down to the floor of the warehouse. He was wearing a hard hat, as required, but he ignored the audible warnings that were triggered by his entrance onto the warehouse floor. He had arranged for Maya and her troops to arrive via one of the loading bays. He was expecting it to be impressive, maybe two or three transports filled with poorly equipped and slightly bemused security personnel, who had suddenly, somehow, found themselves in an army. He would shower them with brand new super up-to-date equipment and send them back out as the defenders of Mars. He smiled at the thought.

He had been there a few minutes when an alarm bell rang out and yellow lights started flashing, signalling that one of the big bay doors was about to open. He had sent security clearance to Maya. Her comdev was all she would need to open the door. It had to be her.

Slowly, the huge door started to lower into the ground. At first Kostovich could only see the lights in the ceiling of the tunnel beyond, but as the door got lower it revealed the first transport then others behind it. He walked towards them. He could see that the driver had assumed she would be coming into the warehouse. She had not expected it to be as full as it was. She looked to Foveaux, sat to her right, as if asking what she should do now, but Foveaux was already climbing down from the cabin and walking over to meet Kostovich, hand outstretched.

"You must be Kostovich," she said.

"You must be Commissioner Foveaux," said Kostovich. "Please, come this way. I think the easiest way to do this, for the uniforms, helmets and rifles, anyway, would be for your troops to just get kitted up right here. What do you think?"

"Sounds good to me," said Foveaux. "What have you got for us?"

"Everything I said I would in the documentation I sent over. It's all here."

"Everything?"

"Some of the field artillery is still being fabricated, and the armoured transports, too. But all the stuff for your troopers is right here."

"That's great," said Foveaux. "Where do you want us?"

"Uh, I guess if you start forming a queue here," he gestured to a pile of crates. "These are the basic uniforms. I've had the forklifts make various piles down there. This is uniforms, next pile on is boots, beyond that is helmets, beyond that is rifles and so on down the line. I guess the easiest thing is for people to work their way down the line picking stuff up as they go."

"Very good," said Foveaux, "I'll get them out of the transports." She spoke into her comdev and the transports started emptying into the warehouse. Her troops slowly coalesced into a line in front of the first pile of crates. The two troops at the front of the queue looked expectantly at Kostovich as if he was going to help them.

Kostovich gestured at the crates. "Go ahead," he said, "it's self-service."

The two troopers looked at each other somewhat disappointedly, but moved forward and opened the first crate. They pulled out uniforms, rummaging through looking for the right sizes. They scoured labels and held the uniforms up to themselves until they were satisfied. They took the uniforms and moved to the next pile. Two more troopers stepped forward to take their places. Seeing that the system, crude as it was, appeared to be working Kostovich spoke to Foveaux. "I thought you would be first in the queue," he said.

"Plenty of time for that," she replied. "Will you be training us on these weapons and coms systems?"

Kostovich looked shocked. "No. I've provided very comprehensive IVR routines for training. I sent them to you, I assumed you'd been training already."

"You did? I'm so sorry, I'll look into that. I guess I'm just a bit practical minded. An IVR is never quite like the real thing to me."

"Well," said Kostovich, "if you like I could quickly walk you through the Enhanced Battlefield HUD and the plasma rifle?"

"Thank you," said Foveaux, "I'd like that, can we make a time?"

Kostovich tried to act like this was the most natural thing in the world to him. "Let me know some times that are good for you and I'll check with my diary," he said, but he knew he was prepared to clear anything.

"Okay, I'll do that, thanks," said Foveaux.

Kostovich nodded toward a group of troops who had changed into their new uniforms and were carrying plasma rifles and EBH helmets. "They look like proper soldiers," he said.

Foveaux nodded in agreement.

Foveaux watched the strip lights on the roof of the tunnel fly past her and thought about everything she needed to do. Her army, such as it was, was less than two months old. Its main role, aside from being the de facto Martian police force, was to keep the old USAN Army on Mars neutralized. The MSS was a police force without police officers and an army without an enemy. At least it was no longer an army without weapons. Within days, she hoped, it would no longer be an army without base. She had been operating out of one of Venkdt Security's buildings, but it was not fit for purpose and certainly not big enough.

The tunnel opened out to the familiar scrubland before the gates to the garrison. The guards at the garrison's gate were two of her own troops. The transport paused and, despite the troops obviously recognising their leader, they dutifully went through the process of checking her bona fides via an automated handshake process with her comdev. "Welcome to the garrison, Commissioner Foveaux," a guard said, waving to her colleague who opened the gate. The transport proceeded into the parade ground in front of the main garrison building.

The transport had barely come to a stop when Captain Claudia Gibbs bounded from the main entrance towards it. "Commissioner Foveaux," she was saying as Foveaux stepped down from the transport, "it's good to meet you in person. Welcome to the garrison."

"Thank you Captain Gibbs," said Foveaux. "Is there somewhere we can talk?"

"Certainly," said Gibbs, "come right this way." She led Foveaux into the building and up the stairs to what had been Shaw's office. The blood had been cleaned up but Foveaux immediately noticed the fresh plaster in the wall by the window. The bullet hole, which had been made in the wall rather than her own head, had been patched over but not yet painted. The reminder gave her a chill but she quickly put it out of her mind. Gibbs immediately picked up on her discomfort. "I'm so sorry," she said, "I didn't think about that, shall we go somewhere else?"

"No, no," said Foveaux, "it's fine, really."

Gibbs looked mortified. "I hope you don't think this was a stunt. I'm so sorry, I should have thought."

"Really, it's fine," said Foveaux, sitting down.

"Can I get you anything? Tea? Coffee?"

"Water would be fine," said Foveaux. Gibbs tapped her terminal.

"I'm so glad you've come over. The way I see this whole thing is that we need to work together. I mean, obviously, there's a big disagreement here, and we're in the middle of it, but I still think we can handle this together without things getting out of hand. Let the politicians think what they think; we're the ones at the tight end and I think we can rub along together just fine until this thing is sorted out."

Foveaux took a bottle of water off the droid that had entered the room. It carried on to Gibbs, who took a steaming mug of black coffee and set it on her desk. "I'm glad you see it that way," said Foveaux, "I'm thinking along similar lines myself. In fact, that's what I've come here to discuss." She took a swig from the bottle.

"Do go on," said Gibbs.

"Well," said Foveaux, "strictly speaking Martian forces are in command here. We have Shaw and Edley under house arrest, and you and your troops in pretty much the same position."

Gibbs nodded philosophically. "I guess that's true," she said.

"That works for me tactically, but there are still some other things I need from you."

Gibbs was troubled by the words but she covered it well. She thought the stand-off position was a good place to be in. She was happy to be in command of a neutralized battalion. She knew that under the terms of the surrender she could no longer respond to any gung-ho orders from politicians or generals a hundred and forty million miles behind her, and her force had been stripped of arms. To her, the current position worked well for all sides. Now it sounded like Foveaux wanted to mess with the balance. These thoughts all flashed through her head at once, but instead of grimacing she smiled sweetly and said, "Of course, how can we help?"

"One thing I don't have and really need," said Foveaux, gesturing with both hands, "is a garrison. We're currently based in one of Venkdt Security's buildings. We have the offer of an old warehouse on the edge of town; I don't much fancy that either. I'm trying to put together an army and would like for it to be based here."

Gibbs knew that she didn't have anything to negotiate with. In fact the entire meeting was a charade. Foveaux could, if she wished, simply order her out. She decided to play along with it. At least that way she could leave with dignity. "I see," she said, "that does make a lot of sense."

"What I was thinking," said Foveaux, "is that you could move your troops out to the warehouse, and I could move my troops in here. Does that sound reasonable to you?"

'*Of course not*,' thought Gibbs. "Yes, that sounds like a reasonable arrangement," she said.

"That's great," said Foveaux, "I'll have one of the assistant commissioners come over right away to arrange the details."

"Yes, do that," said Gibbs.

"One other thing," said Foveaux.

"Yes?"

"I'd like to offer any of your people who would like to accept it a role in the MSS. You've been performing this role much longer than we have and your experience and advice would be invaluable."

Gibbs nodded. "I see," she said. "Of course, for any USAN troops to volunteer for the MSS they would be committing treason. You understand that?"

"I suppose," said Foveaux. "Would you like us to handle it from our end?"

Gibbs looked distinctly uncomfortable. "Commissioner, we can't really have anything to do with that. Do you really think it's a good idea? We have a comfortable situation at the moment. If you start asking people to switch sides things might turn very ugly. Families, friends feeling betrayed. I really don't think it's a good idea, and I certainly can't be a party to it."

Foveaux nodded. "I understand. I shouldn't have asked."

"Well, we're reasonable people," said Gibbs, "that's why we have these discussions; to figure out those sorts of things. Thank you for understanding."

"No problem," said Foveaux. "We won't ask for volunteers until you're settled into the new facilities."

Gibbs forced a smile. She didn't like it one bit, but she wasn't in a position to argue.

The warehouse facility was barely suitable as a base for two hundred troops. Under Gibbs' supervision they had requested and received building materials. The warehouse itself, apart from a single office high up on one side, was basically a huge empty box. Gibbs' plan was to build a two storey structure on one side of the warehouse. There would be a space in front of the building, much like the parade ground at the old garrison but far smaller. The new building would house the refectory, day room and living quarters. Gibbs had elected to make the overseeing office hers. She would have a view across the parade ground to the quarters beyond.

The two access points to the warehouse were below her office. They were large gates leading directly to tunnels, connected to the main Martian road-tunnel network. They were guarded by MSS forces, four troops either side of both gates. As soon as she received them Maya planned to position two armoured troop carriers in the tunnels, too. She didn't expect trouble from the USAN forces but she wasn't taking anything for granted.

As well as being necessary, the work on the new garrison buildings in the warehouse gave Gibbs' troops something to do. They had been at work for six days and the outline of what was going to be was taking shape. The floor plan was clearly visible and some of the ground floor walls were already in place. Scaffolding reached ambitiously upwards, and it was possible to imagine what the finished building might look like.

Gibbs was looking out of her window, satisfied that the troops were occupied and that the building of their own accommodation would give them sufficient ownership over it to make up for the fact that they had been evicted from their true home. She even thought they might be enjoying the task, hard as it was.

She heard one of the huge gates clanking as it sank into the ground and assumed it was another truckload of building materials. She was surprised to see one of the MSS's transports rolling in. She saw Maya and Assistant Commissioner Matthias Schroeder step down from the cab. She watched with rising alarm as they walked to the front of the building project. Schroeder looked like he had something in his hand. She couldn't make out what it was until he lifted it to his mouth and began to speak. She hurriedly opened one of the windows in her office to hear what he was saying.

"Soldiers of the USAN. You are all aware of the recent change in status of the planet Mars. Until recently you had been charged with keeping order on our great planet. That proud duty has now fallen to the Martian Security Service, the MSS, of which I am assistant commissioner. Commissioner Foveaux and I would like to offer all of you the opportunity to serve in the MSS. Your knowledge and experience will be invaluable to us. We understand that taking up this offer will present you with significant difficulties. You've all sworn an oath to the USAN, which you would necessarily have to break in order to join us.

"We are living through turbulent times, and at such times it can be difficult to see things clearly and understand what is really happening. Mars is now an independent planet. That is a plain fact, and will not change. It will take some time for our former colonial masters to come to terms with that fact, and until then they may view some of our actions through a distorting lens, seeing them very differently to how they actually are. We are not asking you to become traitors to the country to which you have sworn an oath. We have dissolved your unit. We do not regard you as an alien or enemy force. For us, you are welcome guests on our planet. As part of our courtesy towards you, we offer you the opportunity to join with us and help us forge the MSS."

Gibbs glanced to the microphone hanging from a hook next to the window. It was connected to loudhailers on the roof of her office. She thought about grabbing it and screaming, '*If any one of you dog-faces steps forward I'll have you thrown in the stockade and court-martialled to within an inch of your lives.*' But then she thought about the conversation she'd had with Foveaux and knew she couldn't afford to antagonise the Martians. On top of that, the troops hadn't even got round to building the new stockade yet. Her hand physically twitched as she looked at the mic, but she let it go and carried on listening.

"If any of you would like to join us as officers of the MSS on pay equal to current MSS officers, please step forward now. We can take you immediately to the garrison - your old garrison - and induct you into our new service. If any of you would like further time to think this offer over you can contact either myself or Commissioner Foveaux for further details or for an informal chat. We will be leaving in the next thirty minutes. If any of you would like to come along with us please know that your help would be greatly appreciated. Thank you"

Schroeder dropped the loudhailer to his side and took a few steps until he was beside Foveaux. He leant in and spoke to her. Gibbs scanned the building site opposite. The men and women there had been working until five minutes ago, carrying, lifting and bolting. Now they had coalesced into little groups and seemed to be debating. She saw that some groups quickly finished their debate and went back to work, while others seemed to carry on discussing. In a couple of groups the discussion seemed quite heated, with fingers jabbing and wild gesticulation. She saw, in some places, her troops leave their work and disappear toward the region where their kit bags and equipment were temporarily stored.

It was ten very long minutes before the first of her troops ambled over to Assistant Commissioner Schroeder. The man had a kitbag slung over his shoulder and was carrying another bag in his right hand. As he reached Schroeder he dropped the bag and thrust his hand forward, shaking Schroeder's hand vigorously. He had a broad smile on his face and she could see them exchange a few pleasant words. As they finished up Schroeder grabbed the man's upper arm, and patted it twice. The man then walked over to the transport. Looking up Gibbs could see another couple of troops walking from the storage area, and behind them one more. Behind him there were at least half a dozen rummaging amongst the kit bags.

There was a knock at the open door. Foveaux looked up. It was Schroeder. "Come in," she said, "sit down."

Schroeder came into the room and walked over to the chair in front of Foveaux's desk. He sat down as requested.

Foveaux was engrossed in her terminal. "I'll be with you in a second, I just need to finish this up," she said.

Schroeder glanced around the room as he waited. It was still not familiar to him.

"Okay," said Foveaux, looking up, "how many did we get in the end?"

"Seventeen. Not bad, from two hundred. I'm surprised we got even that."

"That's great. Obviously, I need thorough background checks and ongoing monitoring on anyone who comes to us from the USAN. But these first seventeen are our bankers. They've made this decision quickly; no one made it for them. These are the ones we can trust. Any that come over in the next few days or weeks may be sent as double agents. They're the ones we'll *really* need to keep an eye on."

"Of course. We've done background and personnel checks on the ones we have and we'll be doing psych evaluations later today."

"Good. I want these people distributed around the service as much as possible. We don't need any factionalism. Also, we want to get the greatest benefit we can from their experience. They might be able to help with the training, too. The kit we've been supplied with is fundamentally upgraded USAN stuff, so they should be familiar with it. How's the training going?"

"It's going very well. The IVRs are extremely accurate and the live training is good, too."

"Good. And the new accommodation?"

EPHIALTES

"No problems. The kitchen staff are unhappy about the state of the cookers; that's about it."

"Okay, I'll see if Venkdt has any kitchen equipment we can have. But that's it? No other problems?"

"None I can think of. We're getting the field artillery and troop carriers soon, right?"

"Should be in the next couple of weeks or so. I'll contact Kostovich and see where we are on that."

"For now, you want us to carry on with the training?"

"Yes, training is the number one priority. Get the most senior USAN trooper to come over and find out how they did their policing. At the moment we're just muddling through. We really need to firm that up; patrols maybe, and certainly a central control and dispatch office. Find out what they did and start doing it."

"Yes, Commissioner. Anything else?"

"Yes, there is one more thing." She rose from her chair and stepped to the window. She pointed to the fresh plaster on a patch of wall there. "See this?" she said. "This is a repair. As you can see, it's not finished. I want to make sure that it doesn't get finished. In fact, if it's possible I'd like this new plaster to be dug back out."

Schroeder kept a poker face. "Yes, Commissioner," he said.

Foveaux felt compelled to explain. "The bullet that made this hole skimmed my head on its way there. It should have ended up here," she pointed between her eyes, "rather than there. I'd like that hole there to remind me two things about this job. One is that, in the broader scheme of things, we're not here by popular consent; it was by struggle and force of will that we got here."

"And the other?"

"Well, the other is the most important thing we should all try to keep in mind; that due to the nature of our role there will always be people around who want to kill us."

CHAPTER 18

Robust Diplomacy

Farrell had his intelligence teams do a thorough job on Anthony Karjalainen. Anthony had never stepped out from his father's shadow. As the younger son he had always been the apple of his father's eye. Where Bobby had been boisterous and cheeky, Anthony had always managed to do the right thing. He was the boy who would tidy up his toys, rather than leave them scattered about the living room. He would get up on time, where Bobby might laze in his bed until he was good and ready. Bobby's school reports would often mention how he had great ability but didn't apply it. Anthony's ability was less but his application was unquestioned.

He had left school early and gone straight into the family firm. His record was unremarkable and it seemed to the analysts that his meteoric rise through the company could not be justified by his actions alone. It was his name that had got him close to the top.

Anthony rarely demonstrated original thought. He took on the ideas around him. His father loved to use him as a sounding board. Anthony could make suggestions which appeared insightful but were in fact superficial. It made it seem like he was applying a critical eye to the ideas that Jack Karjalainen was bouncing off him, when in fact he was just giving back uncritical approval. Jack had managed to kid himself that Anthony had a sharp mind. That opinion was a product of his own arrogance. Because Anthony appeared to think what Jack did, Jack took that as a sign of Anthony's great mental faculties rather than what it was; a product of the lack of them.

Consequently, he had risen to a senior role in Hjälp Teknik very quickly despite his mediocre abilities and tender age. This flagged him as an ideal candidate to the USAN intelligence analysts. He was senior, respected and had a veneer of intelligence, but he was also shallow and unimaginative. Exactly what they would need for their puppet government. They wanted to maintain what had hitherto been the status quo, and someone like Anthony Karjalainen, who was conservative and dull-witted by nature, was ideal for them.

They had pulled up a few other potential candidates, all senior managers at Hjälp Teknik, and had done thorough analyses. These people were the reserves, though. Anthony Karjalainen was the prime candidate. Not only did his personality match their ideal profile but his name carried weight on Mars, particularly amongst the limited band of loyalists.

Farrell took the report to Cortes. "I think he's our man," he said. "If you don't have time to read the report I'll summarise it for you; he's senior, people respect his name, he is very resistant to change and he's also his father's son. His father was the only prominent Martian to speak out against independence. If it came to it he would make a credible political leader for us."

Cortes laid his copy of the report on the table in front of them. "This is good work," he said. "Have you approached him on any of this?"

"No Mr President, we haven't made any approach as yet."

"Okay, is there any way we can make a soft approach? Have someone sound him out in person?"

"We don't have anyone on Mars who could do that for us. We could approach him through coms systems but, of course, we might be vulnerable to interceptions."

"Of course," said Cortes. "Are our lines insecure?"

"We don't know for sure but out of an abundance of caution we have to assume so. We had a highly secured encrypted line into the garrison, but the garrison is no longer in our hands."

"So how do we approach him?"

"I'm thinking through Colonel Shaw. Her comdev has military grade hardware encryption codecs by default. She is under house arrest but she still has her comdev. We are in daily communication with her."

"So we can get to Karjalainen through her, somehow?"

"I think so. The house arrest is pretty slack. She's allowed visitors. If we communicate the information to her she can select a trusted visitor and pass the information on to them. They would be the intermediary between her and Karjalainen, and we have direct secure access to her."

"That's great, Farrell," said Cortes. "So we still have some sort of a foothold on that damned planet, however small."

"We do, sir."

"When are you going to put this into action?"

"Well, we're still months away from having the *Aloadae* in orbit. That's when our hand really gets strengthened. I would advise holding off until then. The intelligence indicates that Anthony Karjalainen will be receptive to our suggestions. But if we wait until nearer the time there's less chance for him to waver or be compromised."

"Okay. What happens if Colonel Shaw is compromised in the meantime? What if they realise her comdev isn't standard issue?"

Farrell frowned. "I guess that's a risk we have to take. Colonel Shaw is a good officer, we know we can trust her. Karjalainen seems like a great option, but he's still something of an unknown. On balance, I think it would be better to wait."

"Okay, we wait. When the *Aloadae* are in position we can get our proposal to Karjalainen, and he can start making noises on our behalf."

"That's exactly the plan, Mr President."

"Great, thank you," said Cortes, standing up. He shook Farrell's hand and returned to his desk.

Andrews had indeed, as predicted by Rawls, been shocked that the work on the *Aloadae* was proceeding according to schedule. It was common knowledge that defence contracts ran way over time and way over budget.

Winning a defence contract was similar in some ways to winning the lottery. The main difference was that the payout from the lottery remained fixed. With defence contracts the bottom line could keep growing and growing. Once the client was on the hook for billions of dollars it was difficult to walk away. If another few hundred million were needed that might seem a small price to pay given what had already been invested. And so it went on. Budgets snowballed, projects mutated and the money kept flowing from the public coffers.

This case seemed to be an anomaly. Everything was proceeding as planned. Helios was hitting milestones with unerring accuracy. Deliverables were being delivered on or before the dates projected. It seemed miraculous.

Andrews had known of Askel Lund's work before, but she had paid little attention. Back then she had been focused on the biggest war in generations. Now her focus was taken up with this small *potential* war. Lund, it appeared, was able to work miracles. Twelve weeks ago the idea of getting the *Aloadae* into Martian orbit within half a year seemed fanciful. Politically useful, on paper, but unlikely to become a practical reality. Now she was looking at reports suggesting that the two vessels would be ready to ship out within the next four weeks.

She watched as Cortes skimmed the conclusion of the report. He took his glasses off and looked at her. "I'm very impressed," he said.

"Thank you, Mr President," said Andrews.

"Have Helios ever come in on time and on budget before?"

"I don't think they have, Mr President. And as yet, they still haven't. Let's not put a hex on it."

Cortes laughed. "Quite," he said. "But seriously, it looks like we're going to be on schedule with this?"

"It does, sir. The commanders have been training extensively for Martian environments. They're working on scenarios similar to those we discussed previously. They will be able to take the necessary facilities by force, should it come to it. They're being shipped up to the *Aloadae* this weekend. As soon as the final works and testing are finished in the next few weeks they will be ready to leave immediately."

"This is terrific. I can't quite believe you've managed to pull it off."

"Thank you, sir. I can't quite believe it myself. Helios' lead on this project is a woman called Askel Lund. She seems to be quite the miracle worker."

Cortes nodded. "Could you arrange for a note of my personal thanks to be sent to her?"

"Of course, Mr President, I'll organise that right away."

"Thank you, Audrey. Secretary Farrell is making good headway with the diplomatic plans. I feel that we have a strong two-pronged approach to this problem. Farrell has diplomatic backdoors which sound extremely promising. When we get these two ships in orbit we will really have something to work with. We'll be flanking them from both sides, and of course we'll look strong. You've done great work, you and Farrell. It's important that we are seen to be the superpower that we are. These are very uncertain times. Any weakness we project will be seized upon by our enemies. As you know, we didn't manage to get quite the peace we wanted. I want our enemies to see that we are strong and decisive. You're helping me to deliver on that, so once again I thank you."

"Thank you, Mr President. I'll see that you're kept up-to-date daily on the developments." Andrews stood up and left.

White didn't really have much of a stomach for burgers but this place was something of a favourite for Sherman and he often suggested it. White's Secret Service detail were familiar with it, and were happy to remain on guard outside.

White took his seat and ordered a hamburger and fries with a cola. Sherman picked something more elaborate, with a side of deep-fried Monterey Jack cheese. White hid his mild disgust at the fatty order. He noted that Sherman had also ordered a non-lite soda. It was these little things that made him uneasy about Sherman. He knew, of course, that Sherman lived in a shady underworld but things like his poor diet seemed to advertise it unnecessarily. He put all that to one side and tried to remain civil. "So our man's being shipped up this weekend. He's fully briefed, I take it?"

"Of course," said Sherman, "he wouldn't be much use if he wasn't."

White smiled. "And we can contact him once aboard, if necessary?"

"If strictly necessary we can do that, but each time you open a channel of communication it makes us vulnerable. Those ships are state-of-the-art military, so who knows what type of electronic defences and decryption systems they have aboard? As far as we know we have a secure channel in, but let's not use it if we don't have to. The mission parameters are pretty clear; disrupt, delay, harass. That's it, isn't it?"

"I guess it is. I just want to know that we have lines of communication should anything change."

Sherman took a big bite from his cheeseburger and chewed a bit before answering. "You have that, if you really need it, but it would be in your best interests to not need it."

"I understand," said White.

"Are we done here?" said Sherman.

"I guess so," said White. "You know we had a meeting the other day, a very high level meeting with the president and defence and foreign secretaries. They said that all of this is just a show of force. They said it's part of the diplomatic process, but I don't know. It all sounded very hawkish to me. They've made very clear military plans to attack the Martians with those ships. If they do that it would be an absolute catastrophe. We can't let that happen. We've just spent seven years pissing away trillions of dollars and hundreds of lives - hell, millions of lives, if you count the enemy losses - on a war that achieved just about nothing, and now the president seems to want to go through the whole process again, only this time more expensive and further away."

Sherman munched on his burger. He nodded to White, aware that he was now being used as an unofficial therapist. He didn't mind too much. He was hungry and wanted to eat, and it was easy enough to nod here and there and look sympathetic while White droned on.

"If it comes to a hot war it would be even more disastrous than the last one. At least there we were fighting foreigners, people who could legitimately be seen to be enemies of the USAN. If this thing kicks off we'll be fighting our own people, and on what many of us still consider to be USAN soil. Can you imagine that? The absolute calamity of it. It would be like a civil war. I just can't bear to think about it. And it would give Cortes a plausible reason to continue with his Restrictive War Measures. I know he only needs the slightest excuse to extend them. He's trying to wriggle out of resuming elections as it is. He actually *needs* a crisis - it suits his agenda. If we can take the sting out of this, defuse the whole thing, I think we'll be performing a great public duty. We can deprive Cortes of his war and get him kicked out of office."

Sherman thought he'd toss a little barb into the mix. "And who would replace him? You?"

White took it in his stride, dodging with the ease of a career politician. "If the people elected me then yes, why not? But that's the whole point; it should be down to the people, there should be elections. This whole thing stinks, it's just not right. Everyone was scared during the war so they ate it up like it was just a normal thing, but it's not normal. The people should be electing their president. He got them so scared they gave up their fundamental rights willingly. He told them he was going to do the right thing on their behalf, and they trusted him. Well, I wouldn't be so trustful. I've seen him close up. I've seen it in his eyes. He *wants* another war, and he's hell-bent on getting it. We can stop him." He ran out of steam at that point and absentmindedly picked up one of his fries and ate it.

Sherman took a long sip from his soda. "You don't have to worry about it," he said. "We've got good people on this. Those ships will never get to Mars. Not in time to be useful, anyway. This whole thing will blow over. In two years no one will give a shit about it. There'll be no war, and Cortes will have no excuse to continue with the War Measures. There'll be an election, Gerard White will be elected president by a huge landslide. And they all live happily ever after, The End."

White threw a fry at Sherman. "You son of a bitch," he said, "this is serious. There are lives at stake here, the whole future of the USAN could be decided by this."

The fry hit Sherman on the chin and fell into his lap. He stopped eating and looked directly at White. "Hey," he said, "we've got our best people on this. It's going to work out exactly how you want it, okay?"

White looked at him.

"Okay?" Sherman said again, with a low menace in his voice.

"Okay," said White. "I'm sorry about the fry, I don't know what came over me." He looked flustered. Obviously, he had a lot on his mind.

"I accept your apology," said Sherman, unconvincingly, and he carried on eating.

Meeting with Sherman made White late to his appointment with Zelman. As usual, per the rules of the arrangement, she had booked the hotel and sent him the details. When he arrived he had apologised for his tardiness and showered. He was wearing a bath robe now and had calmed down. It had been a stressful day and the champagne he was pouring would, he hoped, calm his nerves further. Madeline always had a soothing effect on him. As he handed a glass of champagne to her he said, "For you, my dear." She took the glass from him and took a sip before setting it down on the bedside table.

"Tough day?" she said.

White shook his head like he was trying to clear it. "Like you wouldn't believe," he said. "I feel like I'm the only person in this country who gives a shit any more. We're sleepwalking into a dictatorship, and no one seems to give a damn."

"Oh, come on, it's not that bad. The war's been over for months now. He can't hold out much longer, there's no justification any more. You worry too much."

White came around and lay on the bed next to Zelman. "I wish it was that simple," he said. He took a slug from his champagne flute, which he then rested on his belly with two hands clasped around it as if it was some holy object. "He's handling this Mars thing all wrong, way too heavy-handed. I think he's looking for a fight. He's got so used to fighting over the last few years he can't think of any other way of dealing with things. And a fight plays right into his hands. He can go on about security issues and continue stripping away liberties here at home while he does it. He'll continue with the suspension of elections on the pretext of national security again."

"You don't really think that, do you?" said Zelman. "I mean, he's an asshole, that's not in question, but he's not that sort of asshole, is he?"

"I don't know," said White, "I hope not. But it bothers me. I mean, it truly bothers me. The powers he instated for himself during the war are still in place. Not a single one of them has been rescinded. If he gets into a fight with the Martians that will be just the excuse he needs to hang on to them, maybe even add more. It's not right, it's not democracy, and it feels like no one gives a shit but me."

Zelman put a hand on White's arm. "That's because you're a good person," she said, "and that's why it's so important that you're his number two. A heartbeat away, remember? It's part of your job to balance him out and keep him in check."

"It is," said White, "and I think I'm failing at it. I haven't been able to do a damn thing to stop him fixing up those carriers and sending them to Mars. It's the exact opposite of what he should be doing and I've been powerless to stop him."

"It'll blow over," said Zelman. "It's just one of those things that seems like a big deal at the time. A year from now you'll look back at this and wonder why it all seemed so important. I'm sure the Martians will back down, or we'll be able to broker some sort of deal or leaseback or something. Cool heads will prevail, you'll see."

"It's just that sort of thinking I'm worried about," said White. "Everybody thinks these things just work themselves out and turn out okay in the end. That's why they ignore every small incremental step towards disaster; because they think it won't matter in the long run, but it does. We've seen that happen close-up within the last ten years. Everybody thought we wouldn't go to war because it seemed we had too much to lose, and they had too much to lose, and that it wouldn't benefit anyone. But what happened? Somehow we just wandered into it despite everything. And you know why? Because too many people who had the opportunity to do something just sat around saying, '*Well, it'll never come to that.*' But you know what? Sometimes it *does* come to that, and by then it's too late. And it's happening again now, and there's nothing I can do about it."

"Oh come on," said Zelman, "you've had your war. No one's that unlucky. And Cortes had his fingers burned, too. The last thing he wants is another war."

White looked despondently into the distance. "I hope you're right," he said. He put his champagne glass on the bedside table after draining it and rolled over onto his side to face Zelman. "Do you really think I'm being paranoid?" he said.

Zelman looked down at him. "Not paranoid," she said. "Maybe a little over concerned. But that's what makes you such an effective politician; you look out for the things that other people miss. You're just doing your job, and doing it well."

White closed his eyes. "I'm so tired," he said.

"There, there," said Zelman, stroking his hair. "You go to sleep, if that's what you need."

"It is," said White sleepily. "I need to sleep."

Elspeth had been following the streams from Earth as well as Mars. She kept her eyes on streams from government departments and business news. She had followed the developments with the *Aloadae*; there were live streams from the USAN's defence department showing the refit. Occasionally the streams would cut off when there was material which was considered sensitive, but unclassified data on the refits was freely available.

Helios also published information and streams about its business. Information about the *Aloadae* and the personnel working on them was easy to come by.

Elspeth had used the information she gleaned from the various sources to put together stories on her own stream, detailing the political and military manoeuvrings of the USAN government and the newly formed Martian government.

Things on Mars were moving so fast it was difficult to keep up with them. All the senators and the president were new, of course, and their roles were too. There were many issues where people didn't really know what they were supposed to be doing or how to proceed. They were making things up as they went. It was exciting and fun for Elspeth as there was an almost endless supply of news each day regarding the machinations of the senate and the office of the president. There were comic stories too, where people no longer knew who should be responsible for what. For all that, it seemed like the new Mars was forging ahead on a wave of optimism.

Elspeth was unusual for her age in that she was interested in such things. Most of her peers, like people of a similar age on Earth, didn't pay much attention to the way their countries were run. They were comfortable, fed and housed, and had a myriad of distractions to keep them busy. The low-level underpinning of all that was of little concern to them. To Elspeth it was endlessly fascinating. She knew she was living through an incredibly important part of history. Mars would surely go on to grow and become a hugely important planet at the forefront of human expansion into the solar system and beyond, and here she was right there at the moment of independence. She was a keen student of history and could see that after the announcements and parties had come and gone the baby steps of the new Mars were unlikely to be without incident.

She could see the way the government of the USAN had been moving back on Earth. The government, and particularly the office of the president, had taken on more and more powers during the war and seemed reluctant to relinquish them now the war was over. She could see that the war had put a huge stress on the USAN's economy and that the country was in eye-watering debt. Its population was spending more and more money that it didn't have without even knowing or caring that it was doing it. The loss of one of the powerhouses of its economy, and its main source of energy, was going to make that situation far worse. The way she saw it, the USAN had to do something about its Martian problem. Looking at the USAN's recent track record in foreign affairs, which had been conducted largely by its military, and watching the *Aloadae* slowly mutate day by day into interplanetary attack spacecraft, she figured that things were going to get interesting very soon. She put all this into her streams, but viewing figures were low. The revenue she made from advertising was barely enough to cover her hosting fees, but she enjoyed what she was doing and knew that she had to start somewhere and just keep pressing on. She had an exclusive interview with Bobby Karjalainen coming up soon. She thought that would bring her to a much wider audience. If the interview went well she planned to chop it up and stream it over consecutive days, almost like a miniseries. She hoped that people who sought her stream out for Bobby might then get a feel for it and come back for some of her other items. It was unlikely, she knew. Most of the people tuning in for Bobby would be there for his all-American good looks and his exciting war stories. But what the hell. She lived in hope.

CHAPTER 19

An Act of War

Steiner, Foley and Johnson were recovering from the bone-shaking experience of being fired into space from the surface of the Earth when the alarm sounded.

"What the hell is that?" said Johnson.

Steiner shrugged, "I don't know, a test, maybe?"

"It's no drill," said Foley.

"Please remain in your seats and await further instructions," said an amplified voice, seemingly coming from nowhere.

"What is it? What's going on?" said Johnson.

"It's a problem," said Steiner. "They're dealing with it, go back to sleep."

"Back to sleep? Goddammit, I don't like no goddamn problems on no goddamn spacecraft. We could all get killed up here."

"It's fine," said Steiner. "It's probably instrumentation or something simple. We'll be at *Ephialtes* in two hours, anyway. After that we won't care what happens to this rust bucket."

"Two hours is a long time," said Johnson.

The unlocatable voice appeared around them again. "We're having some technical problems and are in contact with the ground, who are looking at solutions for us. We will keep you advised of the situation. We'll get back to you as soon as possible."

"Sheeeeeet!" said Johnson. "That doesn't sound like instrumentation to me. That sounds like they've got an actual problem. Sheeeeet!"

Steiner turned to Foley. "What do you think? Serious?"

Foley shrugged, "We're still here, ain't we?"

The lights flickered off and on in the cabin and the spacecraft gave a slight judder.

"I am not liking that," said Johnson.

"I think there may be something up," said Steiner.

They waited a further few minutes and the disembodied voice appeared again. "We have a significant malfunction with one of our life support systems. There is no need for alarm. The malfunction is not critical and we have more than enough oxygen to get to *Ephialtes*. Due to the nature of the leak, and as a safety precaution, we will dock within the next half-hour with *Otus*, which is currently two thousand kilometres away, eight thousand kilometres nearer than *Ephialtes*. Do not be alarmed."

"Damn," said Johnson. "Do not be alarmed. That's just great, I won't be alarmed. Even if I've got no goddamned air to breathe, I won't be alarmed, if you say so."

Twenty-three minutes later they docked with *Otus*, and after a short period of confusion they floated aboard.

Otus was a vast playground to them. *Otus'* own detachment of commanders had arrived a few days earlier, and old friends and comrades acted as happy guides. Despite repeatedly being chased off by Helios engineers and *Otus'* crew the commanders were all over the place. It seemed like a packed ferry, with people wandering about excitedly and wandering back again.

Ephialtes crew were asked to stay in the day areas while Helios engineers helped to ascertain the problem with the shuttle. The airlock through which the shuttle was docked contained data feeds which were pulled over to *Otus* for analysis.

Adam Speight spent some time on the job himself. It soon became apparent that shortly after the shuttle had escaped the Earth's atmosphere it had performed an emergency purge of its oxygen supplies, quickly venting most of them off into space. Speight analysed and reanalysed the data but could not make sense of it. It certainly appeared to be a software glitch, but he ran many simulations and could not replicate the error. As a precaution he replaced the main and auxiliary computers on the shuttle and replaced the software with the version he had set his AIs to modifying. He had added a number of redundant routines that prevented any purges without explicit human intervention. He believed that would make the shuttle safe for its journey back to Earth, where he recommended it underwent a more thorough accident investigation. All that remained was for *Otus* to donate some of its huge oxygen supplies to the shuttle and it would be able to continue on its way to *Ephialtes*.

That meant a few more hours of impromptu R&R for the commanders on board. Steiner had set himself up in the bar area and had amused himself by winding Johnson up. It was so easy he could hardly resist. Foley had disappeared. He said he had run into an old comrade who'd been posted to *Otus* and they were away somewhere reliving past glories.

Twelve hours later they were back aboard the shuttle and headed to *Ephialtes*.

Work on *Ephialtes* was nearing completion. They had taken aboard their complement of commanders and shipped home most of the Helios workers. A handful of software engineers and other specialists remained for the last few days of snagging and testing.

Askel had been working on data from *Otus*. They had made their 0.5 burn for a trip around the Moon. The information from the trip was invaluable. All systems had performed remarkably well. Data from the 0.5 burn, when extrapolated to a full burn, tallied exceptionally closely to the models. There would be no need for *Ephialtes* to run a similar extended test - the two ships and the alterations to them were close to identical. The data for one would suffice for the other.

There were some very minor adjustments to be made, mostly to the guidance systems. Askel had set her AIs to the task. There were also some last minute issues to resolve with the stores. They would have to wait an extra two days for their final delivery due to an unforeseen issue with one of the HLV shuttles. It irked Askel slightly. She and her team had worked crazy hours and with absolute dedication, and she was looking forward to delivering the upgraded *Ephialtes* two days ahead of what was already an ambitious schedule. Now, due to something as mundane as a broken down shuttle, she would be forced to deliver it merely on time. She felt that she had been robbed of her moment of glory. Of course, delivering this project on time was a staggering achievement in itself, but what she had achieved was even more impressive than that. People wouldn't know, or believe or care, if she told them that she would have delivered two days ahead of schedule if not for a minor fault on some crummy shuttle. '*C'est la vie*,' she thought.

Askel's slight fixation on the shuttle's infuriating deficiency grew when she received a call from Speight. He wanted to talk over the final checks before launch the next day. *Otus* was heading out for Mars.

"The data from the trip to Luna looked great to me. Did you drill down into it? Anything we need to know?"

"No, it's as good as it looks," said Askel. "I had some AIs analyse it closely. It looks like a simulation, exactly what we expected."

"It looked good to me too, and it felt good. Just felt right, y'know?"

"There'll be no problem with the full burn. The extrapolations are good too, we've nailed this thing. How are your supplies?"

"We took our last supply drop tonight. The shuttle took the rest of the team home."

"But you're going along for the journey?"

"I am indeed. Rawls made me an offer I couldn't refuse. He wanted a Helios engineer on board to cover any matters arising. I'll be responsible for both ships - we'll be close enough for real-time coms across both vessels. You're going home?"

"Yes," said Askel.

"About that shuttle," said Speight. "When your shuttle docked with us I ran some tests and patched it up."

"I heard," said Askel.

"One of the things I did was replace the main and auxiliary computers. It dumped all its oxygen for no reason. The hardware was all good so it had to be a software failure."

"You put in manual overrides?"

"Well, I made it a lot harder for the ship to mess with life-critical systems without running by an actual human first. I altered the software to be super cautious, just to get them back to Earth. Thing is, I've run a deep analysis on the software on both control computers, and I've found something a little odd."

"What's that?"

"Well, the software is signed by Helios and dated last year, January or February, I think. Last year, anyway. But it makes reference to libraries that were only released last month."

"That doesn't make sense. It's not using the older versions of the same libraries?"

"No, that's what I thought, so I tried it with the older libraries, and it doesn't work. The routines it used to purge the oxygen are only in the new libraries. I mean, you could do it with the old libraries, but you would have to code it in a completely different and more complex way. That's one of the many things that's so good about the new versions."

"So how is an old system making use of new libraries?"

"This is my point, Askel. It can't. The control system, which caused the failure, has to be very recent. But it says it's almost eighteen months old." He let the point hang.

"Sabotage?" said Askel, not really believing it.

"You tell me," said Speight. "I've gone through it again and again. I've put my best AIs on it, and I can't figure what's happened. The software is a year and a half old. It had a minor patch eight months ago, according to all the meta-data, and it's speaking to other systems that it should not be able to speak to, and telling them to be doing things they shouldn't be doing. What do you think?"

"I don't know," said Askel, "there's usually some freaky explanation for these sorts of things."

"That's what I thought, but I've been over it and over it and it doesn't add up."

"Did you take it to Rawls?"

"Not yet. I'm not even sure what it is."

"Send the data over to me. I'll have a look."

"I can send a virtual copy, but it's embedded in the physical systems. You really need the computers themselves."

"Okay. There's no way to get them over here, is there? And you're leaving tomorrow. Keep working on them and let me know."

"I will."

"Listen, I'm going to be around tomorrow when you go. I'll be following everything."

"Good. It's going to be fine. Like the trip to Luna, except we're going right on past the Moon with our foot to the floor."

"I know," said Askel. "I'm not doing it for moral support; I want to see your data. *Ephialtes* is shipping out in a day or two, so it will be useful for them."

"We're leaving at 06:00, Eastern Standard Time, USAN. Set your alarm."

"I'll be here from 04:00."

"Okay. We've done a good job here, haven't we?"

"Good? I'd say we've done an outstanding job."

"A hell of a lot of that was down to you. Thanks, Askel, you've been a great team leader."

Askel fought to hide her smile. "Thank you too, Speight. We all did well, everyone. I'm going to personally thank all of your team when I get back."

"You do that. Goodnight, Askel."

"Goodnight. Askel out."

Askel's comdev woke her at 03:55. She quickly dressed and sat at the terminal in her small cabin. She patched through to the main comcon of *Otus* and listened in on their audio traffic with ground control back on

Earth. She brought up *Otus'* systems console on her terminal and checked all the main data feeds. Everything looked good.

She listened to Commodore Tommy Parks running through checks with his systems leads. Periodically, ground control would answer a query or impart some additional information. After a while she heard Speight's voice too. He was having technical discussions with ground control and giving some observations to Parks. There was less than an hour to go before *Otus* set off for interplanetary space.

"Speight, Askel here. I'm monitoring your systems from over here; looks good."

"Hi, Askel. Very smooth this end. Seems like a nice morning for a trip, huh?"

"Roger that."

Askel left them to it, but kept her eyes on the data feeds. Everything was well within the normal parameters, just like a simulation.

When the clock had counted down to T minus eleven minutes Askel heard Parks take to the com.

"Men and women of *Otus*, this is Commodore Parks speaking. We are about to embark on an important mission and I want to say a few words to you before we set off. First, I would like to say that I am proud to have you all under my command. I have met you all, and read through your records, and I have to say that you are one of the finest collections of fighting personnel it has ever been my privilege to work with. The task ahead of us appears to be a simple one, but it is also a momentous one for this simple reason. This will be the first time in human history that an offensive force has been sent to another planet. We have the honour of being the first fighting force to represent our country in this way. We have all trained for this mission, and we are all aware that good soldiering means expecting the unexpected, adapting and using initiative to overcome any obstacle. I expect no less from you.

"We leave in less than ten minutes, so you still have time to contact loved ones and family if you want to be able to talk in real time. In five minutes there will be a data curfew. Five minutes after that, we leave. Parks out."

Askel scanned the readings. They were all good. She spoke to her com. "Good luck, Speight."

"Thanks, Askel. Won't need it."

Askel listened as the ground station at Dallas handed over primary control of *Otus* to Parks. They would jointly oversee the initial burn that would kick *Otus* out of Earth orbit. There were seconds left on the clock.

"Dallas, *Otus* here, we have control."

"Confirmed, *Otus*."

"T minus thirteen seconds to primary burn."

"Confirmed."

Askel listened to the countdown finish and followed the data flowing into her console as the great engine fired up. She had seen this a thousand times before, but it had always been simulated data. There was something intoxicating about knowing this data was real. This had all come from ideas that she had had, and now here it was, a real thing, happening right now.

She heard the chief flight engineer from *Otus* over the com. "Dallas, looking good. We have good acceleration and a stable burn."

"*Otus*, we're looking good here too, enjoy the ride."

Askel looked at the data for the mirror magnets containing the plasma chamber in *Otus*' engine. They were well within normal parameters.

She heard the flight engineer again. "Ah, Dallas we are experiencing -" The communication ended mid-sentence as all of Askel's data feeds froze.

"*Otus*, this is Dallas, do you read?"

-

"*Otus*, this is Dallas, do you read?"

-

"*Otus*, this is Dallas, do you read?"

-

"*Ephialtes*, this is Dallas, do you have a visual on *Otus*?"

"Ah, negative, Dallas, not from where we are," the *Ephialtes* flight engineer replied.

"*Ephialtes*, please stand by, we have a suspected communications malfunction with *Otus*, if there's anything you can give us in the meanwhile go ahead."

"Understood, Dallas. We don't have the transponder for *Otus* at this time, we will continue to hail across all frequencies."

"Go ahead, *Ephialtes*, same here. We'll get back to you when we have something."

Askel quickly reran the last seconds of data she had from *Otus*. It was normal, right up to the moment it stopped. Instinctively she raised her hand to cover her mouth. As a scientist and engineer she relied on cold hard data. The data was all good, as far as it went. What the absence of data was telling her was too big for her to take in. She knew that there was an abundance of redundant systems on *Otus*. Independent power supplies, independent coms, independent life-support. Multiple systems could fail simultaneously and the ship would still function. It was designed that way. She had contributed to that design. There could only be one possible explanation for thirty or more independent systems to fail at the same time. She stared at the data on her screen. It resolutely refused to update. It sat there on the screen, a frozen record of the last moment of *Otus*' life.

Ground control called out plaintively from her terminal.

"*Otus*, this is Dallas, do you read?"

"As soon as it became clear what had happened I looked at our software on *Ephialtes*. It's a very, *very* sophisticated insertion."

Rawls was listening to Askel's words and she could see he was scanning through the documentation she had sent him.

"As you can see, it's deliberate, and almost impossible to catch. It has been designed to fail, and disguise the fact that it's failing. And to resist detection."

Rawls nodded. "How did it get there?"

"I don't know. The change records show no updates other than those I personally oversaw. I have the latest versions of the control software here - my versions - and this was written over them, somehow, without leaving a record that it had done so."

"You're saying it was deliberate?"

"I'm absolutely saying it was deliberate. Someone fixed the software so that it would allow the magnetic field cage around the fission reaction to fail at the same time as the fusion reaction ran away with itself. The engine is a bomb; it's exploding in as controlled a way as possible in the direction we need it to. The altered software not only told the explosion to run way beyond safe limits, it fed us false data while it was doing it. And then it removed the cage, and -"

"You're absolutely sure?"

"The data from *Otus* is not consistent with what happened to *Otus*. And the hacked software that caused it has been inserted here too, on *Ephialtes*. If we were to go to a full burn now the exact same thing would happen to us. They were murdered, Rawls. Someone set out to kill them all."

"What do I tell Andrews?"

Askel thought. "Tell her the truth. We were sabotaged. It won't happen again. *Ephialtes* will launch, and it will work. I'll make sure of that."

"Askel, I don't want to take any risks on this, however small. Let's take some time -"

"There is no time. That's why we're being paid so much, to deliver this thing on time. And we have. We have been attacked and I will not let that happen again. *Ephialtes* is safe, I put my life on it."

"Let's not be hasty, Askel. Let's take a few days and really think this through. Come over to my house at the weekend and we'll put our heads together."

"What? I'm not coming back, not now. *Ephialtes* needs a senior Helios engineer for this trip. I'm going with them."

"Askel, I really don't think that's wise."

"Why not? I'm the best person for the job. I know this ship inside out. And I know there's someone on board trying to sab us. If I'm here I can protect us against that and I can route that bastard out."

"We have plenty of great engineers who are familiar with this project. Come home. You're stressed, you're overworked and you need a break. The last thing you need to be doing is six months additional work."

"I'm going, Rawls. I owe it to the people here. They've taken down one of my ships. They're not going to get the other."

"Askel, the *Aloadae* belong to the USAN government. Counter-terrorism is their game, not ours. We've delivered the best systems we could, it's up to them to use them."

"I'm sorry, Rawls, I'm going with them. It's in the contract. We promised them a senior Helios engineer to oversee the maiden voyage. It was supposed to be Speight. Now it's going to be me."

Rawls shook his head. He knew it was no use arguing.

"Listen, I don't know if Andrews is going to call this off, anyway, in light of what happened. They'll want additional safety checks on *Ephialtes* at least, and there'll need to be a major investigation."

"They don't need any of that. I've already told you exactly what happened; they injected martial software to deliberately destroy the ship. It's not a safety issue. *Otus* was a casualty of war. It was attacked."

"So how do we know they're not going to do the same to *Ephialtes*!?"

"That's what I'm trying to tell you. Because I will be here to defend it. I've purged the phony software, I've put additional fail-safes in place. I will be here to make it work. Tell that to Andrews. This ship is leaving to carry out the mission and it will be successful. I will personally see to it."

Rawls threw his hands in the air. "I don't know what to say. How do you know they're not just going to inject the malware again?"

"Because they don't know I've removed it. It can't be injected remotely - that's one of our cyberwarfare security measures - it has to be manually copied right here on the ship. A few days ago we received the commanders for the dropships and a few additional crew members as part of the standard rotation. All of them had been aboard *Otus*. You remember that faulty HLV shuttle? It was hobbled in exactly the same way, manually uploaded hacked software. Someone on that shuttle hacked the shuttle. They hacked *Otus*, then they hacked us. One - at least one - of those thirty is an enemy agent and I'm going to stay here to defend us against them and take them down."

Rawls knew he had been talked into a corner. Askel was brilliant, and part of that brilliance was her indefatigable drive and her absolute refusal to be beaten. What made her great also made her infuriating to deal with. He didn't have a choice.

"Okay, Lund, you're on the trip as our senior engineer. But be careful, you hear me?"

Askel smiled, "I hear you."

"You know, Helios, as a company, has a lot at stake with this mission. That ship is one of the most expensive things we've ever made. And the importance of the mission to our client, well, that just ramps it up again. I wish you weren't going Askel. We've just lost Speight. That's a massive loss to us, and not just on a business level. You're the most important person we have. You have to make this work and you have to come back to us. You understand?"

"I think so. You're saying you care about the bottom line and people too, right?"

"I care about *you*, Askel. Be safe."

Askel was taken aback. Rawls was never this open. Maybe it was the shock of the disaster. That sort of thing could disorient people.

"I'll be safe, Rawls, and I'll bring this big lump of metal back to you."

"Make sure you do."

CHAPTER 20

Target Practice

The launches for the orbiting missile system went without a hitch. Kostovich's AI had predicted the probability of one or more launches failing at two thousand to one. Assembly, as per design, was fast and efficient in accordance with the many computer models Kostovich had run for it.

The system was now ready.

The main Martian conurbation of Marineris was defended by the four missile batteries on the surface of the planet, with further coverage given now by the off-planet platform in geostationary orbit above them. The planetside systems had been tested on inexpensive aerial drones. Kostovich wanted to do live tests for the orbiting platform and needed something to test it against. There were many artificial satellites in Martian orbit. Kostovich need one that was live but expendable.

He had designed the system to be as flexible as possible. To that end each battery's missiles were armed with a number of different payloads, from nukes to tactical battlefield warheads. The idea was to limit destruction to the minimum required in a given situation. Venkdt thought their most likely enemy was their erstwhile compatriots, the USAN. He hoped that, if push came to shove, it would be possible to repulse any attack with minimum aggression.

The batteries' missile of choice was the battlefield EMP. The powerful electromagnetic pulse of these weapons was enough to fry any nearby electronics, rendering such systems inoperable. Rather than destroy the enemy they would disarm him.

The second line was standard chemical explosive warheads, necessary for situations where a precise strike was needed. Lastly, for cases where all subtlety was lost, were tactical nukes.

Kostovich needed to test all three systems. He wanted to disable a working satellite with an EMP, cripple it with a standard chemical explosive missile, then annihilate it with a nuke. A working, perhaps soon to be decommissioned, satellite would be the ideal candidate. He set to scanning the records of the satellites available to him. Quickly he settled on *Ares-H 17*, a coms satellite commissioned by S-Com, an Earth based telecoms company, and leased to the USAN Army. *Ares-H 17* had been superseded five years previously by *Hera-3*. For three years thereafter *Ares-H 17* had been kept online as a failover option for *Hera-3*. *Hera-3* had proved to be every bit as resilient as the manufacturers said she would be. Her internal failovers had never been used once. The additional cost of supporting *Ares-H 17* was therefore seen as unnecessary, and was struck from the budgets. Since then it had been doing nothing necessary and was due to be permanently decommissioned in two months' time.

Kostovich gleaned this information from his backdoor into the USAN information systems. The true nature of *Ares-H 17*'s original purpose was shrouded from public view. The fact that S-Com rented it out to the military was not public knowledge; in fact, S-Com maintained some fairly mundane coms traffic through the satellite's systems to help maintain the cover of its military use. Kostovich knew though, and he was anxious about the possible sensitivity around taking out a piece of USAN hardware, albeit one that was no longer used and was weeks away from being scrapped.

Usually he would have just ploughed ahead and done it. He was well aware of the inherent dangers in asking for people's permission to do things. Generally, he preferred to apologise later, where necessary, rather than get bogged down in discussion, argument and counterargument.

EPHIALTES

This time, however, he wanted to get explicit permission from somewhere. He was, after all, going to be detonating a nuclear bomb.

He called from his terminal and got through to Venkdt's PA.

"Hey there. Is Mr Venkdt available?"

"Hello, Dr Kostovich. Please hold while I check." The image switched from the PA to a Venkdt promotional video. Seconds later the PA reappeared. "I'll patch you through."

Kostovich was midway through his 'Thank you' when the screen switched and Venkdt appeared. "Hi, Dan," he said, "how can I help?"

"Hello, Charles," said Kostovich, still feeling uncomfortable using the forename, "I just want to run something by you. For advice, you know?"

"Go ahead."

"As I'm sure you know the orbiting Parry system has now been successfully assembled. I want to test the weapons systems on an old satellite, but, well, it used to be used by the USAN Army."

"Used to be?"

"Yes. It's weeks away from being permanently decommissioned. They haven't used it for five years."

"Okay." Venkdt thought. "But it's a USAN satellite?"

"No, it's owned by S-Com, they rent it to them. We'd be doing them a favour, saving them the cost of the decommission."

"It's privately owned junk, then?"

"Pretty much."

"So why are you asking me?"

Kostovich thought. "Just because of the USAN connection, I suppose. And I guess you now have overall authority over Martian airspace."

"Dan, if it's defunct just use it."

"Yes, that's what I thought."

Kostovich had one of the old offices in his department refitted as the com-con for the missile batteries. He decided that the room should be manned at all times, and that the batteries should be constantly monitored. This was not strictly necessary as the systems were fully automated and capable of making complex decisions independent of human input. He could also tap into the system from his terminal, should that be necessary. But he thought that such an important system, and one with such destructive potential, should be seen to be being controlled by human beings. This was despite the fact that the human element, in reality, added a layer of uncertainty that increased any potential unreliability. Kostovich was canny enough to know that appearances are everything, so here he found himself at the control site flanked by two of his research assistants who had very recently been seconded into the MSS as weapons engineers.

The overall system had been christened "Parry." In a meeting explaining the mechanics, goals and financing of the system Kostovich had presented the name to a less than enthusiastic response.

"Why Parry?" asked Christina Venkdt.

"Well," said Kostovich, "it's a defensive system, so when the enemy tries to attack, we will Parry."

There were some half-hearted nods.

"I did consider The Sword of Ares," said Kostovich, "but I thought that was a bit melodramatic. I have to admit I hesitated over Parry Missile System, because of the acronym."

"I don't know; massive retaliation to any perceived slight - PMS works for me," Foveaux had said.

"Anyway, I think we've settled on Parry Missile System now. Can we all agree on that?"

Because there was a pressing practical need to pursue the building of the system that had been the full extent of the debate over its name. Had a potential threat not been imminent there may have still been a naming committee running even now, thought Kostovich.

The Parry system was owned by Kostovich. Venkdt, for now, and in time the Martian administration, were picking up the bill, but it was Kostovich's project. He had installed himself as Chief Operating Officer, arguing that for the initial period the system could still be considered to be in development. As the Chief Operating Officer he could test the system in operation and tweak it accordingly. It would remove a layer of bureaucracy and potential miscommunication, speeding things up. Plus it was cool to be in charge of a missile system.

The surface batteries had performed well in their testing, matching or surpassing the computer models. Testing the orbiting platform, *Parry 5*, would be much more of a challenge. The distance to the platform would make a difference, and the targets would be smaller and faster, too. Though *Parry 5* was free from the worst of Martian gravity, and as such had many advantages compared to its surface based brethren, it had to cover a much wider area. It had a more advanced and sensitive detection system and its longer range missiles were adapted to the space environment.

Kostovich had run each test many times in simulated models before the day of the actual tests. He knew what to expect and how the tests should run in sequence, one after the other, and he knew what the effects should be. He had a coms line to *Ares-H 17* and could monitor its output. It was mostly redundant data, but it was a steady stream and was useful just for that.

He had briefed his team extensively. They all knew what to expect. The tests would be a straightforward drill, A followed by B, followed by the gathering of data C. It would be just another day at the office.

Parry 5 was in geostationary orbit over the Martian capital Marineris. *Ares-H 17* was orbiting the planet once every hour and ten minutes. Kostovich aimed to run one test for the next three times *Ares-H 17* came past. The tests should last a little over two and a half hours in total. His team were well briefed. Siena Walton was a senior research assistant and Thomas Baldwin was a very promising postgraduate student. Kostovich had picked them himself and had given them a crash course in overseeing his Parry missile command and control setup.

As it passed by *Parry 5* on each orbit *Ares-H 17* would be five hundred kilometres away at its nearest point, and moving at a speed of more than seven kilometres per second. As soon as it cleared the horizon *Parry 5* would be able to track it. The Parry system made helpful suggestions, informing the team that the satellite was unarmed, unmanned and safe to ignore. Kostovich instructed Walton to arm two EMP missiles and continue tracking. They had tracked *Ares-H 17* on its previous flyby and knew there was nothing likely to be any different about this spin around the planet.

Periodically, Baldwin read out some data regarding the satellite. It was entirely unnecessary as all three of them were monitoring the tracking data on their screens. Kostovich let it go. It sounded significant and serious.

"*Ares-H 17* is now at approximately fifteen hundred kilometres range, closing fast," said Baldwin.

"Prepare the EMPs for launch," said Kostovich.

"EMPs ready for launch," said Walton.

"Check the distance for detonation is set for three hundred metres," said Kostovich.

"Three hundred metres, check," said Walton.

"Where is she now?" said Kostovich.

"Twelve hundred kilometres," said Baldwin.

"Okay," said Kostovich. "We'll launch at one thousand kilometres."

"Launch at one thousand kilometres, check," said Walton.

"Eleven hundred kilometres," said Baldwin.

"Whenever you're ready, I guess," said Kostovich.

Walton was staring intensely at her screen. She nodded almost imperceptibly at Kostovich's last command. She watched the tracker's numbers spinning down from eleven hundred. As they hit the magic thousand she pressed a button on her terminal and with a release of breath she got out the words, "Missiles away."

Baldwin could immediately track the EMPs as they streaked away from *Parry 5*. "Missiles away, confirmed," he said. "Readings for both missiles are good at this time. Forty seconds to detonation."

"Confirmed, forty seconds," said Walton.

Kostovich looked to his screen. He could see a blip representing *Ares-H 17*, alternating between green and blue, moving laterally from right to left, and to two smaller red blips moving upwards. The green-blue blip and the red blips appeared to be converging on space in the centre of the screen. Although he had been through this many times he once again explained it to Walton and Baldwin. "Green is *Ares-H 17*," he said, "blue is *Ares-H 17*'s electrical activity. This time around we are aiming to take out blue and leave green."

"Twenty five seconds to go," said Baldwin.

"Missiles looking healthy, adjusting course for rendezvous with target," said Walton.

"I'm liking it so far," said Kostovich. "Just like the simulations."

"Fifteen seconds," said Baldwin.

"I have some late minor adjustments to trajectory here," said Walton. "Looking good."

"Ten seconds."

Kostovich could see the green-blue blip and the red blips almost touching.

"Five seconds, all systems normal."

They all lifted their heads from their individual terminals to look at the large display in front of the consoles. The green blue blip was now joined by the red blips. As they looked, the red blips disappeared. A solitary green blip continued its journey toward the left side of the screen.

Walton looked back down to her console. "I have two successful detonations, final telemetry from both missiles suggests successful detonations three hundred metres from the target as planned."

"Data feed from the target has dried up," said Baldwin.

"This is good," said Kostovich. "Exactly like the simulations. Good work people. Shall we go for a cup of tea while we wait for her to come round again?"

They reconvened half an hour later to go through the same process again. They waited for *Ares-H 17* to come back around. This time they fired standard explosive missiles. Not wanting to destroy the satellite, but needing to test the accuracy of their system, they had set the missiles to detonate at a distance from *Ares-H 17* such that they would be able to knock it very slightly out of its path of orbit.

Red dots and green dots once again converged on the screen and again the green dot continued on its path.

"I'm analysing the trajectory of *Ares-H 17* in comparison to the previous orbits," said Baldwin.

"Missile telemetry indicates successful detonation in the selected areas," said Walton. "Four for four," she added, and Kostovich grinned.

"How's that trajectory data coming?" he said to Baldwin.

"I need a little longer," Baldwin replied. "We've given her such a tiny jog I need her to travel a bit further before I can see if we've made a difference," he said.

Kostovich, having been through this experience many times in the simulations, knew this would be the case. But he was enjoying the novelty of working closely with other people and asking them questions, especially when he knew what the answers should be.

"Okay," said Baldwin. "Her orbit has definitely changed. We gave her a shove."

"That is compatible with my data from the missiles and what I would have expected," said Walton.

Kostovich nodded, "That's exactly right. We just tickled a satellite moving at more than seven kilometres per second, precisely how and where we wanted to. I think we can call this second test a success. Not only can we place our missiles on a postage stamp, we can place them on a postage stamp that's going really fast. Well done everyone. Is it too soon for more tea?"

They had each viewed the previous tests as routine. The systems had been well tested in simulation and were based on systems that had had many practical tests on Earth. The final test would be the first time that any of them had ever detonated a nuclear bomb. They viewed it as somewhat exceptional.

Kostovich had all the data he needed now, from the simulations and the earlier practical tests, to demonstrate that the missile guidance systems were extremely accurate and reliable. A nuclear weapon, being something of a blunt tool, did not rely as the previous two types of missile did on accuracy. The test here was simply to see if the thing would detonate as planned.

When *Ares-H 17* came around for the final time she might well have expected to have continued travelling on her way unmolested. She had been spinning around Mars for many years and had made the journey hundreds of thousands of times. Why should she expect this time to be any different? Maybe she had been tipped off by the odd occurrences on the last two journeys, packed with more incident than the previous thousands. First, she had been stripped of her senses and then, adding insult to injury, she had been most rudely shoved. Surely things couldn't get any worse.

When she was fifteen hundred kilometres off from *Parry 5* Kostovich went through the same routine with Baldwin and Walton. He asked them to feed him data on the well-being of his missiles and the trajectory of the doomed satellite. Baldwin and Walton were well rehearsed from the many simulations they had taken part in.

"Arm the warhead," said Kostovich.

"The warhead is armed," said Walton.

"Twelve hundred kilometres," said Baldwin.

"Prepare to launch missile," said Kostovich.

"Missile is prepped and ready," said Walton.

"Once again, launch at a thousand kilometres," said Kostovich.

Walton looked at her screen, timing the launch to perfection. "Missile away," she said.

"Missile is on track and on speed," said Baldwin.

"Telemetry is A-okay," said Walton.

"We can expect detonation in thirty seconds," said Baldwin.

Kostovich had set the nuclear missile to detonate five hundred metres in front of *Ares-H 17*. The satellite would be within the blast radius and travelling at speed towards the centre of it.

"Fifteen seconds," said Baldwin. "Looking good."

"Telemetry is good," said Walton.

"I'm patching a visual through to the main display," said Kostovich. The display showed the curve of the Martian horizon with the blackness of space beyond. He hadn't bothered with visuals for the previous two tests because, due to the great distance of his monitoring satellite, there would have been nothing to see.

"Five seconds," said Baldwin.

They looked at the main screen and waited. There was a tiny flash, almost like a glitch on the video feed, followed by a small orange blossoming over the Martian horizon.

"Successful detonation," said Walton.

"I concur," said Baldwin.

"I concur, too," said Kostovich. "Did you see that? We got it, three for three. The system is good, the test is successful. Let's set some AIs running through the data and go home."

Kostovich sent Walton and Baldwin home. He had a cursory look through the data but he knew it was good. He'd seen the same data many times before in his computer models, but he set his AIs to it for a deep analysis. He was aware that this was a vaguely historic event, so he needed to be thorough. Before he left for the night he put a private call through to Charles Venkdt.

Venkdt was in a bathrobe, getting ready for bed. He took the call anyway.

"Hi Charles, I just thought you'd like to know that we've just put *Parry 5* through her paces and she is looking really good."

"That's good to know, Dan."

"We did three sets of tests, EMP, chemical explosive and nuclear. I haven't got the deep analysis of the data back yet but it all looks fantastic, exactly like the simulations, exactly what we were expecting. No surprises. The level of protection afforded by an orbiting system is far superior to what we have on the ground. I'd say that we now have an exceptionally effective defensive system in place."

"Well, Dan, all I can say is thank you. And so quick! How do you do it?"

"In this case, Charles, I did it mostly by stealing the designs from someone else, but what the hell. We're covered. And I've got uniforms and weapons to Foveaux, too. The MSS actually looks like a military force now. We're looking at getting battlefield artillery and armoured transports to them within the next couple of weeks. We have an army worthy of the name."

"We do, Dan. You've worked miracles, I can't thank you enough."

"I'm just glad to have played a role," said Kostovich. "These are historic times aren't they? I've always fancied having my name in the history books."

"I'm sure you'll get that," said Venkdt.

"Okay, good night then," said Kostovich. "And remember, the reason you can sleep safely in your bed is because of people like me manning the barricades, forever looking into the dark night and protecting the citizens of Mars."

"You're full of shit, Kostovich, good night to you too."

"I am full of shit, sir, goodnight."

Kostovich hung up, and found it difficult to wipe the smile off his face.

Colleen Acevedo requested an urgent meeting with Andrews. In light of her previous work Andrews found time to meet with her.

Acevedo entered the office with a sheaf of papers clutched in her hands. "I've sent you copies," she said as she walked towards Andrews' desk. "Did you get chance to take a look?"

"Very briefly. What was I looking at?"

Acevedo pulled a chair round and sat beside Andrews. She fanned the papers out on the desk. "It's a report on Martian defence capability."

"Okay."

"As you know - it's not really much of a secret around here - the Martians have been building missile defences around Marineris."

"Yes."

"They've done it quickly, so we don't know how robust they might be. Anyway, they have the whole city covered from the ground. We've figured that into our attack scenarios. The commanders and dropships all have countermeasures, and the new scenarios prioritise the neutralization of the missile bases."

"This is all known to us already, right?"

"Right, but this is something new. Or it looks like something new."

"What is it?"

"We picked this up from one of our Martian surveillance satellites. It's the trace of a weak electromagnetic pulse."

"So what does that tell us?"

"The EMP coincides exactly with an old communications satellite going dark."

"Go on."

"There was some more activity after the pulse, most likely missiles in the same area, and then about an hour after that there was a limited nuclear explosion."

"And you think this is from the missile bases?"

"No, it's not, it's way out of their range. We think it can only be from an orbiting missile base. And the satellite they attacked was, until recently, one of ours"

"Ours?"

"It was a USAN secure coms relay. So you see, they have a weapons platform in space, and they're targeting our satellites."

"They're taking out our satellites. You're sure of that?"

"It would appear to be the case."

"What can we do about it?"

"At the moment, nothing. But I'd like to recommend that if we're sending a warship into that vicinity then taking out that platform is an essential prerequisite."

"Yes, of course. Thank you."

Farrell had high-level clearance, giving him access to military intelligence. He was made aware of Acevedo's report. The *Aloadae* were to have been his big stick, backing up his team of negotiators. Now it looked more like they were headed into a potential hot zone. He didn't like it one bit. The original plan was to preen and bluster. The possibility of getting into an actual fight, however one-sided, had not been given serious consideration.

Unusually, the president had come over to the Ministry of Defence for the meeting. The standard practise was for the president to take meetings at the New White House, or rarely at the Capitol. Farrell guessed the president wanted to look marshal, emphasising his role as commander-in-chief. As the nominal head of the armed forces, why wouldn't he be at the heart of the action?

It didn't bode well for Farrell's side of the table. Andrews had the military and it was looking like that was the way this thing was going. Farrell had very few cards to play for the side of diplomacy. In fact, if this came down to an invasion, his department would only come into play once the smoke of battle had cleared. They would be charged with framing the peace, the far more difficult task. They had made preliminary contact with Shaw, but he wasn't sure how reliable she would be. Maybe she had gone soft, out on that cushy posting all these years and now under comfortable house arrest. What was house arrest on Mars, anyway? It's not like she would be free to go outside at the best of times.

He would need to ramp up their efforts to contact Anthony Karjalainen. Anthony would be the key to securing stability in the post insurrection Mars. It was something he needed to get right. His department had done well to anticipate the troubles as they bubbled up but they hadn't really been active. All he had managed to do was provide a commentary.

He was determined that, once order had been restored, his department would be decisive in handling the re-established peace. For now, all he could do was back up Andrews.

The president arrived five minutes late. If it had been anyone else Andrews would have left, impressing on the tardy that her time was so valuable she couldn't squander a single moment. But since it was the president she waited anxiously, rereading her briefing papers until the door to Conference Room 2 swung open and the president breezed in.

He didn't offer an apology for being late. He strode to the head of the table, greeting Andrews and Farrell along the way, and sat down. "What do you have for me?" he said.

Andrews gripped her papers with both hands. She noticed she was doing it and consciously lay the papers down on the table before beginning. "Mr President, we have some new intelligence from Mars, raising some very important questions."

Cortes looked surprised. "There was nothing in the intelligence briefing this morning."

"We've only just finished working through this, sir. One of our best analysts finished this report not yet an hour ago."

"I see," said Cortes, stonily.

"Well, the analysis shows that the Martians have armed themselves."

"Missile bases. I know, it's a minor military matter. I've been assured that they will offer no serious threat should we need retake surface facilities."

"That's true, Mr President, but we also now believe they have an orbiting missile platform, which presents a number of new difficulties for us."

Cortes rubbed his chin. "New difficulties. What are they?"

"A defensive platform in space would obviously present a threat to *Ephialtes*."

"So what are you saying? That we have to back off?"

"No, Mr President. But before we can put *Ephialtes* in orbit we have to take the missile platform out."

"So we go all that way for some robust diplomacy and the first thing we do when we get there is attack a Martian installation. That makes us look like aggressors, right?" He directed the question to Farrell.

"We're not the aggressors here, sir -"

"Goddammit, I know that!" said Cortes. "I'm asking you what this is going to *look* like!"

Farrell looked chastened, and he momentarily stumbled over his words as he replied. "Sir, it needn't look like that at all. In fact, we can show that Mars has acted aggressively toward us. We would clearly be acting in self-defence."

"Aggression to us? What are you talking about?"

Andrews stepped in. "Two days ago the orbiting Martian missile platform destroyed a USAN satellite. It was an unprovoked attack, without warning."

Cortes slammed a fist down on the table. Farrell jumped, and struggled to cover it.

"Why am I only hearing about this now! I'm the goddamned president!"

Andrews kept cool. "Mr President, we've only just completed our analysis. This is the earliest we could inform you."

Cortes' eyes narrowed, and he jabbed a finger at Andrews as he spoke. "I am the commander-in-chief. When my forces come under attack I expect to know immediately. Not at the next meeting, not when the report has been tied up with a pretty little bow. Immediately. Do you understand?"

"Yes, sir," said Andrews.

Cortes sat back in his seat. "Jesus! So they're attacking our hardware now. What about *Otus*? Are you any further with that? Was that them?"

"All we know for certain at this point is that *Otus* was deliberately destroyed as the result of a very sophisticated sabotage. The investigation is ongoing, but obviously the Martians would have to be prime candidates. They have the motive and they are one of few entities who might have the means for such an attack," said Andrews.

Farrell cut in. "We don't have anything concrete on that, sir. We're following up some leads at the moment."

"Following leads, nothing concrete. What do I pay you people for? Did they destroy our ship or didn't they? They're attacking our other vessels - thanks for letting me know, by the way - so you can bet your asses they're behind it. Sons of bitches!"

"Our satellite was destroyed by Martian missiles in a deliberate act of aggression, Mr President. It's more than possible they destroyed *Otus*, too," said Farrell.

Cortes thought.

"That takes the aggression off us," offered Farrell. "If we have to destroy their orbiting missile platform -"

"There's no if. It's a real and present threat to *Ephialtes*, and it has to go before we can bring her to bear on any negotiations," Andrews cut in.

"If we destroy their missile platform we will clearly be acting in self-defence following at least one but probably two unprovoked Martian attacks on USAN vessels. It doesn't look bad on us. In fact, given the level of provocation they're exposing us to, it would be a very restrained response," said Farrell.

Cortes placed a hand on the table and absentmindedly drummed on it as he spoke. "How do we do it? When do we do it?"

Andrews adjusted her glasses. "*Ephialtes* has her own missile batteries. As soon as it's in range she can take out the Martian platform. It should be a straightforward task, militarily. I take it we have your approval?"

Cortes nodded. "Of course. We can't put *Ephialtes* at risk. And we're responding to aggression, not initiating it. The platform; is it manned?"

"We don't think so. We can't say for sure, but it would seem unlikely."

"Okay. Take it out."

"Yes, Mr President."

Venkdt's PA burst breathlessly into his office. Venkdt was seated at his desk. He looked up, shocked. "You need to hear this, sir," she said, and tapped her comdev.

"What is it?" said Venkdt, concerned.

"Just a minute." She fiddled with the comdev until the wall next to her came alive with an image of Cortes' head and shoulders. Just visible behind him were the flags, one on either side. "Watch," said the PA. She back-scrolled the footage to the beginning.

"My fellow Americans. The loss last week of our capital ship *Otus* and its crew was a terrible occurrence. I watched the streams, like many of you, with a heavy heart and tear filled eyes. It is my unfortunate duty to tell you now that the preliminary investigation into this disaster has made some very disturbing discoveries. It is believed that the loss of our great ship, and of so many of our sons and daughters, was due not to an accident but a deliberate act of sabotage. The investigation is at too early a stage at present to suggest who was responsible for this savage act, but in the fullness of time we will find out. We will not rest until the wrong-doers are brought to account for their crimes.

"The proud *Otus*, as you know, was setting off for the distant planet of Mars, where the interests of peace and fraternity are under grave threat from those who would cast aside the rule of law and allow the reign of anarchy. That noble task now falls solely to *Otus*' great sister, *Ephialtes*. *Ephialtes* has cast off the bonds of Earth and as I speak is travelling at hitherto unimaginable speed towards her task on the other side of our solar system.

"We do not seek conflict with the people of Mars.

"We seek a peaceful resolution to a jurisdictional dispute, and restoration for the crimes committed against our government and institutions. We go to Mars in the spirit of reconciliation.

"Earlier this afternoon I received confirmation that one of our prime spacecraft in Martian orbit has been destroyed by a deliberate and premeditated Martian attack. I have to tell you now; such aggression will not stand. We will not accept or tolerate attacks on USAN property or personnel. We will respond firmly.

"Two of our ships have been cynically destroyed in the last ten days. Such manoeuvring against us cannot be allowed go unanswered, nor will it. I have sent Charles Venkdt, the leader of the Martian insurrection, a proposal that he stand down immediately and submit himself to the mercy of our courts, so that no further action need be taken on our part beyond restoring order to the Martian polity. Should Mr Venkdt fail to accede to this request we will have no other option but to restore order by force of arms.

"The loss of *Otus* has yet to be attributed. The loss of *Ares-H 17* was a deliberate attack on the USAN military, and as such can only be viewed as an act of war. The leaders of the Martian revolt have brought war to us. Excepting for the immediate submission of Charles Venkdt and his illegitimate government, we will respond in kind.

"Thank you."

Cortes stepped away from the podium and out of shot, and the image quickly changed to a young reporter who started jabbering. The PA tapped her comdev and the image disappeared. Venkdt continued looking through the wall where the image once was. "Well?" said the PA.

Venkdt shrugged. "Well," he said. He toyed with a pencil on his desk. "Does any of that sound remotely plausible to you?"

The PA fidgeted. "What part?"

"Any of it. Is it likely that we'd have the manpower, skills or desire to sabotage a USAN capital ship a hundred and forty million miles away? That we'd want to provoke the best armed nation on Earth?"

The PA didn't answer.

"Is it even plausible that the USAN would send a military force to attack us? Would they do that? Really?"

The PA thought. "They have just successfully prosecuted a war. Maybe the thought of one more little skirmish is okay to them?"

Venkdt threw his hands up slightly. "I don't know what to say. Is he kidding? You know, a bluff?"

Again, the PA didn't answer.

"I want people to know that we are not attacking USAN ships. We're just not. And we're not going to be pushed around on the point of some populist frenzy, whipped up with downright lies and misinformation." He paused in thought.

"Can you get the word around that I will make an announcement tonight on the official presidential stream? That is set up, now isn't it?"

"I believe it was set up last week."

"Okay, I'll be doing a live stream tonight at 19:00. Presidential or Venkdt, if it's not available. Can you get word around? Particularly news aggregators on Earth. We have to set this straight."

"Yes, Mr Venkdt. How long is the stream likely to be?"

"I don't know. Say five minutes?"

"Okay. Will you need anything to prepare for it?"

"I don't know that, either. Maybe. Get me Kostovich."

Venkdt's stream was the number one recommended item for its timeslot on the aggregators, beating even *When Kittens Attack*.

"My fellow Martians, people of Earth. The people of Mars recently decided to take command of their own affairs. This was a momentous step, and one not taken lightly. Obviously, there are some who object to the new arrangement, on moral, political or legal grounds. We acknowledge those concerns and continue to work through them.

"I personally, and I'm sure I speak for my fellow Martians here too, continue to see the USAN as our mother country. We bear the USAN no ill will. In fact, we feel a great bond of kinship, expressed through our shared history and continuing business and family relationships. We share a common culture, a common language and common values. We seek to deepen these bonds as we move into the future.

"The Martian government has recently been accused of some heinous acts of aggression against the USAN. I am speaking to you tonight to refute those allegations in the strongest terms. We are a peaceable nation, and we reject outright the calls of those who would reach for the sword rather than seek to resolve our differences through mutual dialogue and conversation.

"I would like to make this point absolutely clear. The tragic loss of the USAN ship *Otus* was in no way connected to any actions by Martian forces. I can state that for you categorically. Mars is a friend to the USAN, and will continue to be so, despite the current difficulties.

"President Cortes has called for the democratically elected government of Mars to step down. It would be doing a vast disservice to the Martian people, who voted with an overwhelming majority for independence, to comply with this request. We are made of sterner stuff than that. I call in return for President Cortes to open diplomatic channels that we may discuss our differences, of which there are many, and work towards finding common ground, that both of our great nations might grow and prosper in peace.

"Thank you. Good night."

The stream ended.

Venkdt stood up from his chair and immediately began pacing. "How was it?" he said.

"Good," said Kostovich.

"Too short?"

"The length was fine. Nobody has an attention span anymore."

"Will it make any difference? To anything?"

Kostovich shrugged. "Who knows? You got your point out there. And maybe no one will notice that you didn't deny destroying *Ares-H 17*."

"That's not even a USAN ship!"

"Exactly. You were right to avoid it. If you'd tried to explain it's not a USAN craft all people would have heard would have been '*Areas-H 17*' and 'USAN'. So just leave well alone, like you did, and hope nobody notices."

Venkdt finished his pacing and sat back down. "What are we going to do, Dan? If they turn up here in that big ship, spoiling for a fight?"

"Well," said Kostovich, "as I believe I have demonstrated, we have the capability to render them harmless. A surgical EMP strike, which we are quite capable of, would turn *Ephialtes* into an oversized tin can and nothing more."

"And then what?"

Kostovich looked confused, briefly. "And then it's over. It's the only interplanetary military craft in existence, and it took four years to build. Once it's neutralized, that's it. We would be, literally, beyond reach."

Venkdt shook his head. "Christ, we don't want to let it get to that."

Kostovich nodded. "You've got six weeks or so to politic and manoeuvre and bob and weave, but you can be confident that as a fallback, and if you have to, you can take them out of the game, militarily. And relatively safely, too. Obviously, there will always be risks when you're detonating weapons in conflict but we should be able to take that ship off the field of play without harming any of the crew. Wouldn't that look great on the streams, too? Powerful *and* benevolent."

Venkdt shook his head again.

CHAPTER 21

Name, Rank and Number

Elspeth had never interviewed a celebrity before. She had hardly interviewed anyone before. She had followed Bobby's exploits on the streams during the war and had bought his book on the day of release. While she was too level-headed to be called a fan she was certainly in awe of Bobby Karjalainen and that added to her nervousness at the thought of interviewing him.

She was eighteen years old and looked even younger. She was worried Bobby would not take her seriously. She thought it important that the impression she made from the very beginning was one of maturity and seriousness. From everything she had seen and read it seemed like Bobby was quite a strong personality, and if she couldn't approach him as an equal the interview would not work. It would end up as one of those bland press calls where the subject spouts a few meaningless words, glad simply to get their face on the screen. Elspeth didn't want that. She wanted to get something unique.

From her research she was fairly sure that no one had thought of asking Bobby about his return to Mars and his relationship with his dying father. That would be interesting on its own, and it came with the possibility that Bobby might get emotional or defensive. Either way, it would make for compelling viewing. In order to put a strong figure like Bobby in that position she would have to establish herself as a solid presence in her own right. Someone like Bobby, she thought, wouldn't be pushed into a corner by a gauche eighteen-year-old who didn't really know what she was doing. It was absolutely vital that she cover that up; that she should appear calm, authoritative and used to dealing with powerful personalities. Although that was the exact opposite of the truth Elspeth believed she would be able to fake it.

She had rented a room at a local college. She wasn't sure if that was a good idea. Maybe it would play badly with her age, making it look like she was doing a school project or somesuch. But it was the only place she could afford. Her own home would make it look even more like a teenager's project and it would be presumptuous to ask to do it at Bobby's place, as well as giving him home advantage.

She arrived early and set up her equipment. She had borrowed a moderately good camera which she set up behind her right shoulder. She had arranged two chairs not quite facing each other, one for her and one for Bobby. She set up her old camera so it would be looking over Bobby's shoulder at her. She planned to cut in shots of her asking questions, nodding and looking interested. She had seen this set-up many times on the more sober streams - the ones that covered politics, business and so forth - and she thought it seemed suitably serious. She shot some test of footage on each of the cameras, sat in each of the chairs, and she was happy with the results.

Bobby was late.

After ten minutes she started to wonder if he was coming at all. Should she send him a message reminding him, or would that seem desperate? Against her impulses she decided not to message him but to wait. She thought that would be what an old pro would do.

After twenty minutes she was starting to feel despondent. Her last message from Bobby had been over a week ago. He was probably busy with glamorous speaking engagements and had forgotten all about it. She started to feel that she had been a fool to have ever believed that she had landed an interview with Bobby Karjalainen. She felt a strange mixture of emotions; anxiety, disappointment and embarrassment. But underneath it all there was still a scintilla of undying hope: maybe Bobby Karjalainen *will* turn up.

At half an hour Elspeth was considering packing her kit away. She had only booked the room for an hour and it looked like she had been stood up. She sat in her interviewers chair and thought about what she might do with the rest of the day. Whatever she did would be overcast with the massive disappointment of having failed at this one thing she had been planning and looking forward to for weeks. It seemed like the only acceptable option she had would be to mope about all day, feeling sorry for herself. That seemed like a plan.

Bobby was already stepping into the room when he knocked on the open door. He bounded towards Elspeth without waiting for an invitation. "Hi, Bobby Karjalainen, you must be Elspeth Ross?"

"Yes," said Elspeth, "it's great to meet you in person at last."

"Good to meet you too, Elspeth, you're a little younger than I expected."

Elspeth had to think fast to parry. "You look a little younger in the flesh, too," she said.

"I'm late, I had some family business to attend to," said Bobby. Elspeth noted that it was not an apology, merely an explanation. She expected that Bobby had never really had to apologise to anyone.

"It's fine," she lied. "Shall we get started right away? I know you must be busy and I really appreciate your making time for this."

"Why not?" said Bobby. "Let's do it."

Elspeth gestured to the chairs. "If you sit there I'll sit here and ask you a few questions. I was going to ask about the war, a little bit about your family history, and about your plans for the future. I've read your book so I'll ask a little bit about that and maybe get you to expand a bit on some of the anecdotes from there, how does that sound?"

"All sounds fine to me," said Bobby.

Elspeth hesitated. She was going to ask one more question before the interview and she wasn't sure whether it would put her at a disadvantage or if it was even the sort of thing a professional interviewer would say. As much as she wanted to be a hard-hitting journalist there was no getting away from the fact that Elspeth was polite and considerate. She felt compelled to ask anyway, but as a further justification she told herself it might be a clever tactic, lulling Bobby into a false sense of security. "Are there any topics you would be unwilling to discuss?" she said, at the same time thinking she may have just shot herself in the foot.

Bobby paused for a second in thought. "I don't think so," he said casually. "If there's anything I don't want to say I just won't say it," he added with a shrug. "Shall we do it?"

Elspeth looked to her camera over Bobby's shoulder. She tapped her comdev to set the camera on preset two, where it framed her head and shoulders. After her intro she would set it back to preset one, a longer shot favouring her but with the back of Bobby's head and shoulder the foreground.

"I'm speaking today to Bobby Karjalainen, author of *Return of the Warrior*, veteran of World War IV and son of Hjälp Teknik CEO Jack Karjalainen. Bobby recounted his experience of war in his bestselling book and became something of a celebrity on the lecture circuit. Since he left the army he has toured Earth extensively, but has now returned to his home on Mars."

She flipped the camera to preset one and turned to face Bobby. "Bobby, *Return of the Warrior* recounts the story of the Commander Program on Earth and your experiences with it. Could you tell us a little about that?"

"Well," said Bobby, "the Commander Program was dreamt up a couple of years into World War IV. The idea was to return to an earlier sense of martial chivalry, which some felt had been lost, and also to give commanders in the field a greater sense of situational awareness that is simply not available to soldiers operating drones through IVR. I don't think we were expecting the controversy we got. To many people it seemed totally unacceptable to be putting military personnel in harm's way. But for most of human history, that's how it was. People forget that. People now think of war as being fought by drones but even in World War III there were soldiers putting their lives at risk on the battlefield. Before the twenty-first century drones didn't even exist; wars were fought between people, face-to-face. I think what's happened is that over time we've lost track of that sort of thing. People expect wars to be sanitary and safe but the truth is that even in a modern war, a drone war, people get killed. We call it collateral damage or whatever, but people get killed."

"And what was your role in the Commander Program?"

"I signed up for the program at the very beginning, before there even was a program to speak of, so I was involved in setting up and testing the hardware, and developing tactics and organisational structures."

"So you were quite heavily involved in shaping the program?"

"I was. We worked with some great designers from Helios Matériel Corporation and adapted existing drones so that they could take pilots. That turned out to be more complex than we thought it would be, so we had to redesign the command drones from the ground up. I was a test pilot for that, so I got input on the final designs."

"Were you happy with the designs?"

"More than happy. Our concerns were listened to and the designers really worked with us to provide the sorts of machines we needed, and that would do the sorts of things we needed them to do. Once we had the hardware, of course, we had to move on to the harder task of developing tactics and training up the pilots to use them. I have to say, the volunteers we got for the Commander Program were absolutely first-class. I think it takes a particular type of person to be willing to walk on to a battlefield where the enemy will be trying to kill them, and the guys we got were terrific."

"Where were you first deployed?"

"Well, initially, I had trouble getting out of instructing at the school. The program was so new we didn't have enough instructors, so I was stuck training for eighteen months or so. But in the end they let me go. I told them that battlefield experience would make me an even better instructor, and though I don't think they believed it, they let me go."

"And you went to Pakistan?"

"I did."

"Can you tell us about that?"

"Well, I think it's pretty well-documented what went off over there. It's all in my book." Elspeth sensed this was one of the things that Bobby had in mind when he said if he didn't want to say stuff he wouldn't say it.

"And the Battle of Lahore?"

"Yes, I was at the Battle of Lahore."

Elspeth guessed this would be a great place to leave a pause. Maybe Bobby would be compelled to fill the silence with something revelatory, but if not the pause itself would be dramatic. It seemed that Bobby wasn't going to step in, so having given the pause enough time to do its job Elspeth continued.

"That must have had quite an effect on you."

"Yes."

Another pause.

"Did it affect your faith in the Commander Program?"

Bobby thought. "It didn't affect my faith in the program, but obviously an experience like that does, as you say, have an effect. We had all trained for war but nothing really prepares you for it. I served two tours at the start of the war as a drone pilot in Kentucky but I quickly found that physically being on the battlefield is another thing entirely. And of course, the loss of colleagues is something that . . ." He stopped, searching for words. "It's something that is very difficult to deal with."

Elspeth knew she was on delicate ground but was eliciting some great stuff. "Knowing what you know now, and with the experiences you had, would you still have championed and supported the Commander Program the way you did at the beginning?"

"Yes I would. We have a way of life and a way of doing things in the USAN that is worth defending. Our enemies deny their own citizens freedom. They are not free to practice their own religions, or to trade with each other, or to say what they want, or go where they want, or do they want. Half of Earth is shrouded under dark, intolerant, ignorant systems of government. Sometimes we forget that our way of life isn't just the natural order of things. We live in a system that allows people to experience freedom of ideas and expression, and economic freedom. It's this system that has brought us great wealth and great privilege. When you look at the other side and the misery and poverty they live in, brought about by their repressive and intolerant governments, I think it's easy to see that it's worth it to fight for what we have. I know that my fellow commanders who died on the battlefields of Lahore and elsewhere would have done that gladly rather than live under the darkness of the Asian Bloc."

"Would you like to take a break?"

"No, I'm fine."

"Okay, what happened when the war was over?"

"Well, after Lahore I was shipped back to the States. I did some more instructing - mainly instructing the newer instructors - and then I was more or less pensioned off. It's no secret that I was the poster boy for the army. I did some calls promoting the army and my book, and then I came home."

"Why did you come back to Mars?"

"I came back because it's my home."

"Any other reasons?"

"I served the mother country when it called. I'd paid my dues, and it was time to come home."

"Your father, Jack Karjalainen, is very ill, is that right?"

"Yes he is."

"So you came back to be with him?"

"I'm able to spend some time with my father now I'm home, yes."

"You touched on your family life a little in your book and it's documented elsewhere that your relationship with your father hasn't always been great. Has that improved since your return?"

"My father is very ill and as a sick old man he has a bit less fight in him than he used to. I guess I'm a bit older now too, so we're getting along a bit better than we used to."

"Is it true that your father more or less disowned you when you decided to leave for Earth and the USAN Army?"

Bobby shrugged. " 'Disowned' may be a bit strong, but he certainly wasn't happy."

"He didn't speak to you for a number of years, did he?"

"No, he didn't."

"Your father's political views are well known. When you left for Earth were you rebelling against him?"

"Not really. My father and me are different people. I guess we're both quite headstrong, and where we have different views we just rubbed each other the wrong way. I didn't go to Earth to spite my father, but I guess he might not have seen it that way."

"Where do you fit into the family now? Will you continue to be part of the Karjalainen dynasty? A place at the family firm, perhaps?"

Bobby laughed. "No, I don't think that's going to happen any time soon. But I'm on good terms with my family, and I'm happy to be back."

"What will you do now?"

"I really don't know. I don't think my skills are likely to be needed here, and I have a little money from my army pension and the book, so I really don't know. I guess I'll just kick back and see what happens."

"There's one more thing I'd like to ask you before I let you go. The USAN ship *Otus* was recently destroyed, believed to be by an act of sabotage. What's your opinion on that?"

"I'm not really well-placed to comment. All I know is what everyone else knows from the news aggregators. But it goes back to the point I made earlier - we have enemies who would be happy to destroy us and they will go to any lengths to do that. It's very important we remember that everything we have, all the freedoms we have, were won for us at great cost by people who stood up to intimidation and fought back."

"You don't have any ideas as to who might have been behind the attack?"

"I don't; I mean I do, but I would just be guessing like anyone else. I expect it would either be dissident factions in the Asian Bloc who disapprove of the terms of the armistice, or maybe one of the other non-aligned organisations - you know, terrorist groups and the like. Just because the war is over we can't be complacent. There will always be people out there who will want to destroy us. It was terrible what happened to that ship. I knew some of the people who died."

"President Cortes has intimated that the sabotage may have been green-lit from Mars, what do you think about that?"

"I think that's very unlikely and it's irresponsible of the president to be putting that idea out there. I know that Martians, even now, are amongst the most patriotic people of the USAN - maybe I should say people formerly of the USAN, but you know what I mean. I don't think the people of Mars bear any grudge or ill will towards the people of Earth. I still feel a very strong kinship with the USAN and I don't think I know anyone who doesn't. This independence mania will settle down very quickly and we'll all get back to doing what we were doing. We'll always have a very special relationship with the USAN. That will never change, I'm sure of it."

As Bobby was finishing his last sentence Elspeth felt a rising panic. She'd framed her previous question as one last thing but she realised she had another 'last thing' to ask. Her mind raced. She thought she would be able to flip the order of the questions when she edited the piece later but she was worried about how it would sound to Bobby now. Maybe he wouldn't notice? She nodded as he finished his answer and launched straight into the next question.

"You probably have more military experience, certainly battlefield experience, than any other person on Mars. In recent weeks we've seen the formation of the Martian Security Service, taking on the role previously occupied by the USAN Garrison. Have you been offered, or have you considered, taking up a role with the MSS?"

Bobby paused. "That's something I haven't thought about. I've been out of uniform for a while now and I'm enjoying it. But this independence thing? The way I see it, it's a good thing for Mars and really, in the long term, probably a good thing for Earth too. I guess I would like to support that in any way I can, and as you say, I do have experience. I guess I'll just wait for the call," he said, smiling.

Elspeth was thinking to herself, 'Great, he didn't notice the extra question' as she calmly said, "Bobby Karjalainen, thank you so much for your time and good luck with whatever it is you choose to do next."

"Thank you," said Bobby.

They both sat in silence for a few seconds. Elspeth tapped her comdev. "Great, that's it, done," she said. "Thank you so much for doing this."

"No problem," said Bobby. "You do know you said you were going to ask me one more thing, and then asked two things, don't you?"

"Did I?" said Elspeth, "I'm sure it'll be fine, I can edit around it."

Bobby nodded.

"It wasn't too awkward was it, talking about the war?"

"It's fine. I wrote a book about it, people ask all the time. Do you need anything else?"

"No," said Elspeth. "I'm sure I got everything. I'll edit this all together and have it up on my stream in a day or two."

"That's great," said Bobby, standing. "I'll look forward to watching it." He offered Elspeth his hand and she took it and shook firmly. She wasn't used to shaking hands and hoped she was doing it right.

"Thanks again, Mr Karjalainen," she said.

"Please, just call me Bobby. Take care now," he said as he turned and left.

Foveaux got the number from Elspeth. She had seen the stream and thought Bobby would indeed be a useful addition to the MSS. Initially, she would run the MSS much the same as its USAN predecessor but very soon it would be necessary to split it into two separate entities, a military and a police service. While the Martian population was small and politically unified they could get away with having a joint military-police force. As the population grew, and as political opinions diverged, having what amounted to military police under control of the government would not look good or be good for their fledgling democracy.

Maya's plan was to start the partition right from the beginning. Although the MSS would be a single organisation it would be split internally into military and police divisions. When the time came for the two parts to be formally split into their own separate organisations it would, she hoped, be relatively painless.

Coming from a background of security Foveaux saw herself as naturally inclined towards the policing side of the operation. That was where her expertise was. But if Mars was to have an effective military someone with Bobby's background and experience would be an ideal candidate to oversee it.

She managed to get through to him shortly after Elspeth's stream of the interview had been published.

"Mr Karjalainen, you probably don't know me, my name is Maya Foveaux and I'm the head of the Martian Security Service."

"Hello, Ms Foveaux. No, I don't know you."

"I'm sorry to call unannounced but I've just seen your interview with Elspeth Ross."

"How was it?"

"It was very good, Mr Karjalainen, and it got me thinking. As I'm sure you know, the USAN is sending a dropship carrier here. We have some defence systems in place and we have the beginnings of a military force which, unfortunately, it appears will be necessary for us to stand toe to toe with our earthly neighbours when we get to negotiate peace with them. I was wondering if you would like to donate some of your military experience to us over here. It would be greatly appreciated."

"What sort of thing?" said Bobby.

"You've been involved before in setting up a new type of unit. That's exactly what we're doing now. We have personnel and we're getting some new equipment, but what we're really lacking is expertise. The MSS consists, at the moment, of ex-security guards. What we could do with is someone to mould them into an army. It sounds like that's the sort of thing you would be able to do for us."

Bobby thought carefully. "So you want me to design training courses, something like that?"

"That would be great, but what would be even better would be if you could implement those courses yourself."

"Wait a minute, am I being press-ganged here?"

Foveaux smiled. "Of course not. If you don't want to be a part of this I understand. But we have a new planet here, and a pressing need we have at this time is for a functioning army. You're the best hope we have of getting that as fast as we need it. I understand, too, from your interview that you're at a loose end at the moment."

"That's true enough," said Bobby.

"Obviously, we can offer you a full salary and other benefits. And you would have tremendous freedom to organise the new force the best way you see fit. It would be good for us and I think it could be a great opportunity for you, too."

Bobby thought. "Let me come over and take a look and I'll tell you what I think. I can't commit to anything at the moment. I'll need to think about this."

"Sure, that sounds great," said Foveaux.

"Where are you?" said Bobby.

"We're based at the garrison."

CHAPTER 22

Buyout

Venkdt was still using his offices at the Venkdt Mars headquarters building. It seemed no one minded the apparent conflict of interest. Most Martians either worked for Venkdt or owed the company some other huge debt of gratitude. The idea that the interests of Venkdt might conflict with the general Martian population simply didn't add up. By a large majority, employees of Venkdt *were* the Martian population.

Still, it was a matter that Charles Venkdt wanted to address. He knew the Martian economy was starting to grow and in time there would be many corporations and small businesses on Mars. His nascent government would need to be seen to be independent from all biases in order to support that happening. The new Martian economy should be free and open, with the lightest touch of regulation.

Government finances initially consisted of generous donations from Venkdt himself and from Venkdt Mars, the newly independent Martian corporation. Raising taxes had to be the first priority, and consolidating government infrastructure close on behind.

With a popular mandate behind him Venkdt had to deliver on the promises he had made to his electorate. One of these was to buy out Venkdt Mars from the parent company. The difficulty facing him was that the parent company did not accept the buyout at any level.

It was an issue that had to be approached from two angles: legal and technical. Though the purchase would never be strictly legal Venkdt needed it to be as wrapped up in legal terms as it could possibly be. For this he employed the counsel of his daughter, Christina. He imagined the technical aspect, though somewhat more complex, would be easier to implement. Kostovich would be able to funnel money into accounts even where the recipients were unwilling to receive it, that much was certain.

The original pledge had been to buy the Martian division of Venkdt Corporation at market rates plus ten percent. The events surrounding independence had knocked a significant amount of points off of Venkdt shares. Market plus ten now would be undervaluing the worth of the Martian enterprise but Venkdt was determined to play fair by his erstwhile associates.

"Market plus ten now would be an insult," he said.

"What then? Market plus twenty?" said Christina.

"No, no, this has to be reasonable and logical. We can't just pluck numbers out of the air. Can you pull up the share value for the day I made the announcement? Early in the day, before the jitters set in. We'll take that price plus ten per cent. That makes sense, right?"

"It sort of does, I guess," said Christina. "It looks like you're making it up as you go along, though."

"I am making it up as I go along. But we have to give them a fair price and it has to be based on sound reasoning. We'll go with the price on that date, okay?"

Christina nodded.

"And where does the money go?" said Kostovich.

"It goes to Venkdt Corp," said Venkdt.

"Obviously," said Kostovich, "but which part? Venkdt's financial organisation is extremely diverse. They have operations across the globe, and beyond. Even without us they have a facility on Luna, Earth's moon."

"Anywhere, I guess. If they have the money, they have the money. It's up to them how they push it around."

"I wouldn't be so sure," said Kostovich. "An organisation of that size, with such dispersed management, may be very good at losing money off the books when it needs to. There could be any number of fake subsidiaries, offshore accounts and who knows what else. We have to put this money somewhere where it can't get kicked under the rug. The point of this exercise is for us to be seen to be doing the right thing. If nobody sees, or worse nobody sees and the money disappears, then there's no point."

Venkdt thought. "Is there any way you can make their accounts public?"

"Not legally. It would be criminally negligent to do so, anyway. They'd kill us in the press, rightly so."

Venkdt paced. "Okay, how about this. We bypass the company entirely."

"We can't pay the company without paying the company," said Christina.

"No," said Venkdt, "we pay the shareholders. Each individual shareholder gets a proportionate pay-off."

Kostovich shook his head. "You're talking about cracking hundreds of thousands of accounts now, rather than just one. That's a different proposition all together."

Venkdt looked at him. "Too hard?"

"No, not too hard. But a lot harder."

Venkdt smiled. "You relish a challenge, Dan. Can you do it?"

Kostovich took a deep breath. "Yes, I can do it."

"How long do you need?"

Kostovich thought. "I don't know. A week. Two?"

"That's great, two weeks," said Venkdt. He turned to Christina. "Can you get all this paperwork tied up in two weeks? Take as many people as you need. And when you have all the paperwork done it needs to be published on an open forum. It's important that anyone can access our documents and see what it is we're doing, and why we're doing it."

"I think we could do that," said Christina.

"Good," said Venkdt. "That means that in two weeks we can publish the documentation, transfer the money and we will be a truly independent planet." He stopped to think. "Planet or nation? I can't decide. We're sort of a planet made up of one nation."

"Plation?" offered Kostovich.

Venkdt looked at him with a mixture of confusion and pity. "I think we'll stay with planet."

Elspeth's plan to gain publicity from the interview with Bobby Karjalainen worked. The stream was extremely popular. For a brief period it was the second most popular stream on the news aggregators. Charles Venkdt wanted to announce his proposals for the buyout on a live stream, and having seen Elspeth's interview with Bobby he selected her to be his interviewer.

Elspeth felt a little disoriented. She had gone from being a cub reporter to interviewing the president of Mars in a matter of days. Admittedly, the president of Mars was someone she might easily bump into out and about in Marineris, but it still felt like something of a coup. The audience for the interview on Earth would be enormous.

Venkdt had a number of specific questions he wanted to be asked but he had given Elspeth some leeway to ask questions of her own. The equipment he supplied was top of the range.

Elspeth set up the equipment and chairs in a similar configuration to the one she had used with Bobby. There was to be a technician who would cut between the three cameras (this time around there was a long two-shot) in real time. The stream was to go out live, but once that had happened it would live forever, being restreamed or otherwise available to anyone with even a passing interest.

Venkdt had appeared friendly enough when they spoke on the phone. In person too he seemed like an amiable old man. He reassured Elspeth again that as long as she asked the questions he needed she could ask others too. It would be a real interview, albeit one that existed in order to disseminate a specific message to its target audience.

The live stream was timed such that it would be available at peak time in the most populated areas of the USAN. Elspeth began by asking Venkdt some fairly softball questions about his family history and their connections with Mars. She stepped it up a bit when asking about how he had come to the decision to run a plebiscite. Had he thought about possible unintended outcomes? Had he thought about running for president right from the start, or had that come later? Venkdt gave political answers; conservative, reassuring and easy to swallow. They were very plausible, too, to the degree that Elspeth thought they may have even been honest.

She asked Venkdt one of his own questions. "You said you will compensate Venkdt Corporation for their Martian division. Can you elaborate on that?"

"I can elaborate on that, Elspeth. I said in my election speeches that I would buyout Venkdt Mars from the parent company at the market rate plus ten percent. Since then, and we have to assume in response to our new arrangement here, the share price of Venkdt Corporation has dropped somewhat. I want everyone to know that my intentions are completely above board, so what I will be doing is buying the Martian arm of Venkdt Corporation for the market rate plus ten percent as it was on the day I made the announcement about the plebiscite."

Elspeth thought this was a good opportunity to chip in with a question of her own. "And what can you tell us about the legality of that arrangement?"

"Oh," said Venkdt, "I understand that in very strict legal terms what we are doing is not correct. There can be no doubt about that. But what is happening here is the formation of a new planet, the birth of a new society. I don't think that can be done within the strict legal framework of the old planet. I know that, strictly speaking, we are breaking the law here, and that Venkdt Corporation are opposed to us doing this. I can't argue with any of that. But what I want to make very clear is that we are not robbing anyone here. We are taking what we believe to be ours and compensating the original owners. I think that most people would agree that is fair. Not legal, according to the laws of the USAN, but not an injustice either. We don't seek to aggravate the USAN or steal anything from them. We hope to remain on good terms and I feel, as I'm sure most Martians do, that the people of Earth and the USAN are our cousins. We will be a good solid ally to the

USAN and will continue to supply them with essential materials, to their benefit as well as ours."

"So you're quite deliberately flouting the law?"

"The old law, yes. A law that the people of Mars have overwhelmingly voted to say they do not believe applies to them. Don't get me wrong here, Elspeth, the rule of law is essential. It's what has made the USAN so successful, and it's what will make Mars successful. But in this very unusual case, and at this particular moment in time, it has been necessary for us to change from one legal code to another. That can't be done neatly. There will always be a point at which things hang in the air, unresolved. What we want to do is move past that point as quickly as possible. Our own Martian constitution and our own Martian laws are now in effect and will be rigorously upheld, just as we upheld the laws of the USAN right to the point of departure. On this one issue - ownership of Venkdt Mars - we've unfortunately had to go through this grey area, but as I've said, and as I hope everyone can see, while we are not complying fully with the legal requirements of the USAN we are absolutely committed to acting in a fair and just manner. That's why our terms are so generous, in part as compensation for the difficulties people may have with our actions."

Elspeth returned to Venkdt's own questions. "How will the buyout work, in practical terms?"

"I'm glad you asked me that. We have our very best people working on this right at this moment and we hope to have a solution within the next few weeks. We are hoping to be able to pay every Venkdt Corporation shareholder a dividend commensurate with the amount of shares they hold. In short, we're going directly to Venkdt's owners and paying them for what we are taking from them."

"This will be happening in the next few weeks?"

"Yes, within two weeks, we hope. Also, we'll be providing documentation explaining the rationale and other technical aspects of the buyout. All shareowners will receive documentation confirming the amount they will be paid, with full receipts for the monies we will have paid them following in due course. If they run into any financial, legal or other difficulties because of our actions we will support them in sorting any of that out. All this, by the way, is covered in detail in our documentation, which is freely available through the Venkdt site. I can assure any Venkdt Corporation shareholders that they will be fully compensated and supported in every way throughout this process. It is absolutely not our intention to cause any harm, financial or otherwise, to Venkdt Corporation or its shareholders.

"We have written to all the shareholders asking them to accept our offer. We have done this as a matter of courtesy, but the plain truth is that we will be buying ourselves out whatever happens. I would strongly encourage Venkdt Corporation shareholders to accept our offer. It would greatly strengthen our relationship with our former company as we move forward, and it would send us a message of solidarity and goodwill that would be greatly appreciated."

"What happens if they reject your offer?"

"Well, we go ahead anyway, but with heavier hearts."

"Okay, and once again the date for this?"

"Within two weeks."

"So I guess what we have here is an honest thief," said Cortes as the stream finished. "But an honest thief is still a thief. What do you have for me?" He looked around the table. "Anyone?"

"We have *Ephialtes*, of course, and we're hoping to open diplomatic channels very soon on the back of that," said Farrell.

"We're all well aware of that," said Cortes. "How do we deal with this? He looks reasonable, almost. How do we counter that?"

An adviser stepped in. "Well, he is admitting that what they're planning to do, indeed what they have done, is illegal. So he's conceded the moral high ground to us, we can work with that."

"Really? How does it help? He's just said that we're right and he's wrong, but he's still going ahead with it, and smiling and sounding reasonable as he does so. Just being right is scant consolation. What can we do, in practical terms?"

"The buyout hasn't gone through yet. We could block it," offered another adviser.

"How do we do that?" said Cortes.

The adviser hesitated. "I'm not sure, sir, I'll look into it. There must be a way to block the money at source."

"Okay, let's go with that, if we can. What else?"

"We can advise the shareholders not to settle. That would be another victory."

"Goddammit! We don't need moral victories! Are we all going to sit around here patting each other on the back telling each other how right we are and how we all did the right thing as we watch this son of a bitch steal a planet from us!?"

"It would lessen their legitimacy. We have to work with what we've got, Mr President. Little things like this will help us in the long run. We have a warship arriving there soon. That's our ace, but we still have to work at these things. They will make a difference."

Cortes let out a pent-up breath. "Okay, go ahead and advise the shareholders not to settle. Is there anything we can do to induce them?"

"Not really, sir. It would look like bribery. I would appeal to their civic duty and sense of patriotism. Anyone taking them up on the offer would be literally selling out to an opposing power. We can play up that aspect."

"That's good, go with that. What about a public campaign, you know, an advertising campaign? 'Don't Sell Out to Mars,' or something like that?"

"It's a risk, sir. If it backfired we could end up giving them even more legitimacy. I think targeting the shareholders and appealing to their sense of national duty would be the way to go."

"Okay. You can take care of that?"

"Yes, sir."

"Anything else? So we're going to advise shareholders to hold out, and we're going to look into freezing Martian assets, right? Physically stop them from paying us off?"

"Yes, sir," the adviser said. "If that's possible we should definitely pursue that."

"I want to be kept up-to-date on this. Any developments, any information should come through my office."

"Yes, Mr President."

"Anything else?"

"Okay then, that's it."

"My fellow Americans. You may have seen the recent stream by Charles Venkdt explaining how he is going to buy Venkdt Mars Corp from the parent company here on Earth without first consulting with that company. Venkdt acknowledges that this is illegal. It is. It would be theft on a grand scale. Mr Venkdt and his compatriots have already set up an illegitimate government on Mars, breaking many other laws. It can be seen from this that Mr Venkdt has no respect for the law and no respect for private property. He is planning to steal one of the jewels of our industrial crown, and the fact that he plans to give us a hefty tip afterwards is no consolation. There is no such thing as an honest thief, as there is no such thing as a legitimate Martian government.

"Our grand ship *Ephialtes* is heading to Mars, alone now that her sister, the tragic *Otus*, was cruelly taken from us, quite possibly at the hands of Martian agents. When *Ephialtes* arrives at Mars we will step up our negotiations with Mr Venkdt and his colleagues and we will seek to redress the grave injustice he is seeking to perpetrate against us.

"We have endured seven years of war and many of you have suffered hardships because of that. We have shown that we are a hardy people and that we will not back down when we know we are right. Venkdt and his cronies have no legitimacy on Mars and they cannot take from us what is ours.

"We will not stand for tyranny.

"When the US began the Martian adventure nearly two hundred years ago we took that journey for all mankind. We were seeking out a new providence, as always pushing ourselves against the very limits of what we were capable. We didn't know then that Mars would grow into such an important outpost of our country, contributing more than four fifths of our energy supplies and becoming an important cornerstone of our economy.

"Mars is important to us now and it will be even more important in the future. Beyond Mars sits the asteroid belt, which is rich with minerals and other raw materials that will benefit us for many hundreds of years into the future. The asteroid belt is ripe for development and our Martian base is a very necessary way station. There is a bright future for Mars. The Martian people are at the very forefront of the human adventure. They will benefit enormously from the trade generated by the exploitation of the asteroid belt. The Martian people are our people. They are us; we are them.

"This current schism has been brought about wholly for the benefit of Charles Venkdt and no one else. I see a Mars united with the USAN growing in the future into a very prosperous region. One man stands in the way of that. That man, in a few short weeks, has already founded a military and built five powerfully armed missile bases. I ask you this: are those the actions of a man of peace? Are those the actions of a man who is confident that he is doing the right thing, and following, as he calls it, 'natural justice'? Or are they the actions of a tyrant? Of someone who knows he is committing a great crime and will need to defend himself against those who would bring him to justice?

"Mars and the asteroid belt beyond are essential resources for the human race as we grow into the future. We absolutely cannot allow an armed fortress to stand between us and our manifest destiny. It is my sincerest hope that the people of Mars will see sense and come to the table to negotiate a resettlement of the Martian situation and the dismantling of the illegitimate Martian government. But I would ask you, my fellow Americans, to be prepared to fight for what is ours. The great *Ephialtes* will arrive in Martian orbit within weeks. If necessary, and with great reluctance, I will call on our service men and women to take back what is ours. Up to that point the people of Mars will be given every opportunity to rectify the grave mistake they have made.

"I would like to finish tonight by telling you that, even as we speak, we are making diplomatic approaches in an attempt to resolve this situation as quickly and as peaceably as possible. But as the last seven years have shown, the USAN will not be pushed around and we most certainly will not be bought off.

"Thank you."

Acevedo had been asked to prepare a report by Andrews. She worked mainly from the telemetry data from *Ephialtes*, which was all normal. *Ephialtes* was travelling through space at unprecedented speed and was coping well. All the data tallied with that from the simulations. The worry was that the rogue software which destroyed *Otus* had been sophisticated enough to feed back false data to disguise its nefarious purpose. Acevedo had had a long conversation with Askel Lund. Lund had assured her that she was closely monitoring all systems and had put some rudimentary fail-safes in place. She had her own isolated system on *Ephialtes* and periodically would update all software on the ship. That was one line of defence. She had also implemented some sophisticated AIs which, she hoped, would monitor any other changes on the system. The rogue software had been extremely sophisticated. She could see that from what it had achieved. But it was impossible to know exactly *how* sophisticated it was. On *Otus* it had avoided detection successfully, but it was difficult to know if it would be able to react to being hunted down. She had so far managed to defeat it on *Ephialtes*, but would it or its creator be able to learn from their mistakes and strike again?

Acevedo was satisfied that Lund was on top of the situation regarding the software, but it seemed likely there was a saboteur on board *Ephialtes*. Maybe rogue software was not the only weapon in his or her armoury. Acevedo ran extensive background checks on everyone who had been aboard the shuttle. They all seemed to check out. There were a handful of crew and twenty-six commanders. Every commander had been hand-picked for the task and had seen combat in World War IV. It seemed unlikely that someone with such a background would be willing to attack a capital ship of the USAN. Extensive deep searches of all their backgrounds threw up nothing.

The slightest shred Acevedo had to go on was that two of the commanders had suffered brain injuries in combat. Commander Hayden Steiner and Commander Alan Meades had both suffered head injuries, but were fully recovered. Meades had been severely concussed and was released after seventy-two hours of observation. Steiner's injury had been more serious, but even he had been cleared for duty within two months. Maybe the injuries could have affected their personalities or judgement? She knew she was clutching at straws.

She gave the report to Andrews, who in turn was going to hand it over to Cortes. In summary the report said that the mission was proceeding as planned and the ship was behaving as expected. Training was continuing in the IVRs and the commanders were all ready for combat. They had been drilled over and over on the missions for recapturing the essential Martian installations. Their morale was good and they were razor-sharp and ready to go.

The issue with a potential saboteur was in hand. There was a system in place to protect the ship from any errant software and Askel Lund was working together with Acevedo to try to find out how the rogue software had been introduced into the system and by whom. They were more than halfway to Mars and in a couple of weeks would begin the deceleration process.

White hated meeting in car parks. To him it smacked of cheap thrillers and low-budget spy films. He also didn't like the way he felt boxed in, with limited escape routes. There were cameras, too, in car parks, but Sherman had assured him they had been taken out. He had his most trusted Secret Service agent double-check on that; he couldn't take Sherman at his word.

When he arrived Sherman wasn't there. He had to sit and wait in his car for five minutes, his anger growing from a low simmer to a controlled boil.

Sherman made no apology for arriving late. He opened the door to White's sedan and slid into the rear passenger seat beside him. He didn't even give a greeting. White waited for him to say hello or to explain what had happened. When it was clear that Sherman wasn't going to start the conversation White spoke. "Tell me that wasn't us."

"I don't know what you're talking about," said Sherman.

"You know exactly what I'm talking about, and I want you to tell me it was nothing to do with your man."

"First of all, he or she is *our* man, and secondly, he or she was just following our instructions."

White paused. He wanted to control the anger he felt. He didn't want to let it get the better of him. "Our instructions were to delay and obstruct the mission."

"I think *Otus'* mission has been obstructed," said Sherman.

"That wasn't obstruction. It was outright murder, as you well know."

Sherman looked out of the window. He wouldn't make eye contact with White. "When you deal with these sorts of people subtlety inevitably has to go out of the window. I got you what you wanted. If you have cold feet now that's your problem."

White snorted. "It's your problem Sherman. Your agent is out of control. Do you think they're just going to let this one slip by? Tens of highly trained military personnel and billions of dollars of the most sophisticated military hardware ever known. They're going to find out who did it and they're going to trace it all the way back to you."

Sherman had already considered this probability. He had been exceptionally careful to maintain distance between himself and his contacts so that should it come to this he would have plausible denial. There was no way he would be able to assure White of that. As far as White was concerned the only thing linking him to any of this was Sherman himself. Sherman had always thought of White as being something of a weakling, but he knew that in extremes people were capable of extraordinary acts. If

White felt threatened enough, and he knew that the only thing connecting him to the attack on *Otus* was Sherman, what was there to stop him from breaking the link?

"If they get me they get you," said Sherman. "But they're not going to get me. You need to relax. I've told you before, I only use the very best. They're not amateurs."

"Not amateurs? Seems to me like they can't even follow simple instructions."

"Hey," said Sherman, "you make a deal with the devil don't be surprised if he comes around and bites you in the ass."

"I didn't make a deal with the devil, I made a deal with you and you screwed up."

"I know you made a deal with me," said Sherman, "I documented it extensively. In fact, the only thing that stops it being published on my site is the fact that I'm still alive. There are places, dates, times and very detailed notes about our conversations. All the times and places will, of course, tally with your diary and the electronic logs of your movements held by the Secret Service. But you needn't worry. None of that stuff will ever go public. I log into my site every twelve hours and reset the auto publishing. So it will never go live, so long as I'm around to keep doing that."

"You son of a bitch. You really think I'd have you killed? What sort of person do you think I am?"

Sherman shrugged. "I don't know. The sort of person who would authorise an attack on his own military to further his political ends?"

White stared at him. "You know that isn't true. I never asked for that, that is not what I wanted."

"You say that now," said Sherman. "There's some very interesting stuff on my website that details exactly what you asked for and the lengths you ordered me to go to in order to achieve it. It's unpublished as yet. Maybe one day you'll get the chance to read it."

"Your people screwed up. This is all on your head. All I asked for was interference, not this."

"Was it? How are you going to prove that? Even just being in a position where you needed to prove it would mean you were screwed. You wanted to play tough guys. Well you did, and here's where it got you. Deal with it." Sherman angrily left the car, the sound of the slam slowly fading in White's ears. White simply stared forward, mulling over his options. Sherman had told him that he was insulated, that there was no way anything could be linked back to him. White didn't believe him, but he had no other option. He hated meeting in car parks; cameras everywhere and only one way out.

White spent the night with Zelman. He found it difficult to sleep, though for periods just listening to Madeline's rising and falling breaths gave him some comfort. He had always known that with high office came great responsibilities, and during the war at many points he had been a part of meetings that lead directly to deaths on the battlefield. With modern fighting methods - drones and remote warfare - this seldom meant the deaths of USAN soldiers, but with the Commander Program it had happened. There had been other decisions which had led to civilian fatalities, deaths which may not have occurred had the decisions made in those meetings gone a different way. It wasn't the first time that he had initiated something that had gone on to lead to losses of life.

It had always been abstract before. It had been a collegiate process, like being part of a firing squad. No one person would be able to claim the fatal shot was the result of them pulling the trigger. Each individual took a portion of the responsibility, and if they needed to they could tell themselves that it was the others who were responsible.

This was different.

There was scant consolation in telling himself that this was not his intention. Sherman had been right, to a degree, that when you go off-piste there are no rules anymore, and certainly no guarantees. He alone had initiated this action that had resulted in many deaths. The commanders who had died on *Otus* had volunteered to put their lives on the line fighting for the USAN and all it stood for and now, however unintentionally, he had sent them to their fate.

He felt guilty too about his own anxieties. He couldn't be sure whether he was worried about being found out for his own sake, or whether he was worried that he was the last person who was in a position to put a brake on Cortes' mad careening toward a new conflict. If he were taken out of the picture Cortes would have free rein, not only to attack the Martian colony but to continue his diminution of liberty at home.

Maybe, he told himself, it was necessary to destroy *Otus*. Maybe the only problem here was that *Ephialtes* hadn't been taken down, too. After all, he was playing in a high-stakes game and the long-term goals maybe justified these sacrifices.

As he lay in bed staring at the ceiling these thoughts span around and around his head. He had no allies in the cabinet. He had no allies at all. As it stood, he was useful to Cortes as he could always be thrown to the public as the dove to Cortes' hawk. He was the spoonful of sugar that would help the medicine go down. But his position was weak. Cortes's popularity had grown with his successful conclusion of the war. White's dovish position simply helped to placate the minority who were opposed.

He tried to remain calm. He thought maybe a good night's sleep would help, but sleep would not come. He tried to step back and take an objective view of the situation he found himself in, and the situation his country found itself in. The president was extremely popular, so popular that the electorate was giving up its rights and freedoms without question. That troubled him deeply. But he was at the heart of government and in a position to fight back for the freedoms the country was initially founded upon. The situation he found himself in now was intolerable, but there was nothing he could do. Maybe Sherman was right and there was nothing to connect them with what their agent or agents had done. All he could do, he realised, was assume that was the case and carry on. He had high-level security clearance; maybe he could keep an eye on the investigation. Would that look suspicious? Probably not.

EPHIALTES

He rolled over in bed again and looked at the clock. It was 04:20. He tried to clear his mind of all thought, but the *Otus* incident and Sherman's threats kept pushing back into his consciousness.

"Try to get to sleep, hun," Zelman called over her shoulder.

"Are you awake?" said White.

"No, I'm fast asleep," replied Zelman.

"I'm sorry if I woke you," said White.

"It's okay," said Zelman, sleepily. She lazily groped behind herself, eventually finding White's hand. White grasped her hand in his, and gently rubbed his thumb against her finger. He remembered holding the hands of his parents when he was a little boy, and how that made him feel safe and protected. He glanced over at Zelman in the half-light. She seemed to be sleeping again now. He looked up at the ceiling and tried to put all thoughts of *Otus* and Sherman and Cortes out of his mind. He tried to concentrate on Zelman's breathing beside him and the feel of her hand in his.

He lay like that for a long while, but still he couldn't sleep.

CHAPTER 23

The Enemy Within

Askel knew she had the software systems on *Ephialtes* locked down. She also knew there was a saboteur on board. Deductive logic told her that much. What she didn't know was what the saboteur might do next. He or she might only have the software trick, and that had been taken care of. But maybe they were more resourceful than that. *Ephialtes* was a precision instrument. Someone with the time or inclination might be able to, literally or otherwise, throw a spanner in the works.

Askel's work took her all over the ship. She was constantly engaged with its various systems. She was vigilant for any changes. She had asked Andrews for the psych evaluations of all the commanders aboard the ship. Commanders were evaluated every six months. She could find no aberrations. Meades and Steiner had suffered head traumas but both had been passed fit for duty. It had been a stipulation that all commanders on this mission should have combat experience. Askel wondered if any had been traumatised by it, or maybe bore a grudge against the government that had sent them into battle.

She noticed the maintenance crews were reporting higher than usual instances of mechanical failures on the command drones. At least two had leaked coolant, and another had a faulty gyroscope. She had been part of the division that designed the command drones and she knew that failures of this nature should be exceptionally rare. Commanders had been given leave to visit the dropships to run simulations directly from their command drones. Most days commanders could be found in their dropships training for the mission ahead.

Apart from the commanders the only people who had come to *Ephialtes* via the shuttle and *Otus* were six *Ephialtes* crewmembers. None of them were dropship maintenance crew. To Askel it seemed there was a strong probability that the saboteur was a commander. Any other *Ephialtes* crewmembers would need special clearance to access the hangar deck. All the dropship maintenance crews who had access were already on *Ephialtes* before the shuttle docked. The saboteur had to be a commander.

Commanders did not have designated dropships of their own; they would be assigned ships for each mission. Askel looked at the logs for the dropships where faults had been reported. It seemed like some commanders had favourites. She crossed referenced the command drones that had reported failures with the commanders who had used them. That gave her a list of eight commanders. These were her prime suspects. She noted with interest that amongst the eight were Steiner and Meades. She decided to read more deeply into their records.

Commander Alan Meades had served in the Asian theatre. He had been on sixteen combat missions, two of them protracted and bloody affairs. He had an exemplary record and was the youngest serving commander in World War IV. He had captured a missile base single-handedly, losing five of his drones in the process and coming very close to being killed himself. His psych evaluations were all good. Even after the missile base incident he had been assessed positively. His command drone had taken a small-bore artillery shell directly to the torso. He had been knocked unconscious momentarily but went on to complete his mission. He sounded like a war hero, in the mould of Bobby Karjalainen. Askel found it hard to believe he might be the saboteur, but she had to keep him on the list. Everyone stayed in the frame until they could be absolutely exonerated.

Steiner too had suffered a head injury on the battlefield. His occurred as he had tried to rescue a fallen comrade. Interesting, Askel thought; more traumatic. Is that the sort of thing that would turn a soldier against his own people? Seeing a friend die? Maybe. Steiner's injuries had been more severe, too. He had been hospitalised and had required surgery. But again, he had a blemish free record and no problems with any of his psych evaluations.

Askel didn't know what to make of it. She felt confident the saboteur was one of her eight. Was the head injury thing a red herring? What about the others? All had served on the battlefield and had been a part of the violence of war. Most had been in fairly routine battles, with massive superiority over their enemies. Maybe that in itself could be traumatising, thought Askel. But she still liked Meades or Steiner for the sab. They had been in heavy action close-up, and had physically suffered for it.

Askel knocked gingerly on Commodore Lucero's door.

"Come," said the voice from within. Askel entered. Lucero was at her terminal with a stack of papers on the side of her desk. She looked up. "Lund!" she said. "Sit down. How are you?" She gestured towards her bed.

"I'm good," said Askel, sitting down. "How'd you like the ship we built you?"

"Pretty good," said Lucero.

"Everything alright?"

"I think so. Shouldn't it be?"

"Well," said Askel, "she was never designed to be out here. I just wondered about your opinion, as a user."

"A user," said Lucero, "I like that."

Askel looked embarrassed. "Well, I mean, as a designer you design things to the best of your abilities and try to anticipate how things are going to be used. But it's the users who will judge in the end if your designs are successful. I'm a designer, and I'm happy with the design of the ship. But you're the commodore. What do you think?"

"Seems pretty good to me. We were floating around Earth for a few months getting used to her. In a while we'll be floating around Mars, which adds up to the same thing. And in the meantime, thanks to your fancy engine, we're floating between Earth and Mars, which is pretty similar, too. It's all good."

Askel nodded. "Okay. No problems then, nothing unusual?"

Lucero turned her chair around from the console to face Askel on the bed. "What is this?" she said. "Is something wrong?"

Lucero hadn't been on the shuttle or *Otus*. Askel was as close to certain she could trust her. "Maybe," she said.

"Maybe what? Something may be wrong?"

Askel hesitated. "The ship's fine. The design is good, the build is good. But there may still be a problem."

"What is it, Lund?" said Lucero. "You can tell me straight out. No riddles, okay?"

"It's . . ." Askel stopped. Lucero waited. "I think there is someone on board trying to sabotage the mission."

Lucero looked at her. "You *think*?"

"Well, I'm pretty sure. Listen, *Otus* was deliberately destroyed. It wasn't an accident. Whoever did it tried to do the same thing to *Ephialtes*. And they're almost certainly still on board."

"Okay," said Lucero. "What are we going to do about it?"

"I don't know," said Askel. "They got to *Otus* through her software systems. I've locked all that right down on this ship. I mean, you can never lock something up one hundred percent watertight, but as far as possible I think I have secured the software systems. But if the person who tampered with the software is still on board they can continue to hamper the mission by other means."

"What sort of other means?"

"Physical means. Violence. Insurrection. Who knows? Whoever it was had no qualms about taking out a capital ship and her entire crew, so who knows what they might be capable of?"

Lucero thought. "And you knew about this before we set off?"

Askel shrugged. "I don't know about it even now, not for sure. All I'm saying is don't trust anyone, and if you notice anything odd, however small or apparently insignificant, let me know."

"Okay," said Lucero. "What happens if we don't find them?"

"I don't know," said Askel. "Let's hope we do."

CHAPTER 24

Secession

The deadline passed. The monies were transferred. It was the final bow tying up Martian independence. The USAN's financial authorities working in tandem with National Cybersecurity had tried to freeze Martian assets. Kostovich was ahead of them every step of the way, not least because he knew exactly what they were doing. Through his backdoor he had daily briefings on exactly what they were trying to do and how they were trying to do it. Even without that information Kostovich was always going to beat them.

He circumvented the USAN's measures in the middle of the night. Shareholders of Venkdt Corporation woke up to find themselves not just divested of a proportional amount of their shares but appropriately compensated with cash in their bank accounts. Literally overnight, without a shot being fired or a brick being thrown, in fact with no physical clash whatsoever, Venkdt Mars Corp had wrested itself free from the parent company. Now Mars was truly independent.

All the companies that recently formed on Mars were Martian. Venkdt Mars Corp was now fully Martian. Hjälp Teknik remained a public company traded on stock exchanges of Earth, but accounted for only a small portion of the Martian economy. Charles Venkdt had often said he welcomed foreign investment in the new Mars and there it was already.

In a matter of months Mars had gone from being a colonial outpost with a ramshackle garrison, half-heartedly enforcing laws from a hundred and forty million miles away, to a new nation, a new planet, with its own fully independent economy and military. It had its own locally elected government and a president with a huge mandate from the Martian people. Charles Venkdt, like many of his fellow countrymen, believed there was a golden future ahead of them. They were sitting on huge resources which they could extract and sell to their solar neighbour. Not only that but they were right next door to the asteroid belt. The asteroid belt was immensely rich with resources which the Martians could exploit for themselves and trade with others. They were right at the frontier of human experience, forging ahead into the solar system, a few short years from conquering the asteroid belt. Who knew where they could go from there? With a big enough population on Mars and with the wealth they could extract from the natural resources around them maybe even terraforming would become a possibility. The great dry oceans of Mars might once again heave with water. Maybe one day Martian children would play in the open air. It seemed the possibilities were endless. The Martian future was bright indeed.

Charles Venkdt liked to read. He had read many books about the founding of the USAN. About how people had crossed oceans, spending long months in relatively unsophisticated craft then landing in a hostile environment. How they had overcome many trials and false starts in order to gain a foothold in an unforgiving new world. Those first settlers would hardly believe what the world they were founding would go on to become. Venkdt saw the early Martians in the same light. Similarly, they had travelled immense distances in barely suitable craft and had faced extreme difficulties in surviving in a hostile and unfamiliar world. They too had triumphed. They had adapted, using their technological knowledge and sheer will to prevail over the environment. He expected that they in their turn were building a future unimaginable to them. Technologies would develop allowing further and faster travel. Mankind would expand beyond the solar system, again facing challenges of distance and environment. Through enduring hardship and by adapting and overcoming all challenges it would prevail once more.

So the cycle would repeat.

Where might it end? Maybe never. Maybe the only limit was the edge of the universe itself.

Elspeth had planned a special stream celebrating the final plank of Martian independence being laid in place. She had expected to be covering parties, like those for the election. Maybe she would do some vox pops and some pieces to camera with madly celebrating Martians behind her. But the transfer of the monies passed largely unremarked. To the bulk of Martians independence had already arrived. They had voted for it and they had received it. They had voted for their president, Charles Venkdt. Martian independence was old news. Some money got moved around in some bank accounts somewhere. So what?

Elspeth still did her piece. Ratings were better now, following the interviews with Bobby Karjalainen and President Venkdt. But there was not much she could do to make a change in balance sheets seem exciting. Elections, competitions such as they were, with winners and losers and all the rest of it, made for good entertainment. Numbers moving around? Less so.

She tried to jazz up the story with some graphics. She depicted great streams of money shooting through space from Mars to Earth, with the little flag flying over Mars in her graphic changing colour. It was pretty tame stuff, and was not popular.

Elspeth wondered what she might cover next. The election and Martian independence had been exciting but it was pretty much all over now. She knew the story of the money transfers was dull but she was still surprised at how low her stream had rated on the aggregators. A few months earlier Martian independence seemed radical and exciting. Now it was just a fact of life, no more remarkable than the sun rising in the morning.

She had always wanted to be a correspondent covering political and business stories and she knew those were not the most glamorous or popular, but after the heady days of her two big interviews she had come to like the idea of being prominent. She had an 'in' with the president now; that might be useful. She knew that the Martian economy would undergo many changes in the coming years. It was exciting to her. Her challenge was to make it exciting to the audience, and she was already discovering how difficult it was to enthuse them.

Venkdt had just stepped out of the shower. He decided to log into his aggregator to catch the news as he dressed. Since the interview he had added Elspeth as one of his favourites, and he noticed her report on the transfer of monies to Earth. He selected it and screened it on the wall of his bedroom. Visually the report was not particularly interesting but Venkdt listened as he selected clothes from his wardrobe and rubbed himself down with a towel.

In a way he was glad that there hadn't been much excitement about the news. It was right because this was just a formal detail and something that people didn't really need to trouble themselves with. He knew that when people got excited they were volatile. The time for that had passed.

Once he was dressed Venkdt moved to his breakfast room. A drone brought him coffee, toast and jam. As he spread jam on the toast he wondered about what the day might hold for him. He had meetings with the senate - they were still thrashing out amendments to the constitution. He wanted to catch up with Kostovich at some point to thank him for all his help with the money transfers and the armaments. When he finished breakfast he decided to call Christina.

"Hi, Dad," she said.

"Hey, kid," said Venkdt, "did you catch any of the bulletins this morning?"

"I didn't. Is something up?"

"No, no, they're just talking about the money. It all went through, Kostovich got them all paid off."

"That's good, Dad."

EPHIALTES

"I think so," said Venkdt. "So that's it now, all done. Venkdt no longer owns Venkdt Mars and the constitution - which is pretty good anyway, thanks for that - is shaping up nicely, too. We're kicking a few more things around later on. So it's all done now, the major stuff. We are an independent, self-determining economy."

"Congratulations, Dad, I'm glad it all worked out for you."

"Not just for me, for us. All of us Martians. This is just the very beginning, for all of us."

"Okay, Dad," said Christina, with the slightest hint of weariness in her voice. "Listen, I'm going to be late for work, I'll call you tonight, okay?"

"Sure, kid," said Venkdt, and Christina was gone.

The younger generation, he thought, just took all this for granted. They didn't appreciate that everything they had, everything their world was built upon, had been put there by hard work by those who had gone before. The systems that maintained their world were not part of natural law, but were governed by the laws of man. Without the supremacy of law, with all held equally before it, the system would come crashing down and the world would revert to a feudal state.

Before he arranged for his car to pick him up he called his PA and asked her to set a meeting with Kostovich for later that afternoon.

It was never good to be called urgently to the president's office. Farrell felt an odd sick feeling in the pit of his stomach as he tried to rack his brains for any lapses or failures his department may have made. He knew that Mars was a top priority at the moment and he also knew that Venkdt's deadline for the transfers had passed overnight. Immediately after taking the call he contacted his most trusted deputies and got them to prepare reports on what had happened. Not only did he need paperwork that covered his ass, he needed it to look like it hadn't been quickly created for that specific purpose.

National Cybersecurity had been tasked with freezing Martian assets. Obviously, they had failed. Farrell kept running through his mind how and when had they been asked to do that. How specifically had the task been framed? How often had the department of foreign affairs requested reports to be made to them? And wasn't defence supposed to be involved too? Maybe some of the blame should be on them. He had an underling looking into all these questions but they were against the clock. It would only take him minutes to get to the New White House. The reports could be sent through to his comdev so they had to be concise, and he had to be able to internalise them before he met with the president.

There was a second task he needed to tackle too; what to do next? He had another hastily assembled team on this. The horse had already bolted but maybe he could distract attention from that by concentrating on what their options were. It seemed to him that they were quite limited. The Martians now owned most of the infrastructure on Mars and seemed to be doing well politically, too. Maybe he could play the legality card? What about collecting all the money that had been transferred and depositing it in a central place? Was there maybe some way to declare it illegal and confiscate it? It seemed unlikely. While it wasn't legal to buy something without the would-be vendor's consent, it equally was not illegal to give someone money for nothing. From a very strict legal point of view the shareholders still held valid shares and had merely been given an amount more than equal to those shares by someone with whom they had not agreed to do business. Maybe there was some way to just let them keep the money *and* the shares as a big screw you to Charles Venkdt?

At the New White House he made his way through security and up to the president's office. On entering he found that Senator Peter Brennan and Audrey Andrews were already there. Farrell made his way to the sofas. "I'm sorry I'm late," he said.

"As far as I'm concerned, these people just got free money. It doesn't change a thing, legally," said Brennan.

"Not the point," said Cortes. "Think about how it looks. He would make us look like the bad guys, taking money for nothing, and him getting nothing in return."

Brennan shook his head. "If some crank wants to give away free money that's down to him. Nothing we can do about it. I say we hold firm. Nothing has changed."

Cortes was clearly annoyed. "What has changed is this; we look like fools, incompetent, impotent fools. We said we were going to freeze their assets. What happened to that?"

Farrell thought that getting in early and controlling the conversation would be a good strategy, rather than hiding from the wrath of the president. "If I could just cut in here, sir," he said. "Cybersecurity is looking into that right now. It appears the Martians used some extremely sophisticated and hitherto unseen techniques to get those monies transferred across. It really is quite remarkable."

"Quite remarkable," echoed Cortes. "We're the most powerful nation to have ever existed. Don't we have software engineers capable of doing remarkable things?"

"Of course, Mr President. Perhaps I didn't convey the extreme level sophistry that was required for this operation. It's something quite unprecedented."

Cortes snorted. "Well the precedent has been set now, and it's made us look stupid. What are you doing about it?"

"Well," said Farrell, "we're looking at all our options. I have two teams who are going over it right now and we hope to have a report ready for you by the end of the day, sir."

"Great," said Cortes. "They've turned us over just how they said they would, but at least we'll have a report by the end of the day." Cortes shook his head disappointedly. "What does defence have?"

"Mr President, I can update you on the progress of *Ephialtes*. The mission is proceeding smoothly and as planned. We hope to have the ship in Martian orbit within ten days."

"What about the missile platform?"

"We are prepared to take the platform out as soon as it's in range. That's a mission priority."

"And we have the capability to do that?"

"I've been assured we have, Mr President?"

"Should that go disastrously wrong, can I have your assurance that you will be able to provide me with a 'report by the end of the day'?"

Andrews was not quite sure how to respond to the president's sarcasm. "Militarily it's a straightforward operation, sir. We are not anticipating any difficulties."

"Good," said Cortes. "It'll be nice for something to go right for a change."

Cortes and Brennan drafted a statement to be given to the news media. The USAN rejected outright Venkdt's buyout, which was not recognised in law. Shareholders of Venkdt, as far as the law was concerned, had been given a generous gift by Venkdt Mars Corp, but the status of their shares remained intact. The statement went on to mention the illegal manner in which the money had been transferred and hinted darkly at the nefarious means the Martians had used. It restated that Charles Venkdt's Martian government had absolutely no legitimacy and was not recognised by the USAN, nor any other country on Earth.

The statement also touched on where the USAN saw the whole situation going. It was absolutely not acceptable for the Martian insurrection to stand. The strong hope was that an agreement, possibly generous to Martian requirements, could be brokered. But if that was not possible force would be used.

The statement mentioned *Ephialtes* by name, also giving its estimated time of arrival. As far as the USAN was concerned the clock was ticking down for the Martians.

Venkdt regarded Kostovich's office almost as a separate land. He had been there before only rarely. On this day he knocked gingerly on the door before walking in. He noticed Kostovich was not at his desk. He wondered if he might be in a lab somewhere, but then as he walked further into the room he noticed the sofa to one side and the snoring Kostovich laid upon it.

He coughed, quietly at first then louder, but Kostovich did not stir. He tried tapping the desk. "Dan?" he called. It reminded him of waking Christina when she was a child. "Dan!" he called again, this time much louder, and Kostovich jumped up with a start.

"Jeez!" he said.

Venkdt couldn't help but smile, though he felt slightly guilty at startling his star protégé. "I'm sorry, Dan," he said, "I didn't mean to wake you. Well, I *did* mean to wake you, just not quite like that."

Kostovich had collected himself a little, and he sat up. "What is it, has something happened?" he said.

"No, no. Nothing like that," said Venkdt. "I just wanted to drop by to thank you for everything you've done over the last few months. I heard about the money going through. Terrific stuff, really terrific. And all your help with the military kit and hardware, it's all been really helpful, Dan. I just wanted to come by and thank you in person."

Kostovich's head was clearing now, but the words didn't quite make sense to him. "Thank me for what? It's just my job. I'm a Martian too, just like everyone else. I'm happy to do my bit for this project."

"That's good to hear, Dan, but I still want to thank you."

"Well," Kostovich shrugged, "thanks for your thanks."

Venkdt looked around the office, noting small knick-knacks and action figures. "Listen, Dan," he said. "This big ship they're sending, *Ephialtes*. We have enough defences to block it, don't we? I mean, in a chess-like sense?"

"Sure," said Kostovich. "And we have the missile defences and field artillery, should they land any dropships on the surface."

Venkdt winced. "I don't like that kind of talk. Obviously, we'll never let anything get that far anyway. What I want to know is that we have enough of a plausible defence to stop them using *Ephialtes* against us. We have that, don't we?"

"I'd say we do."

Venkdt thought. "If you were them, and you were coming at us with that big ship, is there anything you might do or need to do before you got here? You know, communications stuff or logistics or anything like that?"

Kostovich thought. "The ship is a self-contained unit. I'm guessing they have enough supplies for years. What they're trying to do isn't dissimilar to a medieval siege, except we're never going to run out of food or resources. We have or can make anything we need right here. We could bear the siege indefinitely. In fact, the only thing they would be able to stop us doing would be exporting minerals back to Earth, and that's exactly what they need us to be doing. So the siege actually works against their interests, rather than ours. It makes you wonder if they've thought it through, really."

Venkdt nodded. "Unless they're not planning on a siege."

Kostovich picked up his meaning immediately. "I don't think they would attack us. Public opinion wouldn't bear it, and we have all the expertise and equipment necessary for extracting deuterium. All of that could be destroyed in a fight. However pissed off they are at us, they need to keep us onside. It wouldn't make sense to do anything else."

"Well, Dan, you can't rely on people to always do the sensible thing. They're nothing if not unpredictable."

"I guess that's true," said Kostovich.

"If they were planning on landing a military force, what would be the first thing they'd do? And what could we do to stop them doing it?"

Kostovich had run some scenarios in his simulators, so he had the answer readily to hand. "Well, if I was sending a dropship carrier to a distant planet with the intent of landing drone squads on the surface, the first thing I would want to do would be to make sure the carrier itself was safe. If there were any off-planet defences I would have to take them out before I put my prized ship in orbit."

Venkdt nodded.

CHAPTER 25

Gainful Employment

There was something familiar but unfamiliar about the former USAN garrison on Mars when Bobby Karjalainen entered. The garrison had been built by the USAN but was now occupied by the Martian Security Service. The style of architecture and many of the fittings were familiar to Bobby from his time in military installations on Earth, but there was something slightly off about the personnel. It wasn't just the uniforms, which were broadly similar to the USAN's but subtly different, it was the way they carried themselves. On USAN Army installations on Earth they would have been berated for being sloppy. He wasn't sure if what was going on here was that they were poorly trained or just doing things differently. He had to keep reminding himself that this wasn't the USAN Army, it was the Martian Security Service, and that was a different thing entirely.

He had made it through the checkpoint, presenting his identification to the guards and being patted down and scanned before being allowed to enter. They had called back to the main building for someone to come and escort him. The escort was a bright young woman who smiled politely and made small talk as they walked. As she led him to Foveaux's office she asked him what he would be doing for the MSS. He answered honestly that he did not know.

He waited for a few minutes in an anteroom with Foveaux's personal assistant until he was waved through. As he entered her office Foveaux rose to greet him with an outstretched hand which he shook firmly. "Please, take a seat," she said.

"Nice place you have here," said Bobby.

Foveaux nodded. "We're working on it. Okay, let's get straight to it."

Bobby smiled. "Yes, let's."

Foveaux knew of Bobby by reputation and had read his service record. She had an idea that he might be trouble, but from what she had read it seemed likely the trouble would be worth it. She decided she would let the flirty undertone of that last remark pass. After all, at this point Bobby was still a civilian and a guest at her installation. If he decided to join them then maybe later on would be the time to try to rein him in. "You know all about the situation we're in, of course. Everything here has changed. As I'm sure you're aware the former USAN garrison, which was based here, was the de facto Martian police force. That job has now been taken over by us, and by us I mean the MSS, the Martian Security Service. I was formerly head of security at Venkdt Mars Corp and I was offered this position, Commissioner of the MSS, based on the work I had done there. My remit was and is to form the new security service and oversee its development into a dedicated Martian police force and a dedicated Martian military. It was originally thought that the two branches would grow apart organically over time. It was also assumed that the military branch would fulfil a mostly ceremonial role." She paused. "However, we have been overtaken by events to some degree and it now seems that the military side of things is more pressing than we originally anticipated. Venkdt have been terrific in providing us with equipment. We have uniforms, armour and weapons. What we don't have is the training and discipline necessary to use them."

Bobby stirred in his seat. He had a good idea what might be coming next.

"That's where you come in. I don't need to tell you about your record in the military. It speaks for itself. You have something we don't, and that makes you very valuable to us. What I would like to ask from you is that you join us on a senior military rank and oversee our training program. You're the most qualified person on the planet for that role, and it would be a peach of a job. We would pretty much turn the whole thing over to you so you would be able to organise the training as you saw fit. You would be able to organise the entire military, using your personal experience and your knowledge of Martian needs. What do you say?"

Bobby shifted in his seat again. "First of all I have to say I'm very flattered that you would offer this to me. But the second thing I have to say is this. The military was supposed to be symbolic, sitting around polishing their brass and turning up for parades, right? Now you need them to be trained in a hurry. What's that about?"

"There are certain things I can't discuss. As a military man I'm sure you understand that. But you will have seen in the bulletins that the USAN is sending a dropship carrier to us. That is something no one anticipated. Well, another thing no one anticipated is that we will have military capability here waiting for them. Do you see?"

Bobby spoke slowly. "I *think* I see. The most powerful military force that has ever existed is sending a state-of-the-art attack ship, and you want to fight them off with a band of ex-security guards. And the only problem, as you see it, is that the ex-security guards need a bit of training?"

Foveaux was irritated by Bobby's levity but she hid it. "It's not quite like that," she said. "We don't really intend to fight anybody. But as a student of military tactics I'm sure you will know that it will give the USAN great pause if they think that we're prepared to put up a fight. I guess you would call it a bluff, but any bluff worth a damn has to have some substance behind it. I'm not saying that we can mould a force capable of taking on the USAN. But what we do need is some credibility. Are you up for that?" She quickly rephrased the question, hoping to bait Bobby into a positive answer. "Are you *capable* of that?"

Bobby sat back in his chair and thought. He looked over Foveaux's head and noticed the hole in the plasterwork. He nodded towards it. "What's that?" he said.

Foveaux turned in her chair and looked at the damaged wall. "Bullet hole," she said.

"Do you have many firefights in your office?" asked Bobby.

"I've only been here a few weeks," said Foveaux. "There's only been one so far."

Bobby leaned around in his chair and scanned the wall behind him. There were no bullet holes there. "So you didn't return fire?" he said.

"Of course I returned fire," said Foveaux, "I just didn't miss."

Bobby nodded appreciatively and a smile broke across his face. "Sure, I'll help you out," he said. "When do I start?"

"Start Monday after next. Give us some time to find you an office, sort out the paper work," said Foveaux.

"Terms and conditions?" said Bobby.

"Within reason you can write your own terms and conditions," said Foveaux. "As I said to you before, we're starting out from scratch. Essentially, you will be founding the Martian Army and it's up to you how you do it."

"So what would my title be?" said Bobby mischievously.

Foveaux thought. "I don't know. It's your army, so I guess that would be up to you."

"Obergruppenführer?" suggested Bobby.

Foveaux frowned. "Are you going to be trouble, Bobby Karjalainen?"

"I hope so, ma'am."

"Let's be clear on this from the beginning. I'm not ma'am, I'm sir. And though you will be in charge of the army, I'm still in charge of the MSS. When you start here with us, whatever you decide to call yourself, I will still be your superior officer. In answer to your question, no, obergruppenführer would not be an appropriate title for the chief of the Martian Army."

Bobby grinned. "You know," he said, "you look great when you're angry."

Foveaux smiled back at him thinly. "I'm not angry. And I'm not charmed by the cheeky, irreverent work-hard-play-hard type either. I've asked you here to do a job for us. It's an important job and you're more than qualified to do it. I'm glad you've accepted and I hope you will give the role your full attention and the dedication it requires."

"I hope so too," said Bobby, still smiling.

Foveaux took Bobby on a tour of the garrison. It wasn't a particularly large building. Bobby asked many questions and stopped to chat with various personnel along the way. He asked about the organisational structure, which was weak and temporary, and he asked about equipment. He was shown the new kit that had been supplied by Venkdt. It was good stuff, certainly up to the job. Most of the personnel were keen. Bobby guessed they were fired up by the novelty of it all. A few weeks ago they had been security guards, probably staring at feeds from security cameras and patrolling warehouses at all hours of the night. Now, here they were in a military facility with shiny new kit, all pumped up at the idea they were the guardians of an entire planet.

He liked the enthusiasm. He thought it would be something he could work with when trying to mould them into some sort of a functioning army. But there were problems, too. There was a very wide range of ages. Usually, the foot soldiers in any military would be in their teens or twenties. Here there were many in their forties or fifties and a handful even older than that. It was something he would have to take into account, but like all of the new Martian institutions he realised that the Martian Army was provisional and subject to change. At this point just having an army was an achievement in itself. He knew what he might like it to be at some distant point in the future but he accepted what was available to him now, both in terms of materiel and personnel. One of the things that had been impressed strongly on him in his own training was the importance of working with what was available, changing the plan on the fly according to current conditions. There was no point in waiting for ideal circumstances, which would probably never materialise. A good soldier was able to adapt to conditions as he found them and work with what he had. Bobby was going to apply that principle to the creation of the Martian Army. There was no other way of doing it.

At the end of the tour Foveaux saw Bobby to the gate. "Thanks for coming," she said. "I'm glad to have you aboard. And I really mean that. We need you, Bobby. Thanks."

Bobby nodded and shook her hand again. "I'm glad to be of help, Commissioner Foveaux," he said. "I'll look forward to seeing you again in a couple of weeks."

"There's one other thing," said Foveaux.

"Yes?" said Bobby.

"I know you're not starting yet but it would be good if you could swing past Venkdt and talk to someone called Dan Kostovich."

"Kostovich?"

"Yes. He's head of R&D there. He's the one who's developed our uniforms and hardware. He also developed the missile platforms that are defending the city. Maybe you've seen some stuff about him on the bulletins?"

"Maybe. I don't follow the news too closely."

"Well, he's something of a genius and very high up in the Venkdt organisation. He's our hardware guy. I think it would be good if you got together with him and talked over some of the kit we have. If there's anything you need - modifications or additional kit or anything like that - he would be the person to talk to. At the moment he's in charge of the missile batteries he developed. I'd like to think they will eventually come under our authority. Maybe you could talk to him about that, too. I'll arrange clearance for you."

Bobby nodded, "Okay."

Bobby and Foveaux stood facing each other, each waiting for the other to leave or say a final goodbye. Bobby thought he had irritated her in their initial meeting, but he felt that by being serious and sensible during the tour he had won her round again. He liked her and sensed he would be able to work with her. It was easy to see that she was strong, both physically and mentally. "Goodbye, then," he said.

"Goodbye," said Foveaux, adding as she turned away, "Obergruppenführer Karjalainen."

Bobby smiled after her and called out, "Maybe you're right. That is a bit of a mouthful."

Foveaux was smiling too as she walked but she didn't look back or reply.

Foveaux had arranged the clearance immediately via her comdev. Before she had reached the garrison building Bobby Karjalainen was cleared to enter Venkdt Mars Corp headquarters and its R&D Department.

Bobby had called ahead and been advised that Dr Daniel Kostovich was very busy at that time and may not be available. He decided to go along anyway. The R&D Department had even higher security than the rest of Venkdt Mars Corp. Kostovich himself had doubled the security detail in the last couple of weeks. The R&D Department was his personal fiefdom and at the moment it was the nerve centre of the Martian missile defences. Kostovich thought the extra security measures were justified.

The guards posted outside the department initially queried Bobby's clearance. His comdev checked out but they had been told to be extra vigilant. Bobby had to wait while they phoned through to Maya Foveaux. Even after a personal assurance from her they were not satisfied, so they found Kostovich himself.

Five minutes later Kostovich came down to meet Bobby at the entrance. He looked at him suspiciously as he made his way across the forecourt. "You're Bobby Karjalainen?" he said.

"I am," said Bobby. "You must be Dan Kostovich. Commissioner Foveaux has been telling me all about you."

"She has, huh? Do you mind telling me why you're here?"

"Commissioner Foveaux said it would be a good idea to talk to you about the equipment you're providing to the MSS."

"What's it to you?" said Kostovich.

Bobby thought that Kostovich was being needlessly antagonistic, but with his characteristic cool detachment he stepped back from the situation and thought about it from Kostovich's point of view. He realised that he hadn't properly explained what was going on and that Kostovich, probably overworked for the last few months and with the additional stress of having his finger on the nuclear trigger, was possibly right to be suspicious.

"Listen," said Bobby, "I didn't explain properly. Commissioner Foveaux has just appointed me as the head of the military division of the MSS. I'll be training up the new Martian Army and we'll be using the equipment you have provided. Commissioner Foveaux thought it would be useful for the two of us to become acquainted. I'll be able to feed back on the equipment and maybe request modifications and that sort of thing." He held a hand out towards Kostovich.

Kostovich took his hand and shook it without commitment. "Well that all sounds great," he said, "but we're kind of busy here at the moment."

"I don't want to interrupt you if you're busy," said Bobby. "Maybe we can arrange to do this some other time?"

Kostovich squinted at him. "Bobby Karjalainen the war hero, right?"

Bobby looked back at him and smiled. "I guess I've been called that, yes," he said.

"And you're going to be heading up our military division?"

"It looks like I am."

Kostovich looked at Bobby and weighed him up, then spent a few more moments pondering the general situation. "Okay," he said, "you'd better come with me." He turned and led Bobby into the R&D Department. They walked down a few corridors past offices and interesting looking labs before arriving at the provisional missile control centre. At the door Kostovich turned to Bobby. "You have clearance for this, right?" he said.

"Commissioner Foveaux said she was going to see to that. Here's my comdev," he said, lifting his comdev up next to the scanner on the entry panel. The panel flashed green and the door opened.

"I guess Foveaux works fast," said Kostovich.

"I heard that rumour too," said Bobby as they entered the control centre.

Kostovich made cursory introductions between Bobby and Baldwin and Walton. He gave Bobby a brief introduction to the control room and explained what they were monitoring and how the control centre worked.

"So this is purely a defensive system?" said Bobby.

"Of course," replied Kostovich. "We're a nation of just a hundred thousand people. There's no one small enough for us to attack."

Bobby nodded in agreement. "Who are you defending us against?"

Kostovich nodded at one of the terminals. "Our former brothers and sisters. See that ship there? It's a state-of-the-art dropship carrier, and our erstwhile comrades have seen fit to point that thing us."

"That's *Ephialtes*," said Bobby, "I had some very minor input on her design. Well, the dropships really, and the drones."

"Oh yes, of course," said Kostovich. "Then you know how dangerous that thing can be."

Bobby looked across the terminals. Much of what he saw made no sense to him - numbers and graphs. But it was clear they were monitoring the progress of *Ephialtes* and they had missiles trained in her direction.

"Do you think they would actually attack? From what I've heard they're just playing the intimidation game."

Kostovich snorted. "I don't just think they're going to attack us, I know it. In fact, I have their precise orders. As soon as that thing's in range they're going to attack one of our major military installations."

"Where does that leave your defence system?" said Bobby.

"It leaves it perfectly intact after claiming its first kill," said Kostovich.

Bobby knew that Martian independence had caused a huge kerfuffle back on Earth. Destroying a capital ship and all the lives aboard it seemed like massive overkill and unnecessarily provocative.

"You're going to destroy *Ephialtes*?" said Bobby. He felt uneasy about what he was getting into. He had signed up with Foveaux on the understanding he was going to be training an army for a limited defensive role. Now it seemed that the nascent Martian military were being gung-ho about starting a full-on shooting war with the USAN, a country which, until a few short months ago, he had fought for himself.

"Not destroy," said Kostovich, "neutralize. We have the capability of making a pinpoint strike that will render *Ephialtes* useless as a weapon of war. It will still exist. That is to say it will retain its structural integrity, but its martial application will have been removed."

Bobby felt relief at that. "And the crew?" he said.

"The crew will be unharmed. In fact, the biggest danger to the crew will be themselves. After we have disarmed their ship we will attempt to rescue the stranded crew. How they react to that will determine their fate. If they recognise that they've been defeated, and that we have come to rescue them in good faith, all will be good. However, if they don't trust us or they suspect a trap things could go very badly indeed. I've recommended to Commissioner Foveaux that if our rescue team has even the slightest suspicion of the intentions of the survivors they should pull out and leave them to their fate."

"What fate would that be?" said Bobby.

"Well," said Kostovich, "at the present time *Ephialtes* is on a trajectory that will take it close enough to Mars to be captured into orbit, but it has yet to fully apply the brakes as it will need to. That means it's going way too fast for capture to happen. If it doesn't slow down between now and when we disarm it, it will continue at its current speed. Rather than being captured by Mars' gravity it will simply be deflected slightly and then carry on to the asteroid belt and the further reaches of the solar system beyond. And unless it hits anything it will just carry on into deep space."

"So they'll just be stuck on a one way trip out into the galaxy?"

"They will, but they'll be dead. Once that ship is disabled the life-support systems will no longer function. If we can't pull them off within a few days, that will be that.

"A far more likely scenario is that they slam the brakes on and assume a speed suitable for capture into Martian orbit well before we have the opportunity to take them out. But that still leaves them stranded in orbit in what will rapidly become a toxic freezer."

Bobby nodded. "So who is going to be charged with getting them off?"

Kostovich shrugged. "That's down to Foveaux," he said. "I understand she has a team ready and they're preparing one of the shuttles for launch."

Bobby nodded again. Foveaux had told him that none of her personnel had any combat experience or training worth a damn. A rescue mission on board a potentially hostile spacecraft sounded pretty tricky to him. He thought that his first day at work was likely to be more eventful than he had initially supposed.

CHAPTER 26

The Countdown

The cabinet room at the New White House had an enormous single plate window covering most of the entirety of one wall. It afforded fantastic views of the White House lawn and the new Capitol beyond. The glass-like material it was made of was super-strong and could withstand sniper bullets and explosions. It gave the room impressive lighting and an airy feel that lifted some of the oppression from long and difficult meetings.

Today Cortes had the security blinds in place. There was no natural light in the room. The whole cabinet was meeting. Farrell, Andrews, Brennan and White took their places amongst the others.

Farrell had fed back to the room such intelligence as he had about the Martians; that they would be unwilling to negotiate on any terms as they now saw themselves as entirely independent. For them, there was nothing to negotiate with the USAN government. The only negotiations would be between Venkdt and the other Martian companies, and the companies they did business with on Earth. Venkdt in particular was keen to negotiate its new relationship with its former parent company. Previously they had extracted minerals, particularly deuterium, on behalf of the parent company. Now they were doing it as an independent entity and needed partners to trade with. Venkdt Earth desperately needed the supply of minerals but was reluctant to trade with its former self. The problem wasn't restricted to Venkdt Corporation, since they in turn provided these vital resources to the government and power companies. The deuterium, in particular, was essential to keep the nation in power.

"So you see," said Farrell, "we have stocks of deuterium for the next eighteen months but after that it becomes a very grave issue. We can source some deuterium here on Earth, probably enough to supply essential services indefinitely. But for households and the wider community we only have a year and a half to get that deuterium flowing again before we're in real trouble."

"The intelligence tells us there is absolutely no way the Martians are willing to negotiate?" said White.

"That's what we have," said Farrell.

"And how reliable are your sources?"

"We are inside their coms system. Pretty reliable, I'd say," said Farrell.

"They're denying us our essential fuel supplies and they will not negotiate," said Cortes. "Secretary Andrews, can you please take us through our military options one more time?"

"Yes, Mr President. *Ephialtes* will be in Martian orbit within seven days. From orbit *Ephialtes* is able to deliver twenty-four dropships. Each dropship carries eleven Mech-Type drones and a piloted command drone. Each dropship itself is also an independent airborne drone with intelligence gathering and strike capability. We have rehearsed many scenarios, and I've been assured that our military force is more than capable of taking the necessary Martian facilities for extracting, refining and transporting deuterium, as well as other important minerals."

"What about the Martian defences?" said White.

"We understand that the Martians have very quickly built some missile defences. Our dropships and command drones easily have the necessary capacity to take them on. It's something they've trained for. We do not anticipate the Martian defences being high quality. They've been fabricated very quickly and have limited capability."

"What about the orbiting platform?" said White.

EPHIALTES

"We have accounted for that in our plans, too," said Andrews.

"Can you elaborate?"

"Certainly. The orbiting Martian missile platform poses a potential threat to *Ephialtes*. It is therefore a mission priority to eliminate that threat before *Ephialtes* takes her place in Martian orbit."

"You're going to destroy it?" said White.

"Well, what else do you think we should do?" said Cortes.

"It seems a bit . . ." White shrugged, ". . . aggressive?"

"It may have escaped the Vice President's attention but we are dealing here with an insurrection. Revolutionaries who have already destroyed one of our satellites and almost certainly destroyed one of our capital ships without a moment's thought. I don't think kid gloves are necessary here. The Martians have kicked off a revolutionary war. Well, if they want a war we can give them one. I certainly don't have any qualms about destroying an unmanned missile platform in order to protect one of our ships. Does anyone here have any objections?" said Cortes.

He looked around the table and apart from a few people shaking their heads 'no', no one responded to his question.

"And what about when we have taken the facilities?" said Brennan. "Do we have a long-term plan?"

"We do," said Cortes. "Secretary Farrell?"

"Yes," said Farrell. "We're in the process of contacting Anthony Karjalainen, who we feel we could install as an interim president. He is a Martian native with strong Earth sympathies. Our plan would be, essentially, to keep the new Martian constitution - elections suspended, of course - with Anthony Karjalainen as president and Mars as the newest nation incorporated into the USAN. We've looked into it and we think that is a solution that would be acceptable to all sides. Mars would nominally be independent and have its own accountable government, but it would be still part of and answerable to the USAN. In time, obviously, we would reintroduce elections. But until then we would keep a military force on the planet to keep order."

"Good," said Cortes. "I like the plan. Quick, decisive and thorough."

"Expensive, too," said White, under his breath.

"Does anyone have anything else to add?" said Cortes.

"The secretary's plan mentions elections at some point down the line for Mars," said White. "Will we be extending the same courtesy to our own citizens within a similar time-frame?"

Cortes looked at him. "Elections have been suspended due to serious global instability. That period of instability is coming to an end with the conclusion of the last war and the settlement of this minor internecine difficulty. We hope to reintroduce elections as soon as possible, and to that end I would ask all of you for your full cooperation in sorting out this immediate problem. In answer to your question, Mr Vice President, I anticipate that elections here in the USAN will take place in the very near future." Cortes held White's gaze long after he had finished speaking.

"Thank you for that full and informative answer, Mr President," said White.

"Secretary Andrews, you said you expect *Ephialtes* to be in orbit within the next seven days. At what point do you anticipate the strike against the orbiting missile platform?"

Andrews consulted some papers in front of her. "We'll neutralize the missile platform as soon as we have it in range. That should be shortly before we arrive in orbit."

"Good," said Cortes. "I'd like to be kept closely informed on that part of the operation."

"Yes, Mr President."

"Anything else?" Cortes looked around the table. There were no replies.

"Okay, that's it. Let's go."

White met in his office with a group of his most trusted advisers. They had the minutes from the cabinet meeting and the intelligence briefings. "What can we do with this stuff?" White asked.

"You have an assurance here from the president himself that elections are going to be reinstated soon, sir," said one of the advisers. "That's great news, and progress, I would say."

"It's a vague promise. It doesn't mean a thing," said White.

"But it's here in the record," said the adviser. "You can refer to this later, if you need to."

White made derisive grunt. "All of this is constitutional. Well, according to the current constitution. We have an unelected president here -"

"But sir, President Cortes *was* elected," interrupted another adviser.

"He was elected for a four-year term *nine* years ago," said White. "As far as I'm concerned, hell, as far as the original constitution of these United States and Nations is concerned, he was not elected to serve for the last *five* years. He is an illegitimate president."

"Sir?" another adviser cautiously asked. "By that argument you haven't been legitimately elected to the vice presidency either."

White looked at her. "Yes, I know that. How do you think that makes me feel? I'm trying to do the right thing here, to sort this mess out. We are in very dangerous waters, drifting away from constitutional government as mandated by the people. You're right; my position is not legitimate either. But as long as I'm here I'm going to try to bring him in, and I need your help to do it. So does anyone have any useful suggestions?"

One of the advisers spoke up. "Everything the president has done has been with the approval of congress. It may be wrong, but if everyone goes along with it we have no means of challenging it legally."

"That's right," said White. "There's what's legal, and there's what's right, and every now and then the two diverge. So what do you do then?"

His question was met with blank faces.

Kostovich had two streams of information about his approaching enemy. *Parry 5* could look deep into space with tracking systems which were able to monitor *Ephialtes'* deliberate approach. Through his backdoor into the USAN's network he also had very detailed information on the mission, including telemetry from *Ephialtes* which was being sent back to the defence department on Earth. He had access to the minutes of important government meetings and all files from the defence department. He was absolutely aware that *Ephialtes* was going to destroy *Parry 5* at the first opportunity it had. There was no question about it. His only option was to disable *Ephialtes* before it had the chance to destroy his own platform.

He had been aware of this for weeks. Initially, it had appeared to be an abstract problem, way down the line in the future. Rather than face it he had decided to put it to the back of his mind. He knew that there was very little to contemplate. Although the stakes were high and the scale enormous it was a very simple issue at heart; kill or be killed.

Kostovich had happily put that decision off to one side, but he could now see from his data that the time was coming when he would have to address it head-on. *Ephialtes* was hours away from being within range of *Parry 5*'s EMP missiles. There would be no need to physically destroy *Ephialtes*. With the EMPs he would simply be able to render it useless, destroyed in military terms but retaining its physical integrity. No lives would be lost in the initial attack.

One thing that did bother Kostovich was that once all the electronics had been extirpated on *Ephialtes* her ability to sustain life would be severely limited. Carbon dioxide filters, air pumps, heating and cooling devices would no longer work. Once *Ephialtes* had been attacked those aboard would be living in a drifting metal box which would soon become a coffin. He had thought about this and was satisfied that *Ephialtes* would be able to sustain life for a number of days following an EMP attack. He had roughed out a plan to rescue the survivors. He had talked about it in the broadest terms with Venkdt, who had given his approval, but he hadn't really given it his full attention. As he saw the data coming in from *Ephialtes*, showing its inexorable approach, he set his AIs on firming up the plan. It would involve sending a large ship - probably a shuttle - to *Ephialtes* and taking the crew off. The difficulty was that the crew would be enemy belligerents. With no communications it would not be possible to tell them of the shuttle's intent before it docked. Once a team from the shuttle were on board they would be in a hostile environment, attempting to rescue people who might see them simply as the enemy. That was the trickiest part of the mission and something that even the AIs were not able to cope with. That would need great human skills. Kostovich didn't like to think about it.

Kostovich piped all the information he had into one of his AIs, which processed it and gave him a nice visual display of the problem he had. *Ephialtes* would be within range of *Parry 5*'s missiles within six hours. *Ephialtes* would be in range to strike the *Parry 5* missile platform within a few tens of minutes over six hours. The window was small, but there was a point at which the *Parry 5* platform held superiority over the mighty *Ephialtes*. That was the point at which the strike must happen. If it didn't happen then, *Ephialtes* herself would strike immediately after. The moment would be lost, the missile platform would be lost, and following on from that the entire planet was potentially lost. Kostovich had all this displayed on his terminal. He could see *Parry 5* with a large circle around it, indicating the range of its missiles. There was a similar circle around the approaching *Ephialtes*. In the corner of the screen there was a clock ticking down. It was currently orange. Once *Ephialtes* was in range it would turn green. Once *Parry 5* was in range of *Ephialtes*, it would turn red.

Kostovich had read all the intelligence briefings that had been given to Cortes. They indicated that Mars was not open to negotiation and recommended seizure of important Martian installations by force. As a prelude to that they recommended again and again that the orbiting missile platform, *Parry 5*, should be destroyed. Those plans had been signed off by the president.

Kostovich had also read all the communications between the defence department on Earth and Commodore Lucero on *Ephialtes*. There was absolutely no ambiguity. Until *Ephialtes* was in orbit around Mars the mission priority was to destroy *Parry 5*.

That very afternoon Kostovich had spent some time listening in to communications on board *Ephialtes*. Lucero had briefed her senior commanders on the attack. They were going to fire a sequence of three missiles, spaced fifteen seconds apart, at *Parry 5* approximately thirty seconds after they were in range. They had assumed the range of the Parry missiles was similar to their own, and they anticipated that they would not be attacked immediately they were in range. The missiles they had were mostly defensive and would be up to the task, they thought, of seeing off any Parry missiles that might be sent towards them. They were unaware of the avoidance routines that Kostovich had added to the Parry's guidance systems and the increased range he had squeezed from improving the efficiency of their engines. Kostovich estimated that one out of every three missiles he sent towards *Ephialtes* would get through. He had nine missiles prepared to fire, and he only needed one to reach its target.

Kostovich looked at the clock in the corner of his screen. It was orange, and showed 01:37:13.

"Could you put me through to Mr Venkdt, please?"

"Who's calling?"

"It's me. Dan Kostovich."

"I'm sorry, Dr Kostovich, Mr Venkdt is in a meeting right now."

"It's urgent."

"I'm sure it is urgent, Dr Kostovich, but Mr Venkdt is in a meeting right now."

"It's a matter of national security," said Kostovich.

Venkdt's PA was used to fighting off people who wanted some of his precious time, but this line was a new one on her and she hesitated for just a moment. "Mr Venkdt has expressly asked that he not be disturbed in this meeting, Dr Kostovich. I can pass on a message for him to call you as soon as he's finished?"

"I need to speak to him right now. We are in present danger of attack by an enemy force, and I need to speak to the president. Please put me through."

"Hold the line please," the PA said, in a languorous and unhelpful tone.

Kostovich was looking at the orange number counting down in the corner of his terminal.

EPHIALTES

The PA came back on the line. "I'm transferring you now, Dr Kostovich."

Kostovich went to say thank you, but the line clicked before he had the chance and he was through to Venkdt.

"What is it, Dan, I'm in the middle of something here?" said Venkdt, in a not unfriendly voice.

"It's *Ephialtes*, Mr President. She is almost within missile range."

"Okay," said Venkdt. "We talked about this, didn't we?"

"We did, sir," said Kostovich, "but it was all a bit abstract then. Right now it seems very real, and a different proposition."

Venkdt thought. "Nothing's changed, Dan. We agreed what we have to do. And you can do it with no loss of life, right?"

Kostovich hesitated. "I can take out *Ephialtes*, no problem. The issue is what to do with the crew once we've disabled their ship. We can't just leave them up there."

"I see," said Venkdt. "I thought you had a plan for that? For getting them off, I mean. We spoke about that too, didn't we?"

"We did. Yes, we can send a shuttle and some troops and probably get them off. If they're happy to be taken off. Remember, strictly speaking they are an enemy military and we will have just destroyed their major ship."

"Okay, so you're worried that it might not work out?"

"I don't know, sir. It just seems a bit . . . serious, I guess."

"Listen, have Maya Foveaux go over your rescue plan. She has some good people and I'm sure she'll be able to make it work. Go through it with her, and implement our original plan for *Ephialtes* unless you have any reasonable alternatives."

"I don't. I'm listening to their coms. They're going to shoot down *Parry 5* as soon as they have the opportunity. That will be in about one hour."

"One hour?" said Venkdt. "In one hour they're going to destroy our only airborne missile defence system, and you're having qualms about defending it against them?"

"I don't have any qualms about it at all," said Kostovich. "But I'm sitting here with my finger on the trigger and it feels a lot different now to how it did when we discussed it weeks ago. I just need to know that this is what you want."

Venkdt paused. "Kostovich, this is a direct order from the president of Mars. In order for us to be able to maintain the defence of our nation and our planet it is our sad duty to have to disarm *Ephialtes*. I am *ordering* you to do that. In addition to this verbal order I will make a written statement and publish it to the government site."

"Yes, Mr President," said Kostovich, "of course."

"Is that clear enough for you?" said Venkdt.

"Very clear, sir," said Kostovich.

"Good," said Venkdt. "Take her down."

Kostovich immediately took the plans his AIs had written and sent them to Maya Foveaux, along with a message asking her to read them as a matter of urgency and comment on any areas she had issues with. In essence the plan was simple. It was to dock a shuttle with *Ephialtes* via one of the emergency ports. The port would then be breached and a small contingent of Martian military would board the ship. Armed with loud hailers as well as standard military equipment they would search their way through the ship making their benevolent intentions clear. Should the crew of *Ephialtes* remain belligerent they would retreat back to the shuttle and leave. If they were amenable to it, they would be disarmed and escorted to the shuttle and thence to the surface of Mars, where they would be held until such time as they could be transported back to Earth.

Technically, it was a simple mission. The difficulty was knowing what the attitude of the *Ephialtes* crew was going to be. If they chose to be difficult things could turn nasty. A firefight in an enclosed space where the enemy has numerical advantage was not an enticing prospect. Kostovich knew that Foveaux's military were green and that this particular job required great nerve and tact. He wasn't sure if they'd be up to it and he needed to know Foveaux's opinion.

EPHIALTES

Kostovich watched the numbers ticking down in the top right of his screen. He had assigned Baldwin to keep a particular eye on *Ephialtes* and Walton to take care of *Parry 5*. As the countdown clock reached 00:45:19 he spoke to her. "Could you please arm three EMPs," he said

"Arming three EMPs," she replied.

Kostovich saw he had an incoming call from Foveaux. Before he took it he called to Baldwin, "Keep on top of *Ephialtes*' coms."

"Yes?" said Kostovich.

"I have your plans here," said Foveaux, "I've only had chance for a quick read through but it seems pretty simple. When are you thinking about doing this?"

"It would be soon," said Kostovich. "Do you really think your people are ready for something like this?"

"Who else is going to do it?" said Foveaux.

"I know there's no one else," said Kostovich irritably, "that's not the question I'm asking. Can your people do it?"

"Yes," said Foveaux.

"Good," said Kostovich. "Start preparing now. We'll only have a very short window to put this thing into effect. Is there anything you need? Anything you need from me?"

"We have all the equipment we need," said Foveaux. "Thank you for that. Who's organising the shuttle?"

"Don't worry about that, it's all taken care of. I've gone through Venkdt for that, the shuttle is being prepared and should be ready for launch within forty-eight hours. I don't know how long they'll be able to survive on *Ephialtes* once we've destroyed the life-support capabilities. Two to three days would be my guess, but I can't even say that for sure. As soon as the shuttle's ready for launch we need to go."

"I understand," said Foveaux.

"You do know," said Kostovich, "that they may not want to be rescued. They may not even accept that it is a rescue. Your people will be boarding an enemy ship, a potentially hostile enemy ship. It will be a live military situation. You're prepared for that?"

"Of course," said Foveaux.

"Good," said Kostovich. "Get training."

Foveaux was looking through a simulation of *Ephialtes*' interior and thinking about the task she had been charged with. She knew that her people were fundamentally security guards and not military, but she also knew they were keen to assist with the forging of the new planet and any security services it needed. Kostovich was right; this was going to be a military operation and far beyond anything any of them had ever done before. She had told him they were ready, but in truth she wasn't sure herself.

While she was familiarising herself with *Ephialtes* she put a call through to Bobby Karjalainen.

"Hello?" said Bobby.

"Hello, Foveaux here. Listen, I know you haven't even started yet but I have a big favour to ask."

"Go on," said Bobby, cautiously.

"Very soon, *very* soon, we will be undertaking an extremely important mission. As you know, we have very limited combat experience, and this mission will be taking place on an enemy spacecraft. You're the only person in the MSS who has any combat experience whatsoever. You have a knowledge of tactics and weapons too, which is something we don't have. I know we said Monday, but could you get down here as soon as possible and join our training for this mission?"

"Join your training?"

Foveaux spluttered, "Well, you know, lead the training."

"Okay," said Bobby, "I'll get down as soon as I can. I have a few things I have to finish up first."

"Thank you," said Foveaux.

"This mission. Enemy spacecraft? You're talking about *Ephialtes*?"

"I am."

"You're sending a force to attack *Ephialtes*?"

"Not to attack. It's a rescue mission."

"I don't follow," said Bobby. "Who are you rescuing from whom?"

"We're rescuing the crew from certain death. This time tomorrow *Ephialtes* is going to be the most expensive tomb ever built. If we can get a team on there we can save the crew. The difficulty will be persuading the crew that that is our intention."

Bobby thought. "I'm guessing there's some stuff here that you're not telling me."

"Of course, and I apologise for that. I can't tell you now but in the next few hours it will be obvious. The point is this; we will need to get a team to *Ephialtes* and they will need to know what they're doing. It's a rescue mission, plain and simple, but those being rescued may not see it that way."

"Okay," said Bobby, "I think I understand."

"It will become clear," said Foveaux, "but we do need your help, and we need it as soon as possible."

"Okay," said Bobby. "I'm on my way."

CHAPTER 27

Open Fire

Ephialtes had used its ion engines to reverse its attitude in space. It then fired up its main NFJ engine. The braking action had slowed the great ship down to a speed at which the gravity of Mars would capture it and hold it in its orbit.

Askel had triple checked her locked down software but had still been jittery about firing up the engine. It had to be done. The speed of *Ephialtes* on its outbound journey was so great that not even mighty Ares himself would have been able to stop her. If they hadn't slowed down the ship would have skipped past Mars and carried on toward the outer limits of the solar system and deep space beyond.

The firing had passed without incident and afterwards the ship was once again turned around to face its destination. The bridge afforded a panoramic forward view of the rust-coloured planet which loomed large before them.

The lower speed - as well as ultimately ensuring their survival - afforded Askel the opportunity to test some of the other important systems. She had gone to the starboard day room to ask for volunteers. When none were forthcoming she had made a formal request to Soward through Lucero.

"I need a few commanders. Three, at least. I'm going to run through a simulated drop," she had said to Lucero.

"Why do you need commanders if it's a simulation?"

"The drop is simulated. I'd like to do a full rehearsal of everything else, including opening the drop-bay doors."

Lucero thought. "Why? Why can't you just sim the whole thing?"

"I could, of course. But I want to run through the exercise with as much real data as possible. You know that the malware that destroyed *Otus* was adept at feeding back phony data. I want to see these systems physically working. And I'd like real human feedback from the pilots, too."

Lucero paced. "Well, it sounds fine to me. Just drop by one of the day rooms and pick up some volunteers."

"I tried that."

"Oh," said Lucero. "Leave it with me."

Soward had provided Steiner, Meades and Jennifer W Hayes. None seemed particularly happy with the assignment, but they listened patiently while Askel talked them through it.

"I will run data through the systems for a deployment over Marineris. Telemetry data for *Ephialtes* will be simmed, time will be simmed, but you will be using the physical systems in your dropships. That is to say the dropships and drones will be fully armed, and you will run through the full launch procedure. The bay doors will open - that is one of the prime tests we are running here - and you will then launch, but that part of the test will be simulation again."

"So is this sim or actual?" said Meades.

"It's a hybrid test," said Lund. "I need data on a physical run-through of the arming procedure and the opening of the bay doors. I've adjusted the sim to accept actual data for those parts of the test. Obviously, we don't want to launch out here, but apart from that I want this to be as close as we can get to a physical launch. Any other questions?"

"I have a question," said Steiner.

"Go on," said Lund.

"Why me?" said Steiner, with fake theatricality. Meades and Hayes laughed.

Lund took some steps closer to Steiner. "It's your job, commander. Is that a problem?"

Steiner flashed Lund a shit-eating grin. "No, ma'am, not a problem at all."

"Good," said Lund. "Let's go."

Once the commanders were in their dropships the truculence disappeared. Commanders tended to be task oriented and once they had something to do they focused on it and gave it their full attention. The drill they were performing they had done many times before, either simmed in situ in their dropships or in IVRs back on Earth. This case was unusual in that it was a full rehearsal for a drop with real-world overlays. In the sims they would routinely skip over the arming process once they had programmed their loadouts. The simple reason for that was that arming a dropship and its drones took anything up to half an hour. The system was automated, so all the pilots had to do was sit and wait. In a simulated drop they could skip through that part. What was happening now was real - the dropships and their drones were actually being armed by maintenance drones. It made sense from an operational point of view - wars are not fought in simulators, after all - but it was tedious to be a part of.

Steiner considered chatting over the com to Meades and Hayes but he didn't know them well and decided against it. Instead he reviewed the data coming over his com and HUD relating to the arming process. As far as he could see it all looked good. His dropship would be fully armed in ten or fifteen minutes. All other readings looked good, too.

Lund was monitoring the procedure. She had data feeds from all three dropships, all of the drones on board each ship and all of the maintenance drones. She had video feeds from the dropship cabins and the drones, too. She monitored these carefully to see the correlation between what was physically happening and what the data said was happening. It all tallied.

When the armoury drones had finished their work Lund spoke over the com to Steiner, Meades and Hayes. "This is Lund, all my readings are good here, please confirm your status."

"Good here," said Steiner, and the others followed suit.

"I'm depressurising the drop-bays," said Lund.

"Acknowledged," came the replies.

"Dropships four through six, please prepare for launch."

"Preparing."

Steiner ran through some final checks and made some last minute adjustments. He knew that Meades and Hayes would be doing the same thing.

Lund came over the com again. "Drop-bays are now fully purged, standby for bay doors to open."

Lund ran the sequence that would open the doors. As she did so she moved on to the launch program. She knew this part of the process was to be simulated so she had to oversee it manually. Casually glancing back to the door opening sequence she was surprised to see it read 'Complete' when the visuals she had from the dropship cockpits clearly showed that the doors had not moved.

"Commander Hayes, can you please confirm for me that your drop-bay door has not opened?" Lund said over the com.

"Confirmed," said Hayes. "The bay door remains closed."

"Steiner, Meades. Can you please confirm that your bay doors have not opened either?"

"Confirmed," came both replies.

Lund ran the door opening sequence again. As she looked at her display the data showed the doors opening while the visuals showed they were not. For a moment she thought she must be confusing the sim and actual part of the test. She switched the entire system over to manual.

"Commanders Steiner, Meades and Hayes, please do not do anything until ordered. We're temporarily running a fully live system here. I'm just chasing down some bugs, please stand by," said Lund. Now fully in control of the system she ran the door opening sequence again.

Nothing happened.

EPHIALTES

Lund flipped the system back to the simulation and ran the kill sequence.

"Commanders, this exercise is terminated, please stand by for further instruction. You've no breathable air in the bays at the moment so sit tight."

"I'm glad that wasn't a complete waste of time," Steiner said to Meades over the com.

Lund repressurised the bays.

"That's it guys for now, thanks for your time," she said.

Askel Lund was passive by nature and not taken to storming either into or out of rooms. For this particular instance she had decided at some low animal level to make an exception. She entered the day room at a fair clip and launched into her tirade immediately.

"This is a ship of war, about to enter into theatre. Below us will be a hostile planet, prepared if necessary to kill us. We face a common enemy together. I have built you the best ship I could in order that we should prevail over our enemies. The ship is strong. The crew - you - are well trained and equipped. We are more than equal to the task at hand.

"One amongst you is trying to subvert this mission. One amongst you actively wants us to fail. You have succeeded in destroying *Otus* but you will not succeed here. I will find you - we will find you - and you will be held to account for the wrong you have done us."

The room was silent but for the short panting breaths Lund was taking when she'd finished.

A commander stepped forward. "Now listen here, ma'am, I don't take kindly to being called a -"

Askel cut him off. "Traitor? I don't like it either. But until we find who it is you are all under suspicion."

"Excuse me, Dr Lund," said Foley, "I think you mean *we* are all under suspicion."

He looked at her pointedly.

"I know where I stand," said Lund. "I'm the only one I trust. Look around you. Someone on this ship - one of the commanders on this ship - is working for our enemies."

She turned about and left.

Kostovich had noticed an interesting phenomenon. As he looked at the clock on his terminal counting down to zero he had no sense that the crucial moment was approaching. When there were ten minutes left, it seemed that ten minutes was enough for an entire lifetime. Ten whole minutes! The luxury!

The momentous task, when it was ten minutes away, seemed as though it may have been ten months, or ten years away. It didn't seem, somehow, to be immediate. But the *really* curious thing was this; the phenomenon repeated itself at every milestone. At five minutes it appeared that five minutes was broadly equivalent to infinite time. Kostovich waited and waited for 00:00:00 to roll around but the clocked kept ticking languorously down, each second slowly passing like a season in childhood.

When the clock hit one minute remaining Kostovich felt almost serene. He was aware that he had fixated on the clock and that that may have had the effect of some sort of meditation. Each second had filled his consciousness to the exclusion of all other things and now he was feeling mildly disoriented as the countdown entered the final ten seconds.

He heard himself speaking as if he was hearing somebody else, aware yet not aware that he was saying the words, "Are the missiles prepared and ready for launch?"

"Missiles ready," came Walton's reply, inevitably, like the next beat in a piece of music.

"Give me the range on *Ephialtes*," Kostovich said to Baldwin, whose reply, like Walton's, seemed to hit a perfect rhythm.

"*Ephialtes* in range in three seconds."

As the clock flipped over from the amber coloured 00:00:01 to the green 00:00:00 it seemed that time really did stop. Kostovich thought this was the only time that would ever exist that would feature the universe lined up in this particular way; that everything was exactly where it needed to be right now in order for right now to happen.

"Fire the missiles," he said.

"Missiles away," said Walton, her voice now curious for its ordinariness. She was no longer his musical foil but an assistant imparting useful information to him. He had snapped out of his trance and had to focus on what he was doing, which was the most important task he had ever been entrusted with. It was his job to save the planet. Try as he might, he could find no way of arguing that that was overstating the case. No, simply put it was his job, on this day, at this hour, to save the planet.

"Roger that," he said in reply to Walton, who was momentarily confused. Who says 'Roger that' to someone who is in the same room as them?

Back in her cabin Askel tried to calm down, but she was heaving with rage. For most of the journey she had felt that she was on top of the situation. Now that she had been beaten by the saboteur one more time she was deflated. She knew the mission was imperilled all the while the saboteur was out there. She had been so wrapped up in the idea of outsmarting and defeating whoever it was that she hadn't given time to considering what the stakes were. Her life and the lives of the rest of the crew were in imminent danger. She knew she was smart but she didn't know how long she would be able to keep outsmarting an enemy she could not identify. Maybe they were dumb and lucky. Maybe she was. She found it hard to bear.

She brought up her simulation routines and the bay control software and immediately began comparing them to the pristine copies she had behind the secure firewall on her comdev. They all checked out at a superficial level so she began to run another check, this time looking deep inside the software itself. It would take a few minutes. In the meantime, anticipating that the bay control software had somehow been compromised, she also began copying over her known good version. She wanted to complete the tests as soon as possible. She planned to pick up from where they had left off. They had left the dropships and the drones armed - that part of the test had completed successfully. She was already thinking about adding some routines to the bay control software and the armoury software that might help defend it against attack. She was thinking about which other software subsystems may have been compromised. She decided to replace them all on a rolling basis. From now on, at any given time, one software system or another would be being overwritten with a known good copy of itself.

As she watched numbers scrolling up her screen as her AIs did a thorough scan, comparing the sets of software, she thought about her outburst in the day room. She wasn't sure whether it would be useful or not for the commanders to know there was a traitor amongst their ranks. Maybe it would lead to a breakdown in trust and efficiency amongst the teams. Maybe it would save their lives if they knew not to put unthinking trust in one another. Maybe their suspicion would help her trace down the offender. She didn't know.

She was feeling sorry for herself for having made such an outburst. She disliked admitting to herself that she had lost self-control in that moment. As she inwardly berated herself she was startled by her comdev. It was Lucero.

"Lund, are you running any combat simulations at the moment?"

"I'm not," she responded, "although I should be. I'm planning to -"

"You're not running any combat simulations whatsoever, please confirm," said Lucero with steel in her voice.

Lund picked up on the urgency. "I'm not. What is it?" she said.

"Probably nothing, please stand by," said Lucero quickly as she closed the line.

Lund glanced at her terminal. It was three more minutes before the bay control software would finish copying over, and another ten before the deep analysis would be complete. She stood up and made her way to the bridge at pace.

At the bridge she was barred from entering by a guard. "You can't come in here, ma'am," the guard said. "The bridge is off limits to civilians."

"For God's sake just let me in," said Lund, "I need to speak to Commodore Lucero. This is an emergency."

The guard was about to insist that Lund was not cleared to enter when Lucero called out from behind him, "Let her in."

The guard snapped smartly to attention and saying, "Yes, sir," he stood aside to let Lund enter.

"What is it?" she said as she walked towards Lucero.

Lucero did not look up from the terminal she was stood in front of. "It looks like a missile attack," she said.

"Missiles? How many? Are they from the orbiting platform?"

"I'm guessing that's exactly where they're from," said Lucero. "There are three of them."

"You have countermeasures in place, right?" said Lund. "How long do we have before impact?"

Lucero looked at her terminal. "Around three minutes. Of course we have countermeasures. We'll be launching our own missiles shortly. I'm interested in the trajectory of these three coming towards us. They seem to be making fine adjustments every twenty seconds or so."

Lund looked worried. "Are we in range for them? I thought we were taking that platform out at the earliest possible opportunity?"

For the first time Commodore Lucero looked up at her. "We are taking them out at the earliest opportunity; the earliest opportunity will be in about fifteen minutes or so. It looks like they have the drop on us."

Lund was concerned. "Do we know what type of warhead these missiles have?"

"No," said Lucero. "Speed and vector are all we have. Prepare to launch defensive missiles."

"Preparing missiles," replied the weapons officer.

Lund looked at the screens depicting *Ephialtes* and the three missiles streaking towards it. She had been aware of the development of *Ephialtes*' defensive missile systems. Back then it had all seemed quite distant and theoretical. Right now she was desperately hoping that the system was good enough.

Lucero was concentrating on her terminal once more. "Fire three missiles per target."

"Three missiles per, sir, understood," said the weapons officer.

"Fire when ready," said Lucero.

"Aye, aye, sir."

Lucero and Lund stared at the encroaching dots on the screen.

"Missiles away, sir," said the weapons officer.

Lund swallowed. "What happens if we miss?" she said.

Lucero shrugged. "Fire some more, I guess," she said, adding, "some militarily tactics are quite complex. This one isn't. We just keep firing until we've shot them all down."

They waited in silence until the oncoming dots and the dots racing towards them met and disappeared.

"Weapons, give me an update on our status," said Lucero.

"All missiles deployed successfully," said the weapons officer. "There are currently no missiles vectoring towards us."

"Weapons, please confirm, are there any missiles vectoring anywhere at the present time?"

"Negative Commodore, no missiles at the present time."

"Okay," said Lucero, "we are on high alert. Everyone needs to be at their post. This is just the beginning, there'll be more. Until we're close enough to take out their missile platform they're going to keep throwing them at us. We just have to keep batting them away. Full alert, everyone, let's go."

"Commodore Lucero," said the weapons officer, "I think you may want to see this."

"What is it?" said Lucero.

"I have some data on the explosions of the missiles. It appears that at least one of the enemy missiles detonated itself as a reaction to the close proximity of our own missile. We've just read a weak electromagnetic pulse from that explosion."

"Shit," said Lucero.

Lund looked at her. "You'd better make sure that none get through," she said.

Lucero nodded, "I'll do what I can."

"They're gone," said Walton. "I've lost all data from the missiles. That wasn't us."

"Their countermeasures seem to have been effective. They launched nine missiles, they took ours out," said Baldwin.

Kostovich paced. "Okay, okay," he said. "That was just to feel them out. Here's what we do. Walton, prepare three nukes and three EMPs. And three standard explosive missiles."

Walton took her eyes from her terminal to look at Kostovich directly. "Nukes? Seriously? You want to fire nukes at a USAN ship?"

Kostovich couldn't hide his irritation. "Prepare the missiles, please. We're not going to fire nukes *at* it, we're going to fire nukes *near* it."

Walton turned her gaze back to her screen, but she was not placated. Kostovich sat in front of a terminal and typed. "Keep all eyes on *Ephialtes*," he said to Baldwin. "If they fire anything at us I need to know immediately."

"We're not in their range for another ten minutes," said Baldwin.

"That's what we think we know," said Kostovich. "Just expect the unexpected and keep monitoring that ship."

"Will do that," said Baldwin.

Kostovich brought up a missile flight plan and patched it through to Walton. "When those missiles are ready fire them according to this flight pattern."

"You don't want to use the regulation flight plans?" said Walton.

"Did I stutter?" said Kostovich. "Load this flight data into those missiles and launch them as soon as you can. Okay?"

Walton was rattled. "Okay," she said quietly as she thought about punching Kostovich in the face.

"When are those missiles going to be ready?" said Kostovich, anxiously.

"We're waiting on the nukes. Safety protocols in the arming routine take a little longer on the nukes. We should be good in a couple of minutes."

Kostovich scanned his terminal. "How's *Ephialtes*? Any change?" he called to Baldwin.

"Steady as she goes," said Baldwin. "No further missile launches."

Kostovich nodded. "As soon as we've launched this volley of missiles prepare the same again," he said to Walton.

"Same again, acknowledged," Walton replied. "Less than one minute to launch for volley number two."

Kostovich rubbed his chin nervously. Though they were based on the surface of the planet, and protected by a further four missile batteries, Kostovich felt like he was aboard *Parry 5*. He could feel the intense vulnerability of the little platform floating above him, and he could feel the massive weight of the task resting on it. He double-checked the missile flight plans he had sent to Walton and ran through various scenarios in his mind, testing and probing his tactics for weaknesses. He couldn't find any, but something nagged away at the back of his consciousness: *'What if you've missed something? / What have you missed?'* "How are we doing on those missiles?" he shouted across to Walton.

"Ready in a few seconds," she replied.

In sharp contrast to the first volley time now appeared to be running at an accelerated rate, individual moments seeming disjointed. It seemed that immediately - or was it simultaneously or even before? - Walton had said there were seconds left she said, "Missiles away."

At that same now-earlier-later moment Kostovich looked down at his screen. He saw the nine blips streak away from *Parry 5* and then, as planned, they drew closer to each other forming a single large blip on his screen. He felt relieved to see the flight plans working but he worried that *Ephialtes* may have seen the original nine blips on their screens too. What would they have made of it? Would they figure it out? How would they try to counter it, even if they did figure it out?

'What if you've missed something? / What have you missed?'

"Telemetry from all missiles is currently good, all missiles are behaving as expected," said Walton.

"No response as yet from *Ephialtes*," said Baldwin.

"Good," said Kostovich as he watched the blip move across his screen towards a large blip on the other side.

Lund was still on the bridge when the second fusillade was launched.

"We have a fresh missile launch," said a signals officer.

"What configuration?" said Lucero.

"It appears to be just one, but I doubt that's the case. It's probably a very tight formation of multiple missiles."

"How long till impact?" said Lucero.

"Approximately four minutes," came the reply.

Lund checked her comdev; the new routines had finished loading.

"Launch countermeasures," said Lucero.

"Aye, aye, sir, preparing to launch countermeasures."

"Listen," said Lund, "we have three fully armed dropships ready to go right now. I suggest launching them immediately."

"Thank you for that suggestion, but how is that going to help us right now?" said Lucero.

Lund nodded at the screen. "If one of those is an EMP and it gets through we are dead in the water. At least if we have some ships out of the blast range we might maintain some capability."

"If all we have left are three dropships then the mission's a bust anyways. Defending *Ephialtes* is our number one priority here."

"I'm not talking about the mission, I'm talking about maintaining some capability in order to rescue us if we're hit with an EMP."

"Whatever, Lund. Do whatever you think is right," said Lucero before barking, "Are those countermeasures ready?"

"Offensive missiles are in range, sir, launching counter measure in three, two . . ."

"Go," said Lucero to Lund. "Get those birds in the air."

"Missiles away, sir."

Lund barked into her comdev, "Steiner, Meades, Hayes. I need you back in your dropships now, ASAP! This is an emergency," as she ran back to her office.

The commanders had been following the attack on a large screen in the day room. Steiner, Meades and Hayes were still suited up from the test earlier. They ran to the hangar deck, half jumping down the stairs and cursing the artificial gravity as they stumbled to the bottom.

Lund was already loading the bay door opening routines as the three commanders clambered up into their dropships.

"Initiating checks," said a slightly breathless Meades.

"No checks," said Lund. "Follow emergency launch procedure, this is not a drill."

"Emergency launch procedure initiated. Hey Lund, can you decompress?"

"Decompression is happening right now, prepare to launch."

Hayes cut in, "I have a warning for reserve power on drone five here, please advise."

"Ignore it, initiate emergency launch procedure," said Lund, her mind now purely focused on launching the dropships as quickly as possible. Everything else had fallen away from her.

"Initiating launch sequence," said Meades.

"Initiating launch sequence," said Hayes.

"We're about to launch here," said Steiner, "any chance you could open the doors for us?"

Lund keyed a button on her terminal, "Initiating dropship bay door opening sequence," she said as she flipped to another terminal showing the video feed from Steiner's cockpit. The drop bay door was directly in front of the ship. Lund stared at the door with absolute focus.

On the bridge Lucero was staring intensely at her terminal. She could see her missiles moving towards the blip approaching them and she was waiting for something to happen. She wasn't sure what it might be but she felt it might happen at any moment.

Suddenly, the approaching blip forked. There were now two blips, with nine of her own racing out to meet them.

"What just happened?" said Lucero

"I think we have a minimum of two missiles, taking different tracks to us," said the signals officer.

"Send three of ours after the group taking the longest course. Keep six on the one still heading straight for us," said Lucero.

"Aye, aye, sir," said the weapons officer.

Lucero saw three of her missiles peel away, adjusting their course to meet the blip that appeared to be veering away from them. "What are they doing?" she said. "How long until we have them?"

"Twenty seconds," said the weapons officer.

As Lucero looked at the screen she could see the blip headed at them elongate and then split in two. There were now three groups heading toward them; two in line, growing further apart, and one that had split off at a tangent and was now being chased down by three of her defensive missiles.

"Hold three back for that second wave," said Lucero.

"I can't do that, sir," said the weapons officer, "they're all at full speed. We have no brakes."

Lucero saw the tactic moments before it happened. The forward batch of the in-line group detonated as it met her own missiles. They were gone. The rear group of the pair adjusted course, taking it out of the blast radius of the three forward nukes, then adjusted again back on course for *Ephialtes*. There was now nothing standing between them and the approaching EMPs.

Lucero looked at the three missiles that were chasing the decoys. "Can we turn our remaining three missiles back on this pack?" she said.

"Negative, sir, our remaining missiles won't make it back," said the weapons officer.

"Prepare nine more missiles for launch," said Lucero.

"Preparing missiles, Commodore."

Everyone on the bridge understood that the missiles would take a minimum of thirty seconds to prepare. The oncoming enemy missiles would arrive at *Ephialtes* in less than twenty seconds.

Lucero knew she had been outmanoeuvred. "Get on the cannon," she said to no one.

"I have the cannon, sir," said another weapons officer. He had brought up the control program for the two plasma cannon mounted on the front of *Ephialtes*. They had been placed there for largely cosmetic reasons. Having limited functionality their purpose was to look suitably military and to fire the odd salute on special occasions. Now they were *Ephialtes'* last thin hope of surviving a missile attack.

Lucero thought about saying something poignant and understated to the weapons officer manning the cannon but she decided against it. 'Now we're screwed,' would have summed up their position nicely but, she thought, wouldn't reflect well on her in the history books. She decided to stick with the prosaic.

"Fire at will," she said.

"Aye, aye, sir," said the weapons officer.

Lund nearly crumpled as she saw the first drop-bay door start to open. The relief was physical. Until it happened she had no awareness of how tensed up she had been. She quickly flipped up the feeds from the other two bays; they were opening too.

"Bay doors are opening, prepare to launch," she said.

"Ready to go here," said Steiner, Meades and Hayes concurring.

Lund had the radar screen up on one of her terminals. From the corner of her eye she saw *Ephialtes'* missiles disappear and the final wave of attack missiles swerve gracefully as they continued on towards *Ephialtes* itself.

"Launch NOW!" she said.

"Dr Lund, the bay door -"

"NOW! Launch Now! Shoot the doors out if you have to!"

Steiner's ship dropped from its mount and sped out of the bay. "I'm clear," he said.

Meades too dropped and launched, scraping the not quite fully open bay door on the way out. "Clear," he said.

Hayes' door had been the last to open. It was still only halfway down when she dropped from her mount. As instructed she fired a blast of cannon at the bay door as she accelerated towards it. The door broke into fragments and her dropship half flew, half scraped its way through. "I'm clear, multiple debris strikes, will advise," she said.

The junior weapons officer manning the cannon had little hope against the three missiles streaking towards him. Even with aiming assists, the speed of the missiles meant the window during which he would be able to fire would be less than a second. If he hadn't been so scared and focused on his task he may have reflected on his small part in history. It would have something of the flavour of the Alamo, or Rorke's Drift, or maybe Custer's Last Stand. Perhaps it was for the best that he didn't have time to give it any thought.

History buffs and lovers of useless titbits of information would, in future years, revel in the fact that against all odds, and with a greater reliance on luck than skill, he did manage to successfully shoot down two of the approaching EMP missiles, a fact that, while interesting and extraordinary, meant little to him or his crewmates at the time. They were forced by immediate circumstances to look at the incident from another perspective; that one EMP got past him and detonated less than three hundred metres above *Ephialtes'* starboard bow.

CHAPTER 28

Blast Radius

Lund was in darkness. There were no windows in her office. She had been aboard *Ephialtes* and *Otus* before when there had been power-outs. The lights would dim and flicker, and the auxiliary power would kick in, powering only essential lights and thereby changing the ambience of the ship. Lund quite liked the mood of the emergency lighting; it made the familiar seem new and intriguing.

This was nothing like that. It was total blackness and near total silence. Distantly she could hear voices, beyond that nothing. She was *floating*.

She had briefly frozen with fear. She didn't let the fear take control. She let it flow through her and allowed herself a moment of panic. Then she pushed it to one side and thought about what she needed to do next.

She craved light. She had never liked the darkness but until this moment she had never really feared it. Now she did, for she knew what it represented. She was determined to fight against it. Feeling her way, she pulled herself to her office door. Touching the frame she knew she had achieved something; she had taken her first step towards the bridge.

Steiner had accelerated away from *Ephialtes* at maximum speed. It was a drill he had practiced over and over; the emergency launch. He guessed Meades would have done the same, too. He tried to check in with Hayes.

"Hayes, how's that damage?"

-

"Hayes, report on your damage, over?"

-

"I think she's off-coms," said Meades.

"Do you have a visual?" said Steiner.

"Negative," said Meades. "Her transponder has stopped. I wouldn't even know where to look."

"Okay," said Steiner. "What's your sitrep?"

"I have three bogies, inbound."

"Roger that," said Steiner, "I have them on my screen. Those three chasing are ours."

"I know that," said Meades, "I'm taking evasive action and deploying countermeasures anyways."

"Roger," said Steiner. He had taken a different course to Meades and was now hundreds of kilometres away. Meades had turned starboard to follow *Ephialtes'* course. He was now in range of the decoy missiles, which were rapidly closing on him.

"Change your vector," said Steiner. "Those things must be nearly out of juice. You can out run them."

"Can't do it," said Meades. "The speed I'd lose in the turn would be enough for them to catch me. Countermeasures and Hail Marys only."

"How long to impact?" said Steiner.

"Twenty seconds," said Meades. "I'm releasing chaff and flares right now, preparing anti-missile missiles."

"Do that," said Steiner. "I'm coming in."

"Is that wise?" said Meades.

"No," said Steiner as he put his dropship into a tight turn. He prepped his anti-missile missiles and sped towards Meades.

"Missiles away," said Meades.

"Roger," said Steiner, "I'm coming straight at you, make sure your transponder isn't damaged. I'm going to fire missiles, too. Mine won't have to turn like yours and I have a better shot."

"Roger that, transponder is on," said Meades. "Don't miss."

Steiner could see Meades' position on his HUD. As he hurtled towards it he could just pick it out visually through his cockpit window. Meades was racing towards him with three missiles gaining pace behind. Behind those Steiner could just make out three more missiles, trying and failing to catch the three ahead of them. He could see from his HUD that these were friendly. His transponder would alert them that he was friendly too, and they should pose no threat to him. At that moment they posed no threat to the enemy missiles either.

The closing speed of the two dropships was very high. When Steiner pressed the missile release button he felt maybe he was too far out. By the time his missiles were away he worried he had left it too late. "Missiles away," he said, and as he saw Meades' dropship grow large in its approach he broke right.

Immediately he felt the impact of the explosions, and alarms sounded in his cockpit. Before his HUD flickered and died he saw that the enemy missiles had gone. The three useless friendly missiles continued on their harmless way.

"Are you there, Meades?"

"Meades, do you copy?"

"I copy," said Meades, weakly. "Nice try, but I don't think we made it this time."

"Meades, what is your situation, over?"

Meades' unbloodied eye roved around his cockpit. The only console that was working was lit up like Christmas with warning lights. He could see he was venting gas out into space. With all the effort he could muster he lifted an arm and pushed the main control stick. There was no response. Briefly, he lost consciousness but quickly came round and focused all his energies on replying to Steiner.

"Situation is . . ." He stopped to cough, but the coughing hurt and he winced. "Situation is I'm screwed," he said.

Steiner pulled on his stick and managed to bring his ship around enough that he could get a visual on Meades. It was easy enough to do. He just followed the stream of debris and particles from where the missiles had detonated. That area was a huge ball of flame that was easy to pick out in the blackness of space.

"Listen, Meades, I'm going to come by there, okay. Try to stay conscious." He pointed his dropship in Meades' direction.

Meades pressed the button on his com, but was too weak to make a reply.

The tiny portion of the vast universe to which Steiner was headed briefly lit up, then blossomed into another bright orange ball.

"Shit," said Steiner. He looked at his control consoles. The warning lights were still flashing. Guidance systems were compromised and life support, too.

He swung the ship up and to the right. In front of him was a large planet, the colour of light rust. He accelerated towards it.

"What happened?" said Kostovich.

"*Ephialtes* remains on course," said Baldwin. "All communications have stopped. No further missiles have been released."

"All our nukes detonated successfully," said Walton. "Two EMPs stopped transmitting telemetry data before detonation. One EMP detonated successfully."

"Where was the detonation?" said Kostovich.

"The detonation, according to the data the missile was sending back to us, was approximately three hundred metres off *Ephialtes*."

"Other missiles?" said Kostovich.

"The three decoy explosive missiles finished up chasing down three dropships which *Ephialtes* deployed immediately before the EMP blast. They all stopped transmitting before detonation. We have to assume they were destroyed by enemy countermeasures, probably from the dropships themselves."

"And where are the dropships now?"

"One appears to be electronically dead and drifting towards Martian orbit. One seems to have lost structural integrity shortly after we lost contact with our missiles. Friendly fire, maybe? The other is intact and heading towards us."

"Give me the range on that one and keep monitoring *Ephialtes*," said Kostovich.

"The remaining dropship is approximately fourteen thousand kilometres from *Parry 5* and turning away."

"That's still in range. Prepare three more explosive missiles and fire them at it," said Kostovich.

"Preparing missiles," said Walton.

"Fire as soon as you're ready," said Kostovich.

"Fire when ready, acknowledged," said Walton, absentmindedly.

"What's *Ephialtes* doing?"

"It's not doing anything," said Baldwin. "Apart from drifting along its trajectory. I think we killed it."

"I think we killed it too," said Kostovich.

"Missiles away," said Walton.

A Helios dropship was more than capable of taking itself through the thin Martian atmosphere and landing at a designated point on the surface. Despite that, and for fun rather than from a sense of diligence, Steiner had spent many hours manually piloting dropships from orbit to the planet's surface in IVRs. As he glanced at the dead autopilot console he was glad he had. He still had some good orientation data available to him and enough fuel to make the trip. There was no contact from *Ephialtes*, and nothing from its transponder. He had to assume the worst; that the blast that had taken out Hayes and damaged Meades was nuclear. All indications were that *Ephialtes* was lost. That made Steiner the last survivor.

It was as he was concentrating on setting his flight plan that he noticed the incoming missiles. He was a thousand kilometres from the surface. He decided to abandon his route, pulling on his control stick to turn the ship around to face the oncoming missiles. His plan was to use the same technique as he had used with Meades; to face the missiles head on. The closing speed of his ship and the missiles would be far higher than if the missiles were chasing him, and that gave him an advantage: the guidance systems for the missiles would be working at the very upper limits of their tolerances. He planned to head directly at the missiles and then, as late as possible, deploy chaff and flares as he dodged out of the way.

He noticed that the ship was not as responsive as it should be. Although the stick still had a full range of movement one quadrant had limited effect. It was still there, but limited. He guessed there was damage to the aft left ion thrusters.

Pulling out of the turn he lined up with the incoming missiles. They were closing rapidly. His HUD was not working but he could glance down at a console and see the missiles represented there. It would be around ten seconds to contact. He flipped some switches, manually preparing the countermeasures. For a split-second he wondered if they had been damaged, too, before immediately discarding that thought. It didn't help him, and he had no other options. This was the plan, and he was going to execute it. If any element failed - the equipment or his timing or judgement - so be it. He had no time to waste ruminating on the endless possibilities for failure. All his concentration was needed now for one thing only - executing the plan.

He set his remaining engines to full throttle, offsetting the pull with micro navigational ion drives. He programmed the launch of all counter measures to route through to a button on his flight stick. He stared forward through the cockpit window and looked for any sign that the three enemy missiles were about to be upon him.

Steiner knew that with the combined speed of his dropship and the missiles the point at which a visual could be established was likely to be a second or less before contact. He held his thumb over the fire button and stared intently at the point where the missiles should appear.

When it came it was like a new star growing out of the darkness and moving slightly, unlike the others which remained fixed in the heavens. The moment he saw it Steiner fired the countermeasures and thrust his stick forward. Before he'd even finished his twitch response the missiles streaked massively over the cockpit window and detonated.

Though the explosions were behind him Steiner was briefly blinded by the flash. He felt the torsion as the blast passed the ship and the flight stick wrenched itself out of his hand. As his vision returned he noticed a new array of alarms going off. All of his consoles were now dead except for one. He noted that the one live console was one that had been dead before. The second blast had somehow knocked it back to life. Ordinarily he would have dwelt on the weirdness, but with a planet looming above him and limited controls he forgot about it almost as he was noticing it.

Shaking the muzziness out of his head he grabbed the flight stick. Now there was even less response from it. He could drop the nose of the ship a little, and he could pull her to the right, but that was it. No up, no left. He tried adjusting power to the engines. Nothing happened. They were on half power, knocked back from the full they had been on. That was something he could work with. If he had been stuck with the engines on full his prospects might have been very different. As it were, they were not good.

Using his limited controls he skilfully guided the ship down to the surface. He was at one kilometre altitude, with an airspeed of six hundred kilometres per hour, when he started to realise that he had half a chance of making it. Until then he had ploughed on, almost automatically, doing everything he could to make the best of a very bad situation. He hadn't really considered the end point. Now here he was, close to being in position for a survivable landing, and he had to figure out what he needed to do to achieve that. Not hitting a mountain seemed like a good place to start, so he pulled the nose around to the right.

For the landing he could redirect the thrust from two of the engines downward through ports along the fuselage. The dropships were VTOL. The problem was that he had no control over the level of thrust; half-power was far too much for a landing. He would also need to arrest his forward motion. He wasn't sure if hitting the ports with too much power would damage them, or even if the system would let him abuse it in that way. But again, he had no other option open to him.

He used the stick to tilt the nose forward, bringing the ship as close to the ground as he could. He was skimming the surface at a hundred and sixty-six metres a second, barely a hundred metres above it. The landscape streaked past him.

He flipped the switch, sending the thrust into his VTOL nozzles. There was an alarming 'bang' sound followed by two crunching scraping noises in quick succession. He immediately filed those under 'Nothing I can do about that, ignore, move on,' as he felt the ship leap upwards. That wasn't good; he needed to lose height. He needed to lose forward momentum too, so he directed the VTOL nozzles forward. The negative-G was immense, and he felt the ship dropping, too.

With his consoles wrecked Steiner was judging airspeed by eye. As the ship slowed to what appeared to be an acceptable speed he directed the nozzles down again. This arrested the fall but the ship rapidly rose again. With no other options left, Steiner killed the engines.

As the engines died the dropship reached the top of a parabola. Its forward speed now was less than eighty kilometres per hour and as it followed down the falling edge of its trajectory Steiner felt that fairground feeling in his stomach, like he was on a roller-coaster. Four hundred and twenty thousand tonnes of dropship, deprived now of its upward thrust, was being greedily sucked down to the Martian surface.

He had no idea what his altitude reading was but the view from the window suggested the ground was coming up fast. In a mild panic as the speed of the onrushing Martian surface grew ever faster Steiner hit the button to restart the engines. He heard the characteristic hiss and whoosh as the engines started to fire, and he felt their force in argument with the Martian gravity. After that, he remembered nothing.

Lund believed she knew *Ephialtes* inside out. She had spent a good part of her working life pouring over its designs and walking through virtual simulations of its interiors. She would have said that she could find her way around it blindfolded. Now that she actually was trying to traverse the ship in total blackness it was much more difficult than she might have anticipated.

When all electronic systems on *Ephialtes* were destroyed the AG went too. Lund had nothing to orient herself with visually and didn't even have the fundamental knowledge of which way was down. The *Aloadae* were built with artificial gravity in mind so they had very definite floors, ceilings and walls. Those designations were moot now.

Using her hands and guided by distant voices Lund pulled herself along. Quickly she met some maintenance personnel who had made their way from the hangar deck.

"Where are you heading?" said one.

"To the bridge. There may be some light there and that's where the commodore is, I think," Lund replied. "You got out of the hangar deck okay?"

"Yes," a voice replied from the blackness. "We had to manually open the emergency escape hatches. What happened?"

"EMP strike, I think," said Lund.

"Jeez," came a reply. "So what happens now?"

"I don't know," said Lund. "We get to the bridge and figure something out." She knew there wasn't really much to figure out. Without electronics the ship was nothing, and there was nothing they could do to fix it. They had no coms, they had no tools. Without external help they had no hope whatsoever. She let all that go for now. "Come on, let's go," she said.

As they got nearer the bridge the voices grew louder. Lund caught a glimpse of light, dim but to her miraculous. As soon as they had that they headed rapidly towards it.

Floating into the bridge Lund was immediately greeted by Lucero.

"Lund," she said, "what have you got for us? Anything?" Lucero knew the situation was hopeless too but she still clung to the idea that a smart person, someone like Askel Lund, would be able to come up with some sort of fiendishly clever plan. Lund for her part had nothing, but didn't want to appear negative in front of the crew.

"First of all I think we need to make a full assessment of the damage. Hull integrity seems good, as far as I can make out. Were we hit anywhere?"

Lucero shook her head, "I don't think so. The issue is power," she said, somewhat redundantly as a good portion of her crew floated about her. They were lit by a low grey glow streaming in through the bridge window. Mars loomed in front of them, providing most of the light.

"And our trajectory?"

"Trajectory should be good. Speed and vector were adjusted before we were hit. We should hit the Martian gravity field and get captured into orbit sometime in the next few minutes."

Lund nodded. "That's good. So we'll be in range of the Martians?"

"Absolutely," said Lucero. "Any time they want to finish us off they can go right ahead. We're sitting ducks up here, and there's not a damn thing we can do about it."

"They're not going to shoot us," said Lund. "That's why they used EMPs. They don't intend to do us any injury. They have us now how they want us - harmless."

Lucero snorted. "Well, we'd better hope so."

Lund knew their only chance of survival was to be rescued by the Martians. She hoped that the Martians knew it. The EMP avoided loss of life, but only temporarily. *Ephialtes* would remain hospitable for only a day or two at most. With no electrical or electronic systems the oxygen would become depleted and the temperature would fall rapidly to a point where life could no longer be supported. If the Martians had gone out of their way to avoid killing them - they could have just used their nukes, after all - then surely they must have considered that. Part two of their plan had to be a rescue. Hadn't it?

"Can you do it? Will you do it?" asked Foveaux.

Bobby scratched his head. "Well, I guess I'm happy to give it a go," he offered.

EPHIALTES

Foveaux frowned. "Mr Karjalainen, this is way out of our league. I know I asked you to start next week but we just don't have anyone qualified for this sort of thing. I'm willing to go myself -"

"No," said Venkdt, "you're far too valuable." He looked to Bobby. "No offence to you, of course, but Commissioner Foveaux's role here is essential. We really can't be putting her in this sort of position right now. There are many, many vital issues that she has to grapple with right here."

"Like I said," said Bobby, "if you want me to go, I'll go."

"We appreciate that," said Venkdt, "I just don't want you to feel obliged. We have other personnel capable of carrying out this task."

"We don't," said Foveaux. "The only combat trained troops we have are a dozen or so ex USAN Army from the garrison. Even if we assume we can trust their loyalty they've never seen a shot fired in anger and all they've been doing for the last two years is polishing their boots and arresting shoplifters. This is a rescue mission, and it should be a straightforward one. But we don't know how *Ephialtes'* crew are going to react. They may be hostile, they may be resistant, they may even be dead. If Mr Karjalainen wants to go I say that's great. He can pick a team from the MSS and lead them aboard. If there's any resistance he can either overcome it or retreat."

"What do you say to that?" said Venkdt.

"I'm more than willing to do it," said Bobby, wondering why his acceptance was creating this debate.

"Good," said Foveaux. "What do you need?"

"Well, the spacecraft is all booked and ready to go, right?"

"It is. We have the shuttle ready for launch tomorrow. There should be more than enough room to bring the *Ephialtes* crew back on it. That leaves you with around eight other seats, so you can take a team of eight with you. Will that be enough?"

Bobby nodded, "Eight should be fine. We have armour and weapons too? Helmets, HUDs? We'll need to know where we are. We'll need infrared and thermal imaging overlays."

"Of course," said Foveaux.

"Okay," said Bobby, "so who are my eight guys?"

"You can come over to the garrison and make your selection now, if you like."

Bobby shrugged. "You pick them. You know them. Sensible people, no hot-heads. Okay?"

"Okay," said Foveaux.

"Let me know when you've made your selection. I'll come over and run through a few things with them."

"Okay," said Foveaux. "I'll speak to Kostovich about the thermal imaging."

"Thanks."

"Thank you," said Venkdt.

Bobby turned to leave.

"Where are you going now?" said Foveaux.

"Pub," said Bobby.

CHAPTER 29

Checkmate

Andrews was a heavy sleeper and it was unusual for her comdev to ring in the middle of the night. In the first few moments of waking she felt confused and disoriented. She looked at her clock before rolling over to grab the comdev. It was 04:35.

"Andrews," she said.

"Secretary Andrews?" came an unsure voice down the line.

"Of course it's Secretary Andrews. Who else would it be? What is this?"

Andrews swung her feet over the side of the bed and stood up.

"My name is Donaldson, ma'am."

"Do I know you?"

"I don't think so, ma'am. I work in your department, in fact I'm over there right now. I'm calling to let you know we've lost contact with *Ephialtes*."

Andrews had clambered into her dressing gown and was making her way downstairs. "What do you mean, lost contact? Is it serious?"

"I think it probably is, ma'am. You might want to get over here."

"Has the president been informed?"

"No, ma'am. We lost contact just over five minutes ago. It doesn't look good."

"What happened?"

"They were engaged in a missile battle. Logs and recordings from the bridge suggest the enemy were using EMPs and nukes. The sudden loss of communication seems to be consistent with one of those types of weapons being successfully deployed against them. The last data we have shows three missiles approaching from the front. They were going to use a plasma cannon against them. After that there's nothing."

Andrews stopped. "I see," she said. "And you've had no further communications since then?"

"None at all, ma'am."

"Okay," said Andrews, "I'll be right over. None of this leaves the building until I get there, okay?"

The operations room at the department of defence had a direct link to the USAN Army's main ground control centre. It would be possible to transfer the whole ground control operation to the operations room if necessary, or to other similarly equipped centres around the globe. When Andrews arrived she was greeted by Donaldson.

"Anything?" said Andrews.

"Still no contact," said Donaldson. "All indications support the position that *Ephialtes* is lost."

"There's no way this is just a coms failure? Or power?"

"Unfortunately not. *Ephialtes* has multiple redundant power and coms systems. The chances of them all failing simultaneously as a result of anything other than a catastrophic failure of the entire ship are astronomically small."

"Shit," said Andrews, sitting down. "What do we do now?"

Donaldson remained standing. "There's very little we can do. We don't have any interplanetary ships capable of reaching Mars any time soon. There's not another launch window for a traditional spacecraft for another twelve months, and the journey would take a further six. Our HLV shuttles, even if they could be converted to the new NFJ engines - and that remains an open question, by the way - even if they could be converted they are not suitable for interplanetary missions. Any survivors will likely be long dead before we can even arrange a meeting to discuss the possibilities."

"What about the Martians?"

"Excuse me, ma'am?"

"The Martians. What are they saying?"

"I believe we are monitoring Martian coms, I'll get a report to you as soon as possible," Donaldson improvised. He resolved to talk with someone in intelligence as soon as he had finished with Andrews. He hoped they would have something he could take back to her.

"What do we do now? We can't just sit here and wait for something to happen. What can we do?"

Donaldson looked awkward. "There really isn't anything we can do at this time," he said. "I'll be preparing the intelligence briefs for the president. Will you be informing him of the situation before his seven o'clock meeting?"

Andrews thought. "Yes. I'll go to the New White House right away. Put everything you can in the intelligence report; all the details about the run up to the loss of contact and everything you can find about what the Martians are saying. That's particularly important. They have to know more than we do at the moment - find out what that is."

"Yes, ma'am."

"It's very, very important that we achieve a successful outcome to this," said Venkdt. "There is a huge gulf between shooting a man between the eyes and simply grabbing his gun to disarm him. We have to be seen to be doing the latter. Wholesale slaughter - unprovoked, at that - would incur the wrath of the USAN and, I would hope, all decent people here on Mars, too. We are not a murderous people. We are not a barbaric people. We have sought only to defend ourselves.

"Of course," said Christina.

"The future of our new state hangs in the balance. If we fail at this task we fail at the whole undertaking we set ourselves just a few short months ago; to build a new country and a new planet and a positive future for all of us."

"You are writing this down, right?" said Christina.

"Of course," said Venkdt. "The comdev is picking it up and transcribing it. I'll edit it a bit and go through the whole thing on my stream. Do you think I should get that girl to interview me again? Elspeth? She was very good."

"No, not an interview this time. This has to be a statement, it has to look strong and from the heart."

"It is! Of course it is, I meant every word I just said. This will be the defining moment of the whole project. We simply cannot fail, it would be unthinkable. Not to mention those poor people up there. We can't abandon them to their fate."

"I know, Dad," said Christina, "and I know you mean it. I just mean that we have to be sure that everyone else knows it too. Do a piece straight to camera, just as you said it to me just now, and everyone will know exactly what you mean and how sincere you are."

"That's what I'm going to do. I need a few more minutes to get my thoughts in order. I'll do a live stream in an hour or so."

"Good," said Christina. "Lead with the rescue mission. Lots of detail, heavy on the magnanimity but subtle too, and work back from there. Stress the parlous situation the survivors are in. The human interest angle will grab everyone's attention. People will be rooting for them to make it, and our guys will be the heroes when they rescue them. It's a terrific story, people will lap it up."

Venkdt looked at her across the breakfast table. "You seem so cynical. There are people up there in mortal danger, because of decisions that we made. We put them in peril, it's our moral duty to save them. It's not a soap or a reality show."

Christina was shocked. She was reminded of how it felt when her father told her off when she was a child. "I don't mean . . . of course, I know that, of course. How could you think otherwise? I'm just thinking of how it will play, how we can best use it to our advantage. I know they're real people, and I know they need our help, and we're going to give it to them as we should. All of that goes without saying. But you have to think of the other angles too, the bigger picture. You're a politician now, Dad, so politic."

Venkdt grunted, "I suppose so."

Cortes always woke early. Most days when he was staying at the New White House he would take a three or five mile run accompanied by Secret Service agents. He would rise around five o'clock and be out running within minutes.

Andrews pulled through the security gates as the presidential group was leaving the building. The Secret Service agents, acutely aware of any irregularities, immediately bundled him back into the building. Andrews got out of her car and went to walk towards them.

"Hold it right there, ma'am," said an agent with his palm held upright in front of him. He spoke into his lapel mic and half ran towards Andrews, quickly scanning rooftops as he went.

"I'm Audrey Andrews, I'm secretary of defence," said Andrews irritably as he approached.

"It's a standard precaution, ma'am," the agent said.

"Can you please -"

"Just raise your arms, ma'am," the agent said.

Seething, Andrews raised her arms and the agent patted her down. "She's clear," he said to his lapel mic. "It's Secretary of Defence Andrews, please advise."

Inside the building Cortes, flanked by two Secret Service agents, overheard the call.

"Andrews?" he said. "For Chrissake, let's get out there."

One of the agents replied, "Secretary of Defence, please confirm your ID by comdev, POTUS is coming out to make a visual confirmation." By the time he had finished speaking Cortes was already striding towards Andrews with a coterie of nervous Secret Service agents about him, making the most of this exciting opportunity to break the tedium of their morning.

"Andrews, what is it?" said Cortes.

"It's bad news, Mr President."

Cortes' expression did not change. "Go on," he said.

"We've lost *Ephialtes*," said Andrews.

Cortes paused. "Lost," he said, with no inflection whatsoever.

"Around four o'clock this morning our time. She was in a missile battle and suddenly went dark. We have to assume an EMP or nuclear strike."

"Survivors?"

"We don't know."

"Anything we do know?"

"No, sir. All communications, telemetry, transponders stopped at once. We have nothing."

"Nothing," said Cortes. "What are we doing?"

"We're monitoring Martian coms. We have to assume they know more about what happened than we do. It'll be in your intelligence briefing this morning if we find anything new."

"Okay," said Cortes. "I want you in the briefing. Farrell and White too. And I want some ideas, and some answers."

"Yes, Mr President."

"I'm late for my run, get out of here."

Venkdt honed his speech to something that worked for all its intended purposes. It was accurate in reflecting his humanity and his deeply held belief that it was Mars' duty to rescue those aboard *Ephialtes*, despite the potential cost in Martian lives. He restated his belief that the new Mars was not aggressive; that they had been forced to build weapons and found an army simply to defend themselves against the worst aggressions of the USAN, and that they had been loath to use them. That, at great risk to themselves, the weapons they had used against *Ephialtes* had rendered it useless but had preserved the lives of its crew, and that now the absolute priority was to rescue that crew and bring them safely to Mars.

He said that the people of Mars meant no harm to the people of Earth or the USAN and that the rescue mission, which would be launching later that day, was proof of that. At great risk and cost a small force from the MSS would attempt to retrieve the crew of *Ephialtes* from certain death aboard their moribund spacecraft.

He mentioned his great affection for the USAN and for Venkdt Corporation, and said that he very much looked forward to working closely with both of them again in the near future.

He finished by wishing the rescue team the best of luck with their endeavour. He, and the rest of the planet, would be with them every step of the way.

"Great," said Christina as Venkdt cut off the camera. "That was terrific."

"And every word of it true," said Venkdt. "I just hate to think of those poor people up there. And their parents, too. If you were on that ship . . ." He shrugged. "Well, it just doesn't bear thinking about."

"I know, Dad," said Christina. "It's awful, but they're alive, and we're going to get them back. A lot of people wouldn't have done that, you know? Most people would have just blown that thing out of the sky. That's what makes you different. That's why you're going to be such a great president."

"I just hope this thing comes off," said Venkdt.

"It will," said Christina.

"As you know by now, we lost *Ephialtes* this morning, shortly after four o'clock. As of this time we know nothing of her fate, but it's safe to assume a catastrophic failure and associated loss of life. Our best hope is that she was struck by an electromagnetic pulse. If that is the case there is some hope there may be survivors. But if she was struck by a nuclear weapon then we would have to accept that all is lost.

"Whichever it turns out to be we no longer have strike capability in the Martian theatre. We have no prospect of such capability for many, many years to come. The *Aloadae* each took four years to build. Both are now gone. Even if we started building this very day we can't put another offensive vessel in that vicinity for nearly half a decade." Andrews looked down at her papers as she finished speaking.

"What do we do now?" said Cortes.

Something pushed Farrell to try to fill the silence. "We're waiting for some more intelligence to come in. We're monitoring Martian coms to glean what information we can. They're the only source of information we have out there now."

Cortes looked up and languorously replied. "That's waiting. What do we *do*?"

This time no one stepped into the breach. The silence remained unabated.

"I take it there's nothing we can do, is that right?" said Cortes.

Once again Farrell was the only one brave enough, or stupid enough, to get involved.

"We're still working on the diplomatic channels -"

Cortes slammed a fist down onto the table. "Diplomacy is nothing! They've just stolen our planet! We're not going to be able to talk them into giving it back!"

He looked at Andrews. "Defence. What do you have? You had the two most powerful war machines ever built. Where are they now? What use are they now? How did that happen?"

"Mr President, I'm sure you -"

Cortes waved her away. "I don't want explanations. Or excuses. I want us to be able to do what we say we are going to do. When we say, 'We will take back what is ours,' we have to follow through on that. We have to make it so. You know why? Because our lives depend on it. That's right, our very lives. If people see, if the world sees that we are weak, they will destroy us. Our enemies will destroy us. You people," he pointed a finger around the table, "have failed in your duty to protect this country. You have failed your offices and you have failed yourselves. Now you have to live with the consequences, and God help us all." He stood up and left the room.

At 08:10 Andrews was put through to Cortes. On the video link she could clearly see the two flags either side of him. He was seated at his desk in the New Oval Office.

EPHIALTES

"Mr President, Martian news sources are saying that *Ephialtes* is in orbit around the planet. She's electronically disabled and the Martians are going to attempt a rescue."

"Are the sources reliable?"

"They are, sir. Charles Venkdt made a live stream not yet an hour ago announcing a rescue mission."

"We're relying on intelligence from Charles Venkdt now? Can you see what's wrong with this picture?"

"I know this is far from ideal, sir, but it's all we have. And it looks like good news about the crew."

"How is it good?" barked Cortes. "They may as well be dead for all the good they will do us now. They'll be paraded on Martian streams and we'll look even more impotent than we do already."

Andrews did not know what to say.

"Was there anything else?" said Cortes.

"No, sir," said Andrews, deflated. "I thought you'd be pleased to hear that the crew are okay."

"Yeah? Well I'm not. I don't give a shit about the crew. I care about my ship, which is now useless, and I care about my deuterium, which I cannot now retrieve, and I care about the reputation of this country, which is now in tatters. Put out a press release: 'The president is relieved to hear that the crew of *Ephialtes* appears to be unharmed, and hopes and prays for their safe passage home.' But know this, and remember it. I do not give a shit. As far as I'm concerned you've all let me and this country down. They did not prosecute the mission to the full extent of their capability, and now they're paying the price. They should be left in that tin can to rot. It's what they deserve."

White ordered a burger and fries with a cola, though he did not feel like eating.

"Was this our guy?" he said. "Please don't tell me it was."

Sherman put a fry in his mouth and chewed on it. "It wasn't our guy," he said.

"You're sure of that?"

Sherman shrugged. "Can't be sure of anything," he said, "but I'd say this was nothing to do with our guy. They said on the streams it was a missile attack. That's what it looks like to me. You must have access to better intelligence than I do. What are they saying?"

"They're saying diddly-squat. The information they have is coming from the streams, same as everyone else's."

"Then it looks like a missile attack," said Sherman, "just like they're saying."

White watched Sherman eat. "So what about our guy now? They're saying there are survivors. They're going to try to pick them up. Where does that leave our guy?"

Sherman finished his mouthful before he replied. "At the moment, I guess, that leaves our guy floating around the planet with the rest of them."

"But what happens when they get picked up?" said White. "What's he going to do then? Any more tricks up his sleeve? A suicide vest for the rescue craft, maybe? Jesus. You have to call him off. We have to put an end to this operation right now. Cortes was pissed off when *Otus* went down. He's absolutely apoplectic now. If he gets even a hint of this thing there's no telling what he might do. You have to call our guy off, understand? You have to put an end to it."

Sherman had just taken a large bite of burger which he chewed at a leisurely pace. He could see White's anger rising and it amused him to watch him trying not to show it. To add to his fun he popped a few more fries in his mouth. Presently, he got around to answering. "At the moment there's nothing we can do. He or she is there on that ship and there is no electricity or electronics of any kind whatsoever. The ship has gone dark so our contact has gone dark. We couldn't contact him if we wanted to, nor him us. That's just the way it is."

"Well, when can you contact him?" said White, unable now to control the irritation in his voice. "If he does anything, if he makes just one false move, then we're all in the shitter. Cortes is going to look into every little thing that happened on this mission. He's going to turn over every stone and shine a light into every dark corner, and at the moment he's got nothing else to occupy his time. He's taken this whole thing personally, and if he finds out about our involvement that's it for us."

"I understand that," said Sherman, "but at the moment there's nothing we can do. There's no communication in or out until they get those people off that ship. Maybe if they can get them to a rescue ship, or maybe once they have them back on the Martian surface and they're near to communication hubs with relays back to Earth, maybe then we can get some kind of message through. But not before."

"Jesus!" said White. "Do you realise what's at stake here?"

"I do," said Sherman. "That's why my ass is covered. I can walk away from this, I had an exit strategy right from the beginning. Did you?"

"Bullshit," said White. "You can be careful, I know that, that's why I always come to you. But no one is invisible. There's always some trace left behind. You're in this as deep as I am; deeper, even. And you can never walk away."

The waitress brought White's order and placed it on the table. "Thank you very much, Ms," he said, "that looks great."

"Is there anything else I can get you?" said the waitress.

"No, thank you again."

"Enjoy your meal," said the waitress as she left.

"That's right," said Sherman. "Enjoy your meal. Right now there's not a thing we can do, so just relax and forget about it. Maybe they're already dead, who knows? Maybe the rescue goes wrong and they all die then, how about that? Let's not worry about it until it happens. In twenty-four hours, forty-eighty maybe, if our man's still around he'll be on the Martian surface. We can contact him then if we need to. But until then, just eat your food have a great day."

White looked at his order. He knew he was hungry but somehow he didn't feel like eating.

Zelman was seated at a table when White arrived at the hotel suite. There was an array of magazines in front of her, and it looked like she was working her way through a puzzle page in one of them. "Awful news about *Ephialtes*," she said. "It's been all over the streams. They've hardly been talking about anything else all day."

"Yes," said White as he walked over and kissed her on the cheek. "It looks like there may be survivors. The Martians are going to try to pick them up, tomorrow, I think."

"I hope they're okay," said Zelman. "It's awful to think of them up there with no light, heat or communication, not knowing what's going to happen to them. Just awful."

"I'm sure it's going to be okay," said White. "They'll pick them up, and that will be that. It'll certainly put an end to Cortes' little venture anyway."

"How was he about it all?" said Zelman.

"Not pleased," said White. "He only speaks that one language; threats and intimidation. They've taken his voice away from him, and now he doesn't know what to do. We're all just hoping that he doesn't lash out at us."

"I'll bet," said Zelman. "I'm sure he'll see sense in a day or two. It was a ridiculous plan anyway."

"We all know that," said White, "but now it's ridiculous, expensive and failed. I don't know if this might be even worse than him having gone through with it."

"Oh come on," said Zelman, "you don't mean that. I really think this is probably for the best. If they can get those people off, and no one got hurt in all of this, then I think this is probably one of the best outcomes you could have hoped for. He's been forced to put his toys back in the box. He'll have to get round the table with them now, he's got no other choice."

"I don't know," said White. "Maybe this has gone too far the other way. There's nothing for them to discuss now - they have everything they want. There's nothing to negotiate, as far as they're concerned."

"It's probably for the best," said Zelman. "Like you said before, in a few months' time we'll be trading with them and everything will be back to normal."

"It's wiped you out though," said White. "Helios stocks have plummeted. Two ships lost in as many months - that doesn't look good for you."

Zelman shrugged. "I guess it means you'll be needing two new ships to replace them. Who's going to build them, if not us? The stocks will be back up in a week or two. I have the rest of my portfolio, anyway."

White went to the bar and poured himself a drink. "Want one?" he said to Zelman.

"I'm fine," she said. "You go ahead. You look like you need to relax."

"Oh boy, do I," said White.

CHAPTER 30

The Prodigal

The piercing wail of multiple alarms seemed to exist on its own, a thought before there was even a consciousness to think it. The alarms were all that existed. As Steiner drifted back from the darkness they seemed to occupy every space in his head. Every fourth or fifth second there was a powerful lurch. It was these that were shaking him awake.

On realising he had been born again into a world consisting of nothing more than shrieking alarms and sudden violent movements Steiner sought to make an impression on it. He reached out for the flight stick but it was not there. Focusing more now, he realised that the engines were still running, but from the cracked cockpit window he could see that he was on the ground, save for a bunny-hop every few seconds. He realised too that, along with the sound of the alarms, he could hear the engines screaming as though in pain. Reflexively his hand shot toward the manual kill switch for the engines. He pressed the button. Nothing happened.

He was more awake now and was able to process his thoughts in a more orderly way. The kill switch was down, so maybe he could manually isolate the fuel supply. As he reached out for the fuel cut-off switch there was another massive lurch as the ship tried to wrench itself free from the grip that Mars had on it. As it crunched back to the ground Steiner reached out again, this time flipping the switch to the 'Off' position. He waited for the remaining fuel to run out. There was another lurch, but this one was notably half-hearted. When the ship slumped back to the Martian surface Steiner heard the engines splutter before finally dying. The ship was now laying still on the face of Mars.

The alarms still wailed. Steiner released his harness and only then noticed the blood trickling down his forehead. He felt the blood with his hand and looked at it momentarily before wiping it off on his flight suit and proceeding on his way out of the cockpit.

The ship felt unfamiliar to him. It was resting at an odd angle and was in disarray. Various items and panels had broken loose and were strewn about, making the familiar seem new and strange.

His intention was to get into his command drone. The drop bays were accessible from behind the cockpit. The command drone was in the first bay on the right. He figured that the structural integrity of the dropship was compromised but maybe the drones, or some of them, would still be okay. And he absolutely had to get away from those damned alarms.

The hatch to drop-bay one was jammed. He went back to the cockpit to retrieve a crowbar and with some effort he began trying to jimmy the hatch. As he was about to give up the hatch moved a little, allowing him to get more purchase. Pulling on the locking mechanism with one hand and half-standing, half-jumping on the crowbar he eventually succeeded in moving the hatch to a semi-open position. The ship itself had been mildly warped by the impact, and the hatches were no longer true.

Guessing there was enough of an opening to squeeze through, Steiner forced the upper part of his body into the gap. Inside it was dark, but enough light followed behind him that he could make out the shape of the top of his commander mech, held in the grip of a giant mounting bracket. He grabbed at the bracket and pulled his legs through the hatch, swinging them round beneath himself. From that position he climbed and slid down to the front of the mech.

Steiner was relieved to find that the entry hatch on the mech had not been damaged. It opened with a sweetly smooth action as it always had, and he clambered inside the huge machine.

The start sequence for the mechs was usually initiated from on board the dropship. Steiner had to resort to a manual override. As he flipped switches and pressed buttons he felt a rising anxiety that the thing would not start, but his fear was unfounded. His HUD came to life and he felt the low rumble of the internal motors starting up.

He tried to communicate with the dropship's internal coms but there was no reply. He sent a 'Start' command to all of the dropship's drones but only received responses from seven of them. He noted that six of the seven were on his side of the ship and guessed that the other side had been more severely damage by the crash-landing.

Using his mech's computer system he drew a rectangle in the darkness in front of him. He thought this was where the door was, but it was difficult to see in the half-light. He set the mech's laser to follow the outline of the rectangle and watched as the red beam slowly worked its way around the shape, taking several minutes.

As he waited he copied the command to the seven drones he had under his command. He checked visuals from each of them and saw that they were all dutifully cutting their way out of their metal prisons.

As the laser in Steiner's bay came to a stop he saw the rectangle of metal fall slightly in its place. It slipped to the side and back slightly, but did not fall completely out. He commanded the mount to release him, but its grip remained firm. Again, he had to turn to a manual override, and his mech fell to the floor of the bay with a loud clang. The mech absorbed the shock of the landing by bending its knees, then did a small sequence of movements, almost like it was stretching after its long slumber. It was calibrating itself to Martian gravity and orienting itself to the space it found itself in. Familiar yet unfamiliar, it was the shape of a hangar bay, but at an angle it had not experienced before.

Steiner lifted his leg and the corresponding leg of the mech lifted, taking a step forward. At the rectangle, the mech punched the metal and suddenly there was a new, albeit crude, exit.

Steiner walked out through it onto the surface of Mars.

Outside he could see the full extent of the damage to the dropship. It was wedged up against a small outcrop of rocks, with the front higher than the back. The right-hand side was lower too, pressed close to the rocks. It looked wrecked. Steiner was amazed to think that this thing, which had brought him to the surface, was still in one piece. Looking at it, it was hard to see how he could have survived. He had always been sceptical about the quality of Helios' equipment before. Now he felt humbled.

Looking along the side of the ship he could see the lasers working on the bay doors. The last few remained, cutting their way out.

Presently, as he watched, the drones punched and kicked their way out of the dropship, just as Steiner had commanded them to.

The seventh drone was on the other side of the dropship. Try as it might, there was no exit available to it. The way was barred with solid rock. Steiner monitored its video feed and knew there was no hope for it. He commanded it to shut down.

Steiner had data feeds from all his drones available to him in his commander mech, but he elected to make a visual inspection of his squad. The scene resembled parade grounds throughout history, with the drones dutifully lined up and their superior checking them over. Steiner was looking for damage, but if he had said, 'Your buttons are dirty, drop and give me twenty,' to one of the drones it would not have seemed out of place.

One drone was feeding back data suggesting it was damaged. Power levels were inconsistent and the servos in the right foot and thigh were behaving erratically. Visual inspection revealed what appeared to be superficial damage. Steiner wasn't sure if there was a physical problem or just a data issue. Data seemed unlikely and he didn't want an unreliable mech on his mission. He decided that that mech should stay and guard the wreckage. If the Martians found the wreck and gained access to the dropship's data systems they could possibly compromise all his inter-drone coms. It seemed unlikely, but he decided to leave a mech on guard anyway.

He sent the remaining mechs in four opposing directions while he took a drink and some food. The food was an all-purpose nutrient slurry. The commander mech carried enough for two weeks. Steiner favoured chocolate flavour.

The mechs were gathering video data about their location. Steiner had it patched in to software which, after a few minutes, worked out where they were on the Martian surface. Steiner let the drones wander on for a few minutes more, in order to confirm their location. After that, he called them back.

They were somewhere south of Baetis Chasma, roughly eight hundred kilometres from the main Martian conurbation of Marineris. The mechs' top walking speed was twenty kilometres an hour, and maybe they would have to round mountains or avoid craters. It would take them around two days to make it to Marineris. They set off.

Steiner had had no communication with *Ephialtes* since he had left her only a few hours earlier. He assumed that she, like Hayes, had been taken out by EMPs or possibly nukes. That left him as the only surviving member of the mission. He had trained over and over again to take key Martian installations and he still had enough firepower to do just that. The Martians had very few defences and no military to speak of. They had heard news that the Martians had built missile defences and had added those into their training simulations. Outwitting missile defences on the surface of the planet seemed a much more inviting prospect than doing the same in space where there was, literally, no place to hide. In the sims they had successfully used features of the landscape and countermeasures to defeat the missile batteries. He saw no reason why he wouldn't be able to do that in reality. In his mind he was forming a plan.

With no direct communications from his mothership, and with Earth out of range for his mech's coms, he decided it was his duty to proceed with the mission as he understood it. He had been training to capture Martian installations pertinent to the deuterium trade, and in order to do that he would first have to render the Martian missile defences harmless. That was his mission. He found added impetus in the fact that, contrary to everything they had been told on their journey, the Martians had proved to be anything but pacific. The attack on *Ephialtes* had been swift and brutal and had resulted, he supposed, in major loss of life. His friends, Foley and Johnson, were among the casualties and he had been right there beside Meades and Hayes when they had been killed.

The way Steiner saw it he had no other option. He was on the surface of what would have to be considered a hostile planet, even without the presence of enemy missile bases. The environment itself was enough to kill him. He had a mission, or enough of one to work with, and he had the base, animal motivation of revenge. He *had* to attack the Martians. It seemed that was the only course of action open to him.

CHAPTER 31

Mission of Mercy

Bobby took the call in the middle of the night. Anthony didn't even have the good grace to call himself. He asked one of the nurses to do it. The nurse told Bobby he should come as soon as possible. Jack was weakening and this was probably the end.

On arriving at the house he made his way to his father's bedroom, which now bore only scant similarity to the place he recalled from his childhood. He remembered jumping up and down on the bed with Anthony, and he remembered clambering into bed with his father and having stories read to him. The room from his memories was now was overlaid with medical equipment and the people in there, the nurses, doctor and lawyer, made it seem a public space and not the intimate family home of his memories.

"How is he?" said Bobby.

At first no one answered then one of the nurses said, "He's comfortable."

He looked anything but comfortable. A breathing tube was taped to his face and another tube from his arm lead to a drip. He was propped up and his head lolled forward at an angle. His eyes were closed but his mouth hung open and his tongue was hanging out. His breathing was noisy and laboured.

"Is he awake?" said Bobby.

"No," said the nurse. "He's been like this for the last four hours or so. The doctor thinks he's very close to the end now. It's good that you're here."

Bobby moved around to the side of the bed where Anthony was sitting. He put a hand on Anthony's shoulder. "How're you doing?" he said.

"I'm fine," said Anthony. "Thanks for coming."

"Is there anything you need me to do?"

"No, it's all taken care of. We just need to be here now. For Dad."

"Okay," said Bobby, and he pulled up a seat next to Anthony.

They sat like that for a few hours. Bobby went to get them some water at one point. They sat and looked at their father, occasionally entering into a whispered exchange with one of the nurses or the doctor. The doctor had nothing to do. His patient was far beyond help and the nurses were more than capable of administering the painkilling medication he had prescribed. In truth, the only reason he was there was that Jack Karjalainen was rich enough to afford a personal physician and his imminent death, as the ultimate health crisis, required that physician's presence. In order to look busy and medical the doctor, from time to time, would look at the instruments monitoring Jack Karjalainen's state of health and then refer to his comdev to make a few notes. He would then whisper into one of the nurses ears and the nurse would nod back at him with a serious face. It was all pantomime. Everyone in the room knew why they were there. They were simply waiting for Jack Karjalainen to die. Nothing they could do would make a difference. He was unconscious now so even pain relief, the one thing they did have some control over, was superfluous. They went about their business, playing their parts in a drama over which they had no influence.

It was during one of their pointless performances, this one being a nurse whispering to Anthony about maintaining Jack's hydration, that he leaned forward slightly and appeared to be wincing as if in pain. He fell back on the bed and moved his head, the first time he had done so since Bobby arrived. He let out a long breath and appeared to stop breathing. The nurse went to him as if to adjust his breathing tube, but the doctor gestured for her to leave it alone. For a long time there was no sound of breathing and it seemed to Bobby like his father was gone, but then there was another gasp and Jack's face twisted into a weird shape. He exhaled slowly and seemed to slump. After that there were no more breaths.

The medical staff kept a respectful distance for a few minutes. Anthony was holding Jack's hand and tears silently rolled down his face. Bobby sat with head bowed. He gently put an arm around his brother's shoulders.

"I'm very sorry," one of the nurses said and Bobby nodded in acknowledgement. The nurse took Jack's other wrist and held it for a while, confirming there was no pulse. She nodded at the doctor, who made a note on his comdev.

"Would you like a few minutes in private?" said the doctor.

"Yes," said Anthony, "we'd appreciate that."

It's said that important decisions should never be made when tired or angry. After staying up two whole days and nights with his dying father, and immediately after witnessing his death, Anthony Karjalainen went directly to Charles Venkdt's office.

After initially being held up by Venkdt's PA he was finally told that his president was currently busy with an important function. The PA's reticence had wound him up even further. It took some more infuriating pressing to get the PA to reveal what and where the function was. Anthony left the Venkdt building with fire in his eyes.

He had been told that Venkdt was addressing the inaugural meeting of the Martian Trade Association. This quasi-governmental organisation had been put together with the purpose of allowing networking between Mars' emerging business class and forging some sort of unified front in key business areas. All Martian enterprises needed financial resources as well as logistics, communications and regulation. Taxation was another issue. It was something Venkdt thought he would leave to a later meeting. The inaugural session was something more akin to a backslapping session or a works beano, particularly in light of its setting in Gluttony, one of Marineris' premier restaurants.

On entering the restaurant all Anthony Karjalainen could see was his father's sworn enemy, in business for the last thirty years and in a profound ideological sense for the last few months of his life. For Anthony Karjalainen Charles Venkdt represented everything bad.

Venkdt was standing at the head of a long centre table and was making a rambling informal speech. His audience were mostly attentive and a few waiting staff moved about the room clearing plates from the dessert courses and bringing coffees. Venkdt was smiling, having just made a light-hearted remark about something or other.

"Charles Venkdt!" shouted Anthony. Venkdt stopped and peered through the semi-darkness to the figure he could see approaching. Two of Foveaux's MSS personnel, seated either side of the room, snapped to panicked attention. Until now they had been enjoying the cushy assignment and free food. A crowded room such as this was a terrible place to have to subdue an assailant. They both desperately hoped the situation was benign, and each was keenly aware that inaction or overreaction were equally undesirable. One caught the other's eye as they both stood, hands moving towards their concealed firearms. They had the ability to immobilise a target and silently communicated their intention to do just that should the situation deteriorate further.

"First of all," said Anthony, striding across the floor of the restaurant as if he was about to start a bar fight, "I want you to know that I do not recognise you as my president."

"Anthony?" said Venkdt, dumbfounded. All eyes were on Anthony, some of the more distant patrons standing and craning for a better view.

"And I want you to know that when the USAN arrives, as they are going to someday, somehow, they're going to install me as interim president and I'm going to oversee the reversal of everything you've done. You are a threat to peace on this planet and you're a disgrace to your own company, the company that bears your name." Anthony had stopped just short of Venkdt and he jabbed his finger violently as he spoke. The two MSS personnel were silently drifting closer to Venkdt.

Anthony turned to the crowded restaurant behind him. Again, he crazily jabbed his finger as he spoke. "And all of you are complicit. Every one of you. If any of you had any decency, a single shred of patriotism for our home planet and great nation, you would have hauled this man off to the stockade months ago. It's not too late. Here he is, right now, in front of you. The Great Traitor. Are you going to do anything?" He waited in vain for an answer. "Look into your hearts. We will have our planet back. You need to decide which side you're on. When this terrible injustice has been righted I will remember where each one of you stood. With me, or against me."

Venkdt had detected that although Antony's anger was being directed at him it may have bubbled up from somewhere else. "How's your father, Anthony?" he said.

"My father is dead," spat Anthony, "and don't act like you give a shit. You always hated him and you hated everything he stood for. He was a good man, a man who knew right from wrong and would stand up for it. He could see right through you. He could see what your power grab was all about. He wasn't taken in by all your fancy words and that comfortable, matey manner in your streams. He knew what you were about: power. You wanted to seize this planet to use for your own ends, and people like my father could see right through you. Well I can see right through you too, and when the army arrive I'm going to be right there when they throw you in jail."

"I'm sorry to hear about your father," said Venkdt. "He was a good man."

Anthony snorted. "You didn't even know my father, he was nothing to you."

Venkdt shrugged. He knew there was no point arguing and he could see the distress Anthony was in. He hoped the talk was all bluster. He bore Anthony no ill will, but it was hard to deny that talking about throwing presidents in prison wasn't treasonous. "I think you should go home, Anthony. You're very upset and you need some time alone to think things over. I'm sorry for your loss, please relay my sympathies to the rest of your family."

"That's right Venkdt, I'm going home. But the next time I see you I'm going to have an army with me. You'd better be ready." He turned and left, the MSS agents skittering behind him at a short distance.

Venkdt stared at the door long after Anthony had left. He knew the kid was in a distressed state but some of the things he had said would have to be addressed. Was it all bluster? The things he had said about the USAN Army installing him as president sounded unsettlingly specific, and some of the other things he had said had been directly threatening. A loud murmur hummed through the room as the politico-business class discussed exactly that.

Venkdt had always known that being president would mean taking difficult decisions. He had genuine sympathy for a young man who had just lost his father, but openly challenging the president was something he could not let stand. It was well known that the Venkdts and Karjalainens were rivals in business, and that Hjälp Teknik was the only challenger to Venkdt's operation on Mars. He didn't like the way it would look for him to be arresting the new CEO of his erstwhile rival. It could easily be interpreted as an abuse of power, of him using his presidency to silence his enemies. But equally he couldn't let someone threaten the presidency in public with impunity. He knew what he had to do. He did it with a heavy heart.

He tapped on his comdev and spoke to his PA. "Can you get me Ms Foveaux, please," he said. Moments later, as colleagues fussed about him, his comdev buzzed. It was Foveaux. He made his excuses and quickly walked to an anteroom for some privacy. "Hello," he said into his comdev.

"I was asked to call you," replied Foveaux.

"Yes," said Venkdt. "You know Anthony Karjalainen, Jack Karjalainen's son?"

"I do," said Foveaux.

"I need you to arrest him."

"Arrest him?"

"Yes. You need to be quite sensitive about it; his father has just died."
"Okay. What are the charges?"
"Sedition."

Anthony Karjalainen, despite having only grabbed a few hours' rest here and there over the previous forty-eight hours, had not gone home after leaving Venkdt. He had headed to a café to have breakfast. He didn't want to be around people he knew, people who might be asking questions about his father or how he felt. He didn't want to be at home, where the coms would be buzzing and visitors would be dropping by. As well as not sleeping he had not eaten properly either, so he headed for a café where he had a full English breakfast with beans and tomatoes.

He was wiping up the bean juice with a piece of bread when the two officers arrived. He paid no attention to them. The bean juice was mixed with tomato juice and there were also remnants of brown sauce and tomato ketchup, with bits of egg yolk and some bacon oil in there, too. The bread was buttered and it picked up the fabulous liquid, which tasted incredible in Anthony's mouth. He was so distracted by the unbelievable flavours he didn't notice the officers approach.

"Are you Anthony Karjalainen?" said one.

Anthony had a mouthful of delicious buttered bread and breakfast juices. He looked at the officer and continued chewing. He gestured with his hand that his mouth was full as he chewed and swallowed. There was some bean juice on his chin.

"I am," he said. "What's this about?"

"Sir, you are under arrest, please come with us."

The other patrons of the café were paying full attention now and the low-level murmur of their conversations and the chinks of their cutlery had faded.

"What do you mean, under arrest? I haven't done anything."

"Sir, we have a warrant for your arrest right here. Please come with us quietly."

"Let me see the warrant," said Anthony.

The officer tapped at his comdev. "It should be on your comdev right now, sir," he said.

Anthony took another wipe with his buttered bread and put it in his mouth before he looked at his comdev. He pressed the screen a few times and then read, chewing. "This is ridiculous," he said. "On whose authority are you doing this?"

"We're doing it in line with the statutes of this planet, sir. Can you please come with us? If you refuse to do so we will take you in by force and add resisting arrest to the charge sheet."

Anthony was rankled now and he figured exactly what was going on. As far as he was concerned the terrible despot Charles Venkdt was using his security services to silence all dissidents in his police state. It confirmed for him exactly what he had thought; that Charles Venkdt was an evil power grabber who could not be trusted. Having earlier had some doubts about his outburst in the restaurant he now thought perhaps he had not gone far enough. Maybe he should have gone with an armed guard and seized control of the government by force right then and there. But it was too late for that now. He felt the righteousness of the oppressed. "May I just finish my breakfast?" he said, with all the stroppiness he could muster.

The officer didn't want to make a scene and thought it was worth losing face a little to keep Anthony placated. "Yes, sir," he said.

The two officers stood by while Anthony finished his breakfast.

The USAN garrison building on Mars had plenty of conference rooms. Maya had booked one to go over the plans for the rescue. She had her assistant commissioners, Matthias Schroeder, Virgill van Velden and Laura Khadzhiyev with her, as well as Bobby and Kostovich.

"You're all familiar with the equipment by now," said Kostovich, "but if there's anything you need to know just ask. We understand this is going to be a simple search and rescue operation. The helmets will give you thermal imaging or infrared if you need it. There is no power on that ship but you should be able to find your way around with no problem whatsoever. Your coms will work inside and you'll be able to talk back to the shuttle, which will relay your coms back to me. I'll be taking data feeds from all of you and combining them into a real-time model of the ship. I'll feed all that straight back to you, of course, so what any one of you knows the rest of you will know. The data will be displayed in a 3-D model available to you in your HUDs. Obviously, during the mission you will each be focusing on your immediate environment. I will be monitoring the overall situation so if I feel the need to draw your attention to anything I will do that. I will be with Commissioner Foveaux, who will have ultimate control of the operation."

"There are no simple operations," said Bobby. "Our biggest problem is going to be getting them to trust us. Remember, we are the enemy. We destroyed their ship, so there's no reason they should welcome us with open arms. Gaining their trust is at the heart of the mission. They are going to be in the dark, cold and frightened when we turn up, and we'll be suited and booted, with guns too. We need them to know that we are coming to save them rather than finish them off."

"I have prepared a drone. The drone will find them and tell them you're coming, but that might not necessarily help. It's all a question of trust," said Kostovich.

"Okay," said Bobby, "how do we get in?"

"There's an emergency hatch on *Ephialtes*. It's standards compliant so we'll be able to dock onto it. We may need to blow the locks, but we have the equipment to do that if necessary."

"Good. And the shuttle is ready to go?"

"It is," said Kostovich. "You'll launch in approximately four hours. You'll need to be at the port in two."

Bobby nodded.

"You're happy with the personnel you're taking along with you?" said Foveaux.

"Sure," said Bobby, "they'll do a fine job. How many survivors are we expecting?"

"Well," said Kostovich, "*Ephialtes* itself has a crew of forty, and there are twenty-six commanders on board - one for each dropship and two substitutes, one commanding officer and one civilian. So it should be sixty-eight. We've no reason to believe there were any fatalities, though it's impossible to know what's gone on up there for the last two days."

"Why is there a civilian on board?" said Bobby.

"She's the designer," answered Kostovich. "She works for Helios and she came along for the maiden voyage. There were problems with the other ship so she came along with this one to see if she could iron them out."

Bobby had an inkling in his gut as to what the answer to his next question might be. "What's her name?" he asked.

"Askel Lund," replied Kostovich.

Bobby nodded.

"You know her?"

Bobby thought carefully before answering. "I know *of* her," he said, and left it at that.

The stockade at the former USAN garrison was small. Most of the criminals taken down by the USAN's army-police were placed under house arrest, if necessary, before coming to trial or being repatriated to Earth. Rarely was anyone considered dangerous enough to be incarcerated and, where no immediate danger was posed, allowing suspects to remain amongst the general population made sense. The habitable part of Mars was an extremely limited area. There was nowhere for anyone to run to. The only people who were put in the stockade were either mad, drugged or otherwise dangerous.

Anthony Karjalainen was not used to the conditions he found in the stockade. His cell was small. There was a bed, a lavatory, a wash basin and a small desk with a terminal on it. There were high windows, but in order to see out of them Anthony had to move the table and stand on it. The view was not inspiring. He could see the parade ground and not much else.

Anthony found himself in the stockade at the most turbulent point in his life. His father had just died, which was extremely difficult for him emotionally, and at the same time and through that death he had become the CEO of a major company. On top of that, he was involved in some interplanetary diplomatic intrigue, and then to round it all off he had been thrown in jail for sedition.

Luckily he had eaten well moments before he came in. After shouting at the guards when they left him he lay on the bed and closed his eyes. In an odd kind of way, he thought to himself, maybe alone in a prison cell was the best place for him to be at that particular moment in his life. He took deep breaths and tried to focus on his breathing, pushing all thoughts of his father and the situation he found himself in out of his mind. Slowly he began to calm and it became easier to push the thoughts away each time they resurfaced. The bed was not uncomfortable and after lying still on it for a few minutes he had fallen asleep.

He was awoken by the jangling of keys turning in the lock. He turned his head to look and saw Bobby entering. "Hey, kid," said Bobby.

Anthony sat up on the bed and leant back against the wall of his cell. "What are you doing here?" he said.

Bobby half sat on the desk opposite Anthony. "I just came to check that you're okay. You're okay, right?" he said.

Anthony looked at him. "Not really," he said.

"Is there anything I can do?" said Bobby. "Is there anything you need?"

Anthony snorted. "Well, I need to be out of this place. Can you do anything about that?"

Bobby shook his head. "No, I don't think I can. I meant do you need any stuff? Clothes, toiletries? Have you got a lawyer?"

"A lawyer? Sure, we've got Toni."

"Okay," said Bobby, "I'll get her to come down here as soon as possible."

"That's it then," said Anthony, "you've done your big brother part, now you can go. Get out of here."

Bobby didn't move. His arms were folded across his chest and he looked at Anthony. Anthony was looking downward, fixated on his own predicament and paying no attention to the rest of the world.

"You haven't changed much, have you?" said Bobby. Anthony didn't react. "I mean, this is exactly how I remember you. Passive-aggressive, truculent, feeling hard done by. You haven't changed one little bit."

"And you have?" said Anthony. "Travel, experience, the army, war. You went away a boy and came back a man, is that it?"

Bobby didn't reply.

"I don't see you sticking up for the family. Someone has to. Dad's not here now. I'm just doing what he wanted. I guess that never occurred to you, to stick up for the family or to do right by your father?"

"Well," said Bobby, "I'm not one for bearing grudges, but Dad never stood by me. That was his choice. I'm sorry it happened that way, but it did. I made my own choices and here I am. I don't owe anyone anything, and no one owes me. So don't be blaming any of this on Dad. You're in this cell because of what you did and it was your choice to do it. Now deal with it."

"'*Deal with it*'," said Anthony. "That's your advice, as an older brother, '*Deal with it*'? You know, it's too bad you weren't around for the last few years. I could have done with some helpful advice like that while I was growing up. Thanks for coming."

"Don't feel sorry for yourself, Anthony. You're in a lot of trouble and it's your own fault. I'll get in touch with Toni, but I doubt there's much she'll be able to do for you. If you need anything just call me."

Anthony continued staring into space as Bobby knocked on the door. After a few seconds a guard opened it and let him out.

Lucero had known that one of her biggest immediate problems was the simple fact that there was nothing anyone could do. She had resolved almost immediately to make sure that there was so much to do that no one would notice that fact. She had arranged the survivors into four groups and had variously sent them about the ship on tasks. One group was tasked with checking every room and making sure there were no people injured or unaccounted for, and no apparent damage. A second group was tasked with bringing up oxygen tanks from the store on the hangar deck. They needed to find rope and other means of securing the tanks so they did not float about the bridge. The bridge was now the absolute heart of the ship. It was the one area with a window, and thereby the only place on the ship were there was any light. The rest of *Ephialtes* was in darkness.

A third group was in charge of gathering food. There were plenty of supplies in the galley, though nothing could be cooked. They didn't have the power and they couldn't spare the oxygen to heat anything. Food gathering was an important job and again the group was tasked with finding a means of securing the food safely in the bridge.

All the tasks had something of a teambuilding exercise about them, except in this case there was actually a nominal purpose to the exercises beyond the team building. Lucero hoped that no one would notice that the task was secondary.

Once they had secured the food and oxygen there was less to do. There were no more expected events on the way. All that would happen now would be the ship getting colder and the CO_2 levels getting higher. Nothing else was likely to happen, unless the Martians were to attempt a rescue mission.

Lund persuaded Lucero this was likely. "There would be no point in them taking us out with EMPs if they were just going to leave us here," she said. "They had nukes. They could have used those on us. The only purpose of using the EMPs would be to preserve life. I'm sure they must be coming."

"I don't know," said Lucero. "Maybe the EMPs were all they had. They pulled that fancy stunt with the dual speed missiles; maybe they needed the nukes to take out our countermeasures and the only thing they had left to use on us was EMPs. Maybe they've forgotten about us already. Maybe we're already dead as far as they're concerned."

Lund baulked at that. "I don't think so," she said. "It doesn't make sense. They have to be coming for us. Anyway, we need to believe that, because if they're not coming for us nobody else is."

"You can't just think it's going to happen because you want to think it, Lund," said Lucero.

"That's not what I mean," said Lund. "What I mean is that if you're using EMPs it must be part of an overriding life preserving strategy. That strategy will include rescuing us from here, and not leaving us to die. Think about it from a political point of view. The Martians were always saying about how they wanted peace and wanted to avoid a war. Just politically it would be impossible for them to open fire on us and kill us all. That's why they used the EMPs. They wanted to disarm us, not kill us. They want to have us on the bulletins, smiling and looking relieved, and thanking them for saving us. You're right, I do want to believe that because it's our only hope, but I do think it's true, too. It's the only thing that makes sense, logically."

"So what are we going to do about it?" said Lucero.

"Nothing. There's nothing we can do, apart from wait."

Lucero had discovered early on that it was difficult to hold a serious meeting when the participants are floating about the room. It would be even more difficult when the subject of the meeting pertained to the life or death of those floating. Lucero had no choice. With no power the artificial gravity was gone, so it was a floating meeting or no meeting.

"Okay people," she began, "I need to talk to you about the situation we find ourselves in. Obviously, I don't need to tell you that we have no power or electronics of any sort; I think that idea has got through to even the dumbest of you by now. We have food and plenty of it, that is not an issue. We have oxygen to breathe, but we don't have working filters to scrub the CO_2 from it. Of course, that means eventually we will run out of breathable air. We've done some back-of-an-envelope calculations on that and we think we probably have a good few days of air left, so we can put that worry to one side for a moment. A more pressing issue is the temperature in here. It's going to get cold. Again, we've done some rough calculations on that and it looks like we're losing a degree or so Celsius every few hours. You may have noticed it getting colder in here already. Well, that process is not going to stop and it's going to get a whole lot colder. We've brought up extra apparel from the stores and we should be fine even after we've dropped below zero Celsius, provided we are wearing appropriate clothing. But it's going to keep getting colder after that, and at some point it will become too cold for survival.

"So that's the bad news; after a few days we're going to run out of breathable air and it's going to get way too cold in here for us to survive. Don't forget the good news though; plenty of food. Just focus on that, we've got plenty of food."

There were some uneasy laughs.

"I've been in discussion with Dr Lund and she has a theory about the Martian attack. Dr Lund believes that the Martians would not have used EMPs if they intended to kill us. She believes the purpose of the EMP attack was to preserve our lives, and following on from that she believes the Martians will make an attempt to rescue us. Now, don't get too excited about that. That's Dr Lund's theory, and although it appears to be logically sound we have no evidence to support it. In light of that I would like to say this:

"Should it appear that the Martians are attempting to board *Ephialtes* we should make every attempt to make friendly contact with them before assuming they mean us any further harm. If Dr Lund's theory is correct and the Martians do attempt to board the ship I think it's safe to assume they will be armed, and they will appear threatening. They have no means of contacting us prior to boarding, so they will be concerned that we will assume they are attacking us. For that reason we must absolutely not appear threatening to them. In the unlikely event that they come in guns blazing then you have my unequivocal permission to fight back, if you can find any means to. But if they come at all we feel they will be coming to help us, and we will have to do everything in our power to make sure they know that we know that.

"Is that clear to everyone?"

"When are they coming?" came a timid voice in the half-light.

"We don't know. We don't even know *if* they're coming."

"And they'll be able to save us all?"

Lucero shrugged. "Listen, let me say it again, this is all just conjecture. We don't know anything about their plans, they may not be coming at all. Prepare yourselves for that. What I want to make clear is if they do come, unless we see obvious indications to the contrary, we can assume they're coming to help us and we should act accordingly."

"What if they don't come?" came another voice. "What happens to us then?"

"I believe I've already made that clear," said Lucero.

"That's just one scenario," said Lund, trying to keep some hope alive. "In one possible scenario it gets cold and we run out of air and that's that. But there are many other scenarios, and the one I think most likely is that they come for us and we all get out of here and it's okay."

"But when will they come, if they come?"

"Soon."

Foveaux concluded her meeting with the rescue team by wishing them good luck. The briefing had consisted of going over the rescue plan. There wasn't much of a plan at all. It was to dock with *Ephialtes*, send the drone in on a search mission, then follow the drone to any people it found. The plan assumed people were likely to be grouped together. Human nature would dictate that at a time of great stress and danger the people aboard *Ephialtes* would come together in a single space.

The rescue team were equipped with loudhailers, as was the drone. Their primary concern was to convey to *Ephialtes*' crew members that they were coming to rescue them, not to continue the fight they had started two days earlier.

Bobby was to be the team leader. Foveaux thought, and Venkdt had agreed, that having been in combat he would be able to deal with the stress of the mission better than any of their other people. Also, having been in combat he was likely to be less trigger-happy. Having

EPHIALTES

seen the devastation a military can inflict a combat vet can usually be relied upon to be a powerful advocate for peace.

The rescue team was small. It was necessarily so in order to keep maximum space on the shuttle to bring back survivors. There was no particular need for a large squad. One of the mission parameters was that if they met any resistance whatsoever they were to withdraw and leave the survivors to their fate.

Ephialtes was going to be a difficult environment to work in. With zero-g and no light it would be hard to evacuate the ship if the evacuees were not compliant. They had considered flooding the ship with a knockout gas if that proved to be the case, but the difficulties of spreading it around the ship and keeping it in non-lethal dosages seemed insurmountable. They assumed that once they could communicate that they were there to save the occupants, the occupants would comply and be rescued. After all, their only other option was to remain with the ship and die a cold, suffocating death to no purpose whatsoever.

"That went pretty well," Bobby said to Foveaux as the briefing finished.

Foveaux shrugged. "That's just words. You've got the tricky part."

"I think it's going to be pretty straightforward," said Bobby. "They have no weapons and they must know the position they're in. I think they'll greet us with open arms."

"You wouldn't be the first soldier in history to make that assumption and be proved wrong," said Foveaux.

Bobby smiled. "I guess not," he said. "But don't forget that soldiers before me have made that assumption and been proved right, too."

"Are you ready to go?" said Foveaux.

"As ready as I'm going to be," replied Bobby.

"As soon as you're in your flight suit get down to the shuttle bay."

"Yes," said Bobby. "Where will you be?"

"I'll be in the operations room with Kostovich. We'll oversee the whole thing from there. Anything you need - information, advice, backup - just let us know."

"I'll do that," said Bobby.

"Okay then," said Foveaux, "I'll see you at the port in about thirty-six hours' time. I'll get some transports there. We'll take the prisoners off you as soon as you land."

"I'll see you there, then," said Bobby, and he left to prepare for the flight.

The launch of the shuttle was uneventful, save for being delayed for an hour to allow a sandstorm to pass. Once they were in orbit they could see the remains of the sandstorm drifting away from the city. It looked beautiful from that height.

From orbit it would take them another few hours to reach *Ephialtes*, and then some more time to dock and breach the hatch. Bobby took the time to get to know his team a little better. They were not like the soldiers he was used to working with. He had been with the Commander Program for many years and he was used to people who were extremely dedicated and focused. The team from the MSS seemed nice enough, but appeared to lack that ruthless focus and cockiness that Bobby was used to amongst his squadmates.

He had suspected as much from the beginning. In the Commander Program you could expect all of your colleagues to be alpha types, but here he had to allow for a range of different types of personality. He thought they would do a good job, mainly because he thought the job was a simple one. If it hadn't been in space it would be absolutely routine. It boiled down to simply shepherding people off a spacecraft that was going to kill them and onto one that was going to save their lives. Even with the added wrinkle that the people they were rescuing may not trust their motivation it still seemed like a straightforward task to Bobby. At a low level he felt quietly confident that the team would execute the mission with minimal fuss and maximum efficiency, despite the high stakes and their relative inexperience. But for him and him alone there was one additional factor lending the mission an extra frisson: Askel.

Although in his mind he had left Askel far behind and long ago, she had never been far from his thoughts. Hearing her name had been like a strangely pleasant punch to the stomach; visceral, shocking and unexpectedly enjoyable. Knowing that he might soon see her again somehow recast his feelings about her. Where he had believed he had been letting her fade in his memories he now realised he had been holding on to his thoughts of their time together, reluctant to finally let her go.

With a few hours left until the mission he decided to have a kip.

CHAPTER 32

War and Peace

"Defence?"

"Nothing, Mr President. We have no interplanetary craft."

"Foreign?"

"Nothing, Mr President. Anthony Karjalainen has been arrested. Colonel Shaw is still under house arrest. She's our senior person on the planet and as far as we know she hasn't been compromised. But she's not in a position to do anything for us at the moment."

"Okay, defence, no interplanetary craft. If we signed the orders here and now how long would it be until we had one?"

Andrews had anticipated the question. She ruffled through her papers before answering. "A ship of the same class and size as *Ephialtes* and *Otus* would take approximately four years to build, Mr President."

Cortes nodded. "What can we do in the meantime? For the next four years?"

"Mr President, you've recently concluded one of the most damaging wars in human history. For the next four years I think we should consolidate our position and plan for a future with an independent Mars. After all, we are the only market they have for their deuterium, so they need us just as much as we need them," said White.

"Plan for the future," said Cortes. "We planned for a future in which we got our colony back and secured our energy supplies. Didn't work out. I think we need an array of more flexible plans, don't you?"

"Things don't always work out the way one hopes, Mr President."

"No, they don't," said Cortes, his laser beam eyes burning into White's.

"I think it's advisable in a situation like this to look at what we have and try to make the best of it. Yes, our original intentions didn't work out. So what have we got? We need to look at that, think about what our long-term goals are and how we are going to work towards them," said White.

"What we have got," said Cortes, "is the square root of nothing. We have lost our two most powerful warships and along with them any influence we might have in the Martian sphere. We have also lost our energy supplies. Without Martian deuterium our entire economy, our entire way of life will grind to a halt. But even more important than both of those things, we have lost all credibility in an unstable world. Our enemies came to the negotiating table because they believed we possessed the power to destroy them. That is how we achieved peace; by preparing for all-out war. It was partly bluff, as you all know. Well, it looks like the Martians have called us on that bluff and now we look like fools. We have no hand to play. Do any of you think our enemies are not watching this unfold? Do any of you think that this incident is not going to affect our standing in the world? What has happened out there is an unmitigated disaster."

There was silence in the room.

"Where do we go from here, Mr President?" said Brennan.

Cortes paused before answering. "First, the state of emergency and the Restrictive War Measures must continue. The stability of this nation is our absolute priority. I swore an oath to protect it, and I shall. Secondly, and in support of that, we have to suspend all military cutbacks. As of now the peace dividend is over. The Asian Bloc is restless and we cannot allow ourselves to fall back into war. We need to continue strengthening our military. That is what brought peace. The negotiations and the treaties were just the endgame of that policy. We achieved peace by gearing up for massive, annihilatory war. That policy, now revived, must continue. At home we have to increase security. Our enemies, whether Asian Bloc, Martian or independent will seek to probe us for any weakness they can exploit. We have to be ready for them."

"I meant with regards to Mars," said Brennan.

Cortes shrugged. "Well, that's one for the foreign office," said Cortes. "We need the deuterium and they are the only place we can get it in sufficient quantities. It's not a secure source anymore but it's the only one we have. For the immediate future I guess we will have to deal with the Martians. Farrell, I expect you to have something worked out by the end of the month. The deuterium has to keep flowing. I don't want to formally recognise the Martian government, so fudge something if you have to. Just keep the deuterium coming."

"Yes, sir," said Farrell.

"So that's it? A fudge?" said White.

"What do you suggest? There are no other options open to us. We tried and we failed. Goddammit, recognise their sovereignty if you have to, but we need that deuterium. What else are we going to do?"

"We could just talk to them," said White, "like I suggested in the first place."

Cortes looked at White with an unnatural stillness. "Like you suggested in the first place," he said. "We just roll over and let them steal our planet. That's how you'd have played it?"

"Of course not," said White. "I'd have negotiated, talked with them, made various proposals, give-and-take, you know? And I'm damn sure we would have ended up in a better position than the one we find ourselves in now."

Cortes frowned and nodded. "Then I guess we should have done what you suggested. Hindsight is a wonderful thing, isn't it? With hindsight you'd have made a better decision than the president of the USAN. You know what? With hindsight the president of the USAN would have made a better decision than the one he did."

"Yes, Mr President," said White. "I'm sorry, I didn't mean to imply -"

"Don't grovel," said Cortes. "It makes you look weak."

"Mr President," said Farrell, "you said that for the immediate future we would deal with the Martians. Obviously, I'll get onto that right away. I'm sure we can come to an arrangement with them that will be beneficial to us all. I don't see that being a problem. I just want to ask, do we have a policy for the long term?"

"Yes we do," said Cortes. "Andrews, you said four years, is that right?"

Andrews was startled. "Yes, sir. The original *Aloadae* took five years each, drawing board to commissioning. My understanding from Helios is that with the infrastructure now in place, and based on the practical experiences they had of building the first two, they would be able to build one now in four years. And that would be to the new specification, including all of Lund's modifications - the new engines and so forth."

"Sounds great," said Cortes. "Tell them we want six."

"Peter! Peter!" White ran awkwardly down the corridor, his hand raised partly in salutation and partly like a schoolchild who eagerly knows the answer. Peter Brennan was walking away and did not notice.

"Peter," said White, finally catching up.

Brennan did not stop walking. "Hello, Gerard."

"What did you make of that?"

Brennan shrugged. "Sort of makes sense, I guess. I don't know how we're going to pay for it. But needs must, I suppose."

"He'll never get a budget for that past congress. We're trillions of dollars in debt already, we just can't afford it. But Farrell has the go-ahead to negotiate with the Martians. This thing will all be sorted out by Christmas. In a year's time no one, not even him, will give a damn about all this."

"You think so?" said Brennan, giving White a sideways look. "The president I know is nothing if not determined. He'll get those carriers yet and we'll clear up this mess."

White continued walking beside Brennan as they left the building. "Even if that happens we have to deal with them for four years. We'll get used to it, they'll get used to it, he'll get used to it. It's good that we didn't get involved in using force. I mean, putting aside the terrible cost in lives as well as treasure, I think the outcome is pretty good."

"Good?"

"Yes. Assuming Farrell succeeds, which I'm sure he will. We have peace, that has to be a good thing, right?"

Brennan stopped. "I share the president's view that 'peace at any cost' is a faulty position. There are some costs that are too high to bear. He's right, you know, about what our enemies will make of this. It was the *Aloadae* that brought the Asian Bloc to the negotiating table. They're gone, squandered on this internecine spat. That leaves us weak at home and abroad. Farrell might be able to patch up the deuterium supplies, so we're out of the hole on that, but we're now in far greater trouble than you seem to be able to see."

"Peter, come on. That's a lot of bull. We avoided getting dragged into another conflict. It's good, you know it is."

"You're privy to the intelligence briefings. You know what they think in Beijing. If they don't see us building new carriers right away they'll know we are ripe for the taking. Hell, even if we start building tomorrow they might just speed up their plans to get in before the four years are up. We are in a very parlous state."

"Well," said White, "I just wanted to thank you for all your support. I disagree with you, but I look forward to working with you in getting all this back on track."

"I don't think we'll be working together. You're politically valuable to the president. You represent something he doesn't, and the public like you. You appeal to the middle classes. But following this screw-up you're going to be confined to PR stuff. You know, popping up on the bulletins saying the stuff the liberal intelligentsia likes to hear, opening schools and that sort of thing. Leave the difficult stuff to me."

White looked at Brennan. "I'm the vice president. I know my influence is limited, but I am part of this administration. I intend to execute my role to its fullest extent.

Brennan took White's hand and shook it. "I wish you the very best of luck with that." He didn't add 'And you'll need it,' but his meaning was clear. He turned and carried on walking. White remained still.

The timing of a live stream from the New White House could be used to gauge its importance, or its perceived importance to the president and his advisers. Cortes had had this stream set up for eight o'clock in the evening such that it would be after most people were home from work but would not yet have gone to bed.

Live streams were not widely watched. People whose aggregators were set to pick up on politics, or current affairs, or maybe just 'Cortes' would find the stream at their leisure. The commentators might make a note of the timing, which was a traditional hangover from bygone eras, and relay that to their audiences. Really, it had just become part of the ritual. A serious announcement had to go out at 'Prime Time', an anachronistic concept that few even understood the meaning of.

So it was that President Cortes began his address to the nation, in a mainland USAN prime time that no one understood the meaning of, and to a country that spanned around the globe, so the time it went out may have been prime or not, depending on where the viewer was. At least the tradition was upheld, so there was that.

"My fellow Americans. I, like the rest of you, have been following the news streams from Mars. The crew of our great and stricken ship *Ephialtes* are, as I speak, in grave and mortal danger. It is our hope that the mission, announced by Martian representatives, to rescue the crew will be successful. We all hope and pray that they make it out of there, and that they are eventually returned to their loved ones here on Earth.

"*Ephialtes* and her crew were going to Mars to protect all of our futures. Martian secession, based on a spurious election, and with no mandate in law, was and remains a crime against our great nation. Had *Ephialtes* and her sister *Otus* not been so cruelly struck down we would have sought to redress that crime in the coming months. That, now, shall not pass.

"I would like to take this opportunity to thank those on Mars who will be saving our sons and daughters, fathers, mothers, sisters and brothers from the fate that would otherwise await them. But I would also like to remind you that it was the criminal Martian revolutionaries who did this to us and our kin. They have compounded their original great crime by attacking USAN ships and personnel, and no amount of magnanimity will atone for that.

"In light of this attack on the USAN I have decided that the current state of emergency will not be rescinded as we had all hoped it would be at the conclusion of the last great war. Our enemies have been able to use underhand tactics against us, and it seems likely that our information systems are compromised. We believe that information useful to the enemy has been leaked or cracked from our systems. Until we route out these weaknesses, the state of emergency will have to remain, and I thank you for your understanding on that.

"We will continue to have diplomatic relations with the Martian state, while not recognising the legitimacy of that state. We will embrace the practical necessity of maintaining relations in the hope of building on those with a legitimate Martian government at such time as one may come to power, and we hope very much that that will be the case in the future.

"We owe the people of Mars, who we still consider to be citizens of the USAN, the protection that all Americans deserve and expect. To that end we will be commissioning the construction of six new carriers, built to the specification of the modified *Aloadae*. All such vessels will now be known as 'Ares Class'. We will not abandon the true patriots of Mars.

"Finally, I would like to say to you all that myself and Mrs Cortes will be watching the streams of the rescue tomorrow, as I'm sure many of you will be, and we will be praying for a positive outcome to this terrible situation.

"Thank you, good night."

Venkdt made a stream that night, too. He expressed regret at having to cripple *Ephialtes*, explaining that there was no other option open to him.

The warmongers of Earth had sent a military instrument to deal with a diplomatic crisis, and Mars' hand had been forced. He said that he too would be following the streams, and that he hoped for a successful resolution to the *Ephialtes* incident.

He made a succession of thanks. To the Martian people for believing in him, and for believing in themselves. To Maya Foveaux and her MSS, for organising the rescue attempt at short notice and with minimal resources. And to his supporters on Earth, from whom he claimed to have received many thousands of messages of support.

He spoke about the asteroid belt, so close to Mars and ripe for exploitation. There were practically limitless resources in the belt and the people of Mars were perfectly placed to seek them out and further add to Mars' wealth. This truly was a great time to be a Martian. Many great things awaited them.

He finished up by saying that Mars was now free from the military intimidation of the USAN, and that the new Martian state could get on with going about its business, re-establishing trade and other links with the home planet. Venkdt looked forward to the massive growth he expected in the economy, and he hoped that Mars would soon be able to welcome even more newcomers who might come to the planet seeking to make their fortunes, and who would add to the growing prosperity of all Martians.

White was surprised to be called to a private meeting with the president at the New White House. He had taken the impression from Brennan that he was out of favour, and the way things had panned out he could understand why. He decided that he didn't mind being frozen out. He always took the long view; what people think and say varies from moment to moment, and the fact that Cortes was seething at him now didn't necessarily mean he would remain that way indefinitely. White expected the whole thing to come off the boil over the next few months, and he would be able to reassert his influence and go back to trying to rein in the president's excesses.

EPHIALTES

The way White saw it, his play, even though it had gotten out of hand, seemed to have worked out. Conflict with Mars had been avoided, and they were now in a position where they had to rely on diplomacy. Of course, he never anticipated the destruction of the two carriers, and he would never have condoned or commissioned such things, but politics is a messy business and through some shrewd manoeuvring and a bit of luck things had ended up where he wanted them. Part of the price was that he would be out of favour for a while, but that was well worth paying.

On entering the Oval Office White was surprised to see Cortes in an apparently buoyant mood. "Come in, Gerard," he said, waving White over. He gestured to the sofas. "Shall we sit here? I think it would be more comfortable."

"Of course," said White, following Cortes over and taking a seat.

"Gerard," said Cortes, clapping his hands together, "I expect you're wondering why I asked you here."

"I assumed it was to do with the Mars thing?" said White.

"Well, sort of," said Cortes, smiling.

"So what is it?" said White.

"Where to begin?" said Cortes.

"Brennan said you wanted me to lay low for a while. To stay out of your way."

"Certainly that, yes, Gerard," said Cortes, "but there's so much more, too."

White saw the excitement dancing in Cortes' eyes. He had never seen the president like that before, except at the height of the war. When the president knew he had an overwhelming advantage over an enemy he got animated. The knot, which had been slowly forming in White's stomach, tightened.

"Okay, let's start here," said Cortes. "Do you know someone by the name of Rodney Sherman? Well, don't answer that, because I know you do. Some of my core Secret Service detail have been in conversation with Mr Sherman, and Mr Sherman has been persuaded to make a full and frank disclosure about his and your involvement in the *Otus* incident."

"Now just wait a minute," said White, "Rodney Sherman is a business associate of mine, and I know he's mixed up in some pretty shady stuff but what's he saying about *Otus*?"

Cortes looked at White and smiled. "Don't even bother, Gerard. We know everything. You'll just be embarrassing yourself, okay?"

White looked at him and knew that continuing with the denials was pointless.

"We never meant for it to happen like it did. The *Otus* thing was Sherman's guy getting out of hand. You have to know I would never have been party to a terrorist act like that."

"I'm sure you're right, Gerard. It doesn't seem like your style, so I'll give you that one. But it did go down like that, and that makes you guilty of treason, doesn't it? On top of mass murder, I mean."

"No," said White. "All we were trying to do was stop another war. Sherman's guy got out of hand. He's the traitor."

"No, no," said Cortes, "he was just following orders. Illegal orders, crimes nonetheless, but *your* orders. Traitorous orders against the government you swore to serve."

White sat deflated. He was backed as tightly into a corner as he had ever been. There was no way out. "So what are you going to do? Take me in? How about a show trial? I bet you'd like that."

Cortes waved a hand. "No, nothing like that. Just relax, we're not going to do anything with you. You spoke to Peter, he told you what we want. Go to your speaking engagements, open a library here and there, be the voice of reason for the media when they're on my back about whatever it might be. Good times."

"So that's it? You accuse me of high treason, of murdering tens of USAN military personnel, and tell me you're going to let it slide?"

"Well, not let it slide exactly. We have it all on you, if we need it, which I hope we won't. I'm sure you see the nature of our little compact."

White stared at Cortes, unsure what to say. He thought he had never seen the president so happy.

"That's it, you can go now," said Cortes.

White stood. Usually under these circumstances he would automatically shake the president's hand. On this occasion, he didn't even say goodbye.

As he reached the door and put his hand out to open it White heard the president call after him. "Oh, Gerard, one more thing."

White turned to face him.

"I was sorry to hear about Madeline. Please accept my sincere condolences." He grinned so hard it looked like his face might split.

"Hi, Dad," said Christina, kissing Venkdt on the cheek.

"Hey, kid," said Venkdt in reply.

"I brought some food, is that okay?"

"Sure, what is it?"

"I picked up some of that salmon. Remember, the stuff you told me about?"

"Oh, yes, I remember."

"I'll have the kitchen prepare it. How are you? I saw your stream."

Venkdt sat back down in his armchair. "I'm great. Tired, but great. You?"

Christina took off her coat and threw it on the sofa. She sat next to it. "I'm great, work is good."

Venkdt nodded. "You want me to take care of that fish?" he said, tapping his comdev.

"That would be great. I thought we could eat together."

A drone came into the living room and Christina placed the wrapped salmon on it.

"Just like last time, please," said Venkdt and the drone left.

"I really liked what you said. You hit just the right tone. Positive, but not gloating."

"Oh," said Venkdt, "I didn't really think about it like that. I just said what I thought. I am worried about those people. I hope we get up there in time."

"I'm sure it'll be fine, Dad. Kostovich has it all worked out. That's what he does. It's terrible, obviously, what happened, but I'm sure it's going to be okay."

Venkdt nodded.

"And now we're home free."

"Yes," said Venkdt. "I wish it could have happened some other way, but you're right. We're beyond their reach again. All that stuff I said in the streams is true."

Christina nodded sympathetically.

"You know," said Venkdt, "A lot of times it's easy to take things for granted. To just assume that something is just the way it is, and that it has always been and will always be that way. But it's often not the case. The first people who came here were risking their lives on a long, dangerous and uncomfortable journey. Many hundreds of the people after them, too. You know, this planet is a hostile place. It's not like Earth, where you can go outside and roam about. This planet is frigid. No flora or fauna, no atmosphere to speak of, breathable or otherwise, and desperately cold. But people came here and made it work. With ingenuity and graft they made a home here. They built something. Where there were problems, they found solutions."

"I know, Dad. It's amazing," said Christina, not really listening.

"This was not an easy place to come to. There were myriad problems and difficulties, so many reasons to not do it. But they came anyway, and here we are now with the future wide open to us. We have the resources here, we have the asteroid belt, we have a fully established and functioning colony. You're right. It's amazing what has been achieved here. Just amazing."

"Will you be watching the streams of the rescue?"

"What?"

"Will you be watching the rescue tomorrow?"

"Oh," said Venkdt. "Probably. I might go by Kostovich's mission control centre."

"It's going to be fine," said Christina. "You might want to be there when they bring them back. It would be a great photo-op, you posing with the grateful survivors."

EPHIALTES

"I don't think so. Those people will have been through enough without having to pretend to look pleased to see me. I just hope they're okay."

"Let's not dwell on that now, though. Let's just have a nice bite to eat together. Even the president is entitled to a night off every once in a while."

"Yes," said Venkdt, "I'll check the fish."

There was no answer at Zelman's house. Her PA said she'd had a lunch date but nothing booked in for the afternoon. She had received a message in the morning, but apart from that she hadn't heard from her all day.

White tried the restaurant where the lunch was. She had left there in the early afternoon. It was now four.

Zelman had disabled tracking on her comdev. White thought about asking one of his Secret Service detail to override her security settings remotely, but didn't want them to see his panic.

White put the name 'Madeline Zelman' into the news aggregator on his comdev, and left her another voicemail.

A while later the aggregator flagged up a news story about an accident on the Stemmons Freeway. A car had crashed, blocking two lanes. It was understood that Madeline Zelman, the noted philanthropist, had been in the wrecked car and had died in the fire. There were no suspicious circumstances.

The time of the accident was given as 15:05. White had finished his meeting with Cortes shortly before 14:30.

Usually White could stride right into the New White House with minimal checks. Sensors picked up his comdev, which was biometrically coded to him, and allowed entry. Any security or Secret Service agents were happy to let him by on facial recognition alone, happy that the scanners were checking his comdev in the background.

Now his security clearance had been revoked. The silent alarm sounded as soon as he was within thirty metres of the main gate. Automated radio messages were relayed to the security staff on the door, and one stepped in front of White as he tried to enter.

"I'm sorry, sir, but you do not have clearance to enter this building."

"What are you talking about?" said White, "I'm the vice president. Of course I can enter the White House."

The security guard held out a hand. "I'm sorry, sir, my instructions are quite clear. Please turn around and leave."

"This must be a mistake. Let me in."

"Sir." The guard gestured for White to leave.

White looked through the iron gate at the New White House. When the old White House had been destroyed back in 2087 this new one had been built here as an exact replica. The original site was still considered a hot zone at that time, but it was thought that a new location, with the old design, would represent a kind of continuity, and that was believed to be important. The White House, they seemed to be saying, is not a place but a concept. It is the seat of the president and it will always exist, withstanding even nuclear attack. Knock it down and it will just rise back up. He had always liked that idea when he believed that his country had the finest constitution in the world, and that it had a government of the people, by the people, for the people.

The thought of that resilience, allied now to the eighty-ninth president, filled him with a foreboding fear. He turned and walked away.

CHAPTER 33

Hostile Inbound

With his commander mech programmed Steiner had little to do for the two days it took to walk to Marineris. The cockpit was comfortable enough and could be set to a sitting position when the drone was on autopilot. Steiner slept a lot of the way, occasionally waking to take sustenance. The other mechs under his command were handling well. Their data suggested they had not been damaged in the crash. Steiner was confident he had enough of a squad to mount a successful attack on any Martian installation he chose.

The installation he had chosen to attack first was the Parry base to the west of Marineris. It was on the outskirts of the city, near the Allentown spaceport. It was just dumb luck that Steiner had crash-landed on that side of the city, but it presented a great opportunity. He would be able to neutralize the missile base and take control of the port, the single most important communications link on the planet. From that position he would be able to dictate terms and maybe arrange a relay so he could communicate with Earth to get further orders. It seemed like a great plan and eminently doable. He had practiced ground based assaults on the missile batteries repeatedly on the journey to Mars. Now all that practice was about to pay off.

In the simulations he had made use of the aerial capabilities of the dropship. He had used it for reconnaissance and as a distraction. In those scenarios he had a full squad of eleven mechs under his command. Here he only had four. He still felt capable of succeeding. He would use the landscape to hide from the battery, which was primarily looking to the sky, and he would disable it from a distance with his laser. Following that it would be a simple case of advancing on the installation and dealing with any resistance as and when it arose.

He programmed the specifics of the plan into the other mechs and checked on his ETA. Seven hours to go. He went back to sleep.

Steiner was startled awake by an alarm. 'Warning,' it repeated, 'hostile inbound.' He immediately turned on his HUD to check. About twenty kilometres distant there was an aircraft approaching. He commanded his mechs to stop.

Looking at the display he guessed the aircraft might be an observation drone. It was headed on a vector that would intersect with the crash site of his dropship. It was possible that, now the storm had cleared, the Martians were sending an aircraft for a look-see.

He thought about programming the damaged mech he had left on guard to shoot it down if and when it got there. That way the Martians might think his force was still out there, and it would throw them off his tracks. However, if they then sent another force to take them on where they supposed they were, at the landing site, they would have to pass right through where they actually were. He thought the best course of action would be to take the aircraft out himself.

If he fired a missile the aircraft would detect it before it got hit. Even if he took it out with his first shot it would relay that information back to base; that there was a hostile force firing missiles to the west of the city. He wanted to take it out instantly, so as to give no clue to his presence. That would still strongly suggest deliberate action, but would at least allow the possibility of mechanical or software failure.

The only method available to him for achieving such an end was his laser. The greater the distance the less accurate his laser was likely to be. He thought he should wait until the aircraft was nearer - say five kilometres or so. That way he had the highest possibility of success. The risk, though, was that he didn't know what type of monitoring equipment might be aboard the aircraft. There was nothing he could do about that. As in all battles he had to make do with limited information, working on assumptions and best guesses.

He programmed his laser to fire in a zigzag pattern, starting ahead of the aircraft and running down the length of its fuselage, then back up. He hoped this would be enough to destroy it, but couldn't be sure if it would be carrying any armour. He was working on the assumption it would be an intelligence gathering drone with no armour at all.

When the aircraft was a few kilometres out he got a visual on it. The cameras mounted on his mech were able to zoom in and reveal that it was, indeed, a standard information gathering drone aircraft, blithely flying along in a straight line at a steady speed. Steiner readied his laser.

When the drone was in range Steiner fired. Watching the visual feed on his HUD he saw the drone suddenly engulfed in a grey cloud, which quickly dissipated. The drone rapidly lost height and any semblance of stable flight. Steiner followed its course all the way to the ground.

Steiner was satisfied with the takedown. He thought he had executed the stealth kill well but even if the drone didn't see it coming, had it seen him and his mechs before then? Maybe it was headed to the crash site and was reserving power for its monitoring equipment until it got there. Or maybe it was monitoring all the way. It was quite possible that, as far as the drone's masters were concerned, it was on a routine mission and had suddenly gone dark for no discernible reason. That was what he hoped, but he couldn't know.

He didn't know if his enemies had any idea he was coming for them. With no other options open he pressed on toward the missile base.

CHAPTER 34

Rescue

"You're approximately fifteen minutes away from *Ephialtes*," said Kostovich.

"Okay," said Bobby.

"The docking procedure is entirely automated. If there are any difficulties with the hatch just cut through it with the laser drill."

"Just cut through it? A *hatch*?"

"Well," conceded Kostovich, "it might take a little while, and it might get a little hot, but you should be able to, if you have to. I don't see there being a problem. Anyway, you should just be able to open up the hatch and float right in."

"I hope so," said Bobby.

"I've asked the pilot to do a full sweep around the ship when you get there. Get as much visual information as you can. We're assuming full integrity of the hull, but it would be good to confirm that if we can. Who knows what might have happened? Maybe they've tried to scuttle her, or maybe tried to manually launch escape pods."

"Manually launch escape pods? Would that work?"

"Of course not. But we don't know what they might have done, is the point I'm trying to make. That's why we need as much additional information as we can get, hence the sweep. Visual information is still information."

"Is Foveaux with you?"

"She's right here," said Kostovich.

"Hello," said Foveaux.

"Hi," said Bobby, "I'm just trying to remember; did we discuss my compensation the other day?"

Foveaux smiled. "We didn't. Put in a good showing today and I'll be able to make a case for starting you on a higher grade."

"Okay," said Bobby, "so this is like a probationary task?"

"Something like that."

The solid clunk of two large vessels joining in space reverberated through them both. As soon as the connection was made Bobby and his team released themselves from their harnesses and made their way to the hatch.

The pilot gave clearance and Bobby opened the shuttle's hatch. Below it was the hatch to *Ephialtes*.

Bobby turned to one of his team. "Prepare the drone," he said and turned back to begin the process of opening the hatch. Eventually the hatch fell away inwards revealing the cold, black interior of *Ephialtes*.

Bobby nodded at the team member with the drone. "Send it in," he said.

The woman with the drone launched it like she might have thrown a dove into the air. In the zero gravity environment the drone halted for a moment and spun round, orienting itself to its surroundings. Once it appeared happy it disappeared into the darkness, and after a few seconds the whir of its guidance fans had faded.

"It's them," said Lund as she half heard, half felt the reverberation of the shuttle docking.

"Everybody, stay right here," said Lucero. "If they're coming in I want them to come and find us here, in one place. Everyone stay put." Although she had always known they were coming, she hadn't *really* known it until now. She kept up the facade of cool control but inside she was filled with relief. From internally questioning whether they would actually come, she now found herself questioning their motive. What if they had come with weapons to finish them off? What if they had used the EMP not in order to save their lives but to save the ship for themselves? Maybe their plan was to simply capture the ship and now all they needed to do was wipe out the remaining unarmed survivors. She put all those thoughts to one side as she said, "Keep quiet and await contact."

"This is it." said Lund. "We're safe. They've come to rescue us."

"We don't know that for sure," said Lucero. "Let's just wait and see."

When the drone appeared the crew scrabbled away from it like primitives before a totem. People pushed and pulled their way as far from the drone as possible. As it moved around the bridge people made way, like it was repelling them.

"Crew of *Ephialtes*." The sound came from the drone, causing some in the bridge to actually gasp and others to hush them so they could better hear the message being delivered. "This is Bobby Karjalainen of the shuttle '*Europa*.' We are about to board your ship. Please do not be alarmed. We have the capacity to take all of you to the Martian surface, where you will be treated fairly and courteously. We are here to help you. Do you understand this message?"

A very low murmur of whispered conversation spread about the bridge. Askel barely heard it, reeling as she was at the sound of the voice coming from the drone. *Bobby Karjalainen?* She wondered for a second if the oxygen was running out and she was starting to hallucinate. A small floating robot claiming it was Bobby Karjalainen coming to rescue her? Surely that couldn't be real.

Lucero spoke up. "Karjalainen," she said, and the drone turned toward her like a little terrier. It floated through the bridge toward her, stopping a metre or so away from her face. "I'm Commodore Lucero, I'm in command of this ship."

A video screen flickered to life on the front of the drone, and Lucero could see Bobby. He was flanked by a group of people who seemed to be crowding round him to look at his screen.

"Hello," said Bobby, "how are you today?"

"Been better," said Lucero. "You're going to get us all off here, is that right?"

"That's the plan," said Bobby. "You just stay put and we'll come to you. We have flashlights and food. We'll lead you back to our ship."

"Understood," said Lucero.

"Are there any injured amongst you? Anyone there need medical help?"

"Negative."

"Listen," said Bobby, "I need to know that you're not going to try anything stupid. All of my people are armed and we're prepared to put you down if we have to. I would very much appreciate your cooperation, Commodore Lucero. When we get to you, I'd like you to tell your people to come with us in an orderly fashion. We'll escort you back to the shuttle in groups of ten, okay? If anyone gives us any trouble, any trouble at all, we're out of here."

"Understood, I guarantee you our full cooperation."

"Okay, we're coming in."

Bobby had left four of his team on the shuttle. Two were guarding the hatch-bay entrance and the others were guarding the main passenger area. The three with him were bouncing and pulling their way through corridors and stairwells towards the bridge. Their HUDs were providing guidance.

The number of people crammed into the bridge surprised Bobby when he got there. It was brighter than he expected, but still dim, and it seemed oddly surreal that these people were in mortal danger. The floating gave the whole thing the air of fun, when in fact the situation was imminently life threatening.

Bobby recognised Lucero from the video feed. He made his way to her. As he approached she held out her hand.

"Welcome aboard *Ephialtes*," she said.

EPHIALTES

"Thank you," said Bobby. "It's great to be here." Looking over Lucero's shoulder he said, "Hi, Askel. You turn up in the damnedest of places."

Askel wanted to launch herself at Bobby and squeeze him until he squeaked. "Hi, Bobby," she said casually, like she had just noticed a neighbour at the supermarket.

"Commodore Lucero, I'd like the first ten people please," said Bobby.

"Yes," said Lucero. She pointed out ten people, "You, you, you . . ."

"We'll be back in a few minutes. Do you need anything?"

"We're fine here," said Lucero.

"Okay," said Bobby, "don't go anywhere."

Bobby and his team ferried the crew in groups of ten back to the shuttle. At the hatch they handed them over to the team on *Europa*, who then handed them off to the team in the passenger area. At the passenger area they were asked to find seats and strap themselves in, and then wait.

Lund and Lucero had remained at the bridge and were taken back with the last group.

At the hatch Bobby waited, floating, to guide the last of his charges through. He saw Askel into the hatch and finally only Lucero remained.

"Up you go, Commodore," said Bobby.

Lucero gestured for Bobby to go first. "After you, if you don't mind. I'd like to be the last to leave."

Bobby wondered if Lucero may be playing some angle, and he was tempted to insist that she go ahead of him. He decided to let it go. "Okay," he said, and he pulled himself aboard the shuttle.

Lucero took a look around, though there was little she could see in the scant amount of light available from the hatch. The drone made its way past her and back through the hatch. She heard it report to its masters, "There are no further personnel aboard *Ephialtes* apart from Commodore Lucero, who is boarding *Europa* now."

Lucero tugged on the hatch rim and glided effortlessly into the shuttle. She patted the hatch as she passed, saying, "She was a good ship."

Bobby personally oversaw the sealing of the hatches, both on *Ephialtes* and *Europa*. He messaged the pilot that it was safe to disengage and the pilot acknowledged him. "We have a few more things to do then we'll disengage and head home," she said.

"Okay," said Bobby. "We'll move back to the passenger area."

"Do that," said the pilot. "Strap yourselves in."

In the passenger section Bobby scanned the rows of seats for Askel. At first he couldn't see her and he didn't want to be seen to be looking, so he was relieved when he noticed her and saw that she hadn't noticed him.

Bobby's seat was at the front of the cabin. He had two of his team with him, with the rest sat along the back of the cabin where they could observe those in front of them. Bobby didn't expect any trouble. He thought Lucero seemed like a straight-up sort of character and he could sense the relief in the cabin. However humiliating it might have been to have been defeated, he knew the crew were glad to be alive.

Bobby was about to float over to Askel. He had decided to ask her something technical about *Ephialtes* - about what might happen to her over time as she remained in lonely orbit slowly atrophying - just as an in. But as he went to unbuckle his harness he heard the pilot's voice over the cabin's strange omnidirectional speaker system.

"This is your captain speaking. We are about to disengage from *Ephialtes*. We will then manoeuvre to a position ready for descent. Please remain in your seats until further notice."

Kostovich had been so engrossed in the live feeds from *Ephialtes* and *Europa* that he hadn't given much time to the data from the drone he had sent to investigate the crashed dropship.

The data he had suggested that while *Parry 5*'s missiles hadn't totally destroyed the only dropship to make it into the Martian atmosphere,

EPHIALTES

they had damaged it enough that gravity would do the rest. The ship had crashed at a safe distance, anyway, so there seemed to be no hurry to investigate. Soon after the crash a sandstorm had swept the area making any recon impossible at that time. The drone had only been launched that morning, when weather conditions were more favourable.

The feeds from the helmet mounted cameras of Bobby's team and the rescue drone were fascinating. *Ephialtes* was in much better shape than Kostovich would have predicted. He thought that, judging by what he had seen, they may have been able to survive much longer than he had predicted. He marvelled at human resilience.

As the feeds showed an external view of *Ephialtes* from *Europa*, still looking mighty as she receded into the distance, Kostovich glanced at the terminal displaying data from his own recon drone. None of the feeds were updating and in the corner of the screen the words 'Data Interrupted' slowly flashed in amber.

He looked at the time on the screen. There had been no new data for forty minutes. He tried a few things to communicate with the drone - manually contacting the auxiliary coms system, sending a soft reset command - but nothing worked. He ran the data back to the moment he had stopped receiving transmissions and looked for any anomalies. There were none. The drone had simply and suddenly stopped.

Kostovich took Foveaux by the arm and guided her to the terminal. "Look at this," he said.

"What am I looking at?" said Foveaux.

"This is a recon drone I sent out to the crash site a couple of hours ago. It's gone dark."

"Is that unusual?"

"It's not entirely unheard of. Weather conditions aren't great at the moment but I would have expected some indication of any problems before losing contact. This one just went out," he snapped his fingers, "like that."

"And that was at the crash site?"

"No, that was on the way to the crash site. In fact, it wasn't that far out from the city. On a direct line from the city to the crash site."

"Do you think it was shot down?"

Kostovich shrugged. "Don't know. You'd expect some warning even with that. You know, see the missile coming or something. It just feels a little . . . odd, to me. What do you think?"

Maya didn't know what to think. But she could see that Kostovich had concerns.

"I'll send some people out there right away."

"Good," said Kostovich, relieved. "You know the troop carriers can go outside, they're fully sealed. The flight suits are designed for low pressure, too. It's late afternoon out there, about four degrees Celsius, I think, so your people won't freeze to death either."

"I'll tell them to suit up," said Foveaux.

"Great," said Kostovich. "I'll launch another drone. It's probably nothing, just a mechanical failure or whatever. I'll let you know if I see anything."

"Okay," said Foveaux, "me too. Can you send me the coordinates for the area the drone went down?"

"I'm sending them now," said Kostovich. "It's forty kilometres or so west of *Parry 4*. Head out to the spaceport and just keep going."

CHAPTER 35

The Horizon

Kostovich's second drone had just taken off as *Europa* was touching down. The loading bridge swung around and connected. Bobby's crew escorted their charges off the shuttle and into the loading area, where two of Foveaux's transports awaited.

Foveaux approached Bobby. "Well done," she said.

"Simple recovery mission, no problem," said Bobby.

"We'll take them back to the garrison and hold them there for processing. Listen, can you come with me?"

"What is it?"

"Kostovich has picked up some suspicious activity. He wanted me to check it out. I'm taking some troops over there right now."

Bobby noticed the armoured troop carriers near the transports. "Okay," he said, "I need to finish up here, just hold on a moment." Bobby walked over to his crew and congratulated them on their deportment during the mission. He shook hands with them all.

When Bobby returned to Foveaux she was talking on her comdev. "Yes, hold on," she said, "I'm putting you on speaker. Bobby Karjalainen is here."

"Karjalainen?" said Kostovich.

"Hello, Dr Kostovich," said Bobby.

"I was just telling the commissioner. I've just lost another drone. It's not mechanical failure. I made a visual on five dust columns just before I lost contact. I think the dropship made a successful landing, though maybe a little off course. The mechs are a few minutes west of the spaceport. I've roughed out their speed. They may be in missile range in the next fifteen or twenty minutes. I'm going to send another drone to the crash site - we'll go the long way round this time - to see if they've sent another squad in some different direction, and I have all my missiles ready to go on them as soon as they breach the horizon. But the Parrys are primarily an air defence. You need to get out there and stop them from making contact with the city. You're a commander, right?"

"I was," said Bobby.

"Then you know their tactics. Figure out what they are going to do and stop them from doing it. I've got reasonable odds with the missiles but their countermeasures are pretty good. If you can get eyes-on you have artillery and other battlefield weapons you can bring to bear on them."

"We do?" said Bobby.

"Yes. The troop carriers have plasma cannon. If you can get line of sight there's nothing they can do to defend themselves against them. But you're vulnerable to their missiles. Let me take care of those, I can deal with the air. You have to get eyes-on and hit them with the cannon."

"Anything else we need to know?"

"If all else fails, I might have a Plan B."

"You're expecting this to fail?"

"Not expecting. But good to have a fallback, eh?"

"Not really," said Bobby. "Not if the failure of Plan A means I get my ass kicked."

"Don't worry about it now. I'm still working on it. Take those mechs out, and hurry."

"Will do," said Bobby.

"Take one of the troop carriers. I'll take the other," said Foveaux.

"Do you have any kind of plan?" said Bobby. "At all?"

"Not really," said Foveaux. "Split up, if necessary abandon the carriers and carry on on foot. We have some RPGs and light personal GG missiles in the back. We can work with those if we have to."

"Okay," said Bobby. "Lock down the hangar, we don't have any time to waste."

Foveaux spoke into her comdev and yellow lights and claxons sounded around the hangar bay. "Decompression in thirty seconds," said a disembodied voice, repeating with the seconds decreasing in decrements of five.

Foveaux shouted above the din to Bobby, "The transports will have to stay here for now. Let's go."

Bobby and Foveaux climbed into their respective troop carriers.

"Hi, I'm Bobby," he said as he entered, "the commissioner has just placed me in charge of this vehicle."

"Not a problem, sir, good to have you aboard," said the driver.

"Have you had much training in this vehicle?" said Bobby.

"Just picked her up this morning," said the driver.

"Great," said Bobby. He noticed an indicator on the dashboard showing that external air pressure was dropping. He rummaged around the back of his seat and found a helmet, which he put on. "Foveaux?" he said into the com.

"Go ahead," said Foveaux.

"We'll break south and you break north, okay?"

"Sounds good."

Bobby saw the huge hangar bay doors opening. They retracted slowly to the floor until he had a clear view of the shuttle and the runway beyond it. Beyond that was the untrammelled surface of wild Mars. He punched the driver gently in the shoulder and said, "Let's go."

Lund and Lucero had seen the intense conversation between Bobby and Foveaux, and the pointing at the troop carriers, from their seats in the transports.

"What do you think it is?" said Lund.

"Some sort of emergency?" said Lucero.

"Is it a trap? Are they just going to leave us here?" said Lund, hiding the panic in her voice.

"I don't think so," said Lucero. "They've left the drivers and guards with us. Unless they're planning on bumping those off, too."

"They're reacting to something," said Lund.

"I can't think what," said Lucero.

"How far out were we when we got hit?"

Lucero shrugged. "Forty, fifty thousand kilometres?"

Lund nodded. "We launched three dropships. Maybe they made it. We would have been in range - just."

"I doubt it," said Lucero. "The blast probably caught them too. And if it didn't the Martians have other missile defences. I'm sure they would have picked them off."

"That's a missile battery there," said Lund, nodding at the Parry base on the far side of the spaceport. "But no defence is infallible. What if they got through? What if just one got through?"

"What if one what got through?" came a voice from across the aisle.

Lund was startled by the aggressive tone. "We were just discussing the -" said Lund, but Lucero hushed her.

"Do not presume to interrupt a superior officer's conversation," said Lucero. "What's your name, soldier?"

The man straightened in his seat. "My name is Commander Foley," he said.

Though he had his suspicions before, Steiner now felt certain the Martians were onto him. The second drone, he thought, was no coincidence. He had taken that one out, too. That act would have alerted them to his presence, even if the drone had not been able to detect him. He checked the details with his HUD. He was now within a handful of kilometres of the spaceport. As soon as he had a visual on the missile battery his plan was to attack it with lasers and take it out. After that the spaceport would be there for the taking. It would be a simple matter of walking up to it.

He checked the data coming from his mechs. It was all good. A scan of all radio frequencies picked up various rubbish, but one group of transmissions stood out. It was coming from the region of the spaceport and although he was unable to decrypt it he was fairly sure it must be military. The position and frequency suggested as much. That, together with the presence of the drones, told him that they were onto him. From now on timing was crucial.

What little information he had about the Martians' missile batteries told him they were aimed primarily at the sky. Until he made it over the missile battery's horizon he would be relatively safe. But he needed to get over the horizon in order to have line of sight for his lasers to do their work. The mechs would have a small window in which to fire, and during that time it was likely that the Martians would fire missiles at them. The mechs' missile defences were pretty good. They had a ninety-five percent success rate in protecting against missile attack. They had chaff, flares and most impressively their lasers to take out an incoming missile once it was locked on and headed at them in a straight line. The mechs' camera systems could guide their lasers, and an incoming missile provided a relatively stable target.

Steiner had detailed maps of the area around the spaceport. There was an outcrop of rocks that they would be able to approach in the lee of. They would be able to prepare the attack and then step from behind the rocks to launch it.

Steiner had managed to sleep as his mech had trundled from the crash site to the spaceport. It had not been comfortable or refreshing but he felt his mind was clear enough to engage in battle. He had taken on sustenance too, in the form of the chocolate sludge. He had also managed to make use of the commander mech's commode facilities. Although he was tired and dirty, and the smell inside the cockpit was strong enough to kill a horse, he felt ready for battle.

On seeing the outcrop appear over the horizon Steiner felt his resolve stiffen. Where he had allowed himself the luxury of self-pity on the journey to the spaceport he now cast all such thoughts aside. Once more he had become a single-minded warrior and all his focus would be on winning this battle.

He scanned the skies for drones; there were none. He scanned the horizon for troops or vehicles; there were none. He proceeded with his mechs towards the outcrop.

As they crossed the plane Steiner looked first to his left and then to his right. He knew the mechs were automatons, machines under his control, but anticipating the battle ahead he couldn't help but feel a brotherly attachment to them. He could feel their strength and resilience, and watching them stride together with him filled him with an esprit de corps that he couldn't really explain. He was the unit and the mechs were merely an extension of his battle capability, but somehow he felt they were his comrades; that they would look out for him if he was in trouble and he would do the same for them. It was all he could do to resist giving them some sort of rousing speech to encourage them in the forthcoming fight. In the end, he settled for a few words to himself. "Let's get these sons of bitches," he said, and his troupe of towering metal warriors continued stomping towards the horizon.

On reaching the outcrop Steiner sent three of his mechs to the left while he and the other one went to the right. If this had been a simulation he would have sent the dropship on a reconnaissance mission way overhead, giving him a view beyond the outcrop. But this was no simulation and his dropship had been destroyed. He knew they would have to proceed Wild West style, dodging out from behind the outcrop and firing at the Parry battery before dodging back. While he didn't like the risks it presented, something about it appealed to him. It would be like playing one of those IVR games.

He programmed his HUD to overlay a visual image of the missile battery where it should be, so it appeared he could see it through the outcrop. He programmed his laser to fire in a figure of eight pattern centred on the middle of the battery, and he set similar configurations in his mechs.

One last time he checked on his radar for incoming missiles and saw none. Finally, he made a visual inspection of the sky. He knew it was pointless. His electronic detection aids were far more accurate than his puny human eyes, but in the martial spirit at the heart of the Commander Program he somehow felt connected to the battlefield at a human level, and visually checking the skies in that way felt necessary.

Sensing that the coast was clear he prepared to step out from the protection of the outcrop and begin the attack. As if to the mechs under his command, but in fact to no one but himself, he said, "Let's go," and began the attack.

CHAPTER 36

Assault

From his position in the control centre Kostovich was scanning the horizon. There were high resolution cameras on the *Parry 4* battery allied to radar and thermal imaging cameras.

"Eyes on the skies," he said to Walton.

"On it," came the reply.

"There's a heat signature flowing upwards and backward and somewhat to the right of that outcrop," said Baldwin. "It's doesn't look right to me. It's very subtle, could be geothermal or even the sun heating a rock maybe, where the sand has been taken away by the dust storm. Or it could be enemy forces."

"Yes, it could be," said Kostovich. "Keep trained on that region."

As he watched, Kostovich saw Bobby's troop carrier streak off towards the left side of his screen.

"Karjalainen, keep an eye on that outcrop. We believe the enemy may be positioned there."

"Roger that," said Bobby. "Any chance of a pre-emptive strike?"

"Negative, we don't know what we're dealing with yet. If you can get eyes-on, or even in a good position for ground radar, we'll know what we can do. Please proceed as planned."

"Foveaux here, we can call in fire from you if we have coordinates, right?"

"Correct, Commissioner. If you can tell me where to fire, I can fire."

Bobby turned to the trooper next to him in the cabin. "Have you used one of these before?" he said, indicating the controls for the plasma cannon.

"Sure," came the reply, "in IVRs. Hell, *Mech Azimuth 4* is my favourite game."

"Could you scooch along and let me take over?"

The man looked at him. "I don't think I can. I don't even know who the hell you are."

Bobby nodded, tight lipped.

A voice came over the com. "This is Commissioner Foveaux. Give Commander Karjalainen the goddamned cannon, that's an order."

The man begrudgingly shifted seats and Bobby took the controls. As soon as he held them a video feed from the cannon appeared in his HUD. He selected 'Aim Assist' and swung the cannon around to face the outcrop.

"Listen, Kostovich," he said, "can you pick up my cannon's video feed and follow it? The moment I see anything at all I want fire support. Rockets, missiles, lasers, anything. Can you do that?"

"Baldwin," said Kostovich, "follow Karjalainen's video. If he starts shooting at something we start too, okay?"

"Okay," said Baldwin. "I'm picking up the video now. Looks good."

"You've got it, Bobby," said Kostovich.

"I'm turning back in toward the outcrop," said Foveaux, "I'll be there in about four minutes. Do you have anything, Kostovich?"

Kostovich glanced at his battlefield model. He had data and video feeds from *Parry 4* and both troop carriers and all the helmet cameras from the troops. All the data fed into his three dimensional model so he had an overview of what was going on with as much information as the sum of all friendly players. Right now he had a lot of information about terrain and the position of friendly troops. The one thing he didn't have was an enemy.

"Negative at this time," he said. "Proceed as planned, I'll feed information back to your battlecoms as soon as I have anything."

"Shit, that's it!" said Baldwin. He saw the two mechs moving and instantly released missiles.

Bobby saw the mechs. "Mechs! Two o'clock!" He fired the plasma cannon.

The mechs implacably fired lasers at *Parry 4* as the plasma bolts hit. One collapsed in a cloud of dust and debris, momentarily obscuring the second one as Bobby turned his fire to where it had been. He wasn't convinced he had managed to hit it.

"Get back into cover!" Bobby shouted at the driver. She swerved the troop carrier and tried to take them across the front of the outcrop, but before she could put it between them and the remaining mech it had fired its missiles.

"Brace!" said the driver. Bobby swung the cannon around and flipped it to full auto. The mech remained out of sight but the sound of screaming missiles and cannon fire filled the cabin. There was a series of loud bangs.

"Are you okay?" said Bobby.

"Still here," said the driver. "Where are the mechs?"

As she spoke *Parry 4*'s missiles streaked past them. They heard two loud explosions.

"One's still there, I think," said Bobby. "Care to take a peek?"

"Commander Karjalainen, are you hit?" said Foveaux over the com.

"Negative," said Bobby. "We have contact with the enemy and are pursuing."

"I'm coming round the back," said Foveaux.

"Good," said Bobby. "We can take them from both sides at once."

The driver reversed the troop carrier and lined up for another attempt at the edge of the outcrop.

"Kostovich, lay some more missile fire on the southern edge of the outcrop."

"Negative, Commander. We're blind."

"We've lost all contact with *Parry 4*. I think they hit us," said Kostovich.

"What about the other batteries?" said Bobby.

"We can try that. Gonna take a little longer to get the missiles to you."

"Stay here," said Bobby to the driver. "What's the ETA on those missiles?"

"Just launched from *Parry 3*. Twenty seconds, I'm using the last good coordinates I have. They may have moved, can you keep them pinned down?"

"We'll try. Keep those missiles away from us."

Bobby looked at his plasma cannon display. "Edge us forward," he said.

The driver began moving the troop carrier forward.

Foveaux first saw one mech as her troop carrier rounded the outcrop. Her plasma cannon fired immediately and struck the mech before it had time to get its missiles away. The cloud of smoke the plasma strike generated partly obscured the second mech, but the cannon's sensors picked it up and fired. The third mech, reacting to data from the second one, fired a full volley of missiles before Foveaux had even seen it. With the carrier moving at full speed the sensors did pick out the mech once it was clear of the rock and the plasma cannon fired two bolts to the centre of its body mass. Its missiles were already away.

The troop carrier continued its curve around the rock with the cannon remaining trained on the three smoking mechs. The missiles the third mech had fired had gone directly upwards and were now coming down at a variety of angles.

"Switch defences to auto," Foveaux said to the gunner. She hesitated for a moment on the new equipment before she switched the cannon to auto. Once engaged, the cannon took out four of the five missiles raining down on the troop carrier.

"What was that?" said Kostovich.

"Foveaux's carrier just went dark," said Baldwin.

"What about individual coms?" said Kostovich, somewhat desperately.

"Nothing," said Baldwin. "They could be rerouting if the carrier's relay is out of action. Could be switching to direct transmission."

"Where are those missiles?"

"Seconds to impact," said Walton.

"How about the coms?"

Baldwin stared at his terminal. "I have one. Two, three. All twelve individual coms are back on line."

"How's their vitality data?"

Baldwin looked down at the feeds. "I don't know. A couple look pretty bad. Could just be instrumentation."

"Foveaux, do you copy?" said Kostovich.

"Foveaux, do you copy?"

There was a flurry of explosions in the air and on the ground around the corner. Bobby gestured for the driver to wait. "I like this," he said to Kostovich, "send more missiles."

"Are we hitting anything?" came the reply.

"Probably," said Bobby.

"Let me know what we're hitting."

"We were counting on waiting here until you'd hit it," said Bobby. "What's happened to Foveaux?"

"Her team is good. Carrier is out of action, though."

As he heard the words Bobby saw a commander mech run from cover in front of him. He pressed fire on the cannon controls but even as he did so he saw a red line shoot from the shoulder of the mech to a point above his cabin where his cannon was mounted. He heard a muted creak above him and as he pressed down on the fire button nothing happened. The mech moved from right to left in front of him. As it passed it didn't even look back.

"Kostovich, missiles! Can you see this? Put some missiles on that mech!"

"Launch missiles from Parrys 3 and 2," Kostovich said to Baldwin. "Commander, we're launching now but you need to keep that mech in contact or we won't know where we're firing."

"Decompress the cab and hit that mech," Bobby said to the driver.

Foveaux coughed. "Everyone okay?" she said. She could see from her HUD that the cabin was decompressing and the troop section was fully decompressed. She quickly brought her visor down and sealed her suit. She was dizzy from the blast and it took a few seconds to register that the troop carrier was on its side. She assumed that the main section was breached. That would explain the decompression. In the cabin the cannon operator and driver were slumped but stirring. The cab was filled with a thin grey smoke.

"Are you okay?" she said to the driver, shaking her.

"I . . . I think so," said the driver.

The cannon operator stirred. "I'm good here," she said, unconvincingly.

"Good," said Foveaux. "We have to get out."

The driver looked at her, unsure.

"We're sitting ducks in here, we have missile launchers in the back, let's go."

The driver heaved the door over her head and pulled herself out. Foveaux followed. She glanced over and could see the three mechs smoking in the Martian dusk. They did not move but stood upright

EPHIALTES

like futuristic wicker men being offered up to some great metallic god. She could see the scorch marks around the carrier where the remnants of missiles had struck the ground, and behind her she could see smoke rising from her own carrier.

"Foveaux," came Kostovich's voice over the com, "do you copy?"

"I copy you," said Foveaux.

"Please advise of your situation, over."

"Carrier is down. Possible casualties. We're continuing the pursuit on foot. We've destroyed three enemy mechs."

"Foveaux!" Bobby's voice cut in. "We need your support. We have a mech proceeding towards the spaceport, we have no cannon."

"Roger that," said Foveaux. "We're on our way."

Bobby's driver gunned the engine and took off in pursuit of Steiner's mech. Steiner was striding as fast as he could across the open scrub between the rocky outcrop and the spaceport. He had exhausted his supply of missiles, but knew that his laser was a formidable weapon and enough to take control of the port.

That he had managed to get away from *Ephialtes* and land on the planet seemed remarkable enough. That he had fought off two armoured vehicles and further missile attacks was remarkable, too. All that remained was for him to make it across the scrub and secure the port and he would have done it, against all the odds. He would be the last man standing, the last survivor of his mission, and he would have achieved what he, and all the rest of them, had set out to do. This was to be his final push to glory.

"Kostovich, put your missiles down in front of the mech. Stop him from proceeding forward and we can take him down," said Bobby.

"You're too close, hold back and leave him to me!" came the reply.

"He's out in the open, he'll take out any missiles headed toward him. Send them short, make a trench. Slow him down."

"Jesus, did you hear that!" Kostovich said to Walton.

"I did, what do you want me to do?"

Kostovich shook his head. "Send them short. No, send five at him and five short. Give him something to think about. Just make sure none go long; that's Karjalainen right behind him."

Foveaux had retrieved the personal missile launchers from the troop carrier. Two of her troops had been injured in the explosion and remained behind but with the rest she set off at a light run towards the mech she could see about five hundred metres distant, which was running toward the spaceport with Bobby's troop carrier in pursuit.

"I have a visual on your mech, Bobby," said Foveaux, "should I fire?"

"Yes," said Bobby.

Foveaux turned to a trooper next to her with one of the hand-held missile launchers. "Take out the mech," she said. "You two too," she said to two others.

As they stopped to allow the grenadiers to drop to one knee and fire they heard, quietly through the thin Martian atmosphere, the roar of approaching missiles.

"Any time you like," said Bobby.

Foveaux saw brief red streaks as the mech tried to take out Kostovich's incoming missiles. "Fire!" she said, and at first one then two and three missiles streaked away, hugging the ground as they sped toward the mech.

While the mech was firing its laser into the air, still running, the second wave of Kostovich's missiles struck the ground in front of it. A huge plume of light brown dust was thrown into the air. Steiner lost visuals in the dust cloud but his radar showed that he was about to enter a newly appeared missile crater. Keeping his momentum he went to jump it.

At the moment his trailing foot left the ground the first of Foveaux's missiles struck, quickly followed by the other two. The mech was strong enough to resist their explosive force but was pushed, just slightly, off balance. As the mech landed on the far side of the crater instead of carrying on with its stride it fell, hitting its right shoulder on the crater wall before spinning and landing on its back.

Bobby continued with his chase. The troop carrier jumped the ridge of the crater and landed on top of the fallen mech.

Steiner struggled to move. He twisted and turned, but it felt like there was a huge weight on his chest. There was; it was Bobby's troop carrier.

Bobby and the driver were shaking about in the cabin as the mech writhed beneath them.

Steiner tried to bring his laser to bear but he couldn't get the angle he needed on the troop carrier.

"Do we get out?" said Bobby's driver.

Bobby was about to answer when, with an almighty twist, the mech span around so it was now laying on its side. The troop carrier slid partly off its back and sat at a forty-five degree angle, half on the mech and half in the crater.

"Yes," said Bobby. "Bring all the ordnance you have."

As his crew scrambled out of the troop carrier Foveaux appeared at the rim of the crater. "Take out the laser!" she said to one of her grenadiers. The trooper squatted and sent a missile directly to Steiner's laser. Steiner felt the blast as keenly as if it had hit his own shoulder. Now he was utterly defenceless. He pressurised his suit and pulled on the emergency evac switch.

Bobby circled around the troop carrier as the dust thinned and cleared. He saw Steiner stagger from the belly of the mech and he saw the pistol in his hand.

"Don't shoot!" said Bobby across all frequencies.

Steiner heard him clearly but ostentatiously banged the side of his helmet like he was having trouble picking up the transmission.

Bobby's crew fanned out beside him. They had plasma rifles, RPGs and personal missile launchers. Steiner pointed his weapon at them suspiciously. He held it two-handed. From his cautious movement it looked like he was controlling the situation. Bobby held a plasma rifle aimed directly at Steiner's head.

"It's over," said Bobby.

The dust cleared further and Steiner could see Foveaux and her fireteam ranged across the far edge of the crater. He had considered taking his chances with Bobby. Now he could see that, as well as being outnumbered, he was at the apex of a perfect field of crossfire from two well-placed fireteams. He dropped his gun and put his hands in the air.

"You've got me," he said.

"Please report on your situation," said Kostovich.

"The area is secure. We have one prisoner. We're bringing him in," said Foveaux.

Bobby approached Steiner. He held out a hand. "Welcome to Mars," he said, "how do you like it so far?"

Steiner looked at the outstretched hand. "I thought *my* hometown was grim," he said. "I need a shower."

"We can sort that out. Come with us." Bobby guided Steiner to the top of the crater. His troops followed behind. Foveaux walked around the edge to greet them.

"Nice work," she said to Bobby.

"Thank you, Commissioner," he replied. "I hope to be compensated accordingly."

"Pay is basic. No bonuses," said Foveaux.

"Is it too late to reconsider?"

"It is now. You're signed up. Welcome to the MSS."

They trudged toward the spaceport.

As they passed *Parry 4* Bobby noticed the crisscross burns on the radio domes. Steiner had done a job on them. He thought he caught Steiner glancing in that direction too, and smirking.

They walked across the runway and into the hangar.

"Are we all here?" said Foveaux. "Raise the doors and repressurise."

They saw the yellow lights spinning and felt the rumble as the powerful motors started to push the doors up from the ground.

As the doors reached a height of two metres Steiner span around and planted a fist into the chest of one of Bobby's troops. He grabbed another and threw him at a further three. Before anyone had time to react he was streaking across the hangar bay towards the doors. A handful of troopers stepped forward and raised their weapons.

"Don't shoot!" said Foveaux. "We can't damage the doors!"

Bobby and some others chased Steiner but he pulled away easily. Bobby had played high school football and his rushing game was excellent, but Steiner's speed seemed unreal. He pulled away from Bobby as if he was standing still.

As he reached the rising hangar door, which was now nearer three metres high, Steiner jumped. He sailed gracefully over the door and was away. Bobby and the troops were left standing, looking as foolish and confused as if Steiner had literally vanished into the thin Martian air. Bobby turned back to Foveaux and made an elaborate shrugging gesture. He started a slow walk back as the doors finally clanked into position and warnings signalled that the hangar was repressurising.

"Don't worry about him," said Kostovich. "He'll never last more than an hour out there. It's dusk - the temperature will be through the floor in a couple of hours. I'm launching a drone. I'll track him and you can recover the body in the morning."

The repressurisation finished and Bobby pulled his helmet off.

"He got away," he said to Foveaux.

"He must know what's waiting for him out there. His choice, I guess. Is that all part of the commander code? Avoiding the dishonour of surrender?"

"Not that I know," said Bobby. "He was going to have a shower. That's what I'd have gone for."

The personnel from *Ephialtes* had been watching from the transports.

"I think that was Steiner," said Lund. "Why would he go and do a thing like that?"

"Steiner? You think he made it?"

"It was him. I know it. That was the emergency. He must have made it through and tried to attack. Why has he run off now, though? He's going to die out there."

"I don't know," said Lucero. "He's one tough son of a bitch. If he made it down here then who knows what he has planned? He's a pretty resourceful guy."

Lund looked at the place Steiner had escaped from. It was like a warehouse in style, but it was warm and light with a breathable atmosphere. The outside had none of those things.

On the drive to the garrison Kostovich's voice came over the com. "Foveaux?" he said.

"Go ahead," said Foveaux.

"I got a drone overhead and I picked up the heat signature of your guy."

"Go on."

"Well, I followed him for a couple of klicks and then he went dead."

"He died? From the cold?"

"Probably that too," said Kostovich, "but the signature just disappeared. Boom, it was gone."

"Fell down a hole, maybe?"

"Who knows? Anyway, I'll give you the coordinates and you can get out there and have a look tomorrow."

"Okay."

"You did a great job today, by the way."

"Thank you. But it wasn't just me. It was all of us. You too."

Kostovich nodded. "Maybe. Maybe we all did a great job, you're right. Congratulations us."

"Congratulations us," said Foveaux.

At the garrison the transports were unloaded under guard.

"There's really no need for all this," said Lucero, "it's not like we're going to go anywhere."

"It's standard procedure," said Foveaux.

"You have a procedure for this?" said Lucero, incredulously.

"We do now," said Foveaux, "I just made it up. In the stockade and secure quarters for now, and we'll sort something out for the long term in a few days."

Lucero rolled her eyes.

Bobby pushed his way through to Askel.

"Askel?" he said.

"Bobby," Askel replied.

"I wanted to catch up on *Europa*. I was kinda busy, though."

"I saw. So you're on the other side now?"

"Well," said Bobby, "I'm just a simple Martian boy, sticking up for my planet."

Askel laughed. "I guess you thought you could get away from me here. Well, look right where I am."

"I'm looking," said Bobby.

"Yeah?"

"Yeah. Looks pretty good to me."

"Oh, that is *slick*. You haven't changed, Bobby Karjalainen."

Bobby smiled at Askel. "What are you doing tonight?"

"Are you asking me out?"

"I might be."

"I'm sorry, but I'm going to have to turn you down."

Bobby was taken aback. "Why?" he said.

"Well," explained Askel, "tonight I have to be a prisoner of war. So I can't make it. But some other time, okay?"

"Hey," said Bobby conspiratorially, nodding toward Foveaux, "I think it'll be okay. I know the commissioner."

A small voice startled Bobby. "Commander Karjalainen, could I have a few words?"

Bobby turned and saw Elspeth standing, camera in hand, beaming at him.

"How did you get in here?" he said.

"I'm accredited now," said Elspeth, pointing to badge attached to her lapel. "Just a few words, for my stream? Could you tell us about the rescue? I understand there was big firefight out at the spaceport? Were you there?"

"I'd love to talk to you, Elspeth, but it's been kind of a long day. Can we do this tomorrow?"

Elspeth looked disappointed. "Okay," she said. "How about something for tonight's stream? Just a picture or something? Who's your friend?"

"This is Askel Lund. She's a spacecraft designer of some repute."

"Could you kiss her?"

"*What!?*" said Bobby.

"It would be a great picture. You rescued her, right? Give her a kiss, I'll make it the number one aggregated image before the end of the day."

"What do you think?" Bobby asked Askel. "Feel like making news?"

Askel looked at him. "C'mere," she said.

Epilogue

Another dust storm was gathering in the dusk as Steiner walked towards the horizon. He felt strange. It was cold, but he didn't feel it. He felt removed from his body, like he was looking down on himself. He felt an urge to rip his helmet off, like the urge he had felt to run towards the hangar doors, only this one he was able to control, to start with anyway.

It had seemed like he was watching a film as he had run to the doors. It seemed like he was going too fast, and he knew he had no chance of clearing the doors with his jump. But somehow he had. He had leapt like a gazelle and somehow landed outside, and had kept on running far further than he would have thought possible.

He wondered if he had some sort of altitude sickness. Maybe there was a leak in his suit and he was losing air. Maybe the lack of oxygen was addling his mind. He felt all wrong and once again came the powerful urge to take the helmet off.

He looked at the HUD. He was now more than fifteen kilometres from the spaceport, in open terrain where they would never find him. Without even considering the consequences, he pulled the helmet off and laid down.

In some weird dreamstate he knew he didn't need the helmet to survive. He dropped it by his side and forgot that he had ever resisted removing it. He noticed for the first time that he was no longer breathing and that the HUD remained, even though the helmet was gone.

Staring up into the deep black sky, and with the dust already blowing up around him, the dream part of his mind, the other self, calculated the length of time it would take the USAN to build and send new ships. Allowing for setbacks and errors, five years seemed reasonable.

The dust was starting to cover him.

His other self was now dominant. It set himself to reactivate in five years, sent himself the deep sleep command, and closed his eyes. Within a few minutes he was covered by the sand. A passing person, or even a survey satellite, would never even know he was there.

Coming soon from Reflex Books:
PHOBOS RISING
EPHIALTES PART II

The peace delivered in the wake of the *Ephialtes* incident is more fragile than many suppose. The USAN's rearmament program continues apace, hindered only by the harsh economic realities imposed by the Martian deuterium embargo.

On Mars, Askel and Bobby have to come to terms with an uncertain future while Foveaux and Kostovich brace themselves for the crisis they dread but know is coming.

When a shocking act of violence sends two planets careening towards conflict there is nowhere left to hide. The cold war between Earth and Mars is about to get hot, and there can only be one winner.

> "Conflict, both military and ethical, abounds in the mid-23rd century, setting the scene for a swashbuckling military science fiction saga with intricate subplots and more characters and points of view than a Russian novel. Parker writes well, the action riding a high-speed rail through layers of technology, deteriorating chains of command, moral dilemmas, and military insight."
>
> *US Review of Books*

Coming soon from Reflex Books:

DEIMOS
EPHIALTES PART III
The epic conclusion to the Ephialtes trilogy

Thirty years after the *Ephialtes* incident a new dawn of peaceful prosperity is breaking. A reformed Asian Bloc is pursuing a meaningful détente with the USAN, and the spectre of war has long since receded.

When a voice from the past is heard across the solar system contemporary assumptions are shaken to the core. The sheen of modern civility is torn asunder as an ageless foe is revealed to be a threat not just to the USAN and Mars, but to the entirety of human civilisation.

An enemy of unprecedented magnitude is coming, and humanity must decide how to confront it. If there is to be even the slimmest hope of prevailing some ugly truths will have to be dragged back into the light. There can be no rules in a fight for survival.

Don't miss out on news, updates, special offers, and giveaways for all things *Ephialtes* - join the Ephialtes Trilogy Mailing List:

https://landing.mailerlite.com/webforms/landing/i4t4l3

Follow Gavin E Parker on Twitter and Facebook

https://twitter.com/gavineparker_

https://www.facebook.com/gavineparkerauthor

For more information visit our websites:

www.gavineparker.com

www.reflexbooks.co.uk

A Note from the Author

Thank you for reading my book *Ephialtes*. I hope you enjoyed it.

If you did, I hope you'll be able to find some time to post reviews on Amazon, Goodreads, Smashwords, LibraryThing and elsewhere.

Finding an audience for a book is the toughest thing a writer has to do, so if you feel that you're a fan please spread the word.

Oh, and if you didn't like it . . . . *sssh!*

Gavin E Parker